The Truitts of Texas Book One

What Brings Us Joy

TERESA WELLS

Scrivenings PRESS
Quench your thirst for story.
www.ScriveningsPress.com

Published by Scrivenings Press LLC

15 Lucky Lane
Morrilton, Arkansas 72110
https://ScriveningsPress.com

Printed in the United States of America

Paperback ISBN 978-1-64917-484-0

eBook ISBN 978-1-64917-485-7

Editors: Amy R. Anguish and Linda Fulkerson

Cover design by Linda Fulkerson - www.bookmarketinggraphics.com

This is a work of fiction. Unless otherwise indicated, all names, characters, businesses, events, and incidents are either the product of the author's imagination or used in a fictitious manner. Any resemblance to actual persons, living or dead, or actual events is purely coincidental.

Scriptures are taken from the KING JAMES VERSION (KJV): KING JAMES VERSION, public domain.

To Rick.
Your love and encouragement made this
book a reality.

Chapter 1

The Victorian crazy quilt, a fad a hundred years ago, was an American invention in vogue for about a quarter century from 1875 to 1900. Like giant jigsaw puzzles, they were made of irregular pieces of silk, satin, velvet or plush sewn onto a solid backing of a lighter material and further decorated with embroidery stitches.—The San Francisco Examiner (San Francisco, California) Sunday, September 01, 1985.

June 4, 1895

As far as the neck could crane, dry prairie grass and squat trees dotted the dusty landscape. Delia Truitt pressed her forehead to the glass and groaned. Texas was worse than she'd imagined.

As the train's steady rhythm slowed, the steward opened the compartment door, accompanied by a whoosh of air and the clackety-clack of wheels on tracks. "Next stop, Blooming Grove."

Delia's pulse skittered. She'd lived in one home all her life.

After eighteen years, she knew every creaking stair, each branch of the magnolia trees, and could walk the lane to her grandparents' home with her eyes closed. She knew every shop owner in town and which one would slip her a swatch of silk or satin for her crazy quilt. How many times had she bicycled alongside her school chums and debated the merits of women's suffrage? But all that changed the day Papa told them the bank was foreclosing. In Texas, Uncle Robert agreed to provide shelter and work for six months.

It was after the six-month time period that worried Delia.

Her fourteen-year-old sister, Hazel, snapped her book shut with a sigh. "What if nobody likes me in Blooming Grove?"

Delia waved away the words as if they were gnats. "Don't be silly. You'll make pals in no time, especially since you're still in school."

Hazel's blue eyes widened. "Oh! Maybe I'll have a beau."

Delia lifted a brow. "Don't you think you're a little young?"

"Better too young than eighteen with no prospects."

Delia dipped her chin. "I don't care one whit about courting and marriage." Not entirely true, but her snippy little sister didn't need to know.

The train's pace slowed, reigniting the nervous sensation in her stomach. Delia touched the quilt piece lying on her lap. She'd been too lost in her anxious thoughts to complete the border of Herringbone stitches. Now the needle hung suspended on the white embroidery thread she'd stopped working. She completed the stitch, then secured the thread before reaching for the scissors.

Before she could open her sewing box, her attention snagged on movement among the other passengers. Murmurs and gasps grew louder. Across the aisle, a man pointed to something outside.

Hazel grabbed Delia's arm. "Look outside. That man is too close."

Just beyond their window, a weathered man on horseback scowled at the passenger train, rifle propped against his leg. When their car slowly rolled past, Delia's gaze connected with his. She drew back with a gasp. "What an awful man."

Hazel rubbed her arms. "I know, like he wanted to murder every one of us."

"Betcha he's gonna rob the train."

Delia started, and Hazel whirled to glare at their mischievous older brother, seated behind them. "Rabb Truitt! That's downright mean. I'm going to sit next to Thomas. He's my favorite anyway."

With a huff, Hazel flounced up the aisle, and Rabb slid into the vacant seat next to Delia, grinning. "Works every time."

"You shouldn't tease like that, especially when it might be true." The man had scared her, too, but if she admitted her fear to Rabb, he'd tease her mercilessly.

"Shoot, he's just a cowpoke. Besides, y'all coddle Hazel. She's gotta have leather skin iffen she aims to survive in Texas."

"Iffen? You sound like you have had no education."

"And you sound like a proper school marm."

Outside, the brakes screeched, and the locomotive jolted to a stop alongside a brick depot bearing the sign Blooming Grove. Before she could save it, her quilt slid to the dirty floor. Rabb reached for it, then yelped. He put his smallest finger in his mouth, frowning. "You oughta be careful with them needles, Red."

"I hope you didn't bleed on it." She examined the fabric, relieved when she found it unblemished. "I've worked too hard on this to have it spoiled."

"Can't figure why. That thing wouldn't keep a mouse warm."

She gave him a sideways glance. "You know very well it's not supposed to keep anyone warm, human or otherwise. This is art." She blew a speck of dirt from the fabric before folding it into a small bundle and tucking it into her carpetbag.

Departing passengers formed a line to exit, and the air filled with eager chatter. Delia pulled on her white gloves and stood, placing her hand on her stomach. If only she'd had breakfast. But her appetite had disappeared somewhere outside Georgia and everything familiar. "I suppose we must go." She patted her straw boater. "Is my hat straight?"

"Yup."

She swatted his arm. "You didn't even look. What kind of woman makes her first appearance with her hat askew? Please, Rabb."

With a roll of his brown eyes, he pulled his lanky body to stand and studied her. "It's straight."

He placed his derby on his wavy hair before stepping into the aisle with a gesture for her to precede him in the queue. She peered out the compartment windows for a view of the town. "I can't see anything for all that steam."

The young woman in front of her peeked over her shoulder with a giggle, obviously aimed at Rabb. This kind of silly flirtation happened all the time when her brother was around. She supposed Rabb was decent looking, if one liked tall men with square jaws.

The locomotive steam dissipated, and she could make out the town through the smudged windows. Horse-drawn wagons and pedestrians made their way along the broad street lined with two-story brick buildings and single-story clapboard storefronts.

Rabb tapped her shoulder and gestured for her to close the space between her and the rest of the line proceeding up the aisle. Close behind her, he said, "Listen, I been doing some thinking."

"I hope your head doesn't ache from the effort."

He nudged her forward. "Hey, now, I'm serious. I need to settle down."

"Ha!"

"What's funny about that?" Hurt dimmed his brown eyes.

"I'm sorry. It's just the idea of you as a responsible husband and father seems a little far-fetched." She winced and tried again. "You can't blame me for being surprised. You've never said anything about a family."

He snorted. "Don't you think it's time? I'll be twenty in a couple of months."

"Hmm."

"Problem is, I need a good woman."

"That's not a problem. Women practically fall at your feet." She inclined her head toward the girl ahead of them to illustrate his effect on women.

He grimaced. "Naw, that's just flirting. That ain't what I'm talking about. You gotta help me out, Red."

Her shoulders fell. "Why me?" The last thing she wanted was to be responsible for him. She'd had enough of trying to corral his antics during their school years. This fell to her simply because they were always in the same class, despite him being a year older. "In fact, you owe me plenty for all the homework I finished for you."

"And one of these days, I'll pay you back. Meantime, help me get a good woman, like you."

She splayed her fingers over her high collar. "Like me? Well, if you aren't the sweetest thing."

"Only, my woman's gotta know how to cook."

Delia dropped her hand. "Very funny." Of course, he would bring up her lack of talent in the kitchen.

"And I want a woman who can keep a house. Darn my socks. Mostly, she's gotta be pretty. So, once you make friends, bring them around."

She turned to face him. "Absolutely not. You want a maid, not a marriage."

"Come on, you know what I mean. Do it for your favorite brother. Please?"

An idea sprouted. Perhaps she could budge a little, as long as she got something out of the agreement. After all, any friend of hers would be too clever to fall for his schemes. "If I agree to introduce you to my new acquaintances, what will you do for me?"

He shrugged. "What do you want?"

She pretended to consider this, though she knew exactly the task she had in mind. "I suppose I could introduce you to my new friends, if you'll keep my bicycle in working order."

"Is that all? Sure."

Was that all? It was everything. That bicycle gave her freedom. She could go where she liked, all around the town, without asking one of her brothers to escort her. But the maintenance required to keep it in working order was bothersome.

"We have an agreement, then." She thrust her hand toward him, and after a few seconds, he took it in a firm shake.

At the exit, she stepped through the narrow door, pausing on the top step to gaze at the people below. She shaded her eyes against the glare.

"Here we go." Papa extended his hand to help her down the steps and onto the uncovered platform. Self-conscious, she touched her straw hat and glanced down at her green travel suit.

Coming to stand beside her, Rabb whistled low. "Look at all these folks!"

She'd expected to see a smattering of grimy gunslingers, especially after encountering the horseman earlier. But this group resembled the people she'd just left behind in Georgia. Men held umbrellas aloft to shade their women, who laughed and chattered in their puffed-sleeved, pastel finery. A sudden gust of hot wind caused most to clutch the brims of their feathered hats. Voices rose in a cacophony of joyful greetings, sharp directives, or sing-song advertising, the latter courtesy of the knickered boys hawking newspapers or shoeshines.

The tension in her shoulders relaxed. Maybe this move wouldn't be so bad.

Papa's brother, Uncle Robert, arranged for delivery of the few pieces of furniture they'd brought, and told them to go ahead to the carriage. "We don't want to keep Mary waiting, you know."

Mother frowned, her hand on the growing bulge in her midsection. "Children, let's not dawdle."

Delia exchanged a look with Rabb. "Children? Who's she talking about?"

Hazel tossed her head. "Me. I'm her baby."

Rabb yanked Hazel's hair. "Enjoy it now, kid. That baby's gonna be here sooner than you think."

"Shush!" Wasn't it just like him to speak of such an indelicate topic? She quickened her pace, much too interested in their new town to hang back with her siblings. Men in dapper suits tipped their bowler hats as she passed, their glances unmistakably admiring. Delia smiled to herself.

Just ahead, a middle-aged woman in a carriage waved a white handkerchief at them. "Hello, hello, this way."

Mother rushed forward to embrace the woman, presumably Aunt Mary. After introductions were made, Aunt

Mary waved them aboard the large, open-air carriage. "What an auspicious group of young people. You all were just little tikes when we left, and just look at you now."

Capturing Delia's hand in hers, Aunt Mary smiled warmly. "Your beautiful auburn hair reminds me of your grandmother's, when she was young."

Now this was a woman she could love. "Really? My cousins said as much, but since I only knew Grandmother with white hair, I wasn't sure."

"And your papa wrote us about your talent with needle and thread."

Mother sighed. "If only she'd use her talent for something more practical than crazy quilts."

The comment stung. True, Mother frequently chided her for spending so much time on her pretty quilts, but to criticize in front of this relative was different.

Delia was relieved when Aunt Mary broke the silence by changing the subject. "Looking at you young folks is like looking at the faces of home. Like I said, Delia takes after Mama Truitt with those brown eyes and red hair—you, too, Rabb. Thomas, you are the image of your father when he was young, with your dark blue eyes and hair. And Hazel, you favor your mama." She winked at Mother. "We shall see who the babe resembles. When will he or she arrive, dear?"

Mother's cheeks reddened. Before she responded, Hazel said, "October."

Aunt Mary clapped her hands. "An autumn baby! Right in time for the county fair."

County fair? Delia started to ask her for details, but Uncle Robert and Papa joined them, saying the wagon with their belongings would deliver the goods later this afternoon. With great flourish, Uncle Robert put the carriage into motion.

Aunt Mary clasped her hands. "Our first stop is our home. I

thought y'all must be hungry, seeing as it's noon. My cook has prepared luncheon."

The journey to their grand Queen Ann-style home didn't take long. In no time, the family sat in upholstered chairs around an ornately carved wooden table. Delia traced the rim of the fine china, remembering luncheons back in Georgia. She tamped down the longing for home.

The chicken sandwiches were the best Delia had ever tasted, and the lemonade was just the right blend of tart and sweet. Conversation was easy and relaxed until Uncle Robert lit a cigar and squinted at Papa.

"Will, what do you think of Texas so far? Not as primitive as you'd thought, eh?" His baritone chuckle sounded without waiting for an answer. His meaty arm gestured to the elegant dining room. "As you can see, I've done well for myself. If you play your cards right, I think you can overcome your foolish financial decisions and make a decent life out here."

Goblet to her lips, Delia froze. Did she hear him correctly? One look around the table confirmed it. Papa coughed into his napkin, no doubt stalling his reply. Mother's lips pressed into a hard line. Delia lowered her drink. How dare her uncle speak of their impoverished circumstances? The breeze from the open window gently ruffled the tassels on the velvet curtains, the only movement in the dining room.

She had to say something, take up for her father. But before she could, Papa spoke. "Let's speak about this in private."

"Come now, Will, we can talk plainly. Surely you see how foolish it was to trust our cousin with your funds. Of course, our father always said you were too gullible for your own good." Uncle Robert laughed. He thumped Papa's arm as if to coax his agreement, though Papa didn't respond.

Mother's fork clinked against the glassware. When she spoke, her words were low. "I beg your pardon, my William is neither foolish nor gullible. He is the kindest, most thoughtful man I know." Her voice broke. "I knew this move was a mistake."

She started to rise, but Papa stopped her, speaking too quietly to discern. Delia held her breath. She should stop all this. But what could she say?

Uncle Robert puffed on his cigar, blowing a stream of smoke over the table. He watched Mother and Papa's whispered conversation, tapping his bulky gold ring upon the wooden armrest. "Esther." He waited until she and Papa reluctantly met his gaze. "Do you really think I would bring your family all this way, at considerable expense, I might add, if I thought so little of my brother? I'm a businessman, and a good one. I brought you out here expecting your success."

The knuckles on Mother's fists were white, but her voice was level. "I'm well aware of our obligation to you. My husband and I will not only meet your expectations, we shall exceed them."

Aunt Mary chuckled and patted Mother's hand. "Of course you shall, dear. We have no doubt of it. Now let's stop all this serious talk and enjoy the meal, shall we?"

Oh, this was dreadful. They just arrived. Why all this dissension? Delia knotted her napkin in her fist and stared at her brothers, willing them to take action.

But it was Hazel who took center stage. Yawning loudly, she pouted. "Can we go now? I'm exhausted."

Aunt Mary sprang up. "Well, of course, dear. How very rude we've been, keeping you all from your new home." She cast a side-eyed glance at Uncle Robert. "Come, let us be on our way."

He smushed the cigar on a porcelain bread plate. "But there's chocolate cake for dessert."

His wife arched her eyebrows. "Robert, the child said she is tired."

The steely words hit their mark. Uncle Robert's expression sagged. "Oh, fine." He tossed his napkin onto the table and hurried from the room, his wife on his heels.

Everyone rose to follow them. Delia glanced at her parents and watched as Mother reached for Papa's hand. Papa lifted her fingers to his lips, and Delia turned away, touched at the rare show of affection. How often she took for granted the way they supported each other. These last weeks had been so difficult, but she never doubted her parents' love for each other. Perhaps that was more important than a comfortable way of life.

Delia hurried to her sister and took her aside. "Was that real, or did you purposely distract all of us?"

Hazel's eyes brightened with mischief. "You be the judge."

Delia laced her arm through Hazel's and followed their brothers out of the room. Just then, the door to the kitchen swung open, and Mrs. Van Dyke, the cook, entered the dining room bearing a tall layer cake in her hands. She stopped short. "Where'd they go?"

Turning back, Thomas pushed a dark lock of hair off his forehead and cast a longing glance at the confection. "Ma'am, is that chocolate cake?"

Mrs. Van Dyke beamed. "Would you like to take some with you? It'd be a shame to let it go to waste."

Thomas lit up. "I'd sure appreciate it, ma'am."

The woman returned quickly with a brown paper-wrapped parcel and placed it in Thomas's big hands. "There you go."

Rabb clapped Thomas on the shoulder. "Looks like uncle's not getting his cake."

~

Clarence Parker wiped his brow, standing after attaching the last wheel on the carriage. He had to admit, the conveyance was a beautiful creation. This was the finest piece of work he had ever crafted, thanks to Mr. Hardy granting him unrestricted creativity in making carriages. The coach was constructed for the banker and mayor, Clive Waldrop. The man was hard to satisfy, but this level of craftsmanship left no room for criticism.

Maybe this would persuade him to give Clarence an opportunity for a loan. Time ticked away before Mr. Hardy would retire and sell the place. Hopefully, his employer would be patient as he raised the funds to buy the business. No doubt, others would want a shot, considering how profitable the hardware store had become.

He took his handkerchief and mopped his face. Footsteps sounded behind him, and he turned, surprised to spot Thad Lewis. "Hey, there, Deputy. You come to admire my work?"

The wiry man didn't return the grin. "Sheriff wants to talk to you."

Clarence tucked the kerchief into his shirt pocket. "Can it wait until I get off in a few hours?"

Lewis shook his head. "He said now."

Worry coiled in Clarence's gut. What did the lawman want with him?

He glanced past Thad, toward the door to the hardware store. "Let me tell Mr. Hardy."

"I'll wait."

Clarence walked back into the store. He found Mr. Hardy seated at his desk, scattered bits of paper before him. The man looked up, blinking behind thick glasses. "Just the person I needed to talk to. I can't seem to make sense of these numbers." He chuckled apologetically, gesturing to the ledger book.

"Yes, sir, I'd be pleased to go over them. Only, I need to head over to the sheriff's office for a bit."

The older man stood with effort, concern in his expression. "Is something wrong?"

Again, dread corkscrewed in his belly. Clarence lifted his shoulders. "I'm not sure. Okay if I go with the deputy now?"

"Son, can I do anything to help?"

Son. Clarence swallowed. Mr. Hardy acted more like a father than Pa ever had. "Thank you, sir, but I'll be fine. I promise I won't be gone long."

Mr. Hardy nodded. "Take your time."

Clarence walked with the deputy along Second Street, no words exchanged between them. The departing locomotive was visible at the end of the road, the rhythmic chug-chug gaining speed to match Clarence's heartbeat. At the lawman's office, which also contained two jail cells, Thad held open the door.

Sheriff Akin stood, directing his gaze upon his second in command. "Deputy, go walk the town."

Hanging his hat on a peg, Thad chuckled. "A little early for that, don't you reckon?"

The sheriff's droopy white mustache hid his mouth, but the muscle in his jaw pulsed. Finally, Thad threw up his hands.

"Aw, fine." Thad shoved his hat on his cropped head. The door slammed behind him, making the window glass shudder.

Sheriff Akin's eyes shifted to Clarence. "Pull up a seat."

"Yes, sir." Sweat dampened the fabric under his arms. He grabbed a ladder-back chair in the small lobby and situated it before the desk. Removing his hat, he let it rest on his lap. Glancing up at the wall behind the sheriff, he noticed a new Wanted poster. His insides went cold. So that's what this was about.

Akin thumped the newspaper lying on his desk. "Seen today's paper?"

Clarence shook his head. The older man wordlessly passed him the weekly issue of the *Blooming Grove Gazette*. The headlines confirmed his fears: **Big Jake Killed in Jail Break Out**. In the smaller typeset below, Virgil Mason Escapes.

His mouth turned cotton dry. He willed the tremor from his voice as he returned the paper. "They're coming here."

He hadn't been aware that he'd spoken his thoughts until the sheriff leaned over his desk. "And just how do you know that? You got a tip this was gonna happen?"

"What? Oh, no, sir. I haven't seen any of them since that day in court."

"Then how do you know their plans?"

"I—I don't." He swallowed, unable to admit that this very thing had occupied his nightmares for the last eight years. "It makes sense. I testified against the gang." Against Virgil. And if he was certain of anything, it was the depth of the outlaw's hatred of turncoats.

The sheriff stroked his mustache thoughtfully. "And they want revenge."

Clarence gripped his hat brim and nodded. How was this happening? He never should have settled down and grown comfortable. Not here, at least. He should've gone far away, to California or Oregon or Canada.

No prison was strong enough to hold Big Jake's gang.

He needed to go. "Is that all, then? Mind if I get back to the store? Mr. Hardy needs me."

The sheriff held up one hand. "Soon enough. Before that, I need you to do something for me."

Clarence's gut tightened. Was this some kind of test? The lawman hadn't wanted his help before. He used his shirtsleeve to wipe the sweat from his forehead.

Tension eased from the sheriff's expression. "Look, I'm not

looking to cast stones. I've watched you. Old man Hardy trusts you. Reckon I can too."

"You said you needed something?"

Akin speared the newspaper with his finger. "These varmints are headed to my town, and you're the only man who can spot them. If Virgil Mason comes to town, or any of his associates, I want to know. Can you do that?"

Was that all? "Yessir."

Sheriff Akin didn't wait for a response. "He likely does not resemble the boy you knew. He's a man in his mid-twenties."

His glance flicked to the Wanted poster. Even with a drawing as lousy as that one, he'd recognize Virgil. That sneer was etched in his memory.

He stood. "If that's all, I need to head back to work."

With a curt bob of his head, Akin dismissed him.

Clarence rose, eager to leave the cave of a room. Just as he laid his hand on the doorknob, the sheriff spoke.

"By the way, you might oughta keep an eye on the seamstress shop."

An incredulous guffaw rose to the surface. Did the sheriff seriously believe outlaws would come to Blooming Grove for a new set of clothes? The little lady who spent her days at the sewing machine looked terrified whenever he'd nodded at her through the window. "No offense, but that's probably the least likely place the group would go."

The lawman blinked. "Don't you know who the seamstress is?"

Clarence shook his head. Why did he care?

"She's Eleanor Baskin. Big Jake's widow."

Aunt Mary filled the ride to their farm with chatty gossip. Delia, still reeling from the tense luncheon conversation, gazed unseeing at the town, her eyelids growing heavy after the filling meal.

She started when Hazel nudged her. "We're here."

Wrapped in the web of slumber, Delia wiped a trail of saliva from her cheek. Her gaze caught on the wrapped cake in Thomas's hands. Her stomach gurgled. How wonderful to eat that delicious cake with a steaming cup of coffee.

"Where are we?" Tall grasses gently swayed on both sides of the narrow road. She inhaled the clean air, a needed contrast to the days of riding in a stifling rail car.

Uncle Robert hopped down from the carriage and faced the family with a sheepish expression. "This is the farm. I realize it looks a bit overgrown. But you'll have the weeds cleared and a new crop planted in no time. Folks around here won't recognize it."

For a long moment, no one spoke. What could they say? A strong breeze might collapse all the shacks within the tall weeds —the home, outhouse, barns, and other indistinguishable structures. A windmill provided a squeaky backdrop. There was nothing fine about this place. Certainly nothing to beckon them home.

Papa climbed down from the driver's seat and came to stand beside his brother. "This is what you brought me here to farm?"

Delia held her breath. Surely Uncle Robert would clap Papa on the back any moment and declare this a great prank.

Instead, the big man frowned. "I told you it needed a bit of work."

Papa let out a heavy breath and grasped the back of his neck. "More than a bit."

"You wanted work, and—"

Papa held up his hand. "I'm grateful for all you've done to help us. But this? There's no way we can put this place in working order, especially if you expect to sell it in six months."

Uncle Robert said nothing.

Thomas hopped to the ground and strode to Papa. "You got me and Rabb. The three of us, we can do it."

Papa straightened, as if fortified by the quiet words. "All right, then."

Movement on the road caught Delia's attention. The wagon bearing their possessions halted in the middle of the lane. The driver called, "Where do you want this stuff?"

Papa walked to the wagon. "Just unload it here. Reckon we'll have to cut a path to the cabin before we start hauling the beds."

Uncle Robert took Aunt Mary's elbow. "Let's be on our way so they can settle in." He helped her into the carriage and took the reins in hand. "Let us know if you need anything."

Anything? By the looks of the place, they needed *everything,* beginning with a scythe to cut a path to their house through the tall weeds. From the road, she saw nothing that resembled a home.

In the hush that remained after the clip-clop of horses' hooves receded, Delia tried to tamp her frustration, pacing the rutted dirt road. This couldn't be their future. No one deserved to be dumped in the middle of nowhere and told to make the best of it.

Mother and Papa stood apart from the group, but Delia stepped nearer so she could hear their conversation.

"It's not so bad, is it?" Papa's face creased with worry as he stroked Mother's arm. "You and the girls can make the cabin nice and cheerful, can't you?"

"What cabin? You mean that leaning building barely visible through the overgrowth?" She scoffed and wiggled out of his grasp. "I can't believe Robert would ask it of me. Of any of us." When Mother's gaze met hers, Delia looked away. She should leave them to their privacy. Yet her desire to know his answer rooted her to the spot.

"Esther, we have no choice. We're beholden to him."

Delia's hopes sank. They weren't leaving this place. Sickened, she returned to her siblings. "We're staying."

Rabb scoffed. "What'd you think?"

She rubbed her face. "I'm so weary, I can't think of anything."

Thomas gestured to Rabb. "Come on, let's have a look at this place." He pulled a small notebook from his shirt pocket, along with a pencil. "I'll make a list of things that need repairs."

Delia put her hands on her hips. "That's simple. It's spelled e-v-e-r-y-t-h-i-n-g."

Hazel leaned on Delia. "This is a nightmare."

It was. Nothing had prepared them for the disrepair of this place. And to think, not so long ago, they'd lived in a large, bustling home with gas lights and an indoor water closet. A mansion, compared to the hovel before them.

Delia's gaze caught on her mother's bulging waist, and guilt assailed her. She nudged her sister. "Look, we both hate this place. But they need us to be brave. Especially with Mother's delicate condition. We don't want to upset her more than she is."

Hazel shrugged. "I don't want to trouble her. But I also don't want to live in this horrible place."

"I understand. But right now, don't focus on this place. Mother needs us." Delia lifted her skirt and, with mincing steps, made her way through the tangle of grasses and vines that caught at her feet, making her stumble. She halted in front of a log structure. "Oh!" Strong odor lay like fog around the place. Delia pulled a handkerchief from her sleeve to cover her nose.

Hazel cried out and squeezed her nostrils together. "Disgusting!"

Just behind them, Papa said, "An animal must've died." He cupped his hand around his mouth. "Boys, see anything?"

Deep voices echoed from inside the cabin. A grinning Rabb emerged, holding a decomposing opossum by its long tail. "This." He tossed it into the tall weeds on the side of the house, causing Hazel to squeal.

Mother raised her voice. "You two be careful in there. Watch for rotten floorboards."

"And pray that roof doesn't collapse," Delia murmured. She swatted at a buzzing insect circling her head before turning to Papa. "How long has it been abandoned?"

Papa cleared his throat. "Not sure. Robert said some of the first settlers to the area built this dogtrot fifty years ago. They constructed it with summer's heat in mind. That covered breezeway that connects the two cabins is where we'll sleep, just like they did in the old days."

She blinked. "With insects and rodents and wild animals?" To say nothing of the stifling heat. How would anyone sleep in such miserable conditions?

A curious bumblebee circled around the four of them. Hazel turned to Mother. "Please tell me this isn't where we'll live."

Mother glanced at Papa. "I'm afraid it is."

As if to punctuate the awful truth, the whine of locusts grew deafening. Delia covered her ears, though she could wail right along with them. This cabin, along with every other building on the farm, would suck the life out of her family.

Thomas and Rabb emerged from the dilapidated house. "Where's that cake? I'm hungry."

Rabb was perpetually hungry.

"How can you think about eating with that horrible stench in the air?" But even so, Delia followed the brothers back to the wagon. Maybe the dessert would lift her spirits a bit.

First to arrive, Thomas reached for the parcel that sat on top of a wooden crate, then jumped back. "Ow!" " He wagged his hand. "Bees got to it."

Sure enough, ten or more honeybees swarmed the treat. Not even a chocolate cake could survive this wild place.

Texas was much worse than she imagined.

Chapter 2

"Never has there been such intense interest in a particular quilt style as there was in the crazy quilt during the period 1876 to 1900 ... The Singer Sewing Machine Company used crazy quilts as a symbol on their trade cards; women's magazines gave directions for making crazy quilts as table covers along with patterns for decorating them, and silk manufacturers promoted the use of their scrap waste in making crazy quilts"—The San Francisco Examiner (San Francisco, California) Sunday, September 01, 1985.

T he odor of dead animals made Delia's stomach heave. Grasshoppers sprang up all around her, clinging to her clothing before she brushed the creatures away. She'd never seen so many spider webs. It was hard to avoid the wispy remains, and countless times, Delia shivered just thinking of the arachnids crawling up her skirts.

After working tirelessly to clean both sides of the dogtrot, Delia, Hazel, and Mother laid six pallets side by side in the covered breezeway between the two rooms of the cabin. Though Delia was weary from the endless labor, sleep eluded

21

her that first night. So, she sat on the steps and let her gaze wander to the wondrous, star-filled sky. One by one, her siblings joined her, crying out when a falling orb zipped across the indigo skies.

"Why haven't we ever done this before?" Hazel voiced the wistful question, but everyone experienced the same emotion. Had they been too immersed in their own worlds to pay attention to creation's beauty?

Though the existence was grueling, the time spent talking and laughing with her family buoyed her spirits. In Georgia, when needs and desires were easily met, she'd taken her family for granted. Here, desires were little more than fanciful wishes. This was a land where basic food, shelter, and clothing were all that mattered.

At the end of each day, she'd collapsed onto her pallet alongside her family, grateful for the air that wafted over them in the covered breezeway. Soft snores lifted within minutes.

All in all, it had been a challenging first week in their new homeland.

By the time Sunday arrived, Delia was more than ready for a Sabbath. Starting before dawn and continuing until well after dusk, all six of them had worked together to make the cabin habitable. Delia hadn't known what hard work was until she'd swept, scrubbed wood floors and cabinets, caulked the chinking between logs, and helped lift heavy timber to brace the falling porch roof.

The prospect of church both exhilarated and overwhelmed her. She longed to meet their neighbors and future friends. Though she'd brought only one Sunday dress, it was a stylish light blue poplin with leg-of-mutton sleeves. The pastel shade brought out the coppery tones of her auburn hair.

Thanks to Uncle Robert's provision for a wagon and two horses, the Truitts rode together to Valley Creek Church.

Seated close in the wagon bed, Hazel turned to Delia, frowning. "I'm nervous."

Compassion melted Delia. Poor Hazel. Fourteen was an awful age full of insecurity and swirling emotions, all happening in a body shifting from child to woman. A fierce protectiveness rose within her, and she grabbed Hazel's sweaty hand within both hers.

"There's no need to worry yourself over making friends. Just be friendly, and you'll have a bevy of chums."

"Think so?"

"Why wouldn't you? You're smart, pretty ... sweet." She swallowed. Sweet wasn't exactly true of Hazel Truitt. But what would a little fib hurt? It might even encourage a milder disposition. "And fashionable. I love the way you've swept up the front of your gorgeous dark hair and left the rest to cascade in curls down your back."

Hazel rolled her eyes. "That's only because Mother won't let me pull it all up until I'm sixteen."

Delia put her finger to her lips with a pointed stare at Mother, sitting within earshot on the wagon seat beside Papa. "And you're clever to boot. Mark my words, you'll have friends galore." Hopefully.

The crease in between Hazel's perfectly shaped eyebrows disappeared. "I've been praying like crazy."

Delia tucked the damp hand under her arm with a final pat and nodded at their dozing brothers. "Those sillies are the ones you should pray for. How can anyone sleep in this wagon bed with all this jostling?"

As if on cue, Rabb snorted loud enough to wake himself and Thomas. He straightened, frowning when the girls laughed.

Mother turned and cast them a warning look as the wagon came to rest in the churchyard. "See to it you enter quietly, as we are noticeably late." She directed the last comment toward Papa, who ignored the jibe as he jumped to the ground.

Delia gazed up at the white church. An unidentifiable hymn poured through the open windows. Nervous pangs tightened her stomach. Would she find new friendships here? Taking Thomas's hand, she carefully stepped to the ground and brushed bits of hay from her pale blue skirt.

Hazel blinked rapidly as she surveyed the building before them. Delia summoned a cheery tone. "Smile your brightest, dearie. Everything will be fine."

They walked in a line up the stairs to the door, first Papa, then Mother, Delia, Hazel, and Rabb, with Thomas bringing up the rear in his easy-going, no-hurry saunter. With every step, Delia tried to school her expression to one of serenity, the very opposite of the dread that churned inside her.

The air was still and warm when they entered the church building. People crammed elbow to elbow on both sides of a center aisle, singing in lackluster fashion to an out-of-tune piano at the front. An urge to flee caused Delia's step to falter. Maybe all the seats were taken, and they could slip out, unnoticed.

But that hope fizzled as the last discordant note ended, and the door snapped shut behind them, causing heads to swivel their way. A girl who looked to be no more than five years old stepped into the aisle to face them, shaking her chubby index finger. "You're late!"

Laughter worked through the stifling congregation as a woman grabbed the child and cast the Truitts an apologetic look. Delia's cheeks burned. If only these people would stop staring, and she could crawl under a rock.

A short, stout man rushed up the aisle, hand extended to Papa. "Welcome, friends. I'm Pastor Swenson." He turned to the crowd with a broad smile. "Who will make room for these folks?"

Shuffling of feet and belongings broke the silence. Someone called from the front, and Pastor Swenson gestured for the Truitts to follow. "Here we go, the Browns kindly gave up their front-row seats. Plenty of room for all your family."

Delia kept her gaze on the wooden-plank floor as they filed up the aisle to the front pew.

Standing between Rabb and Hazel, Delia shifted from one foot to the other as the congregation belted one hymn after another. Was there a rule about standing for the whole time? If so, she'd never return.

When the minister finally gestured for the congregation to sit, Delia could have cheered. Until Pastor Swenson said, "But let's have our visitors remain standing so we might get to know you better."

No, no, no. This was not the way she wanted to be introduced into the community. Heat crept up her neck. No doubt the tips of her ears were as red as a tomato. She stole a glance at Hazel, sure she would be on the verge of tears, bless her heart.

But her younger sister wasn't tearful or shy. Instead, she faced the congregation with a bright smile, waggling her fingers.

Delia hissed, "Turn around this minute!"

Hazel blinked. "I'm being friendly, like you told me to."

Chuckles fluttered through the room.

Lord, if You care about me at all, bring forth a tornado, or a herd of squealing pigs. Even a pair of skunks. Any diversion will do.

Pastor Swenson clasped his hands. "We are happy you're joining our fellowship this morning. Please, tell us about yourselves."

Papa gripped his bowler hat and directed his words to the

people sitting behind them. "I am William Truitt, just here from Georgia. This is my dear wife, Esther. My oldest son, Thomas, Rabb, Delia, who's eighteen and unmarried, and Hazel."

A groan caught in her throat. Papa might as well have put a sign on her back: *Eighteen and Desperate for a Man.*

She twisted her fingers together and willed the preacher to move on with the service.

Instead, he kept up the questioning. "Truitt, you say? Any relation to the Truitt's Dry Goods?"

"Robert is my brother. He told me good things about this town."

Pastor Swenson grinned. "Ah, yes, I thought so. Too bad they aren't here today."

Someone called, "Remember, they took a little trip to Dallas."

Another voice piped up. "Don't worry. Mary said they'd be back and have the store open Monday morning."

Delia glanced at Rabb with a frown. Was there no end to this interrogation? She longed to ease her right foot out of its too-snug slipper.

After a few more questions, the pastor smiled. "We're having a potluck on the lawn after services, and we'd love for your family to be our guests."

At last, Pastor Swenson turned his attention to the sermon, and Delia sank onto the mahogany pew, tugging on Hazel's sleeve when the girl remained standing, seemingly transfixed with the congregation's attention. This might be the longest morning ever.

An hour later, when the service was over, Delia followed her brothers up the crowded aisle. Keeping her gaze on the shoes all around her, she ignored any comments until she crossed the threshold and gulped in the fresh air. Just one moment to relax, then she'd be ready to face the church members who knew far more about her than she'd like. Except the most important thing. How would she hope to offer her services as a seamstress if all they knew was her age and marital status?

Maybe Papa thought the only way she could help their financial predicament was to marry her off. She'd have to prove him wrong.

She stood beside her brothers under the shade of a pecan tree. Thomas's serious gaze on the crowd contrasted with Rabb's grin. Delia realized, with a start, how much like Thomas she was in this moment. How had she ever considered herself a social person?

Rabb nudged Thomas. "Would you look at them girls? Come on, let's talk to 'em."

Thomas shook his head.

Rabb shrugged. "Fine." He reached for Delia's arm. "Come on, Red."

"What are you doing? Let me go!"

She wrenched away, and he faced her. "We're gonna be friendly. Can't let Hazel have all the fun." He gestured to a group across the lawn, where their sister laughed and chatted as if she'd never been worried about breaking into a new group.

With a mix of pride and envy, Delia watched the confident way her sister tossed her head. Had her words given Hazel such confidence? Maybe she should heed her own advice.

"I hate to admit it, but you're right. We can't let her outshine us."

After all, the worst had already happened. Might as well venture out.

~

Walking beside her dashing brother was a sure way to make friends. The circle of young people chatting and laughing opened to include them. Delia forced herself to smile with every introduction.

Her gaze caught on a tall man who stepped forward and removed his hat. "I'm Clarence Parker."

She placed her hand in his. "I'm ..." She blinked, captured like a moth to the light. What an amazing color for eyes. Like looking into the grayish green of sea waves. Or was it the waft of cologne or his dapper suit that held her suspended as if she had no notion of how to daisy-chain words into a sensible message? Her gaze landed on his large hand enveloping hers.

"I'm ..." She swallowed. What was wrong with her?

His lips curved upward in a kind, patient smile. She'd never liked mustaches. Until now.

"Your name is Delia, yes?" His smile was kind.

"Yes, that's right." He released her hand, and she searched for some way to keep him in front of her. "Your eyes remind me of the ocean." She blinked. Why did she say that?

A flicker of surprise crossed his face. "I haven't seen it."

"Me too. I-I mean, I've only seen it once. It was beautiful."

Her cheeks burned. She'd just told a stranger she thought his eyes were beautiful. One minute, she couldn't speak. The next moment, she couldn't stop the babble of lunacy. What must he think?

Rabb held out his hand to the man, his expression anything but friendly. "Rabb Truitt."

"Rabb, this is Mr. Clarence Parker."

The two men shook hands. Rabb glanced at her from the corner of his eye and turned his body so that his back faced her. "So, Clarence, you gotta job?"

Of all the nerve. The one time she wanted more than anything to speak with a man, he came between them.

"Delia?"

She looked up at a young woman with light hair, spectacles, and warm smile. "I see you've met my brother, Clarence. I'm Sallie."

Deila's lips parted in surprise. Where he was dashing and fashionable, his sister wore a simple yellow dress with a plain straw hat, and wisps of her fine, blonde hair escaped from her chignon. She held a Bible but no bag, and from behind her wire-rimmed spectacles, her blue eyes exuded sincerity. Delia liked her at once.

"I'm glad to know you. It's a bit overwhelming, all these new acquaintances." But this one, she'd remember.

Sallie adjusted the Bible to her left side. "I hoped you'd be at church today. I just knew we'd be friends when I saw y'all move in next door."

Delia cocked her head. "Oh?"

Sallie shook her head with a self-deprecating chuckle. "Sorry. I should've said we're the next farm over, maybe half a mile down the road."

Before Delia could respond, Sallie grasped her hand. "Come with me. The girls are dying to meet you."

Delia allowed herself to be dragged once again, but this time, she didn't mind. Five or six young women dressed in pastel dresses and fashionable hats chirped enthusiastic greetings.

"We're delighted a new family has moved in," one girl said.

Another added, "We've been bored to tears with the male population in this town. Until now." They giggled.

And Rabb thought he needed help finding a good woman?

A willowy blonde lifted her chin. "You spoke to Clarence." Her gaze flicked over Delia.

"Is that not allowed?"

The blonde narrowed her eyes. "If I were you, I'd be careful not to flirt with men who are taken."

"But—"

A curvaceous brunette playfully pushed between them. "All right, that's enough, you two." To Delia, she said, "Pay no attention to Gert. She thinks all the men are hers."

Delia folded her arms. "I'm not here to get a man, if that's what you think—"

The petite woman between them laughed. "Oh, we're all after a husband, aren't we, girls?" Her lighthearted manner diffused the tension. "Our slightly possessive friend here is Gert Waldrop, and I'm Lucy Grant. I spoke to your mother a few minutes ago. She tells me you are an expert needlewoman."

"My *mother* said that?"

The girls around her giggled, and Delia flushed. "It's just that she thinks my efforts should be spent on more practical things." Directing her words to Lucy, she nodded. "I'm working on a crazy quilt."

Lucy's mouth formed an O. "Another crazy quilter. I'd love it if you'd teach me how to do that elaborate embroidery."

Gert placed her gloved hands on her hips with a huff. "Well, I like that, Lucy Grant. You know I can teach you all the latest stitches."

Lucy patted Gert's arm and winked conspiratorially at the rest of the group. "Yes, but you get rather impatient, you know. But here's an idea—invite Delia to our sewing bee next Sunday."

A chorus of approval rose, and the willowy Gert managed a tight smile in Delia's direction. "You may come."

What a limp invitation. But Delia refused to let it dampen her spirits. "I appreciate your generous offer. I accept."

Gert's lips flattened. "Our simple little gathering might not impress an Expert Needlewoman."

Delia blinked at the jab. Was all this about one brief, though magical, conversation with Clarence Parker?

Sallie scoffed. "Gert! Don't tease. Your sewing bees are not simple affairs." She turned to Delia. "You won't believe the fancy little sandwiches and cakes she has for us. And Gert's sewing is exquisite. I can't wait to see what she's entering in the fair this year."

The fair. She'd forgotten to ask Aunt Mary for details.

Heads moved in agreement, and someone said, "She's bound to win another blue ribbon. She's famous for her samplers, lace, and beautiful crazy quilts too."

Someone across the churchyard called for everyone to gather for the meal. Once the blessing ended, people queued up on either side of the long wooden tables that held a bounty of food. Delia walked behind Sallie Parker and Lucy Grant, who chatted and laughed.

But Delia's gaze tracked Gert Waldrop as she hurried to catch up to Clarence Parker. As she tucked her hand into the fold of his arm, Gert cast a sly look back at Delia.

The situation was as plain as dry toast. Gert considered her a rival. For Clarence Parker's attentions or fancy needlework? Perhaps both. One thing was clear, though. Gert didn't appreciate competition.

Well, too bad. Delia thrived on it.

Clarence shoveled chicken salad into his mouth and tried to tune out Gert Waldrop's shrill voice. Clever trick, inviting him to sit with her family in front of her influential father. Her pa was the mayor of the town, as well as the banker who stood between him and the loan he needed to purchase the hardware store. He'd been trying to get in front of Waldrop for weeks, and the man had no time for him. So of course, he'd jumped at the chance to discuss a loan with the man, even if it was at a church picnic with curious folks listening.

Only, Gert blocked all his efforts at conversation. Her father and mother had finished eating and had left to mingle with others, leaving Clarence alone to endure Gert's flirtations.

Laughter drew his attention to the blanket where his sister sat with Delia Truitt. Her movements were graceful, like she'd been through finishing school. With her thick hair piled on top of her head, she looked like that Gibson girl from the magazines. He couldn't keep his eyes off her.

Judging by the way other men were staring, he wasn't the only one interested in her. He needed to make his move, before someone else won her heart first.

Whoa. Where did that thought come from? At twenty-four, he wasn't looking for a wife. Not yet, anyway. First, he'd put all his efforts into building his business and making a profit. Then he'd build a little house. After that, he could think about a wife and children. Maybe by then, he'd have figured out how to be the kind of loving husband his father had never been. Better to live alone than in an unhappy home.

Besides, what kind of woman would want to marry a former outlaw? Not many around here knew about that part of his life, but he'd have to confess it to the woman he loved.

His gaze caught on the auburn-haired beauty.

"Clarence! Are you listening to me?"

With a start, he focused on Gert. "I'm sorry. What did you say?"

She sighed. "You haven't said a word about my new dress. I wore it just for you." Gert's mouth pinched in an exaggerated pout.

"For me?" Alarm bells sounded in his brain.

"Of course I did. Don't you think it's pretty?"

Clarence took a swig of cool tea. He hoped she didn't have designs on him. But she sure was acting like she did. "It's fine."

Gert's laugh pierced the air. "Oh, Clarence, you say the sweetest things."

What?

She smirked in the direction of the new girl. Ah. So this was a little show of possession courtesy of Gertrude Waldrop.

Well, he'd put a stop to that. He gathered the remnants of his meal and got to his feet. "If you'll excuse me, Miss Waldrop, I need to speak to my sister."

"But—"

He ignored her protests and returned his dishes before walking to Sallie and her lovely friend "May I join you?"

"Sit down, Clarence." Sallie patted the quilt.

The most beautiful woman gazed up at him. "Please do, Mr. Parker."

His heart flipped. Aw, crumb. Two minutes in her presence and he couldn't think straight.

What kind of enchantment was this? He really shouldn't be talking to her. He had a past to redeem and a future to grab with both hands. He ought to walk away.

Instead, he folded his legs underneath him. "May I call you Delia?"

Chapter 3

The ritual of the quilting party in rural communities and along the frontiers gave a woman a chance to dress up a little, to spend a day in the company of her friends and to work at something to be used more gratefully and remembered longer than most of the fruits of her dull repetitive household chores—and was a means of creating something of her own self.—The Daily News (Lebanon, Pennsylvania) April 29, 1977.

A week passed with no sign of the handsome Mr. Parker. Which was fine. After all, hadn't Delia told her sister she had no interest in a beau? She didn't need any man, not even the intriguing Clarence Parker. She didn't.

When he hadn't shown up to church this morning, her hopeful attitude vanished. To make matters worse, Sunday lunch had run long, and she'd scrambled to clean the dishes in time for the sewing bee every young woman in town was sure to attend. Then she'd had to wait ten minutes for Rabb to quit shooting cans and drive her to town.

As they boarded the wagon, Mother hurried over. "Delia, take this along to Gert's mother."

She handed up a glass jar covered with brown paper and tied with twine. "My peach preserves, straight from home."

"Ma, save them for us. I've had a hankering for preserves."

Mother batted Rabb's hand. "There are plenty. Delia, don't forget."

Delia agreed and placed them inside her sewing bag. "Let's go."

Progress along the road was slow, and Delia repeatedly asked her brother to speed up. "It would've been quicker to ride my two-wheeler."

Without sparing her a glance, Rabb shrugged. "So why didn't you?"

"I don't know my way around this town."

"Pretty simple, if you ask me."

She crossed her arms. He knew very well she had no spare time to study a map of the town, much less go exploring. The only reason she knew Gert Waldrop lived at Number Five, Banker's Row was because Sallie had told her.

"There's no missing it. It's the fanciest house in town."

When the wagon drew close to the road marked Banker's Row, she told Rabb to let her out. Surely she could walk faster than he drove.

Banker's Row turned out to be a lonely road inhabited by few homes. Good thing it was a sunny day, or she might be skittish. Not far ahead, though, a wire fence outlined a lush lawn. A copse of dense cedar trees obscured the house itself, but surely that was Gert Waldrop's home. She peered at her gold watch. The watch hands showed a quarter past three. Fifteen minutes late.

She dropped the timepiece and it swung back and forth on its long chain as she strode toward the home. The carpetbag grew heavy, and she shifted it to the other hand, wincing when something solid thumped her leg. The peach jam. She'd make sure to give it to Mrs. Waldrop first thing.

A few steps more brought her squarely before a manicured lawn, with formal flower gardens framing the most magnificent house she'd ever seen. Sallie's words took on new meaning. It was far fancier than any other home she'd seen in Blooming Grove.

It was as if the architect patterned it with filigree in mind. Three stories of latticed adornment. The veranda on the first floor stretched the entire width of the house and around one side of the soft yellow home, where a castle-like turret sprouted from the second floor, the kind that brought Rapunzel to mind. She counted no less than three balconies on the third story. Brick chimneys jutted from various sides of the pitched roof, and shining glass windows stared as if daring her to stride the length of the brick walkway, climb those six stone steps, and approach the imposing double doors.

She fanned her face. What was she doing here? She, who slept alongside her brothers and sister in the breezeway of an old dogtrot. The bedroom wasn't fancier, with hanging quilts dividing the space for privacy. Her large home back in Georgia had been auctioned away, along with her pride.

Or so she thought. Wasn't it that very same pride that kept her moving up the sidewalk? Dented. Wounded. Raw. But pride, nonetheless.

What did Grandmother used to say? "Where the Lord wills, He gives the way."

Saying it aloud kept her feet in motion. She climbed the grand steps and arrived on the porch, winded. She looked back along the path.

Do not retreat.

She was here to sew, not gawk at the garish house. Finally, she'd have two whole hours to work, undisturbed, on her fancy stitches that joined one silk patch to another. She only hoped her calloused hands wouldn't snag the fine fabric.

Sewing bees were famous for gossip, and hopefully, this one would help her spread the word of her exquisite needlework. Once people knew her capability, they would trust her with their sewing needs. And maybe, with her added funds, her family would never again endure the heartbreak of a public auction.

Six months. That's all the time she had.

But first, the sewing bee, on the other side of these towering mahogany doors. Taking a deep breath, she rapped three times.

The door opened and Mrs. Waldrop, an older version of her daughter, smiled pleasantly. "Good afternoon. Delia, isn't it?" With a sweeping gesture, she indicated Delia should step over the threshold into the grand entryway.

As she entered, taking in the high walls lined with floral wallpaper and polished woodwork, the brown-paper-wrapped jar of preserves once again thumped against her leg, a painful reminder of their presence in the carpetbag. Where they would stay.

Mrs. Waldrop glided past a round table that held a tall vase brimming with colorful flowers, no doubt freshly picked from her garden. "The girls are in the morning room."

Delia followed in her footsteps, more like a little child than a young woman. All her pluck had seemed to vanish within these gilded walls.

At the doorway, feminine laughter wafted to her. Mrs. Waldrop turned to her. "How is your dear mother?"

"She is well."

Mrs. Waldrop clasped her hands together and made a tsking sound. "One more mouth to feed, with so many living in that tiny cabin." She cocked her head to the side in feigned sympathy, as if to provoke a rush of confession. Was that what she wanted? For Delia to spill some sort of secret?

For one heady moment, Delia thought about baiting the woman with some contrived story, just to see the reaction. Instead, she smiled. "We're very eager to welcome this baby. Mother says all babies are blessings from the Lord."

Mrs. Waldrop's eyebrows arched. "I see. Please tell your mother I plan to call on her this week to welcome her to our fair little town."

The woman turned, leaving Delia to wander into the spacious morning room alone. Young women sat in clusters and chatted while crocheting, tatting, or embroidering. Gert strode to her with a tight smile. "I see you made it."

"I'm sorry I'm late."

"Were you? I hadn't noticed. Well, go on, sit somewhere. Our maid will serve cookies and lemonade in a bit." Gert darted away, leaving Delia to scan the room for an empty space.

She settled on the brocade divan beside a girl who introduced herself as Milly Akin. With wide eyes, she leaned to speak in Delia's ear. "This is your first time here, isn't it? This is the grandest home I've ever seen. I'll bet you're just like me, dying of jealousy. Some girls have all the luck." Milly's sigh was long and wistful. Turning her gaze to Delia's carpetbag, she said, "What did you bring?"

Glad for the subject change, Delia smiled. "My crazy quilt. It's been a year and it's still far from finished. Would you like to see it?"

She reached into her bag, avoiding the preserves as she withdrew the quilt from the carpet bag. As she unfolded it, Milly squealed, attracting other admirers. Delia couldn't help beaming.

"This is gorgeous." Lucy Grant gingerly touched the bit of

white silk that bore soft green watercolor strokes. "I read about this method of painting on silk. It's the Japanese style, isn't it?"

"And just look at all those complicated stitches," Milly said.

"Girls, look at the way Delia has combined the herringbone stitch with lazy daisies," Lucy said. Echoes of appreciation brought gooseflesh to Delia's arms.

Sallie chuckled. "Well, I don't know anything about fancy stitches or any other kind, for that matter. I can hardly hem a skirt."

Delia's heart warmed to Sallie and her open humility. "I'd be glad to help you."

"Help me too," echoed around the room. Except for Gert, who stood across the large room, hands on her hips. Then, snapping her fingers, she approached the group.

"I have an idea. Girls, why don't we ask our new friend, Miss Delia Truitt, if she will teach us her big-city techniques?"

"Oh, I'm not from a big city, just Pine Mountain, Georgia."

Gert's smile was saccharin. "I'd never have guessed."

There was no mistaking the dripping sarcasm, especially when the girls around them exchanged glances. Delia's face heated. The girl might as well have called her a country bumpkin.

"You don't mind helping us, do you?" Gert arched her eyebrows. She had the upper hand and it was clear she knew it.

Delia hesitated. She needed these hours to stitch. Too many chores awaited at home to ever have a chunk of time like this. Yet she wanted to get to know these women, make friends. What better way than helping them create beautiful art with needle and thread?

Lucy shook her head. "Gert, don't put Delia on the spot like that. She came to sew, not tutor."

"That's right. She works hard all week." This from Sallie. "She deserves time for fun."

Gert batted her light blue eyes at Delia and raised her voice so all could hear. "I'm sorry, I was under the impression you wanted to help these sweet women. Was I mistaken?"

Delia forced a smile. "I'd be glad to help. Who'll be first?"

For the next two hours, Delia rotated around the room to help anyone who needed her. She did everything from demonstrating how to thread a needle, to sketching out an assortment of fancy stitches, to discussing the strategy of piecing a crazy quilt while making it look effortlessly random.

When two hours came to an end, Delia realized the refreshments had come and gone without her tasting any. Her empty stomach could attest to that. As she and her friends were packing their projects, she peeked at Gert's.

Unlike the others, her sizable quilt was a work of art. Delia stepped closer to examine the even stitches that connected each swatch of silk and velvet.

"It's lovely."

Gert lifted her chin. "Another blue-ribbon winner, I'm sure." She narrowed her gaze. "You're not considering entering the county fair, are you? I'd hate for you to be disappointed."

"I might, if there's time to finish my quilt. When is it?"

Lucy looked up from her seat on the divan. "It's in October. You ought to enter." She cut her eyes at Gert. "Competition is a wonderful thing."

Sallie came to stand next to her. "The grand prize winner in each category gets a cash prize." When Delia met her gaze, her friend nodded. "Fifty dollars."

"Oh." What a difference that kind of money would make to her family.

Delia glanced at her quilt, lying on the sofa where she'd abandoned it. It was far from finished. Worse, she'd just lost the only two hours where no one called her to cook or clean or milk cows. The chances of finishing by October seemed bleak. With a sigh, she folded the quilt and opened her carpetbag to tuck it inside.

Before she could catch it, the jar of preserves tumbled out, dropping onto the wooden floor with a sickening thud. Glass and sticky peach preserves oozed onto the expensive rug. Delia clasped her hand to her mouth, horrified.

Over her shoulder, Gert cried out. "What on earth is that?"

Cheeks burning, Delia attempted to wipe up the gooey mess. A fragment of glass pricked her finger, but it didn't hurt as much as Gert's scorn. "I'm so sorry. I'll clean it."

Gert shooed her away. "Stop all that before you do more harm to my mother's imported carpet. Leave it for the maid."

Delia sat back on her heels and apologized once more.

"A lot of good that does. Don't you know better than to bring something like this to a sewing bee?"

Delia set her jaw. It would never happen again.

Chapter 4

"Farm and country women did not have easy access to silks and other fancy fabrics, but this certainly did not diminish their love for crazy quilting. These humble crazy quilts were made mostly of wool, cottons, and a few special fabrics. Some farm women worked like men in the fields, but still found time for needlework. Their crazy quilts are a tribute to every woman's basic need to beautify her surroundings."—Judith Baker Montano, The Crazy Quilt Handbook, Revised 2nd Edition.

Delia tried to erase the mishap from her mind and focus on the hope of the fair. The more she thought about finishing her project, the more excited she grew. This could be the perfect way to spread the word about her skills. If she won a ribbon, then her crazy quilt would hang for everyone in the county to see for the duration of the fair. Plus, there was a chance of winning enough cash to ensure her family could relocate to a decent home at the six-month deadline.

That tipped the scales in favor of entering the fair. Today was July 3, leaving her more than enough time to finish her quilt, as long as she purposed to work every evening after chores and every time she found a short block of time at her disposal. Like now.

Delia retrieved her carpetbag and strode outside to make use of the midafternoon sunlight. She settled on the top step and sighed. How strange, though nice, to be alone. The distant lowing of cattle and an occasional bee buzzing past provided a tranquil backdrop as she threaded her needle with gold embroidery thread.

The methodical movement of her fingers soothed her. In and out, up and down, slanted, and straight. She lost herself in the chevron stitches that secured the meeting of pink silk and gray velvet. This was what she loved, creating beauty from swatches and samples that otherwise would have found their demise at the bottom of a waste bin. The quilt redeemed the scraps.

She froze as fingers brushed against puckered fabric. Alarm filled her as she secured her needle and peered at the colorful rectangles that formed a lady's fan. She gasped. It was torn.

"No!"

How had this happened? She'd been so precise when constructing the fan, her best and biggest scraps of silk going into the effort. Now it was ruined. Her fingers trembled as she touched the scar-like puckers next to feathery edges of raveled silk.

Long ago memories drifted through her mind of Rabb and Thomas tossing her quilt between them, taunting her. But even they had been careful not to harm her piece.

This was done with vicious intent. But when? How?

Tears blurred the colors and shapes of the quilted fabrics she'd so lovingly stitched together. Entering the fair wouldn't be possible with this kind of damage. But where would she get a replacement, especially when the slash was almost as long as the distance between her wrist and elbow? Silk was scarce in this town. People here valued practical fabrics. With three cotton gins within a half mile of each other, the material was economical and in abundance. But ordinary cotton had no place in a crazy quilt alongside velvet, satin, and silk. Especially in a fair entry.

If only she could go back in time and bring more swatches from Grandmother's cast-off dresses. She had opened her wardrobes and trunks to Delia, revealing an array of ballgowns from decades past.

"Oh, the fun I had as a young woman. But what good is any of it to an old widow? So, take these, darling. Anything you see is yours to cut apart and remake," she'd told Delia. "It pleases me to know I had a hand in my granddaughter's beautiful creations."

But the fine gowns had been left behind when the family moved away. She'd only gathered what she needed at the time, as if she would always have the silk and satin garments to choose from, courtesy of her wealthy grandmother's long-unused clothing. No one could have predicted they would suddenly be forced to relocate so far away.

She pressed a hand to her lips to stifle her raw emotions. There had to be a way to fix this. Everything hinged on the fair. But fixing it would take money she didn't have. No money, no repair. No repair, no fair entry. And without that exposure, she had little chance of building a business that could help her family.

Mother spoke from behind her. "May I sit with you?"

Delia averted her face to swipe away tears. "Of course."

Mother slowly lowered herself to the top step and heaved a sigh. "One day soon I'll not be able to do this."

Delia couldn't speak. She prayed her mother would leave her be.

"What's wrong?"

Before Delia could respond, Mother groaned. "Oh, so you know. I'm so sorry. I meant to tell you earlier."

Delia looked at her mother. "What are you talking about?"

"My mind isn't what it used to be, what with this baby's incessant kicking in the night. This slipped my mind ..."

"What?"

"I'll help you mend it. Don't you think with a clever slipstitch, it will be presentable?"

Delia shook her head, trying to make sense of Mother's words. "A-are you talking about this hole?"

Mother clasped her forehead. "I can't understand how it happened, though. You left it on the chair last night, you know. And when I picked it up, it must have snagged on something."

Her *mother* had done this?

For a moment, Delia's anger surged. All Mother's reminders that crazy quilts had no practical value, only frivolity. That no gentleman in his right mind would value her hours of effort. And now, she admitted to ruining the one thing of Delia's she scorned.

"Delia, will you forgive me? I know this little quilt is important to you."

Important? "This is everything to me." Her voice broke on the last word. She pinched the silk between her fingers and swallowed back her sorrow. But the anger tumbled out. "You've always hated this."

The words dizzied her in their disrespect. Yet she could not, would not, take them back.

Mother shifted. "Hate is a strong word."

But it's true. Delia pressed her lips together. In the silence that stretched between them, birds chattered noisily and the rattle of locusts grew to an almost deafening pitch before fading away.

Finally, Mother sighed. "Whether you choose to forgive me or not, I am sorry I didn't come to you before now."

She pushed herself up from the wooden steps and paused. Delia sensed her mother's stare at her back. She wished she could just smile and wave it off. But discovering that jagged hole taunted her. *You're a failure.*

Maybe she was. Maybe she was kidding herself to think this hard work would lead to anything of value.

In the silence, Mother's voice gentled. "I would never hurt you, Delia, no matter how I view your quilt. I hope you know that." Her shuffled steps melted away in the direction of the main room.

In the afternoon's growing heat, perspiration trickled down Delia's back. Sighing, she searched for the needle and thread she'd dropped. Finding it still dangling from the last stitch, she anchored it at the edge of the quilt and gently folded it. Maybe tomorrow she'd figure out the next steps. For now, she had to let go of her driving need to finish, to enter, to be the best.

The next day, tension reigned between her and Mother as they worked side by side with few words spoken. She knew she should accept the apology. After all, she'd been partly to blame. If she'd put away her quilt, kept it safely out of reach of splintering wood or jutting nails, the accident wouldn't have happened.

Still, she couldn't bring herself to bridge the chasm that had grown between them.

Midmorning, Delia used her free time to take her crazy quilt outside, where she could better examine the tear. Sick at heart, she traced the ragged edges. When Sallie walked up with her sewing bag, Delia had lost all track of time. The clouds shifted across the sun, darkening the sky to match her spirits, making Sallie's light green bonnet bright in contrast. Delia attempted a smile as she greeted her.

Sallie said, "I thought I'd see if you could help me with my sewing. I'm glad to find you here. Is everything all right?"

Delia shrugged. No, it most certainly was not all right. But she couldn't bring herself to say the words, so she laid her finger alongside the gash.

Sallie leaned closer and gasped. "How did that happen?"

Delia inhaled. The less said, the better. "An accident."

Sallie pushed up her spectacles, her blue eyes full of sympathy. "Can you fix it?"

A large, tan grasshopper landed on her hand, and Delia whisked it away. "I don't see how."

Sallie hugged her knees. "What if you cut it out and put another swatch in its place?"

"There's not a lot of silk in this town." A gross understatement.

"So use another fabric. Or an old tie or handkerchief."

Delia considered before nodding. "That might work."

"Let's ask your mother if she has anything that might fit."

"No." She grimaced at her harshness. "Sorry, it's just ..."

She glanced behind her to make sure Mother was nowhere near, then relayed the story. Sallie's sympathetic murmurs did little to soothe Delia. She wanted to move forward and forget the reason for the predicament.

"I suppose we could go into town and beg Uncle Robert for swatches. But last week, he only had cottons and wools to choose from."

"Then let's go somewhere else. Truitt's isn't the only dry goods store in town, you know. Maybe next week."

Delia plucked at a stray thread. Next week seemed an eternity from now. "Why not tomorrow?"

Sallie's chin dropped. "Did you forget it's the Fourth of July?"

Delia looked at her blankly. "So, the stores will be closed, I guess."

Sallie laughed. "I would hope so! Don't tell me you haven't heard about our celebration?"

Delia shook her head. A deep need for joy stirred. Enough ruminating. For now, anyway. "Tell me."

Sallie clasped her hands. "You won't believe all the activities. First, everyone decks the town out in red, white, and blue bunting and folks wave flags as the parade goes down Main Street. There's foot races and speeches. And then there's the box social lunch, where we girls decorate boxes and make a very special meal to put inside. Then the boxes are auctioned off to raise money for a town library. Whoever wins your box gets to eat it with you. Then at night, there's a dance. You must come!"

"It does sound fun." An idea formed in Delia's mind. "You said the women decorate boxes?"

"The prettiest boxes go for the most money."

Interesting. But a meal? Cooking up something to be savored was asking a lot of her rather primitive skills in the kitchen.

Sallie leaned forward. "I'm making steak sandwiches. How about you? It's got to be good. Everybody talks about the food."

Delia scrunched her nose. It always came back to a woman's ability to prepare a meal. "Do people also talk about the creative way the boxes are decorated?"

"Sure."

Delia nodded slowly, a finger to her lips. An opportunity to put her talent in front of the town. Not in food preparation, of course. Maybe Mother would help with that. But Delia could have tongues wagging about the artistic presentation. And she needed to build her reputation if she were going to open a sewing business. The trouble was she had few materials on hand.

But what if she got a sponsor? Ideas whirled in her mind. It wasn't too late to go to town and talk with her aunt. Wouldn't it be clever to advertise Truitt's Dry Goods at the same time she showed off her skills?

Sallie pushed up her spectacles. "Do you think Rabb will be there?"

Delia rolled her eyes. "Where pretty women and tasty food are, there Rabb will be."

Something about the wistful look on her friend's face made Delia pause. "What is it?"

Sallie blew out a long breath. "If I ask you something, will you give me an honest answer?"

"Of course."

"Do you think Rabb could ever like a girl like me?"

The earnest look on her face squeezed Delia's heart. "Why wouldn't he? You get along with everyone."

"Not like that. I mean, romantically."

Delia blinked, biting back the *no*. Practical, forthright Sallie wasn't the kind of girl who attracted Rabb's attention. Though he probably needed her more than he knew. But stating the brutal truth would crush her friend. Sallie wanted an honest answer, but Delia couldn't trample on her tender feelings. "Rabb isn't the man he will be someday. Right now, he's a tease and a flirt. Maybe someday he'll be ready to settle down with a good woman."

"And maybe somebody who doesn't wear these." Sallie held up her spectacles.

Delia bit her bottom lip. Her friend hit on the truth. Rabb was a good-looking man and loved beautiful women. Why couldn't he be a man who looked beyond the surface?

"Sallie, you are beautiful, inside and out. And if Rabb is too thick-skulled to see that, he doesn't deserve you."

The wistful smile faded, and Sallie returned her glasses to her sun-kissed face. "In other words, no." She pulled at a clump of grass. "I guess I knew that. I was just hoping ..." She stood and brushed the dirt and grass from her calico skirt. "I should probably go."

Delia scrambled to her feet. "Please don't. I didn't mean to hurt you."

"It's all right. I asked for an honest answer, and you gave it."

"But what about our sewing? And plans for the box social?"

Sallie lifted her hand but kept walking. "I'll see you at the parade."

Delia watched her friend for a moment. Maybe she should have lied. The truth delivered a slap to the face. She ached to say something to ease her friend's disappointment.

But she couldn't change the situation, no matter how badly she wanted to force her silly brother into noticing Sallie. She had work to do for the celebration tomorrow. If only she'd paid attention to the goings on in town, she wouldn't be caught off guard. A box lunch auction. That meant preparing a meal—and not just any meal. A delicious lunch. The idea might make her giggle if it weren't so important. All the girls would create a beautiful box to go with their best efforts at a meal, with hopes of convincing an attractive single man of their talents.

Or in her case, create a fascinating box to make the food contained within more palatable.

This called for a bicycle trip to town right away. Perhaps her uncle and aunt would be open to a sponsorship of sorts. If everything went as she hoped, she'd return with plenty of materials to make her box a thing of beauty.

Chapter 5

It is entirely unfair for a man to sneer at a woman's inability to understand a baseball game until he has proven his own ability to grapple with the mysteries of a crazy quilt social.—Mitchell Daily Republican (Mitchell, South Dakota) July 1, 1886.

Delia strolled down Main Street, her decorated box lunch clutched in both hands as though she were offering it up for the town's admiration. It was a beautiful creation, to be sure. Judging by the admiring glances, she wasn't the only one who thought so.

After Sallie left yesterday, Delia had ridden her bicycle to Truitt's, where she proposed a little trade. She would advertise Uncle Robert's store on her box lunch if her aunt and uncle would supply her with the materials. They happily agreed, and Delia returned home with more supplies than she'd imagined. She'd worked long into the night arranging colorful cotton bits to resemble her crazy quilt. On paper, she wrote, "Truitt's Dry Goods, the only place to shop for fabrics," and glued it front and center on her box. This box would call attention to the store while showing off her artistic talent. Free publicity for them both.

Mother had been only too happy to cook for her basket. "It's my chance to repent for tearing your quilt."

"You don't have to do anything. If I hadn't left it out, it wouldn't be ripped."

"That's gracious of you, dear. But your father just received a couple of hens in payment for chopping wood for Uncle Robert. How about I fry one and donate some to your basket?"

The lump in Delia's throat made speaking impossible, so she nodded her approval. When Mother finished, she handed over a plate of golden fried chicken. "For your box. May the most eligible bachelor win the bid."

The aroma of fried chicken made Delia's stomach growl as she wove among the growing crowd. She had never seen such a festive place. Every owner had draped their storefront in red, white, and blue bunting. Delia admired the array of American flags rippling in the breeze. Though the parade was still a half hour away, chattering families lined each side of the road, waving handheld flags.

Delia heard her name called from across the street. Lucy and Sallie hurried to cross in front of a wagon full of people and came to stand with her, laughing and breathless. She admired their artistic boxes. Lucy's was white and trimmed with red ruffles, and Sallie's bore ribboned flowers around the edges.

Lucy winked. "I hope a certain dashing redheaded man bids on mine."

Rabb, no doubt. Just like every other unattached female in town. Delia glanced at Sallie to gauge her reaction. But she only nodded. "That would be wonderful."

Lucy hiked her box on her hip. "We'd best hurry down the road to the entry table. I'd hate to miss the start of the parade."

At the end of Main Street, long tables stood underneath a canopy of green trees. They joined the line of chatting women.

Gert Waldrop approached the trio with a sugary smile. "My, what cute little boxes." She plucked at Delia's miniature hand-lettered advertisement. "A shameless plug for your uncle's store. How quaint."

Delia shifted her box away from Gert's reach. But the movement didn't stop the snide commentary.

"And look at the tiny little patchwork." She hummed in mock sympathy. "Men despise crazy quilts, you know. I wonder if you'll get any bids at all." She batted her eyelashes before turning away.

Delia narrowed her eyes. How many times had she suffered her brothers' taunts? *Crazy girls make crazy quilts.*

You must have a patchwork brain.

You can't do nothing with that fancy thing.

But Gert was a crazy quilter, so why the taunt? Could she still be annoyed by the spilled jam? Or was this about competing against each other in the county fair?

The woman at the table said, "Next." When Delia hesitated, she made a circling motion with her hand. "Come on, don't be shy."

Delia stepped up to the table and handed over her creation, aware of Gert's nosy presence just behind her. The woman seemed not to notice, though, and lifted the box to assess all sides. "This is beautiful. Sure to garner top dollar."

Delia turned from the table but not before hearing, "We'll see about that."

Warning bells jingled in Delia's mind, but she extinguished the inner noise, catching up with Lucy and Sallie to walk back the way they'd come and find a place to view the parade. Lucy spoke in a low tone, glancing over her shoulder. "Careful, Delia. Gert isn't a kind adversary."

Delia shrugged. "It's nothing. Just a little competition."

Sallie made a humming sound, which Delia ignored. They found a place on the sidewalk alongside a family with four boisterous children. Delia allowed her gaze to roam up the street. The whole town must have turned out. Her family was here, somewhere in the crowd. A man jogged by, distributing small American flags, and they each took one. Laughing, the three raised their flags and waved them with vigor. Delia let the energy that pulsed through Blooming Grove swallow her up.

A burst of trumpets from the far end of Main Street hushed the crowd. The band, clad in dark uniforms, marched with military precision. The bass drum echoed against the tall brick buildings that lined the street.

Something jostled Delia, making her stumble forward with a cry. She turned in time to see a woman beside her fall to the sidewalk. The crowd gasped, but no one extended a helping hand. Aghast, Delia crouched. "Are you hurt?"

Bonnet askew, the woman moaned. "My arm!"

"Let us help you." Delia took hold of her and gently righted her. Face florid and hair awry, the woman batted away her hands. "I'll be fine."

Delia exchanged a glance with her friends. The woman's fall had torn her sleeve, and blood trickled down her wrist. "Nonsense. We'll walk you to the doctor."

The protests grew weaker as Sallie and Delia encircled her and walked her in the direction of the medical clinic. Dr. Taggert stood outside his office watching the parade and jogged to help them inside. "What happened?"

"I fell. Clumsy of me."

The doctor looked surprised. "But Mrs. Baskin, this is twice in two days."

She ducked her head and mumbled something. The doctor

glanced at the girls before escorting Mrs. Baskin to the examining room.

Delia turned to her friends. "Did you hear that? She's fallen before, poor thing."

Sallie and Lucy exchanged a look. Sallie said, "Pushed, more like. There's rumors, you know ..."

"What kind of rumors?"

Lucy's voice was dry. "The kind that link her to a murderer."

Delia gaped. "That sweet old lady?"

"You might change your opinion when you hear who she was married to." Lucy crooked an eyebrow. "Big Jake Baskin. Rumors have it she's the mastermind of the gang and has all the loot stashed in her apartment above her seamstress shop."

Delia blinked. Mastermind? Loot? A guffaw burst from her lips. "What's next? Is the cavalry going to ride into town and surround her until she gives up?"

Lucy placed her hands on her hips. "Fine, laugh if you want. But I'm telling you, once we discovered her identity, everyone stopped going to her shop."

Sallie nodded. "I kinda hope she has the loot. She might need it to keep from starving."

After the doctor assured them Mrs. Baskin would be fine and would rest there in the clinic, the girls left and headed to the park for the box social event. Though Delia had scoffed at the rumors, a niggling doubt made her wonder about the woman.

"Hurry! They're about to start." Lucy lifted her skirt to jog the rest of the way, and Delia joined her, with Sallie trailing behind, laughing. They slowed their pace as they neared the overhang of shade trees, joyous voices and laughter cutting through her troubled thoughts.

As if reading her mind, Sallie hooked Delia's other arm, connecting the three of them as they walked the last steps to the park. "Let's turn this day around. We put a lot of effort into our boxes. Now it's time to have fun."

Delia gave her a quick smile. "Yes, let's. I'm excited about the auction."

Excited and nervous. The thought of some man bidding on her box, and then actually sitting down with this unknown male and eating with him ... well, it was enough to make her stomach do flips. Not that she cared, really, who it was. But it would be so nice if Clarence was that person.

She scanned the crowd for a tall, handsome man, but scolded herself when she didn't see him. It didn't matter. Besides, if she really wanted to know where he'd been these last couple weeks, she could've asked his sister. Still could.

Which undoubtedly meant he didn't mean that much to her after all. Shaking her head of his image, she willed herself to pay attention to driving business to Truitt's Dry Goods. Her aunt and uncle had sponsored her box lunch, after all. She owed it to them to represent them well.

As they moved toward the long table loaded with the lunches, Delia scanned the crowd once more before chiding herself. She would go look at her attractive box one more time, just to take her mind off the elusive man she couldn't forget.

Only, her box wasn't there.

She stopped Sallie. "I can't see my box on the table."

Sallie shrugged. "I'm sure it just got pushed out of the way."

Delia strode to the table, concern heightened. Gert's veiled threat played through her mind. Would she hide it from view? Worse, take it? She gritted her teeth, blood pounding in her ears. She stood before the exhibit of pretty box lunches, pulse quickening when she couldn't locate hers. Each basket or decorated box held its own place of honor, with none out of sight. Except hers.

Sallie scooted to look behind the display, and gasped, bending to the ground.

Delia hurried to stand beside her. Her heart thudded at the sight of her toppled creation upon the grass. With both hands, Sallie picked the crushed bundle up and held it out. "Oh, Delia."

Fingers trembling, Delia took it. Clumps of dirt clung to the top, which had lost the bits of fabric she'd painstakingly attached. The wooden box was splintered and broken in places. "It's ruined."

"It seems to be damaged mostly on the outside of the box. I'll bet the food is relatively undisturbed." Lucy placed a gentle hand on Delia's shoulder.

Lifting the handkerchief, Delia saw it was true. "I can't believe anyone would be so evil."

Sallie's eyebrows shot up and her fingers stilled. "You don't think someone would purposely ruin your entry, do you?"

"Not just anyone. Gert Waldrop."

She heard the quick intake of breath from her two friends and faced them. "You know I'm right. You told me Gert wasn't a kind adversary."

Lucy frowned. "No doubt she's spoiled and a bit self-centered, but this?"

"Yes, this. Ever since I came to town, she's been hostile." Delia swallowed. "Now she ruined my box lunch."

"It's not so bad ..." Sallie's gaze faltered.

Lucy stooped to pick up a wad of crumpled paper. "No, it is bad. But it's not hopeless. Let's try to repair it."

Rage simmering, Delia worked with fumbling fingers to

tack on the fabric bits. No hope for the advertisement, though. Not that Uncle Robert would want the store associated with such a pitiful box. He'd probably never trust her now that she hadn't delivered her part of the bargain. If only she'd stuck around the table to keep her box safe from harm. Why hadn't she heeded the warning bells in her head?

Behind them, applause peppered the air, and a man spoke to the gathering. Gert's father, the mayor. The crowd hushed in expectation.

Delia lowered her voice. "I ought to show him what his daughter did."

"You can't prove she did it." Sallie's eyes beseeched her. "Just try to put this aside and have a nice time."

Delia folded her arms. Easy for her to say. These people wouldn't forget her forlorn box lunch. First impressions were never wrong, according to the adage. It might take months, even years, to overcome Blooming Grove's first impression of her abilities.

"Citizens of Blooming Grove, Happy Fourth of July!"

Cheers lifted, but Delia ignored them. Arms tight around her chest, her mind whirled in blind rage.

The mayor talked on. "Men, there are some mighty fine smells up here. The winner of the basket gets to sit with the pretty gal who made it." He winked at the crowd in an exaggerated way, causing folks to laugh. "And if we play our cards right, we'll be hearing wedding bells within the year."

Milly Akin giggled and leaned close to Delia. "I hope so. That's what happened to my parents, you know. And they've been blissfully wedded for twenty-five years."

Delia tried to smile.

The mayor continued. "I've invited Robert Truitt to help me auction these fine box lunches. Fellows, get your wallets out, and let the bidding begin!"

The clang of the gavel made Delia start. She put her hand to her forehead and took in a deep breath. Not so long ago, she stood alongside her weeping mother as they witnessed their possessions seep away at ridiculously low prices. That day last spring, she'd sworn never to be the victim of someone else's greed. Yet, wasn't she, even now?

This day had soured. Maybe she should leave.

The mayor lifted a blue-painted basket with a big blue ribbon on top, and the crowd hummed approvingly. Lucy growled. "That one's Gert's. I'd know her gaudy workmanship anywhere. I've a mind to rip that box to pieces after what she did to you."

Sallie said, "Me too. But let's not cause trouble."

Delia's mouth flattened. "You believe me now?"

Lucy thumbed to the blonde standing at the foot of the stage. "Just look at her. There's no doubt. She acts like she's already been declared winner of everything."

Sure enough, Gert stood alongside the raised platform, smiling triumphantly. Delia balled her fists.

The bid started at ten cents and built from there. When the bidding slowed at seventy-five cents, Uncle Robert frowned at the crowd. "Come on, you men can do better than that!" The bids increased to one dollar, twenty-five cents when one man claimed Gert's basket.

Rabb.

Her own brother. She watched him strut to the stage, and before she could stop herself, Delia shouldered through a cluster of men to stand in his path. "How dare you?"

Rabb's jaw dropped. "What's a matter with you? All I'm doing is buying a basket of food."

"From her." She narrowed her eyes at Gert.

"So? That's how you do this thing." He skirted around her to pay while the crowd buzzed around her. Delia's face heated.

Everywhere she glanced, wide eyes looked back at her. Her anger melted into humiliation, and she bit her lip. What was she doing? If her box didn't make a bad impression, her behavior would. Delia wove through the whispering crowd to stand on the outskirts of the gathering.

She clasped her arms and stared into the distance. A question dawned on her. Where did Rabb get money to bid? He certainly hadn't saved anything. He spent every dime as soon as he earned it.

She scanned the crowd for her sibling. There he was, still in the midst of the bidding, only it was for someone else's box. She tuned her ears to the fast-paced auctioneer. Sallie's floral box was on display. Rabb's hand lifted in the air, and shortly after, he was declared the winner.

Her brother, who never had two pennies, bought not one, but two box lunches—at a pretty cost. She watched, aghast, as he won two other boxes as well.

"Rabb Truitt, how are you going to eat all that food?" Uncle Robert laughed. To which Rabb, standing amidst the crowd, lifted his shoulders. "I'm hungry!"

The crowd chuckled, but Delia's gut clenched. Something wasn't right. Rabb had some explaining to do, and she hoped he'd tell the truth about his money. Like as not, though, he'd tell her it was none of her business.

She fanned herself. When would this auction end? All she wanted to do was go home. Then another deep voice snagged her attention. Thomas? She drew closer to get a look at whose container was up and recognized Lucy's. Her lips parted in surprise. Her shy brother was making his bid. Pride filled her, and she found her way to Lucy.

Lucy's eyes sparkled, and she grabbed Delia's arm. "This is so exciting! Your brothers are fighting over my basket!"

"But surely he's out of money by now."

Lucy shook her head with glee. "No, he's not! See?" She pointed over the crowd, and sure enough, there was Rabb, raising his hand to bid against Thomas. Yet, this time, he failed.

The mayor announced, "Thomas Truitt, you win Lucy Grant's box lunch!"

Her happiness for Thomas was short-lived as her attention was snatched by Uncle Robert, who called to her. Seeing her pitiful box in his hands, she walked slowly, dreading his reaction to her lopsided, dirt-stained container.

In a low voice, he said, "What happened?"

Swallowing, she looked beyond him to Clive Waldrop. "S-someone ... it fell."

Uncle Robert studied her. "This was purposeful, then." He brushed away the crumpled advertisement in disgust. "Who did this? I'll give them a piece of my mind. Maybe more."

Words caught in her throat. Would he resort to fisticuffs over this crumpled box? This was her chance. But for some unknown reason, she couldn't utter Gert's name. Uncle Robert seemed to sense her hesitation, and he nodded his head once. "Very well, then." He stood and handed the ruined box to the mayor.

Clive Waldrop pantomimed shock as he held the forlorn box up for all to see. "Well, I must say, I've never seen an entry like this. Looks like it had a bumpy ride on the way to the social!"

A few people laughed at his joke. Delia wanted to run, and fast. But pride kept her feet planted.

"Who will give me one cent? Anyone?"

Silence. Delia squeezed her eyes shut. This was horrible. She fisted her hands to keep her shaking fingers from showing. She wanted to shout, "It looks bad, but the food's delicious."

Surely these men could see beyond the pathetic appearance. Yet the seconds ticked by with no bids.

Nervous titters grew. She pressed her eyes shut. What a way to introduce her artistic abilities. The bitter thoughts circled like buzzards.

"One dollar!"

The crowd gasped. Delia held her breath.

From the stage, the mayor prompted, "Do I have one dollar, five cents?"

Delia stood on her tiptoes to scan the crowd. The silence held expectation.

"One dollar. Going once. Twice. Sold! To the gentleman in blue."

That could be anyone. When she saw a tall figure in a natty blue suit making his way to her, her pulse rabbited. Clarence Parker.

He paid at the table, and came to stand before her, box lunch under one arm, grinning. "Yours?"

A puff of laughter pushed through her lips. "You're a brave man to bid on such an ugly box."

A smile twitched his lips. "I like rooting for the underdog."

She touched her throat, blinking fast. Here was a man who looked beyond the outer covering.

He offered her his arm. "Shall we?"

Smiling, she took it. "Lucky for you, my mother fried the chicken. If I'd done it, you might have demanded your money back."

Chapter 6

The average woman's mind is like a crazy-quilt, and she gives
her husband irregular pieces of it at irregular intervals.—The
Washington Post (Washington, D.C.) June 18, 1905.

Walking beside Clarence gave Delia time to think without having to face him. It was hard enough not to dwell on his muscular arm under her fingers as they made their way to picnic. She couldn't put two words together when he looked into her eyes.

He cleared his throat. "If I'm not mistaken, this box has seen better days."

Delia groaned. "That's a nice way to put it. I promise, it looked beautiful when I turned it in."

"That's a shame. But it smells like heaven."

"My mother's a wonderful cook."

"And you?"

"Me? Oh, I'm hopeless in the kitchen."

He chuckled. "Most girls wouldn't admit that."

Delia shrugged. "It's the truth, so why not own up to it?"

They approached a large circle of their peers, already eating and chatting. Clarence turned to her. "Is it all right if we sit here?"

She nodded, careful to sink to the ground in a ladylike manner.

"Hey, Red."

Delia turned to see her brother, the last person she wanted to sit near. Surrounding him were the four women whose boxes he'd won. Gert Waldrop sat inches from him, clutching his sleeve.

Gert's mouth dropped. "Red? What kind of name is that? Oh, wait. Is it because Delia has red hair?"

Clarence leaned close. "She's not the brightest person, is she?"

Delia giggled, shaking her head.

Gert waggled her fingers and sing-songed, "Hi, Red."

Rabb shook his head. "That's my name for her. You get your own."

Gert smirked. "I'll do that."

Clarence lowered his head. "Would you like to move somewhere else?"

Delia's shoulders relaxed. "Very much."

As they were leaving, Rabb called, "Hey, Parker. You know what you're getting yourself into? Might oughta throw that food out."

Delia whirled. "For your information, Rabb Truitt, I didn't make a thing inside this box. Mother did."

Gert's eyes almost popped out of their sockets. "You mean you let your mommy do the work for you? Seems like that's cheating."

Clarence glanced at Delia before telling Rabb, "Your sister's very honest about her capabilities."

Rabb shrugged. "It's your funeral," and turned his attention back to the gaggle of women.

She set out for a spot far from her nemesis, not waiting for Clarence. She sank to her knees on a carpet of verdant grass closer to the creek underneath the green canopy of mature trees. Clarence joined her, setting the box on the ground between them. "Ah. This spot has a great cross breeze."

She filled two glasses with lemonade and passed him one, then loaded both their plates with fried chicken, buttered sweet cornbread, green beans, boiled summer squash, and sliced tomatoes. "Here you go. And save room for dessert. Mother's Egg Custard Pie is delicious."

They tucked in without speaking except for the occasional appreciative nod for Mother's meal.

Clarence drew a napkin along his mouth and looked at her. "I hear you have one of those bicycle contraptions." One side of his mouth tipped. "We don't have many of those around here. You're quite a modern woman."

She lifted her chin. If he only knew how this modern woman had to beg her parents for permission to ride to town. "Is that good or bad?"

He choked on a laugh. "Are you always so direct?"

"When it's important."

His smile faded. "And I suppose being a modern woman is important to you?"

"I've got big dreams. I want to open a dressmaker's shop. To make money, of course, but also to make women feel extraordinary. A pretty dress can change a woman's outlook, you know. Just like a lovely painting or a lilting voice can lift the soul. If that makes me a bit progressive, so be it."

"I'd like to hear more."

"You would?"

"Sure. Most girls around here are all the same. But you're different."

Her cheeks burned. "Different usually translates to odd."

"Not at all. Unique is a better word."

Was he poking fun at her? He looked earnest, but she could be wrong. Better to find out now. "I suppose I am a bit unique. I love creating art from discarded materials. I suppose that's why I take such pleasure in crazy quilting." She paused, waiting for a moan. When he simply waited for her to continue, she plunged ahead. "When I make a crazy quilt, I gather up little bits of fancy fabric, useless to most people. I arrange them every which way and connect the pieces with fancy stitches. It might take months to finish, but the end result gives me great joy."

He nodded slowly, as if in thought. "You bring beauty from ashes."

She blinked. What a poetic phrase. "I've never thought of it that way."

"What about a marriage and children?"

She laughed, surprised. "That's quite a change of subject." And he said she was the direct one. "I want those things. But it would be a shame to waste my talent."

He unfolded his legs and leaned back, arms propping him. "You want both a happy home and a successful business?"

She refilled his glass. "Does that idea shock you?"

"I've heard of such things." His words held a tone of restraint, as if he didn't want to cause a rift. Delia held her breath, waiting for an objection. Would he be like other men, who expected women to be solely devoted to domestic duties?

His gaze met hers. "But may I ask why it's important for you to work outside the home?"

Now they were getting deep. She wasn't ready to bare her soul. "Independence appeals to me." That was true enough. She ruffled the soft grass with the palm of her hand.

Slowly, he sat upright. "Independence is a powerful drug, Delia. It can be life-giving, and it can be lethal."

"I don't understand." If he didn't look so somber, she would have thought he teased her.

"Someday you will." Those gray-green eyes reflected an emotion she couldn't pin down. She had a feeling even if she knew the circumstances behind his wisdom, he would still be a mystery.

He took the lemonade glass and drank until it was empty. When he spoke, his tone was light. "My sister said you are entering the fair this fall."

"I think it's a good way for people to see my work. After all, I'll have to drum up interest before I can start my business."

"Why not enter a dress you've sewn?"

"Most women can make a dress. But crazy quilts? It takes time and skill, and many don't finish." She snapped her mouth shut. She'd already told him all this. "I could go on and on when it comes to crazy quilts. Let's talk about you."

He shifted, his arms circling a knee. "Don't believe anything Sallie says."

She'd said very little, actually. "I've told you my dreams. It's your turn."

"I want to buy out my boss at the hardware and carriage company."

"Really? Tell me about that."

In the distance, a bell jangled, and men and women all around them rose. "I'd like that very much, only it's time for the foot races. Will you come to watch me run?"

She stuck out her bottom lip. "If only I could. But I promised to accompany Mother home so she can rest. She's in a delicate way."

His cheeks reddened, and she hid her smile. They gathered

the leftovers and stood with the box between them. He smiled down at her. "Thank you for the delicious meal."

She opened her mouth to object, but he lifted his hands to stop her. "I know, you didn't make the meal. It doesn't matter. I just wanted to spend time with you."

Happiness welled inside her. "Thank you for seeing beyond my little box's appearance. In doing so, you made a generous contribution to the library fund."

He inclined his head. "Glad to do so. The food was delicious, and the company, delightful."

Her heart fluttered. His open admiration made her giddy.

"I'm sorry you won't see me run in the footrace. Will you return for the dance tonight?"

"I'm not sure."

"If you do, will you save me a dance?"

Only one? "I think I can arrange that."

While Mother napped, Delia sat on the porch and mentally replayed her time with Clarence. No other man inquired about her plans. It was as if he not only accepted them but was also in favor of her progressive ways. Of course, he hadn't said that outright. Still, he listened, and that was more than she could say for most people.

Clarence confused her. She thought her plans were straightforward, set in stone. After meeting him, she wasn't sure.

Father, show me Your plans for me. What's the right path?

She stilled, waiting, like she always did after praying. But instead of a booming voice from the skies above, birds trilled from the trees, crickets chirped, and cows lowed.

Tonight was the community dance, and Clarence would be

there. One dance was all he asked. His question tempted her to go. But doubt niggled. What if he turned his attentions to another?

Her quilt lay untouched in her lap, and she ran her finger along the torn part. A sense of hopelessness threatened to overtake her when she looked at that gash. How could she garner favorable attention for her work when each time she tried ended with disaster? First, this tear. Then, the sabotaged box lunch. What was next?

Without money, she couldn't repair the hole. Perhaps she could ask Uncle Robert for a job at Truitt's Dry Goods. But Mother needed her to help around here.

She blinked as realization flooded her mind. Mrs. Baskin, the frail woman who'd fallen in town, was a seamstress. Perhaps she had scraps from commissioned dresses. Possibilities ricocheted in her mind, edging out her guilt. What if she called on the woman tomorrow? Maybe she could bring her something to soothe her injuries. And once she'd done the right thing, she'd be free to ask her for scraps. Surely she had some.

Mother's step sounded behind her, and Delia turned. "Did you have a nice nap?"

Mother shaded her eyes. "Did you lose track of time? We should leave soon, and you haven't dressed for the dance."

Delia folded her quilt and got to her feet. "Will you help me with my hair?"

Surprise fluttered her mother's face, followed quickly by pleasure. "Does your sudden concern about your appearance have anything to do with that handsome man who purchased your box?"

Wonderful. Now she'd be hounding her about Clarence. "Do I need a man to want to look my best?"

But Mother wasn't deterred. Delia endured a half hour of

71

questions, which she tried to evade, and advice on the proper behavior when in a courting relationship. When they returned to the park around six o'clock, Delia sat with her family for a cold picnic dinner before joining her friends near the dance area.

She gazed at the festive dance floor, illuminated by many lanterns hung on wooden posts. The park had transformed for the evening, tables and chairs surrounding the dance area. She inhaled the sweetness of freshly cut wood. Underneath the overhanging canopy of pecan and oak trees, the effect was magical. She heard the wheezy sound of a fiddle and noticed a small group of musicians readying for the dance. Her heart fluttered as she imagined dancing in Clarence's arms beneath the stars.

Soon, a jolly tune erupted from the musicians. Her gaze flitted over the crowd. No sign of Clarence. She touched Sallie's arm. "I thought your brother would be here."

"Me too. I don't know where he is."

"Welcome to the Fourth of July Dance Under the Stars!"

The crowd cheered and clapped, and the caller, Gus Dolan, waited for the applause to subside before he gestured to the three musicians standing beside him. "This here's Abe Heath on guitar, Ernest Mahaffy on banjo, and a newcomer on fiddle, Will Truitt."

Delia gaped. Papa? How had she not known he was playing tonight?

Lucy turned. "Your father is a musician?"

Mutely, Delia nodded. "But it's been ages since I've seen him play." Before worry knotted his forehead and layered his words. "He used to play at night after we'd gone to bed. Nothing rousing, of course. Just sweet, soft tunes. I've missed that."

The caller admonished the crowd with an upheld finger. "Fellas, you'd best claim your dance partner right quick."

A frisson of worry settled in Delia's stomach. Clarence wasn't here. Who would she dance with if not him?

A strong hand clutched her elbow. She whirled, only to see Thomas standing before her, the dark cowlick hanging over his forehead. "You gotta dance with me."

"But—"

"Please, Delia."

His voice was low and he glared at something beyond her. She followed his gaze. Oh, no. Lucy laughed as Rabb whirled her around the dance floor. "Didn't you ask her?"

"He got to her first."

A moment ticked by. There seemed more going on here than he was letting on. "Did something happen earlier after you bid on her box lunch?" Besides Rabb trying to outbid him and add one more lunch to his collection.

Thomas looked away. "Just dance with me, sis."

So, something *had* happened, and her oldest brother wouldn't discuss it. "Fine."

They stepped onto the dance floor. His grip on her hand was like a vice. When the music started, he stood stiffly, as if he'd forgotten how to dance.

"What are you waiting for? Come on," Delia urged, picking up his inert hand and placed it on her waist. Red stain crept up her brother's neck. "Sorry."

They joined the river of dancers in a quick waltz. She'd forgotten the exhilaration of feet moving in rhythmic agreement, although Thomas's sense of rhythm could use some practice. She lifted her head to smile with encouragement. "Do you remember the way we all used to dance back home?"

One corner of his mouth lifted. "Those were fine times."

The remembrance didn't last long, though. Something

changed in Thomas's grip on her hand. Rabb and Lucy were close. Delia's heart wrenched at their flirtatious banter.

Thomas stumbled, causing Delia to turn her ankle. She cried out in pain. Thomas pulled her out of the flow of couples, his face pale. "You all right?"

She shook her head. "Help me to a chair."

She bit her lip against the tears that pricked.

He laced his arm under hers and helped her limp off the dance floor. "I'm mighty sorry. Something about seeing Rabb with Lucy gets my blood boiling."

"Next time, just ask her to dance."

"Rabb always gets there first."

Delia winced with every step. "If you don't try, she's going to think you don't like her."

By the time he'd managed to get her to a chair, tears coursed down her face. Thomas kneeled beside her. "I'll fetch the doc. You gonna be all right here?"

She nodded and thumbed moisture from her cheek as she stared after him. Why didn't she tell Thomas to take her home? Now he was gone, and she was alone, surrounded by joyful voices and peppy music. Worst of all, Clarence was nowhere to be seen. Delia leaned her elbows upon her knees, covering her face. What an awful turn this night had taken.

"I brought the doc."

Relief flooded her. Beside Thomas stood the kind man who'd helped Mrs. Baskin. He took a knee beside her chair, concern on his face. "May I take a look at your ankle?"

She flushed. "Could we move to a more private spot?"

With the aid of the doctor and her brother, she hobbled to a chair farther away from the crowd. After examining the offended ankle, the doctor bandaged it and ordered her to rest for several days. As he turned to leave, she remembered something. "Is Mrs. Baskin all right?"

"She will be fine. But I'd like someone to check on her." He paused, as if weighing whether to tell her something. "Maybe when your ankle's better, you can stop by her home."

After the doctor left, Delia turned her attention to Thomas. "Go have fun."

Part of her hoped he wouldn't leave her alone. Thomas leaned forward, patting her arm. "I'm just sorry I caused this."

She sniffed. "At least you didn't promise me a dance and skip out on me." She clapped her hand over her mouth. Where had that come from?

Her brother's eyes took on suspicion. "Some fella let you down?"

Why hadn't she kept quiet? "It's nothing."

"Doesn't look like nothing to me. What's the fella's name? I'll show him."

"Thomas, no. It's fine. Please, just sit with me. Tell me about your crops."

Anything to keep him from giving Clarence a workover. Though why did she want to protect him? He'd all but promised to dance with her.

Thomas narrowed his eyes. "Don't tell me. It's that Clarence Parker that's got you teary-eyed. And here I thought your ankle pained you."

"I'm not crying because of him."

"Uh-huh."

She sighed. "He just seemed like a wonderful man, that's all. Not at all the sort who'd promise something and forget." But maybe she'd been wrong. Perhaps Clarence Parker had fooled her into thinking he was a man to be trusted.

Thomas patted her shoulder. "You leave him to me and Pa. We'll get to the bottom of this. Ain't nobody gonna break my sister's heart."

Chapter 7

Nell—A lovers' quarrel always reminds me of a crazy quilt.
Belle—How's that? Nell—Always patched up.—Edwardsville
Intelligencer (Edwardsville, Illinois) March 10, 1909.

The day after the festivities, Clarence must've looked at the store clock twenty times within an hour. At noon, he would go out to Delia's. Set things straight. Which meant he would apologize for not showing up at the dance last night. Thankfully, the boss granted him a couple hours off, since not many customers came in the hardware store on a Thursday afternoon.

The closer it came to leaving time, however, the more he mopped the sweat off his neck. He couldn't remember the last time something had him tied in knots like this.

Apologizing was no trouble. Clarence prided himself on being humble, and if he'd done something wrong, he needed to own up to it. But how would he say it? Seeing how the clock said eleven fifty-five, he'd best do some fast thinking.

After renting a horse from the livery, he rode out of town, slowing as he came into view of the old Bernard place where the Truitts lived. Instead of turning in, though, he continued on until he came to his family's place and dismounted, tying the reins on the hitching post before gazing up at the two-story farmhouse.

He took the broad steps two at a time and knocked on the screen door. Something savory—fried onions, maybe—wafted out to him. He should've thought about it being dinner time.

"Clarence! Why'd you knock? Come on in, honey. Have you eaten anything?" Ma swung the screen door as wide as her smile. He leaned down to peck her cheek.

"Hey, Ma." His gaze wandered to the dim hallway that led to the kitchen.

As if reading his mind, Ma said, "He's not here. It's just me."

Relief poured over him like a cool glass of water. "I don't mean to disturb your dinner. Just wondered if I could borrow some of your roses."

Pleasure lit her face. "Son, I'd be delighted for you to take some. Don't have to bring them back, though."

He blinked, not getting her joke until she nudged his arm with a chuckle. He followed her to the kitchen in the back, where a single plate lay on the small table. "Why don't you let me fix you a plate of beans and cornbread? Made peach cobbler for dessert."

Just the suggestion made his stomach growl. He paused only a second before hanging his hat on a peg and plopping in a chair. "Where's Sallie?"

"Oh, here and there. Probably bottle feeding the calf who's way too big for all that nonsense."

She handed him a plate heaped high, and he shoveled the food in with appreciative grunts. He drained his glass of milk, then sat back with satisfaction. "Thanks, Ma. That hit the spot." Like always.

She smiled, extending her hand on the table, and he covered it with his own. His throat thickened, the way it did when he thought of her acceptance. It took running away to convince him of her unconditional love. He'd been wild and mixed-up, seeking comfort on a hard pew in a faraway church. But when she'd found out where he was, there was no stopping her letters of encouragement.

He cleared his throat and stood, breaking the recollection. "I need to get going." He squinted through the window at the garden. "Sure you don't mind if I take some?"

"I'd be mad if you didn't, son."

When he'd chosen the prettiest red roses, his mother tied them together with a ribbon. He recognized the question in Ma's gaze, but didn't offer an explanation.

He gave her a quick hug. When he let her go, she patted his arm.

"Take care of yourself and drop by more often."

He clutched the bouquet and mounted his horse, dreading the greeting he'd get from Delia's family. Who could blame them, though? If somebody had left Sallie high and dry at the dance, no telling what he'd do. Which didn't make this easier. With every plodding step down the dirt road to the Truitts' place, the roiling in his gut intensified.

He groaned as he came within a few feet of the farm, spotting Mr. Truitt and Thomas hacking away thick brush with sickles. Great. Angry men bearing weapons.

He pulled on the reins and halted. "Afternoon, Mr. Truitt. Thomas."

The men exchanged glances. Then Delia's father wiped his face with a sleeve and slowly approached the road, Thomas following. Clarence had seen softer expressions on a granite mountain.

Mr. Truitt spoke. "What do you want, Parker?"

Clarence swung down off the horse and faced the men, still clutching the handful of posies in his right hand, like a fool. "Sir, I've come to talk to Delia. To apologize for not showing up to the dance."

"No."

Clarence froze. "Sir?"

"You heard him." Thomas glared.

Clarence's jaw sagged. Surely they wouldn't turn him away. "I'm really sorry. I know I made a mistake. I just want to set things right and tell Delia how sorry I am."

Mr. Truitt twisted his mouth like he worked a chaw of tobacco, though he didn't spit anything. Clarence returned the man's stare. Seconds passed. The horse nickered and shifted.

"I'm sorry." If he looked away from Truitt's unblinking stare, he'd lose the man's respect—if there was any to be had.

Finally, Mr. Truitt spoke. "Son, you'd better have a good explanation."

Hope surged. "I do, sir. But it'll take a few minutes to explain, if you don't mind taking time away from your work."

As Delia darned socks with her sore foot propped on a stool, she mentally replayed details from the night before. Why had Clarence asked for a dance if he didn't intend to show up? Every time she thought about his absence, her heart squeezed. Sallie dropped by this morning and mentioned nothing about some horrible accident, so surely the man was fit enough to attend the dance. And he hadn't sent word.

But it was just one dance, after all. Did she have any right to be hurt when he didn't come? She had no claim on him. She was disappointed, certainly. But she shouldn't be angry.

She shifted, and pain radiated from her lower leg, causing

her to wince. The throbbing ankle was a constant reminder of the botched evening. Her bruised heart might not mend as quickly as the physical injury.

If Clarence had come to the dance like he promised, she wouldn't be in this predicament. But she'd believed his intentions with no questions, making her a fool who scanned the crowd for a man who probably never intended to dance with her.

Steps sounded on the path, and she looked up to see the man himself. "Clarence?" She fumbled with her needle and thread. "What are you doing here?" She had a good idea, considering the flowers he clutched. His white-knuckled grasp on his hat left no question. She put aside her sewing and tried to steady her breaths.

He offered her the bouquet, which she accepted, taking note of the sweat that beaded his forehead. Stalling to gather her chaotic thoughts, she brought the velvety roses to her face and drank in their fragrance.

"They're from my mother's garden." He looked down, a slight frown creasing his brow. "Delia, I'm sorry I didn't make it to the dance."

His pleading gaze made her stiffen. "That makes two of us."

"I feel awful, after I practically begged you to go. But you got my note, didn't you?"

"What note? I spent the whole night wondering if something catastrophic had happened to you."

Clarence's jaw sagged. "You didn't get the note? It explained everything."

She arched her eyebrows. She wouldn't make this easy, not after all she'd been through.

He muttered something before repeating his apology. "It's just, I've been wanting to talk to Clive Waldrop about a loan so I could buy the hardware store. So when I heard the banker wanted to meet me at six-fifteen to talk, I thought it was finally happening." His ears turned a deep shade of scarlet. "I should have known it was a prank."

"Who would do that?"

He shrugged. "I'm guessing the fellas I work with. See, for months, I've been talking about buying out my boss, but I can't get Clive Waldrop to give me a loan. Reckon I got so excited, I didn't think logically." Clarence shook his head. "I wrote you a note saying I'd be a little late. I ended up waiting for him more than an hour. And here I find out you didn't even get my message ..." He allowed the words to trail. "Bet you thought I was pretty rotten."

"Something like that."

"I hope you'll give me another chance."

Delia met his pleading gaze. The anger she'd harbored faded. The truth? She admired his tenacity. He wanted something, and he wouldn't stop until he had it. Isn't it what she would have done?

And he'd tried to let her know he'd be late. "I'll forgive you, on one condition."

"Anything."

She cocked her head and batted her eyelashes to break the tension. "Next time you want to get a message to me, Mr. Parker, don't send it with one of your mischievous coworkers."

He didn't return her grin. "That's the thing. I wouldn't have trusted one of those guys. I sent that note with Gert Waldrop."

Gert Waldrop struck again. One day later, it still grated. What did the girl have against Delia? Besides competition for the best crazy quilt, that is. Or the attentions of a fine-looking man.

Sitting once more on the covered porch between the bedroom and the living room with her leg propped on a stool, she turned to find her parents pulling up chairs across from her.

Usually at this time of the morning, Papa was in the fields. Yet here he was, sitting in a chair as if he had all day. "Is something wrong?"

"Of course not." Mother's tone held a false brightness. Like she knew something Delia didn't.

Papa glanced at Mother. He cleared his throat. "Clarence Parker came to see me yesterday."

"He spoke to me too."

He sat forward in the chair, his face earnest. "He wants to court you. But seeing how he let you down the other night, I wanted to speak with you before I gave him an answer."

Delia softened. "I appreciate that, Papa."

Mother smiled. "Delia, the man is interested in a future with you."

Excitement bloomed, making her heart flutter. She shouldn't be surprised, after the way he'd begged for a second chance. But they barely knew one another. Courting was serious and usually led to marriage within a year. Was she ready to be a wife?

And there was the little matter of helping her parents financially. Of course, she'd made no progress in opening a business. It was starting to feel more like a dream than a goal.

"Well? What do you want me to tell him, daughter?"

"Courting is a big step, and I'm not sure I'm ready for that. Oh, I like Clarence." Maybe more than she was willing to acknowledge. "I just wonder if it's too soon to focus on marriage. After all, you might need me to help financially. Uncle Robert's deadline is approaching." Papa stiffened, and she rushed on. "I could earn money sewing. I'm entering my crazy quilt in the county fair, you know. The prize money could really help us."

Mother sighed. "This again? Please, for once, be reasonable. Marriage and family are what every woman needs."

"Leave the money matters to the menfolk and consider the young man's request. With you married and gone, there'd be one less mouth to feed."

Papa's words hit Delia like a knife to her heart. How could he be so callous? She blinked away the rising tears. She tried to rise, but Papa held up his hand to stop her.

"Sit back down." He leaned closer to Delia. "Before you get mad, you should know I gave him what for about that dance business. If I can forgive the man for letting down my little girl, you can too."

She folded her arms and stared at the slightly bowed wood planks at their feet. It wasn't Clarence she needed to forgive.

Mother clucked her tongue. "For pity's sake, Delia, Clarence Parker is the most eligible bachelor in town. Don't throw away his attentions."

"It's not that."

"Then what?"

How could she put into words the heaviness lodged deep at her core? For weeks, she'd focused on taking action to help her family out of this predicament. To contribute. She could do more than just milk cows and feed chickens and clean dishes. Now, shifting her sights to marriage seemed premature. Yet, she liked Clarence. *Really* liked him. If she turned him down, told him to wait just a bit while she followed her plans to open a business, she'd be treating him like a task on her list, to be checked off at the proper time. Her heart stirred at the memory of him standing before her yesterday.

"Papa, I'd be pleased for Clarence Parker to call on me."

After all, if their courtship progressed into a proposal, her leaving home would be—how had Papa put it? *One less mouth to feed.*

Maybe that was the best way to help the family after all.

The conversation looped through her mind that afternoon while she lengthened a skirt for Hazel. Clarence wanted to court her. Not only was he the most handsome man in town, but he was kind and witty. Yes, he'd broken her heart when he hadn't shown up at the dance, but he'd apologized. Even brought her a beautiful bouquet.

But he'd trusted Gert Waldrop to deliver his note, evidence that perhaps he was too trusting. It hadn't taken Delia long before she knew two things about Gert. First, she was the unofficial princess of Blooming Grove. When she wanted something, she got it. After all, she was the mayor's daughter and lived in the most lavish home Delia had ever seen. Second, Gert had a mean streak, and even though Delia had no proof, she was certain Gert had destroyed her box lunch. No telling what else she might do, especially when she discovered Clarence's romantic plans didn't include her.

A breeze lifted bits of dry grass and silty dirt into a miniature cyclone on the path, dying out just before pounding feet sounded, and Hazel appeared. She climbed the three steps and sank into a chair, wiping her red face with her sleeve.

Delia held the skirt aloft. "Look, I altered this for you."

"Is that one of Mother's?"

Delia shrugged. "She thought you should have it, since you've outgrown most of your dresses. I would've given you mine, but you've passed my height."

Hazel's face softened. "Thanks for doing that."

"You really ought to let me teach you to sew, you know. Nothing fancy. Just enough so you can get by."

Hazel shrugged, and they sat in silence for a few moments.

"Papa tells me Clarence Parker wants to court me."

Hazel squealed. "I knew it!" She clapped her hands. "He's so dreamy."

"Oh, he's lots more than just a handsome face. He's warm, and he has this sense of deeper things." *Beauty from ashes.*

"So, you like him?"

"I do."

"Remember how I did your hair that first Sunday? I'll bet that's what got his attention. You should let me do it more often."

"I might just do that."

Chapter 8

Good size, great variety of shapes. All colors, 1/2 cut of silk by yard. Send four three-cent stamps for samples. Gilmore's Purchasing Agent, 261 Wabash Avenue, Chicago, Ill.—The Hawk Eye (Burlington, Iowa) July 26, 1883.

Delia inspected her brothers, who'd changed from their work clothes and dressed in their Sunday suits, complete with rigid collars, vests, and coats. She'd had her fill of their complaining about getting dressed up on a Saturday when they'd repeat it the next morning.

"I don't know why we have to wear fancy duds, anyway. *We're* not courting Clarence." Thomas ran his finger along the inside of his stiff collar.

"Because it's the first time. It's special." And terrifying. Anticipation zinged through her belly. "And if you two do anything to cause a problem, I swear you'll be sorry for it."

"Mother says no swearing," Hazel said primly as she smoothed her skirt.

Rabb dipped his chin. "There's a difference between swearing and ... you know. Swearing."

Hazel arched her eyebrows. "That makes absolutely no sense. You ought to expand your vocabulary. Try reading. I have plenty of books, you know."

"You saying I'm stupid?"

"Well, there must be a reason I've never once seen you with a book. Can you even read?"

Delia stepped between them, spreading her arms. "Hazel! Rabb. Stop this at once. What will Clarence think when he hears you two yelling?"

"Ain't yelling. Just telling."

Hazel rolled her eyes. "See there? You prove my point." She tugged at her sleeves, which were an inch too short. Delia made a mental note to lengthen them. Growth spurts were hideous on the wardrobe.

"Mother, the table looks beautiful." Delia clasped her hands, taking in the transformed space between the two parts of the cabin. Whereas yesterday, the covered breezeway had clumps of grass and dirt littering the area, now it was swept and featured a long table and many chairs. Mother had unpacked the china and washed it. Now it gleamed on the white lace tablecloth, alongside crystal and silverware, remnants of their former life.

But the best part of all was Mother's baked chicken, fried potatoes, green beans, and peach cobbler. Aunt Mary had been happy to donate her canned goods for the occasion.

When Clarence arrived, he shook Papa's hand. "Good evening, sir. Thank you for inviting me to your home."

Papa nodded and returned the handshake. Delia stepped forward with a warm smile. "May I take your hat?"

He handed her his bowler, along with a small bouquet of pink rosebuds. "The color reminded me of you." His neck reddened as his gaze scurried around the group of listeners. "Ma said they'd bloom in a jar of water."

She inhaled the delicate scent. Roses, more than any other flower, spoke to her soul. The graceful petal folds, the light scent that lingered on fingertips, the elegance of the bloom. All surrounded by treacherous thorns. Like a stormy day ending with a beautiful rainbow, the journey was difficult, but the reward surprising.

Before long, the whole family was seated at the table, enjoying the breeze the dogtrot afforded. Papa said grace, then the family passed food around the table, appreciative of Mother's meal.

Rabb said, "Clarence, Ma went all out for you. Hope you aim to come calling every day. I could get used to eating like this." He ran a finger to loosen his collar. "Maybe without the fancy duds."

Mother huffed. "Well, Clarence is welcome here any time. You, my son, are another story. Careful not to abandon your manners. You may find yourself eating a cold cheese sandwich in the barn."

Laughter erupted, along with teasing from Hazel and Thomas. Delia glanced at Clarence. His family's home, with only his parents and Sallie, surely wasn't this noisy. But he laughed along.

"This meal is delicious, Mrs. Truitt." Clarence wiped his mouth with a napkin.

"I must give credit to Delia for helping me prepare it."

Rabb set his glass down. "She only sliced the peaches for dessert. Can't do much harm there."

Hazel leaned close to him and hissed, "Stop it, before he finds out she can't cook."

What Delia wouldn't give for an intimate dinner for two. "Thank you, but I've already warned him."

Mother delicately cleared her throat. "Clarence, I've grown

to enjoy your mother's company. I'm so thankful your family's farm is within walking distance."

"Yes, ma'am. She's happy to have a woman friend close."

"Do you help your father with his crop?"

Clarence shifted. "No, ma'am. I live and work in town."

"Doesn't mean you can't help out." Papa's tone didn't carry the reproof his words did. From the corner of her eye, Delia saw Mother's eyebrows lift.

After a moment, Clarence nodded. "I reckon you're right about that, sir. But my pa won't accept my help."

Papa's eyes squinted as he studied Clarence. Whatever thoughts he had were kept to himself.

The silence grew taut. Delia wanted to stuff the last bits of food into her siblings' mouths and rush Clarence away. Any minute, one of them would say something embarrassing. At last, Mother rose. "Who's ready for peach cobbler?"

Delia stood, almost toppling her chair as she reached for Clarence's plate.

In the kitchen, Mother dished out the warm pieces onto small plates. "Refill the creamer, please."

Behind her, Hazel shushed them. "Did you hear that? Papa just asked Clarence if he used to be an outlaw. What's gotten into him?"

Delia looked back at the table and moaned when she saw Clarence's reddened neck and Papa's intense stare. She took two of the dessert dishes and signaled for Hazel to follow. Setting one before Clarence and the other before Papa, she sat down slowly, looking between the two.

Mother approached with the coffee and filled cups, darting a glance at Papa. "Gentleman, let's enjoy the pie with coffee, shall we?"

Clarence cleared his throat. "Mr. Truitt, I would like to answer your question."

Delia stilled. Rabb caught her gaze and made a slicing motion over his neck.

Clarence continued. "Sir, I'm afraid what you heard about me is true. I'm not proud of it. When I was a teenager, I left home and joined up with Big Jake Baskin's gang."

Hazel drew in a breath and turned wide eyes to Delia. But her shock didn't come near Delia's own. This clean, respectable man, a gang member? Had she misheard him?

"I wouldn't have thought it." Papa's expression couldn't be read, but his words held a hint of compassion. Clarence must have sensed the same, for he continued quietly.

"It only took a week before I knew what a fool I'd been to join up with them. Unfortunately, my involvement with that group caused my brother's death." He paused, and Delia watched him trace the spoon beside his plate. "My father doesn't believe I've changed. But I found God when I didn't think life was worth living anymore. I vowed to be a good man from then on, in Joe's honor."

Papa nodded. "I appreciate you telling me that."

After Clarence made his thanks to her mother and shook Papa's hand, Delia walked with him toward the road. She'd never expected the arrow-straight Clarence Parker to be a man with a dark past.

Their feet moved in step along the path to the road. Locusts purred in the trees. The sun dipped close to the horizon, and the sky held an orangey glow. "I love this time of day."

Clarence turned to her, an expression of regret on his face. "Look, I'm sorry. I'm sure my past shocked you. It kinda shocks me, to be honest. But you don't have to worry about the kind of fella I am. All that is behind me. I just want to live a respectable life and build a business, have a family ..." His words trailed off, leaving the gentle rustle of tall grass in the breeze to fill the silence.

He was right, his story had astonished her. That, in combination with her own future plans, gave her pause.

"You were brave to tell your story, but didn't you think you might have put our courtship at risk?"

His gray-green eyes scanned behind her, then locked with hers. "I have to be honest."

The words hung in the air before he closed the space between them. He pulled her close, his forehead meeting hers. "You make me want to be a better man, Delia."

Longing bloomed within her at the heat of his breath, the nearness of his lips. She turned her face to him, and he lowered his head.

"Hey, none of that stuff."

With a groan, Clarence stepped back from her and glared at Thomas and Rabb. No telling how long they'd been watching.

Delia huffed. "Are you checking up on us?"

Rabb laughed. "Feeling guilty? We might need to stick around, make sure ole Clarence here gets on his way before dark."

Nothing like overprotective brothers to get in the way.

That night, Delia tossed and turned in the bed she shared with Hazel. The thought of kind Clarence Parker as an outlaw didn't make sense. Yet, there was no sign of unrest in the man who'd stood before her. He'd met her father's gaze and told the truth about himself.

People could change, though to go from criminal to reputable citizen was dramatic.

It all came down to trust. Could she put her future in the hands of a man she'd known such a short time?

And what about her? No amount of trust or love or independence could change the fact that she could *not* cook. She'd tried many times, with just as many dismal failures. But with marriage came the expectation of tasty meals. She would have to improve.

And then there was the issue of working for an income. She knew she could help her family by earning an income. So far, the dream of sewing for people had stalled.

She sat up and glowered at the flat pillow. A few good punches reshaped it slightly, and she swished her long braid over her shoulder and fell back onto the cushion.

A whine sounded from Hazel. "Stop moving."

"Sorry," Delia whispered, squeezing her eyes shut. *Lord, please tell me what I should do.*

No use racking her brain about these things now. She'd have an answer in the morning when she was fresh.

The next morning at the breakfast table, she leveled a gaze at her parents. "I'd like to discuss something with y'all."

The door to Truitt's Dry Goods squeaked loudly when she opened it, causing the dozen or so customers to glance her way before resuming their shopping. Like all buildings along Main Street, the store's wooden floors and tall ceilings produced a cacophony of clipped heels and echoed conversations that carried the length of the building.

"Why, if it isn't my favorite niece!" Aunt Mary hurried over with open arms. Delia returned the embrace and held her breath against the profusion of spicy perfume that engulfed her. "Let me show you the new hats we just received."

"Actually, I'd like to talk about getting a job here."

Aunt Mary's mouth fell open. "What a wonderful idea. I

know you want to help your folks, and we can certainly use the assistance."

In truth, her decision to work for pay revolved around the key to making money—the fair. But to enter, she had to repair that gaping hole. If she didn't get some silk, and quickly, she might as well kiss that fair entry goodbye. And this morning, the one thing she knew for sure was that she wanted that blue ribbon and the fifty-dollar prize money.

Her aunt hung back to allow Delia to come alongside and lowered her voice. "Take note of our stock, especially since you don't come in very often. We are the premiere dry goods store in Blooming Grove, you know. Folks trust us to get what they need, and to have ample supplies for all they desire, like the shoes there."

She hesitated. Her surreptitious gaze flitted over Delia's crisp white shirtwaist and dark skirt. "One thing, though, dearie. I've seen you on one of those wheeled machines."

"My bicycle? Why, yes, that's how I came to town."

Aunt Mary frowned, giving her another once over. "Hmm. You don't wear bloomers?"

"Not always." Though what a time she'd had today, trying to keep her skirt from tangling in the spokes and chain.

"If you must cycle to work here, you simply cannot wear those indecent bloomers."

"I understand. I don't particularly like them, but I take a chance on injury if I don't. And my bicycle is the only way to get to town. Unless I was to pull my brothers away from their hard work on your farm. And we wouldn't want that." She let that settle for a moment before continuing. "So, you see, bloomers are essential."

Aunt Mary bit her lip, shaking her head. "I don't think your uncle would approve."

Before she could rescind the job offer, Delia said, "What if I made a convertible skirt, the kind that hides the bloomers?"

"Perhaps. Just be sure not to let the customers see you walking around in those horrid trousers. We have a reputation to uphold, you know. And you don't want to be seen as one of those brazen suffragettes."

Delia'd be proud to side with the brave women who clamored for the right to vote. But she refrained from speaking. She needed this job, after all.

Aunt Mary continued her tour. "Now, see here." She stopped before a counter. "Part of your duty will be re-folding garments, straightening the store, and so on." She gestured to a tall stack of shoe boxes that almost reached the ceiling. The variety of men's, women's, and children's garments, including underclothes, was endless. Ladies' petticoats draped from a suspended cable, reminding Delia of the clothesline her mother had erected to hang wet laundry from. Just below, running parallel, a thin rope boasted several triangles of crisp handkerchiefs.

And something else. Delia opened her eyes wide in assumed astonishment. "Aunt Mary, I do believe I spy the dreaded bloomers right there, hanging from the wire."

Her aunt had the decency to blush as she batted the air. "Yes, we sell the abominable things. That doesn't mean I condone them. Come along."

Across the narrow shop, hat boxes stood one upon the other, with several men's and women's hats on display. Umbrellas, men's neckties, and suspenders were arranged attractively. Every inch of the business was packed.

But it was the center of the store that drew Delia's attention. There, arranged in neatly folded groups, were the fabrics. They beckoned her like a siren's song. As Aunt Mary chatted with a customer, Delia wordlessly stepped closer and ran her finger along the stack. Cotton, wool, muslin, and broadcloth were plentiful, but no silk or velvets.

She scanned the room and found her uncle stacking shoeboxes. "Uncle Robert, do you carry fine fabrics? I'd love to get just a little swatch of silk, if you have it."

He tipped his head to peer at her over his spectacles. "Young lady, do you know how costly silk is? If I gave away samples here and there, I'd be a poor man."

"What about if I made a purchase?"

He sniffed. "I rarely carry the stuff. No one around here is willing to part with their hard-earned money for something rarely worn. Except the Waldrops, of course."

Her ears perked. "Gert's family?"

He nodded, placing the last of the shoe boxes in the tall stack. "In fact, Gertrude and her mother purchased the last fancy fabric I had last week."

"Perhaps you can make an order? Surely someone will need it."

"I won't. But if I did, it would go to the Waldrops."

"Why?"

He shrugged. "I suppose they're having silk frocks made. Gert made a special point of telling me to notify her first when any shipment of fine fabrics came in. Even offered to pay double its worth."

Disappointed, Delia thanked him. It was almost as if Gert wanted to monopolize the materials that appeared in a crazy quilt.

What a strange coincidence. Did Gert know about the gash?

Impossible. Since that day Mother told her how she'd torn the quilt, Delia had told only her closest friends.

But a tiny suspicion swirled in her mind. What if Mother

only *thought* she'd damaged it? What if someone purposely vandalized her beautiful quilt?

She could think of only one person who would be so vicious. But even as the name planted itself in her mind, she shook her head. Surely Gert had a measure of decency.

The fact remained, she needed fabric that wasn't to be found, even in the town's leading dry goods store. If she didn't find a way to fix her quilt, she couldn't enter the fair.

Fifteen minutes later, she walked out the door as an employee of Truitt's Dry Goods. "Be here tomorrow at nine o'clock sharp. We're counting on you," Uncle Robert said. "Especially for the back-to-school rush."

Exhilaration thrummed in Delia's veins. Her spirits were high as she strode down the boardwalk to her bicycle.

"Excuse me. You're one of the young ladies who helped me."

A light touch on her sleeve made Delia turn. Before her stood the small woman who'd fallen to the street on the Fourth of July. "Why, Mrs. Baskin. How are you?"

Though no explanation was needed. This woman was nothing like the frail, bird-like creature who'd been injured the day of the parade. Her papery cheeks had a touch of pink to them, and her eyes danced when she smiled. Even her dress, a light blue paisley, was cheerful. She might not have recognized the woman if she'd passed her on the street.

When Delia nodded, she continued. "I don't know what I would have done without you girls."

Delia clasped the birdlike hand. "I'm glad your injuries have healed."

Mrs. Baskin beamed. "The Lord has blessed me. Won't you come inside my little place?"

Delia followed her in, eager to see the seamstress shop.

Light flooded the small space. A table stood to the side with a bolt of light green fabric atop. A mirror stood opposite, adjacent to a small cookstove where a teakettle blew steam.

"This is charming." And exactly the kind of shop she wished to own.

At the back was a Singer sewing machine situated inside a beautiful wood sewing cabinet, a treadle at the bottom. Delia crouched to inspect an engraving. *"Who can find a virtuous woman? For her price is far above rubies."*

She stood. "What a lovely inscription. Is that from Proverbs?"

Mrs. Baskin's eyes dimmed. "Yes. Proverbs thirty-one, verse ten. My father had it engraved. He said it would remind me of his affection for me."

"How thoughtful."

"He resides in Heaven now, bless him."

She shouldn't have said anything. "I'm sorry to bring up a painful subject."

Mrs. Baskin blew out a breath. "He was a wonderful man. I just wish I'd listened to him more. I have many regrets." She smiled sadly. "But enough of that. Will you have a cup of tea with me?"

Delia's gaze flitted to the window. It had to be close to noon, and she must get home to help Mother. "I suppose I have a few minutes, if you're sure it doesn't put you out."

Mrs. Baskin beamed. "I would enjoy it."

While Delia waited for the woman to pour tea, she studied the small shop. "One day, I hope to have a place like this."

"Oh? Do you like to sew?"

"Very much."

Mrs. Baskin was silent a moment before walking the cups to Delia and nodding to the table. "Please, do sit."

Delia sat and inhaled the fragrant brew. "I appreciate your kindness."

Mrs. Baskin studied her. "If you are serious about sewing for a living, perhaps I can help you."

Delia stared. "You would do that for me?"

Mrs. Baskin smiled. "My dear, I owe my welfare to you and your friends."

Delia brushed away the comment. "Anyone would have helped you."

"Yet no one else did."

Delia met the woman's gaze. Sallie had said something about women taking their business elsewhere. Sitting across from this lovely woman brought weight to the statement. How could people be so heartless?

Mrs. Baskin placed a small plate of cookies on the table between them before sitting with her own cup. "Would you mind if I prayed for our refreshments?"

Not waiting for a response, she murmured words of thanksgiving that Delia could barely discern until the ending Amen sounded. Mrs. Baskin reached across the table and squeezed Delia's hand. "I hope we will be friends."

"I would like that too."

Taking a cookie, she bit into it, savoring the sweetness of molasses. What a wonderful day this had turned out to be. First, the job at Truitt's, and now, a mentor.

Her gaze drifted to the window and caught on a man who stared intently at them from across the street. Delia placed her cup in the saucer with a click. "Do you know that man? He seems to be watching us."

Mrs. Baskin turned in her chair just in time to see the cowboy lower his head so his broad-brimmed hat effectively hid his face from view. Nonetheless, her lips parted, and she covered them with an unsteady hand.

"You do know him."

Mrs. Baskin turned back to Delia, not meeting her gaze as she reached for a cookie. "Not at all."

Her trembling fingers told another story.

Chapter 9

The Crazy Quilt—The new and fashionable device of the young ladies for using up old bits of silk and satin is one of the most popular means of spending spare evenings. The quilt is of more colors than ever appeared in Joseph's coat.—The Vicksburg Herald (Vicksburg, Mississippi) Tuesday, June 16, 1885.

Clarence emerged from the carriage shop, noting the lengthening shadows of late afternoon. He crammed the newspaper into his jacket pocket to heave shut the sliding doors and walked toward the diner, allowing his gaze to settle once more on the bold proclamation on page one.

Gang Headed for Blooming Grove
Inmate overheard vicious gang's plan before breakout

Fear clutched his chest. They were coming for him. Nobody testified against the gang and lived to tell about it. No telling how long it'd take the outlaws to track down anyone who'd betrayed them. Clarence's gut twisted. This was the third day the Baskin gang had grabbed the headline of the local paper. Would his name be in the next edition?

He had a bad feeling. Call it intuition, paranoia, or the prompting of the Holy Spirit, he needed to make sure his mother and sister were safe. He couldn't depend on Pa. Not when his cotton crop demanded his attention.

If he could eat the noon meal quickly, there'd be time to ride out to the farm and get back before Mr. Hardy needed him. He had to see for himself that they were all right.

His steps faltered when he caught sight of Delia walking along Main Street's boardwalk. What was she doing in town? When he called her name, she whirled.

"Clarence."

He lengthened his stride to come alongside her. Seeing her soothed his anxious thoughts. "I didn't expect to see you in town." He cleared his throat, hoping his sour mood wasn't apparent. "You shopping for a new dress?"

Her smile dimmed. "I had some business in Truitt's. But just now, I had a lovely visit with the seamstress."

He stared at her. "The Baskin woman? You need to steer clear of her."

Delia took a step back. "I beg your pardon?"

Thumping the newspaper, he thrust it at her. "She's trouble. Just look at this. Her husband's desperadoes are all over the area. I wouldn't put it past her to be in on their thievery."

Though the paper hadn't named her, Clarence knew those outlaws would drop in on her. The sheriff had told him to watch the shop. And here was the woman he cared about, naively planting herself in the middle of a hornet's nest of trouble. Didn't she know better than to make an ally of a villain?

She pushed the newspaper back, eyes snapping. "I will see who I want to see, whether you approve or not."

Now he'd done it. "I don't want to see you get involved with someone like her."

She shook her head with vehemence, setting loose a dark red lock at her temple. "I'll thank you to let me be the judge of my friends, sir. I am quite discerning."

This woman could argue with a broomstick. "Look, I'm sorry you took it the wrong way. But—"

"You are sorry *I took it* the wrong way? You are too much, Clarence Parker!" She marched away, leaving him slack-jawed.

Aw, crumb. He jogged after her. "I'm sorry, all right?"

She kept walking down the covered walkway, her little feet clip-clopping in a precise rhythm.

"Will you forgive me?" Maybe if he just kept apologizing, she'd settle down.

Which, to his relief, was exactly what happened. It took a good minute, but eventually, her steps slowed, and she faced him.

"Fine. I'll accept your apology. But don't tell me what to do. I'm an independent woman."

"I like independent women." Unless said independent woman raved and shrieked at him.

Her gaze settled on the newspaper protruding from his pocket. "Fine. Let me see it."

He handed it to her, and she unfolded it. Her eyes moved from left to right, then down the page.

With quick, decisive movements, she folded the newspaper in fourths and handed it back. "Quite sensational. Are you afraid?"

"These are bad men, Delia. Men who don't cotton to people like me turning against them." He slapped the paper against his palm. "Besides, this is the third article in a week about Big Jake's gang roaming the area. And as for that woman, who knows if she's involved with them? I know, she says she's not. But I'm skeptical."

She folded her arms across her chest as if holding a shield.

"We need to be careful, is all." His voice soothed.

"How?"

He shifted his feet. Did he water his words, or should he tell her exactly what he feared? "I'm asking—no, making a request. A suggestion."

"What is the suggestion?" No hint of warmth in those chocolate eyes. This discussion was more hazardous than walking through a field of rattlesnakes.

"I think you ought to consider steering clear of that Baskin woman. Just until they arrest those outlaws, that's all."

For a moment, Delia stared at him. Then she stepped forward and jabbed his lapel. "You don't get to ask, request, or suggest anything to me, Clarence Parker. I'm not your *little woman*."

She'd let her temper get away from her. Not that she wasn't right. But walking away to cool off would've been the dignified response. Yet here she stood, trying to calm her racing pulse, while his uncomfortable gaze darted to passing friends and neighbors.

Delia didn't mean to poke him in the chest. But he needed to be mindful of their relationship. They were not married. He had no say over her actions.

Still, she'd overreacted. But she couldn't shake the image of Mrs. Baskin's fear at the sight of that stranger. Clarence assumed that small, defenseless woman was in cahoots with that evil gang, but he hadn't seen her reaction to the man who watched her shop.

Of course, she wouldn't tell him. He'd probably say Eleanor and the cowboy were both members of the Baskin gang. But even though her reaction was strange and unexplainable, Delia couldn't believe such a sweet woman would be involved with criminals.

Delia turned to him with a smile. "Clarence, I appreciate your concern for my well-being. I'll see you Saturday evening, then?"

He blinked. "Yes, Saturday evening. Have a good day, and just ... take care, will you?"

～

Though she'd wanted to ignore Clarence's admonishment, she found herself scanning their farmyard for any cowboys like the one in town. But each day was as predictable as the next. The most recent news was that the gang had been sighted one hundred miles north of Blooming Grove. The town seemed to breathe easier, greeting one another with more cheer than in the previous weeks.

When Saturday arrived, Hazel promised to help with her hair. "Why do you want to look special? It's not the first time he's come for dinner."

To assuage her guilt for the terrible way she treated him. "Oh, I don't know. I just want to look my best, that's all."

Hazel's probing questions trailed her as they made their way to the bedroom. Delia plucked the hairpins from her chignon and ran her fingers through her waist-length hair.

Hazel considered the mane. "How do you want it?"

"Just make me look pretty."

Apparently, pretty was also painful. Delia yelped when

Hazel ran the comb through her tresses. "Ow! Stop pulling so hard."

"I thought you wanted to look your best."

Delia winced as a pin scraped her scalp. "Gentle, please. You don't have to be so vigorous." She sighed, peering into a small mirror. "Although this attempt might be for nothing, as he saw me red-faced and sweaty the other day."

Hazel's fingers stilled, her voice laced with disbelief. "You perspired ... in his presence?"

"I don't know how I could've prevented it, as we were sitting in the heat of the day. The Fourth of July picnic, remember?" Delia held up her hand to the coming protest. "I know what you're going to say, that ladies should never perspire. Ridiculous. Don't believe all those articles you read. Ladies sweat, just like men. Especially in Texas."

"You should always carry a lavender-scented hanky." Hazel attached the last pin and circled Delia, peering at her creation from every angle. "There. Just don't move your head much, and those pins will stay in place."

Delia rose with a wry grin. "Such practical advice."

She admired her reflection. Not bad. Though in half an hour, her heavy mane would probably droop and be a mess, like always. She resolved to check her appearance more often when Clarence was around. She'd never seen him disheveled. He kept his mustache and hair neatly trimmed and combed into submission. Of course, men had far less hair to worry with.

Her heart did a funny little flip when he appeared at the door. She liked the way his eyes lit up when he saw her.

This time, the bouquet he gave her was white petaled daisies. She inhaled the delicate scent. "Thank you. They're so pretty."

"Like you."

Her cheeks warmed, and she smiled, averting her eyes,

allowing him to briefly capture her hand within his big one. Gazing at their intertwined fingers, warmth filled her heart. His tenderness touched her. With this man, she was safe.

Behind her, Rabb cleared his throat, and Clarence stepped back, breaking their connection. Her brother stuck out his hand and pumped Clarence's. "How you doing, old man? How's the hardware business?"

Clarence chuckled. "Sales are steady."

The two men lapsed into conversation about tools, and she turned away in search of a vase for the fresh daisies. The roses he'd given her last week still flourished, so she poked the daisies into the same container and admired them. An unlikely coupling, the elegant rose and humble daisy. She rather liked the contrast. Even more, she loved the gesture. Papa never gave Mother a bouquet of flowers. A flush of pleasure swept Delia.

Before dinner, she found herself glancing over at him. He laughed easily and seemed to fit in with the men no matter what the topic. Once, when Mother struggled to move a heavy chair, he rushed to take it from her with a smile before turning back to the menfolk. It was a kindness unspoken, unobserved by all except Mother. And Delia. It struck her how kind he was, and humble. Nice qualities that Papa had.

Sitting beside Clarence at dinner, she found herself captivated by his long, tapered fingers. No scars or dirt, like the men in her family. But not soft. They were the hands of a hard worker. She shivered when his arm brushed hers.

After supper, Delia and Hazel helped with clean up until Mother shooed her away. "Go on, sit outside with your beau. We will get the rest."

Her beau. The word still felt foreign on her lips and in her thoughts.

She walked beside Clarence to the top step of the wooden

porch. They sat close, but with enough space between them to suit her parents' standards.

She lowered her voice. "I'm sorry I was a little snippy with you the other day."

Clarence's shoulders eased. "I like that you were honest."

"I'm relieved to hear the gang is far from here. I was worried about you."

"I was, too, for my family's safety." He took her hand. "And yours."

"What would they want with me?"

"You're my girl. And anybody who cares about me ... well, I'm just happy they've traveled far from here."

She bit her lip. "Remember when we talked about my crazy quilt? Well, I just want to make sure you understand that I *am* a crazy quilter."

He coughed a surprised laugh. "Okay."

Heat scalded her neck. "I just want you to know."

"It's no secret. We talked about it at the picnic."

"Yes, but ..." She stole a glance at his face. "That doesn't make you want to run away?"

He cocked his head. "Angry bulls, swarming bees, a cattle stampede ... those are things I'd run from. Not sewing." Humor threaded his words.

"You say that, but there's a reason I'm telling you." She swallowed. "It was a problem with boys back in Georgia."

"Well, that's just it. They were boys. I'm a man. And no man worth his salt would let a little hobby run him off."

Her shoulders sagged. Not Clarence too. "D-did you say hobby?"

He frowned in a puzzled way. "That's what we're talking about, right? Something to pass the time?"

"That's what I'm trying to tell you. Crazy quilting is not my hobby. It's who I am." She swallowed and searched for just the right words. "At the picnic, I shared a little about my view of crazy quilts, and you said something I can't forget. You said beauty from ashes. That's a perfect description of the fine art of crazy quilts. My quilts represent how I view the world. Each raggedy scrap symbolizes cast aside people. Alone, they're overlooked. Worthless. But joined with scraps of different textures and vibrant colors, they transform into a thing of wonder." She squeezed his hand. "That's what I want you to know, Clarence. Crazy quilting might seem to many as a frivolous waste of time, but I see transformation. It brings me joy."

The words seemed to echo in the stillness, like the rings that pulsed around a rock thrown into a lake. Her pulse hammered as she waited for his reaction.

"I can see it is important to you."

Surprise and pleasure lifted her spirits. "So, you understand?"

He laid his hand atop hers. "I'd like to. Next time, maybe you can show me your quilt?"

She nodded, smiling. It was the perfect response. And when she unfolded her masterpiece, he'd have no questions about the artistry that went into making it. Well, except for the gash. But maybe by the time he saw it, she'd have earned enough money to purchase a replacement.

He drew out his watch and consulted the time. "I should go. Will you walk with me?"

He drew her to her feet and tucked her hand in the crook of his arm. Their steps evened into a joined cadence, as natural as the setting sun.

At the end of the drive where his horse waited, he drew her closer, casting a glance toward the house. Today, no brothers sauntered their way.

He lifted her hand and pressed his lips to her fingers. A

shiver danced down her neck. His gaze traveled her upturned face and settled on her lips. She held her breath, waiting for his head to dip closer.

But he didn't kiss her. Instead, he gently cupped her cheek. "Good night, Delia."

～

The margin between dusk and dark made the country road ahead murky, but Clarence let the old horse plod at his own speed. He sure couldn't pay attention.

What an amazing woman. Everything square and solid, she changed into curves and liquids. Her way of seeing things challenged him to look at life in a whole new way.

Funny thing was, he liked it.

He liked *her*.

～

Delia's thoughts whirled around Clarence. The days dragged between his Saturday visits. He sat beside her at church on Sunday mornings, but when service concluded, eager friends surrounded them. Gert flirted outrageously with him. He was too kind to ignore her, catching Delia's eye and shrugging as if he were helpless. It wouldn't hurt him to turn his back on the hussy. But he was a gentleman, and apparently, gentlemen didn't give their back to anyone.

Each Saturday evening, Delia counted the minutes until dinner was over so she and her handsome beau could excuse themselves to sit on the porch step, arms touching. Twine their fingers. Murmur low, so as not to be overheard. Catch the stars as they peeked through the hazy dusk and eventually winked, diamond-like, in the indigo sky. And when he left, Delia would slip inside, reliving touches and words, until at last, sleep claimed her.

She'd never dreamed that she could be so drawn to a man— a man who not only condoned her quilting, but supported her artistry. She floated around the house, sighing, dreaming, and longing to be with him. He was everything she'd dreamed and more, just as smitten with her as she was with him.

It was almost too good to be true.

Chapter 10

That's a lovely necktie you have on," she remarked. "Glad you like it; I thought it rather neat myself." "Yes, it would look so well in the silk patchwork quilt I am making."—Elevated Railroad Journal—Stevens Point Journal (Stevens Point, Wisconsin) December 23, 1882.

When Delia accepted the position as a clerk at Truitt's Dry Goods, she thought Mother and Papa would be happy for the added income.

She was wrong.

"I can't have one of the boys driving you twice a day. I need 'em here."

"I'm more than happy to ride my two-wheeler, Papa."

"And what about the house chores, Delia? I depend on you to help out."

"My job at Truitt's won't last the whole day, Mother. I'll still help you. Plus, I can bring home any groceries or goods you might need. You won't have to send the boys anymore."

Papa exchanged a glance with Mother. "I will admit, the

money you bring in will help us out. I wish it didn't. It's difficult for me to send my little girl out into the world for a paying job."

Delia stood and came to his side, kissing his forehead. "Need I remind you I'm almost nineteen? I'm not your *little girl* anymore, you know."

He grabbed her hand and kissed it. "You'll never stop being my little girl."

In the end, they agreed she would ride the bicycle to town, and Thomas or Rabb would come back for her in the late afternoon. They could stow the bicycle in the wagon bed. As for the chores, she'd pointed out how much time Hazel spent with her nose in a book. "Besides, I can do the milking before I leave."

Papa told her to keep a little of her earnings for herself. She smiled and kept the nature of her future purchases to herself. They wouldn't understand buying more silk and velvet. Crazy quilters were scorned in the newspapers as well as in her home. "Crazy women make crazy quilts," was the standard taunt.

Even though working at the dry goods store exhausted her, the variety in her days was exhilarating. Each day brought new customers and new situations, and the diversity of experiences helped buffer her yearning for Clarence.

Plus, he was only a block away in the hardware store at the end of Main Street. Not that she saw him often, but between customers, her gaze was drawn to the walkways lining the busy street in hopes of catching a glimpse of her handsome beau.

As she assisted families with purchases, a happy future with Clarence stayed at the forefront of her thoughts. Would she be like one of these mothers, trying to herd a group of little ones in search of just the right clothing for school? A month ago, she'd have dismissed the thought. But that was before. Waiting on the harried but happy mothers with their chaotic groups of demanding children, she wondered if she'd had the wrong idea of domestic life. Maybe it was bliss, after all.

At the end of a particularly hectic day, she hurried to lock the door behind the last patron and flip the sign to *Closed*. Leaning against it, she surveyed the wreckage.

"I just organized the fabric table, and now look at it. It will take me thirty minutes to neaten this mess." She shook her head and marched to her favorite spot in the store.

Aunt Mary scurried by with an arm full of hats. "And tomorrow at this time it will look just the same, dearie. Welcome to August at Truitt's."

Delia grunted in agreement as she strode to the back for a broom. Uncle Robert counted money from the shiny new cash register. "And thank the good Lord for that. August and December keep us afloat."

Delia swept the gritty floor mindlessly until she came to a mound of worn, black shoes. She stooped to pick them up. Who would forget three pairs of children's shoes?

She held them aloft. "Uncle Robert, what should I do with these?"

He peered over the rim of his spectacles. "Throw them in the rubbish bin."

"But shouldn't we look for the owner?"

"Some beleaguered mother left them, I'm sure. My policy is to throw away anything left behind." He pointed to the back of the store, where the trash bin sat. "Rubbish."

Taking each one by the laces, she carried them to the trash and dropped them one by one. It seemed wrong to throw them away when they still had plenty of usefulness. Her mother never tossed aside worn garments. Not these days, anyway. They made over dresses, darned holey socks, and found a new use for old things.

She stared at the tangled shoes, then scooped them up. She

couldn't let these go to waste. Surely there was a child in need of shoes, no matter how scuffed.

Each day as she worked, she peeked out the plate glass, hoping to catch a glimpse of her beau. But she rarely spotted him walking by. So, when the door to Truitt's opened, sounding the bell, she continued to stack neatly folded bundles of cotton.

"Delia."

The rich baritone belonged to only one man. Heart pounding, she whirled to find him inches behind her.

"Clarence!"

Every time she looked into those eyes, it was like swimming in the depths of the sea. She reached behind her to steady herself, only to topple a tower of stacked cotton.

With a soft laugh, Clarence averted disaster by placing a steady hand to keep the fabric from spilling onto the floor. His chuckle crinkled the corners of his eyes. "I thought maybe I could look at the ties." He leaned near her ear, his breath tickling her neck. She ducked her head, smiling. "That's my excuse, anyway. Mostly I wanted to see you."

"Why, if it isn't Clarence Parker."

He took a step back from Delia, smiling in the direction of the shrill call. "Mrs. Truitt, nice to see you, ma'am."

Aunt Mary's eyes sparkled as she came to stand beside them. "Am I interrupting something? Or did you come to admire one of my best shopgirls?"

Delia averted her eyes, pleasure filling her as Aunt Mary spoke. "I'm sure you'll agree with me Delia is one of the prettiest girls in town. That dark red hair brings out her brown eyes and peachy complexion."

Delia shook her head, as if that would stop the woman.

Other customers glanced their way. She wanted to steer the conversation away from herself. But once Aunt Mary got started, a freight train couldn't stop her before she said her piece. "Isn't she a pretty picture in that pale green dress?"

Clarence smiled warmly, catching Delia's gaze. "She's lovely."

Clarence said, "As a matter of fact, I have the honor of courting Delia."

Aunt Mary knew all about their courtship, of course. But she squealed as if it were the first time she'd heard.

"Oh, I just knew you two were destined for each other. When shall we hear wedding bells?"

"Aunt Mary!" It was too presumptuous, even for her. Clarence's ears reddened as he seemed to search for a response.

This had to stop. "Aunt Mary, Clarence wants to choose a tie." Sure enough, her aunt lost the sly look and turned into a businesswoman, dragging Clarence by the arm to the counter where they displayed men's ties.

Delia busied herself with organizing the table in front of her. *Breathe in, breathe out.* Still, her pulse raced.

Uncle Robert set a box in front of her and brushed his hands together. "New fabric. Try to separate the winter material from the lighter-weight cottons. The blue taffeta I'm holding in the back, for Miss Eula May."

Delia's thoughts flew to her quilt project. Taffeta was a nice enough fabric to make a suitable replacement for the ruined silk. She'd had little luck finding anything other than common materials. Now, here she was, mid-August, with an unfinished quilt and no remedy in sight. A prickle of alarm sobered her. She had to do something fast. It would only take a little of Miss Eula May's taffeta.

Hope must've shone in her face because Uncle Robert lifted one eyebrow.

"The taffeta is spoken for," he repeated. Holding his hand up to silence her, he added, "Despite your begging Mary to order fine fabrics. But as I've told you, all my silks and velvets and satins come nearer the holidays. We just don't have a need for something so frivolous. I told your father so just yesterday."

"You told my father?" Alarm bells sounded in her mind. Like Mother, Papa considered her crazy quilt a waste of time.

"What else could I do? Each day, you beg me to order expensive silk that people around here need only for Christmas. I thought it best to speak with Will. You left me little choice, Delia."

She watched him as he strode to the back stockroom, feeling like a chastised child. No choice? He had plenty of options. It was she who had no choice. No fabric. No money. Not yet, anyhow, as her uncle would pay her at the end of the month. What she did have was an approaching deadline and a gaping hole in her otherwise beautiful crazy quilt.

Delia chewed her nail as her mind sifted one more time through possible answers. There were old flour sacks aplenty at home. But flour sacks belonged in common patchwork quilts, not crazy quilts. She'd considered the band of green silk on her hat, faded though it was. But it was too small to fill the hole.

Perhaps if she spoke with Aunt Mary in private. Surely, she'd view Delia's predicament with more compassion. Casting a look at Uncle Robert, who had stepped in to help Clarence with his selection, she quickly unloaded the box of cottons and headed to the stockroom with the empty crate.

She found Aunt Mary and a woman whispering together just inside the curtain. They fell silent as she approached. Clearly it was a private conversation. Delia placed the empty crate under a counter and turned to go, smiling in acknowledgment of the ladies. To her delight, the woman left.

Delia placed her hand on Aunt Mary's arm. "Might I speak with you?"

In a low voice, she described her ruined quilt. Her time limit. The needed fabric. The desperate search.

Aunt Mary's face fell in sympathy. "If only you'd told me yesterday. We received a shipment of Miss Eula May's blue taffeta, but also some beautiful gold. But unfortunately, your uncle told me to send it up to the Waldrops. Such a shame. It would have been just the thing."

So, they'd claimed the taffeta too. "But there's still Miss Eula May's. Please Aunt Mary. I just need a small sample. Ten inches at most."

"Ten inches?" Aunt Mary's shriek hushed all conversation on the other side of the curtain.

If she didn't hurry, the whole store would know her business. She lowered her voice, hoping Aunt Mary would follow suit. "How about nine? Eight?"

The woman clucked her tongue. "My dear girl, you are testing my patience. Now come along. There's bound to be something fine enough for your project."

Delia trailed behind her, gritting her teeth. How many times had Uncle Robert thrown away perfectly usable things? And now they squawked about a measly ten inches of fabric?

Aunt Mary marched back to the front of the store and Delia had no choice but to follow, knowing full well there was nothing on the table that would suit.

Aunt Mary sifted through the bolts of fabric before lifting a bundle of red wool. "Now look here. This should be adequate. Let me get the shears."

Uncle Robert's head swiveled in their direction. Delia's heart sank as he left Clarence at the counter and hurried over. "No more giving away swatches—to Delia or anyone else."

Aunt Mary stuck out her bottom lip and blinked rapidly.

Delia recognized the ploy her aunt used to talk her uncle into giving in. "But Darling Booboo, our little niece has a hole in her quilt. How will she compete against Gert at the fair?"

He cast Delia an apologetic look. "I must go by what your father told me. No free material."

"But you don't understand—" She swallowed the retort, aware of Clarence's presence nearby. Heat crawled up her neck. He'd probably heard every humiliating word. How childish she must appear.

Aunt Mary turned to Delia. "I'm sorry, dear. Look on the bright side. There's a fair every fall, and by next year, you'll be ready."

"Next year? I can't wait that long."

Lifting her shoulders as if there were nothing to be done, Aunt Mary clucked sympathetically and left Delia standing alone.

A torrent of anger and frustration and sorrow roiled within her. How could Papa do this? She hadn't asked for much, just a few scraps of fabric that every dry goods merchant had on hand. How else would she repair the rip?

It was all Gert's fault. Delia clenched her fists. Oh, she couldn't prove that her nemesis had vandalized her quilt, but Delia was more certain now than she had been when she'd discovered the tear after the sewing bee.

This wouldn't be a problem back in Georgia. There, she was known for her ability to craft beautiful clothing. In this new community, it would take time to prove herself worthy of folks' hard-earned dollars.

Eyes burning, she hurried to the backroom before her uncontrolled emotions further embarrassed her. Swiping away the tears, she took deep breaths. Surely there was another way. Putting off her ability to help her family was unacceptable. She'd think of something.

When she returned, her gaze darted to the last place she'd seen Clarence, but he was gone. Uncle Robert said, "There you are. Clarence sends his regrets but had to get back to the hardware store."

Disappointment landed like a wet blanket. First, the fabric, now Clarence. She'd find him later and apologize for ducking into the back for so long. But for now, she'd attempt a more positive frame of mind and tidy the store. At least she had this job and its slight pay to bring home to her family.

A box of handkerchiefs sat on the counter, and she placed it where it belonged. A pile of fabric remained, and she plucked it up, examining it closer. A cream-colored necktie, frayed and sweat-stained. The subtle baby blue design down the center assured her it was Clarence's. Or had been, before he'd left it here. He must have purchased a new one. It was about time. He'd always been so meticulously attired, with the exception of this worn-out tie.

She turned it over, examining the lightweight backing. The stitches were uneven and amateurish, a contrast to the cream silk that fronted the piece. He must be doing well for himself, now that he was able to buy a new necktie. At least, she assumed he had done so, since he'd left this one behind. She wheeled to ask her uncle what she should do but thought better of it. No doubt he'd order her to toss it in the trash.

But regardless of its condition, this had belonged to Clarence. She pressed it to her face and inhaled his clean scent. She couldn't throw away something of his.

With a tender smile, Delia tucked the tie into her pocket.

Chapter 11

*The "crazy quilt" girl plays sad havoc with her young man's hat
lining and cravats. —Chester Times (Chester, Pennsylvania)
December 5, 1883.*

Delia worked the rest of the day, conscious of the tie
in her pocket. When her day was finished and she
emerged into the afternoon shadows, there was no
sign of her family's wagon. She stood on the boardwalk where
this morning, Thomas had dropped her off for work. She
watched people coming and going, nodding a greeting at those
she knew. If she were honest with herself, she would admit she
looked for Clarence all along Main Street, even though he
didn't leave work until five o'clock, a half hour from now.
Several shops down the walkway, Mrs. Baskin emerged, locking
her door behind her.

Delia quickened her pace. "Mrs. Baskin, hello."

The woman looked happy to see her and paused, bag in
hand.

Delia stood before the birdlike woman. "I'm surprised to
see you closing already."

The woman looked embarrassed. "I'm afraid I don't have a reason to stay open."

Delia frowned. "We've been busy with all the families getting ready for school to open. I would have thought you'd be just as hectic with dress orders."

Mrs. Baskin looked down and massaged her gnarled hands. "Maybe it's just as well that my customers have dwindled. These old fingers aren't as quick with a needle."

Why did Delia have the feeling there was more to this? And it probably tied directly to the rumors attached to the Baskin name.

A couple walked past, nodding as they did, and Delia became aware of their lack of privacy. She touched the older woman's arm, urging her to stand closer to the shop she'd just closed.

"Mrs. Baskin, may I ask you something?"

A cloud passed over the wrinkled face, and she said nothing. Delia took her silence as consent.

"I've heard your husband is ... known." She might as well spit it out. "That he's notorious."

The woman's eyes shuttered. "I'm sure you have heard a great deal about my notorious husband."

Delia blinked. She'd made her angry. "I'm sorry, it's none of my business."

"It's no one's business but my own." Mrs. Baskin huffed, staring out at the street. "Don't let anyone tell you there's a chance to start over. Because there's not. Your secrets will always be found out. Gossip will follow you around every corner. It doesn't matter how many years go by, they will see you as the person you once were, not who you've become."

Delia swallowed. Undoubtedly, "they" were the people of Blooming Grove. She'd touched on a nerve, to be sure, and longed to take back her words.

"I'm really sorry. I shouldn't have said anything. It's just ... I wanted to hear the truth from you. I couldn't make sense of the gossip."

Mrs. Baskin's lips tightened. She shook her head. "There's no telling what you heard. The truth? I left my husband and his life of crime. When he and his gang left to do their evil, I cleared out. I ended up here, within miles of their hideout. A foolish decision. If only I'd boarded a train for California or New York, somewhere far from Navarro County. Be free of the past. But when you're Big Jake's wife, you're never free. No matter how far you travel, people find out."

How could a woman hope to walk forward when the past enslaved her? Images of her own past floated in her mind. The whispers, snubs, and strangling gossip when they lost everything. Only, they'd been able to leave Pine Mountain and begin a new life with no rumors trailing them. Nothing standing in the way of a fresh start, except maybe her own discontent. They had a second chance.

Shouldn't everyone?

At the sound of an approaching wagon, Delia glanced up to see Thomas. "I suppose I should be going." On impulse, she touched the older woman's arm. "Won't you come home with me? I'd love to introduce you to my family."

Now that the hardware store was empty and his duties complete, Clarence finally had time to sit at his desk. The numbers on the paper reflected his personal finances. Though the amount was more than he'd ever had, it still wasn't enough to buy the business Mr. Hardy had built. It wouldn't be long before Mr. Hardy retired, and if Clarence didn't find a way to procure financing, he'd be forced to pass up this opportunity.

He rubbed his face. "Lord, I can't make the numbers work. Please help me find a way to finance this store."

He crumpled the sheet and tossed it in the trash bin. A good meal and rest, and he'd tackle this again. Maybe tomorrow, he'd figure things out.

He secured the store and walked down the street to his boardinghouse. His landlady, Mrs. Johnson, looked up as she cleared the dishes from the dining table. "Supper's over, Mr. Parker."

He sighed, weariness sagging him. "I don't suppose you have anything left?"

She pursed her lips, but despite her stern expression, he could sense her resolve weaken. "You're in luck. But see here, young man. Dinner is served at six o'clock sharp and no later."

"Yes, ma'am, it won't happen again. I'll just wash up and be back in two minutes."

He took the steps two at a time and bounded into his room. He cast his jacket to the unmade bed and rolled up his sleeves as he strode to the washstand. He poured tepid water from the pitcher and splashed his face, and as he toweled off, he peered at the shadow of whiskers. No time to shave, though.

He admired the new blue tie around his neck. A nice purchase at Truitt's. Even better when he'd seen his girl. He still couldn't believe some guy hadn't snatched her sooner.

Like a douse of cold water, realization hit him—he'd forgotten his tie. Joe's tie. The one thing he could touch and sense his brother's presence. He had to get there before they closed.

As he flew down the stairs and out the door, he heard Mrs. Johnson call after him, "Where are you going, Mr. Parker? I refuse to hold your dinner one more minute." But he continued running into the dusky road. He had to get to Truitt's.

Clarence cupped his hand over his eyes, hoping to spot movement inside the dry goods store. But only shadows remained. He peered at the counter where he'd purchased his new necktie. It was too dim to make out whether his old one remained where he'd left it.

He pushed off the window and uttered a word he hadn't used since those dark days, after his brother died. Frustration boiled. How could he have been so stupid? He should've kept it neatly folded inside his dresser drawer instead of wearing it every day. But no, for some crazy reason he wore it daily, as if he needed a reminder of what he'd once been, and what it had cost his family. Now, he'd carelessly left it in the store, which was locked solid for the night.

He jammed his hands deep within his pockets and stared out onto the empty street. Maybe he should go knock on Robert Truitt's door.

Fine plan if he knew exactly which house in Blooming Grove belonged to Robert and Mary. Maybe it was still light enough to ride out to Delia's to ask.

He jogged in the direction of the livery. He'd be lucky if Cal and his men were still around to rent him a horse. It had to be close to seven-thirty.

Sure enough, the only sign of life was the muffled sound of horses.

He let out a frustrated groan and gazed unseeingly at the dirt, hands on hips. What was he thinking? He wasn't presentable without his hat and coat. Her dad would lose all respect for him if he showed up looking like this. Besides, the tie would still be in the store when it opened tomorrow morning.

Might as well go home. He set out for the boarding house.

His stomach grumbled, reminding him of his skipped meal. Not much chance his landlady would serve him now. If he wanted supper, he'd have to get it at the diner. After he went back for his coat and hat, that is. No respectable businessman went to eat halfway dressed.

The sky above had lost all trace of light, and he was glad for the gas lamps that gave the abandoned streets a little golden illumination. It would be just his luck if the diner stopped serving before he made it back to Main Street.

He picked up his pace when the boardinghouse came into view until a shadowy movement between the house and the derelict building next door arrested his attention. His pulse hiccupped. Was that a man hiding behind a tree?

His senses heightened as he glanced around the isolated street. But for the soft glow coming from the windows of the two-story boardinghouse, this whole area would be cloaked in black on a moonless night like this. The boardinghouse was the sole survivor of a fire that consumed the small buildings on the street several years prior. Now it stood sentinel over the charred remains. Wouldn't those hollowed-out buildings make an excellent hiding place?

"Who's there?"

He stood so still he was afraid to breathe. No sound. No twig snap. Nothing.

Maybe he'd imagined it.

All at once, a form sailed toward him from overhead. He yelped and ducked, shielding his head with his arms. The rush of powerful wings moved the still air with a swoosh. Pulse hammering, he whirled to find the creature in the top of a high tree.

An owl.

Clarence stood to his full height, laughing at his cowardice. Shaking his head, he crossed the patchy yard toward the door.

But when he looked over his shoulder to the inky darkness of the tall oaks, the hair on the back of his neck lifted. Was it just an owl?

Or was something, someone, out there, watching?

～

Her family had quickly warmed to Eleanor Baskin, and conversation flowed around the table effortlessly. Having the pleasant woman among them felt natural, as if she were more family than friend. When the dishes were cleaned, Delia pulled Eleanor aside to show her the quilt. She spread the silk medley on the bed and looked on in delight as the older woman murmured praise.

"How beautiful. Your stitches are flawless. But this." Her gnarled fingers touched the marred silk. "What a dreadful tear. Such a shame."

"I'd almost given up hope of mending it." Delia drew the tie from her pocket. "Until this. I think it's the right size to fill in the gap."

Eleanor took the worn necktie, handling it with a thoughtful expression on her face. "It just might work. Where did you get it?"

"I found it on the counter today." She hesitated. "Actually, my beau left it there after he purchased a new one."

"He left it for you?"

"I don't think so. Lots of our customers leave their old things when they replace them. Uncle Robert tells me to throw it all away, but when I found Clarence's old necktie, I just couldn't ..." Instead, she'd breathed in the aroma of the one man who made her heart somersault.

"Well, then, this is answered prayer." Smiling, Eleanor

handed the limp silk back to Delia. "That is, if you are sure he would want you to have it."

Her words planted a sliver of doubt. Would Clarence mind that she'd kept it?

Of course, he wouldn't care. If it were special to him, she would not have found it lying on the counter. He wanted a new one, and that was that.

That night, long after Thomas had escorted Eleanor back to town, Delia stared into the darkness of the room, comforted by her sister's soft snores. Eagerness to get her project underway ruined her attempts to sleep, and finally, she gave in and tiptoed across the breezeway to the living room, carpetbag in hand. After lighting a lamp, she spread the crazy quilt on the table. Breath snagged in her throat. Gorgeous. Except, of course, for the gaping cleft. But she had a solution, and her hopes of entering the fair soared.

Now, as the only soul up at this advanced hour, she welcomed the silence. Better for concentrating, especially when it came to trimming the old torn fabric to make room for the new. New to her, anyhow.

Shoulders and arms taut, she snipped until at last, the ruined cloth fell free, leaving a wedge-shaped cavity. Though she'd dreaded this for weeks, it wasn't so bad. She stood upright and rotated her shoulders.

Fingers trembling, she placed the cream-colored necktie over the opening. Quiet victory puffed from her lips. The best part of the necktie would show, allowing her to dispose of the unsightly frays and sweat stains. With deft stitches, she basted it into the featured applique of a lady's fan comprised of multi-colored wedges.

Perfect. A gift from on high.

All that remained was the fancy chevron stitching to outline the replacement. Not tonight, of course. But by the end of the week, her quilt would be finished.

Thanks to Clarence's cast-off tie, she would take the first step toward establishing her business and making her dream come true.

The next morning, Clarence rushed out of the boardinghouse right after breakfast and hustled to Truitt's. If he was lucky, they'd be open, though it was only six forty-five. Most businesses were still closed for another couple hours. But he knew Robert Truitt got an early start on the business day. Hopefully, he hadn't thrown out the necktie.

Though the door was locked, and the sign proclaimed *Closed*, he tapped on the glass. After peering in and spotting the rosy hue of a lamp at the back, it was obvious someone was working.

Clarence pounded on the wooden door.

Robert's balding head poked out of the backroom curtains. He looked none too happy to be disturbed. Well, too bad. Clarence wouldn't take a *no*.

The jiggle of the lock sounded, and Robert opened the door. "It's early. We're not open."

Clarence stepped on the threshold to block the door's closing. "Can I come in? I'll only be a minute."

Glancing to the street, the store owner stood aside and allowed him in. "What's this about?"

"Yesterday, I left my necktie." Clarence rushed to the counter and frowned when he found it clear. "Did you find it?"

"That raggedy tie? That's why you're banging on my door at this early hour?"

"It's important. Did you see it?"

Robert Truitt sighed. "Only when you wore the worn-out thing into the store."

Clarence ignored the insult. "I remember taking it off right here." He thumped the glass counter.

Robert pursed his lips as he rubbed away the smudge on the pristine case. "If you don't see it, then it's not here."

Clarence inhaled. He didn't want to be confrontational, but this man didn't take him seriously. "Look, I understand you've got other things to do. I appreciate you letting me in like this. But would you just look around for me?"

"Parker, I sold you one of my best ties. I saw that shabby thing you've worn for years. I'm telling you, if it was lying here, it was undoubtedly mistaken for rubbish and tossed away."

Clarence felt the blood drain from his face. "You mean, somebody would have thrown out my tie? That's my property."

"Actually, if you abandoned it in my store, it belongs to me." Robert's tone sparked a fire.

Heat rose within Clarence. Abandoned? Whatever happened to accidents? Or forgetting? He'd like to wipe that self-righteous sneer off Robert Truitt's face. "So, you're saying it's my fault?"

He splayed his arms. "Take it however you will. Nonetheless, the tie you're looking for is not here."

They faced each other as the seconds ticked. Then Robert's shoulders fell. "Fine. I'll check the rubbish bin."

Relief washed over Clarence. "Thank you."

"But I'm telling you, if it's not there, it's gone. I keep a tidy establishment."

In less than a minute, Robert returned, shaking his head. "It's not there. You probably dropped it on the way home."

"Let me have a look."

Robert's jaw dropped. "You surely don't intend to go through my trash?"

"Exactly." Clarence strode to the back room, ignoring all objections.

But after upending the bin and combing through every crumpled paper, a broken fan, an assortment of empty jars, and a pair of holey socks, he admitted defeat. The tie had vanished. After cleaning up the mess he'd made, he lifted a hand in thanks and set out for the hardware store.

The morning sunlight brightened everything but Clarence's spirits. How could he have lost something so important? His negligence sickened him. He'd once again failed his brother. The regret in his chest was an old companion, not easily shed.

Chapter 12

*A Chicago woman was turned out of her happy home for making
a crazy quilt out of her husband's four-in-hand ties. She didn't
realize she was cutting home ties.—The Charleroi Mail
(Charleroi, Pennsylvania) November 25, 1930.*

Though exhausted after each day's work at Truitt's Dry
Goods, Delia was determined to finish the quilt by
the end of the week. In two evenings, she'd added the
chevron stitches to outline the cream tie. That left only the soft
black cotton backing, and that she could tack in a few days.
When she gently withdrew it from her sewing bag each
evening and spread it out before her, her heart swelled.
Glorious. She was in awe of the creation, as if a larger force had
guided her needle.

Perhaps she'd finally show it to Clarence when he came
Saturday evening. He'd be impressed by the attention to detail,
and maybe even appreciate her careful combination of colors
and textures.

She and Clarence hadn't spoken of her project since the

night she told him what crazy quilts meant to her. Now that his tie filled the space where the rip had been, she couldn't wait to show him what a help he'd been to her.

Friday morning, Aunt Mary handed her an envelope with her name written in neat block letters. "Clarence wanted me to give this to you, dearie. I hope it's not bad news."

A strange thing to say. Even stranger that the envelope's seal was broken. One look at Aunt Mary's guilty expression and she had her answer.

"You opened my note from Clarence?"

Aunt Mary rolled her eyes as if the question were ludicrous. "Go on, now. Have a look for yourself."

Delia shook her head as she unfolded the letter. Ignoring the hot breath on the back of her neck, she read the short missive.

> Dear Delia,
> I regret to tell you I will not be dining with you and your family Saturday night. Please tell your mother I gladly accept her generous invitation.
> With warmest regards,
> Clarence Parker

Disappointment weighed her shoulders as she re-read the note.

Aunt Mary poked her shoulder. "What do you suppose that means?"

Delia whirled on the woman. "Really, Aunt Mary. Have you no shame?"

Aunt Mary's face reddened. "Curiosity kills me! Besides, I'm here to protect my favorite niece."

Delia rolled her eyes with a resigned sigh. "In answer to your question, I have no idea what he's talking about. To my knowledge, Mother hasn't invited him anywhere." She blinked. "This is the first Saturday night he'll miss since we've been courting."

Aunt Mary made a sympathetic clucking sound as she patted her arm. "Now don't you worry, dearie. That young man is clearly besotted with you."

Delia folded the note and slipped it back into the envelope. Disappointment blanketed her mood throughout that day and the next, especially when she scanned the busy streets for any sign of him. If this had been a few weeks earlier, she would've scoffed at the idea of a man consuming her thoughts. But that'd been before Clarence had upended her world.

But when they arrived at church Sunday morning, he stood outside the building. Her pulse rabbited as the wagon slowed to a stop.

Hazel sniffed. "I wish I had a beau."

Rabb frowned, offering a hand to the girl. "Talk like that and I'll make sure every boy in town keeps away until you're twenty-five."

Thomas snickered, and Hazel swatted at both brothers.

Delia walked behind her siblings. Even when he greeted her family, he seemed restrained. What if he wanted to end their courtship?

When he smiled at her, her shoulders relaxed. He greeted her parents and siblings as they passed. Waiting until the others had entered the building, Clarence took her hands in his and pulled her close.

"I've missed you."

She let out her breath, all her questions about his absence falling by the wayside. "You have?"

Amusement creased the skin around those gray-green eyes. "Sure I have." He blinked, an expression of growing concern on his face. "You got my note, didn't you? That I'd miss Saturday night?"

She nodded. "B-but you didn't say why."

His grin returned as he squeezed her hands. "I'll tell you all about it." From the open windows, the banging piano keys urged the congregation to join in song. Clarence grimaced. "Guess we oughta get in there."

He loosened his grip on her hands, but Delia shook her head. "Oh, no, you don't. Tell me now. I've waited all week to find out what kept you away."

"All week? It's been a couple days!" He winked. "Have a little patience. I'm saving it for when we're alone."

"But—"

"Patience." He placed her hand in the crook of his arm.

"You drive me crazy, Clarence Parker." She made a show of huffing with indignance. Truth was, she was ridiculously happy now that he was by her side.

As the congregation stood singing a hymn while casting curious glances their way, he walked her all the way to her family's pew. As they passed the Waldrops, her gaze collided with Gert's. Delia couldn't help feeling a bit triumphant, hanging onto Clarence's arm in full view of the church, and she waggled her fingers at her rival. Gert's mouth flattened before swiveling her head.

As they sang along with the congregation, Delia's mind circled back to Clarence's surprise. The way he told her seemed to hold significance. But what?

Had he bought some token to assure his promise to her? A ring? Her knees trembled. That must be it. All the secrecy made sense if for a proposal.

But was she ready for that big step in their relationship?

∿

After church, Clarence came for Sunday dinner, which was apparently the invitation he had referred to in his note. It irked her that her mother had kept it from her. Why the secrecy? She barely tasted the fried chicken and pushed mashed potatoes around on her plate. Just the chance of Clarence proposing was enough to make her insides quake.

Every member of her family sat around the table. As the conversation hummed, she bounced her heel on the leg of her chair, imagining Clarence taking her hands in his, pulling her close. Saying the words any girl would kill to hear. Would he whisper the words and bend his head to place his lips on hers in a kiss? Or would he—

Hazel poked her arm. "Delia! I'm talking to you."

Startled, Delia sat up straight and looked around the table. Everyone stared at her. Had she missed something? "I asked you if you were the one making all the racket?"

"What are you talking about?"

Her sister threw up her hands in disgust and ducked under the tablecloth. Mother's gasp echoed Delia's. Of all horrors, her sister was making a scene, the unpardonable sin in this home. The men smothered their laughter and averted their eyes from the sight of Hazel's oversized bow poking up from the back of her dress.

Delia was speechless. Which didn't seem to matter because her sister's muffled voice drifted to them from underneath the table. "I'm sure I heard something tapping." Then, with a triumphant cry, Hazel's flushed head popped up. She tossed her braids behind her shoulders and pinned Delia with a frown. "Your leg's jumping around like crazy. You are driving me insane with the constant tapping."

Mother choked out a reprimand. "Hazel!"

Heat climbed Delia's neck, and she couldn't meet Clarence's gaze, especially when all the males of her family guffawed. But it didn't stop Hazel from pointing out Delia's untouched food. "Why, you haven't eaten a thing. Are you sick?"

Oh, Lord, make her mute.

"I am perfectly fine."

Mother cleared her throat in a dainty fashion. "I'm sorry for the interruption, Clarence. You were saying?"

Clarence cleared his throat. "I guess my point is that necktie belonged to my brother. I'd sure like to know where it is."

Delia froze. Necktie? The very one she'd brought home? She grabbed her glass and gulped water.

Papa laid his napkin beside his plate. "Clarence, we'll pray this remembrance of your brother shows up." He looked around the table. "Who's interested in a game of horseshoes?"

Oblivious to movement around her, Delia remained in her chair with a napkin pressed to her lips. The tie! He hadn't left it for someone else to dispose of, no matter how raggedy and worn. No, he'd simply forgotten it. Now, he was searching everywhere for the thing. And she'd sewn it into her quilt.

This was awful.

Clarence touched her shoulder, causing her to start. "Are you all right?"

She stared up at him, mindlessly rubbing her arms. "I'm fine."

She was not. She was far, far, from fine.

"Coming?"

"Pardon?"

He cocked his head. "You know, outside. Horseshoes?"

How could he grin at her like that? She'd gone and stolen his tie!

"Delia?"

She shook herself. "Oh, yes. Of course." She stood and focused her gaze on his collar. On his new tie. "No, no. Y-you go on. I'll just ... help with the dishes."

She flashed a smile that she hoped would make him leave before she could answer her pounding heart and blab the truth.

She waited until Clarence quit the room, then fisted Hazel's sleeve. "Tell me quick. What was he talking about?"

Clearly annoyed, she twisted from Delia's grasp. "You were sitting right there."

Indeed. But she'd been too lost in her romantic daydream to hear Clarence speak. "Please, I'm begging you. Just tell me."

"I don't know. Something about losing his dead brother's tie." Hazel huffed and walked away.

Delia sagged against the wall. His dead brother's tie. It was worse than she'd imagined. And now, she couldn't give it back no matter how much she wanted to. Why, oh why, had she sewn it into her crazy quilt?

Sitting on the steps a little while later, Clarence picked up Delia's hand and laid it against his own. "My fingers are almost double the size of yours."

She smiled bashfully. "You make me feel safe."

"You are safe with me. Delia, I'll never let anyone hurt you."

She looked up at him with her chocolate-brown eyes. "You're such a good man, Clarence."

His smile faded. *A good man.* He had a long way to go before that description would fit him.

He gently withdrew his hand. "I guess you might think I'm ridiculous."

"What do you mean?"

Uncertainty layered her response. He'd known this would be hard, but now the moment was here, the words stuck. Maybe if he didn't have to look at her, this would go better. He leaned forward, hands clasped on his knees.

"I've been acting a little crazy after losing Joe's tie. Your uncle probably told you."

He looked at her for confirmation, but she shook her head. At least Robert Truitt thought enough of him to be discreet. "Since we're looking at a future together, you ought to know the whole story."

Her eyes widened, but she said nothing. He took a deep breath. "Everybody loved my big brother. My pa thought the sun rose in him. Joe was pretty much perfect."

He studied his hands. "When I was a teenager, I got fed up with how much Pa favored Joe. I started showing out, causing trouble. Anything to get Pa's attention. But it didn't work. My resentment built up until it seemed about to boil over. That's when me and a couple of friends, Virgil Mason and Eugene Smith, ran away, thought we'd join up with a cattle drive, see the world. Instead, we ended up in Fort Worth, hanging out with a bunch of bad men. Big Jake's gang, which I told you about. But I didn't tell you all of it, especially where it involves Joe."

He forced himself to meet her somber gaze. Guilt swallowed his words. Oh, the trust she held for him. Innocent, blind trust. After what he had to reveal about himself, she likely wouldn't look at him the same again. But he had to tell her the whole ugly story. Otherwise, what was the point in courting her? If she didn't know what he'd been, she'd never understand who he longed to be.

"It was a pretty low place. I did stuff I'm not proud of."

"You can tell me, Clarence."

He wiped his sweaty palms on his thighs. "When I woke up face down in an alley and couldn't remember how I got there, I swore that was it. No more of that kind of life. I wrote my pa, told him I wanted to come home and needed funds for a train ticket. But instead of wiring the money, Joe came. Told me he was there to take me home. I'd avoided my friends, but when Joe and me were waiting on the train, Eugene and Virgil showed up."

Clarence stood and raked his hand through his short hair, the scene playing in his mind as if he were back there, struggling loose of their grip as they dragged him away. "They said I had to go back to Jake's gang, no leaving now that I was part of the gang. But Joe fought them off and told me to run. That's when I heard the shot. When I looked back, Joe was down, and Virgil stood over him, holding a gun."

Hot tears blurred his vision. He sensed her presence and tried to block the comfort of her hand on his arm. He needed to get himself together and tell her everything. But try as he might, emotion clogged his throat.

"Clarence, how dreadful. I'm so sorry."

He rubbed the back of his neck, lost in the memory. "I tried to staunch the blood, but it wouldn't stop. That red stain spread over Joe's white shirt. Before he stopped breathing, he told me to tell his wife he loved her." Clarence had held him, bawling, until deputies pried his arms off so the undertaker could take him. "If I hadn't been such a fool, he'd be alive."

"What happened after that? If you want to tell me, that is."

He clasped the back of his neck. "After the funeral, I couldn't stay around. So, I just wandered from place to place, hiring on at ranches to help with branding or rounding up cattle. Odd jobs. But when I got to Houston, I found shelter from a hailstorm inside a little white church. The preacher found me. Talked to me. He and his wife took me in and fed me." He lifted his shoulders. "Pastor Wilbur saved my life."

"How do you mean?"

"He said God could redeem my past." He stopped pacing and faced her. "Even though I can't go back and change things, I can move forward in the right direction." He took a deep breath, relieved the tale was told. "So, now you know."

"I'm so sorry you went through that, Clarence. It must have been horrible." She paused. "But I'm not sure how the tie is connected to your story. Not that I'm making light of it ..."

He sat up straight. "Sorry, I guess I didn't connect the two things. That tie I lost? It's the only thing I have of Joe's. With it gone, it's like he died all over again."

Her lips parted. "Oh, no ..." To his surprise, her eyes pooled with tears. "Oh, Clarence, I'm so sorry." She buried her head in her hands.

Aw, crumb. He shouldn't have told her the gory details, her being such a delicate female and all. He patted her back helplessly. "There, there ... it's not your fault."

She jerked her head up, revealing her tear-streaked face. "I had no idea it was so dear to you—I never meant—Eleanor asked, but I thought—and the fair is upon us, you see ..."

Huh? This gal jumped from one subject to another quicker than he could blink. "Maybe we'd best get you back to your mother." Great. Mr. Truitt wouldn't let him within a mile of his daughter if he kept upsetting her like this. "I've been inconsiderate. Please forgive me."

"But what about me? Aren't you mad?"

He blinked. Had he missed something? "Mad at myself is more like it." He needed to leave before he did more damage to this fragile creature. "Can I get you anything? Water, cold compress, your mother ...?"

She sniffed, long and rattly, and pressed her hand over her nose. "A handkerchief?"

Relief flooded him. Maybe she was done crying. He dug the square from his pocket. "Here you go."

He slowly sat back down and smiled at her ladylike nose-blowing. She handed it back to him. "Thank you."

He recoiled. "Oh, no. You keep it."

Suddenly, his little beauty looked at him with the biggest, mournful eyes, which sprouted fresh new tears. "About the tie—"

He held up his hand. "Let's just forget about it." He'd already ruined the afternoon. The least he could do was try to steer their conversation onto happier subjects.

To his horror, she dissolved into tears all over again. She was either emotionally unstable or the most compassionate woman he'd ever met. In the future, he'd be careful not to tell her when he got a splinter. It might set her back for days.

"Look, I think it's better if I leave now. This has been a difficult afternoon, I'm afraid."

When she didn't object, he went inside to get his hat and thank her mother for the invitation to join them this afternoon.

At least Delia's tears had stopped flowing when he came out. Wordless, he reached for her hand, and they walked toward the road.

At the lane where his horse waited, he faced her. "I almost forgot to tell you. That trip I took?"

Her smile faded.

"Oh, no, don't worry. It's good. The best, in fact."

"Oh?"

"I took a trip to see a banker."

Her brow wrinkled. "A banker?"

He nodded. "Yep."

"Don't we have one here?"

He couldn't help but sneer. "Clive Waldrop's been dodging my appointments for months. Guess I did something to get on his bad side." Because he'd rejected Waldrop's daughter, no doubt. "I went to Corsicana to get my business loan."

All that came from her was a whisper. "A-and?"

"What if I told you I'm the new owner of Parker Hardware and Carriage Shop?"

She clasped her hands together. "Oh, Clarence! Your dream."

He touched the last trace of moisture on her cheek. "One I hope to share with you someday."

Her lips tipped in a soft smile. "I think I'd like that."

A wisp of breeze lifted a tendril of hair, and it fell across her brown eyes. He gently lifted it. "I knew you were special the first time I saw you. And then, when someone sabotaged your box lunch, you lifted your chin like you dared anyone to tell you it wasn't good enough. Other girls would have run away crying. But not you. You held your head high when no one bid on that sad-looking box." He cupped her cheek and swallowed words she wasn't ready to hear, no matter how ready he was to say them. "I want to be the kind of man you can trust."

She placed her hand on top of his. "You are. I've never experienced such ready forgiveness." Her eyes took on a reddish sheen. Not more tears.

Pebbles crunched on the path seconds before Thomas appeared, grinning ruefully. "Ma says it's time to come in, Delia."

Relief flooded Clarence. He backed away, lifting his arm in a wave. "Okay, then, you folks have a good evening."

He made haste to his horse. Just before he mounted, drifts of conversation floated to him.

146

"Thomas, your timing is terrible. He would have kissed me if you hadn't come up."

A deep chuckle, then, "Why do you think I kicked those rocks when I did?"

Shaking his head, he urged the horse to the road. Delia Truitt was without a doubt the sweetest, most beautiful woman he'd ever met. But life would be lots easier once he figured her out.

Chapter 13

"So behind every young ambitious man working his way up the
ladder to success was a woman working to produce a crazy quilt
to show off in the parlor to prove just how successful they were!"
—Judith Baker Montano, The Crazy Quilt Handbook,
Revised 2ⁿᵈ Edition.

Delia couldn't sleep as Clarence's tormented past played through her mind. Sure, he'd told her about Jake Baskin's gang, but she'd thought he exaggerated his involvement. Now that she knew the whole story, his involvement gave her pause.

And now she knew why the necktie was so worn. Her sweet man had wanted to keep it close, as if it would replace his brother. If she'd known its significance, she would have run after him that day and made sure he didn't leave it.

Now, it was snipped to size and sewn securely into her crazy quilt. He'd said she wasn't at fault. But as she reflected on the conversation, had she been clear about what she'd done with his necktie? He'd been so quick to absolve her guilt. No doubt he was a good man with a forgiving heart. Even so, he should've questioned her at the very least. After all, the tie was the only physical reminder of his lost brother. She needed to tell him in an unemotional, logical manner what had become of the tie.

Riding her bicycle to work the next day, she considered how to tell him his brother's necktie was no more. At least not the way he expected. If only she hadn't allowed him to leave without first showing him the quilt.

Maybe he would thank her for preserving it within her quilt. Wasn't the remembrance safer within her pretty quilt than lying in a trash bin?

Oh, who was she kidding? The plain truth was she'd used his beloved artifact to repair her quilt so she could win a ribbon at the fair. What kind of sweetheart did that?

Ahead, the train rails crossing the road caused her to slow and dismount so she could walk the two-wheeler over the tracks. As she guided the bicycle, movement in the copse of trees to her right caught her attention.

Her breath caught. A man rode toward her, the same man she'd seen outside Mrs. Baskin's shop. The hair on the back of her neck stood up. For a moment, the fifty or so feet between them shrunk. He could overtake her in seconds, and no one would be the wiser. Not on this lonely stretch of road. She had to get away. Scrambling back onto the bicycle seat, she pushed off with a wobble. Was he following? She tossed a look over her shoulder. The bicycle veered crazily.

Senses on high alert, she gripped the handlebars and forced her legs into rhythm. Air skimmed her cheeks and loosed her hair from its bun. Main Street was just ahead. Pedaling fast, she rounded the corner where unsuspecting people went about their business. Gulping air, her shoulders sagged with relief.

This time when she looked over her shoulder, both feet

skimmed the dirt road, keeping her stable at this slow speed. No sign of the brooding man.

She expelled a long breath. Silly, getting so worked up. What if it hadn't even been the same man?

Now that Truitt's Dry Goods stood within sight, she coasted. No more wild imaginings. Though she certainly hadn't imagined the fellow outside Mrs. Baskin's shop the other day.

"Well, well, well, if it isn't our resident lady cyclist. How very modern of you."

Gert Waldrop. But after the scare on the road, even seeing Gert wasn't upsetting.

Delia smiled sweetly as she dismounted. "Thank you kindly, Gert. I do consider myself quite progressive."

Gert harrumphed. "More like a spinster in the making. You can't honestly believe Clarence will condone this—" she gestured to the split skirt—"horribly mannish outfit, do you? Or has he seen you in this dreadful getup?"

"I'm surprised at how old-fashioned you are. Bloomers are the accepted apparel for cycling." She started to roll her bicycle away but thought better of it. "And by the way, I do not need Clarence's permission to dress appropriately. Yours, either."

"How about society's? Or would you rather defy convention?"

"Fine with me."

Gert pursed her lips. Delia pushed the bicycle forward. Over her shoulder, she called, "Have a wonderful day, Miss Waldrop. Come see us at Truitt's, and I'll show you the latest fashion in bloomers."

As she could have predicted, Gert emitted a shrill huff, and Delia grinned as she approached the store.

Inside, Delia entered a private curtained area and unbuttoned the overskirt to hide the bloomers, brushing it clean of dirt. Murmurs sounded outside her tiny dressing room. She recognized her aunt and uncle's hushed voices. When she heard Clarence's name, she stilled.

"He came around again, looking for that tie."

A sympathetic clucking preceded her aunt's words. "Now, don't be impatient with the young man. Persistence is a virtue."

"Persistence, my eye. Obsession is more like it. I warned him not to bang on my door anymore."

Their voices drifted from the back area, and Delia chewed her fingernail. Apparently, Clarence was going to all lengths looking for Joe's tie.

That sealed it. She needed to tell him before he alienated the whole town.

Clarence stood before Hardy's desk. "What's next?"

"We signed the papers, son. I'm mighty pleased to say the store's not mine no more. It's yours."

"Just like that."

Hardy rose and patted Clarence on the shoulder. "Future's just around the corner, son. Yours and mine both." Hardy gestured to the desk. "It's all yours now. Have a seat, Mr. Owner."

Clarence sat down and laughed softly. "I can't believe it. I've thought about this for a long time." Ever since he'd come to work at the hardware store, he'd dreamed of someday buying this business. Hardy'd made no bones about retiring soon. Now that the day had arrived, Clarence couldn't think straight.

"I'm happy for you, son."

"I'm grateful you didn't sell to anybody else, even when I kept hitting a wall." Clarence swallowed. "Thank you."

Hardy chuckled. "Let's see if you thank me a year from now."

"I know I will."

It was the first step toward becoming the kind of man people respected. And after he married Delia, he'd build her a fine house. Raise a family. Settle into this town, and maybe even help run it. Who knew what lay ahead?

~

Midweek, Lucy and Sallie came into the store. When they walked through the doors, Delia ran to greet them. "It's been forever since I've seen y'all."

Lucy rolled her eyes. "You hardly know we exist, Miss I-Have-a-Beau."

Sallie folded her arms with a mock pout. "I have to fight off my brother to come within two feet of you at church."

Delia laughed. It was true. Clarence was always at her side at church.

"She's protecting her man, no doubt." Lucy nodded. "I've seen the way Gert's claws come out around you two. You'd best watch out for her."

"I'm not worried." Though no telling what lengths she'd go to come between Delia and Clarence, like the Fourth of July box social or the torn quilt. Even though Delia couldn't prove Gert had done either, she was certain of it.

"Well, never mind all that. We came with a special invitation." Sallie drew an envelope from her pocket. "Go ahead, open it."

Delia read the words out loud.

Miss Delia Truitt
is most cordially invited to attend a garden luncheon
In honor of the completion of her Crazy Quilt
Wednesday afternoon at 1:00

At the home of
Sallie Parker

She looked at each friend. "All this, just to celebrate my quilt?"

They spoke at the same time. "Of course!"

"We know how you've worried over it, and now that it's complete, we want to celebrate your efforts!" Sallie smiled.

She still hadn't told Clarence about the tie. How would Sallie react when she saw it in the repaired quilt?

Delia's stomach knotted. Glancing over her shoulder, she stepped away. "I need to get back to work. I'd love to come, if I can get the time off work. May I bring something?"

Lucy chuckled. "Your quilt, silly."

"Oh." Her stomach dipped. "It's just ... well, I thought I'd keep it to myself until the fair."

Sallie cocked her head "But not from us? We're your best friends."

Lucy laid an arm across Delia's shoulders. "I still don't know how you fixed the hole, though I'm not a bit surprised. The reason for this little get-together is to celebrate your achievement."

"I haven't won anything. Don't you want to wait and see if I place?"

"Absolutely not. You have won already."

Behind her, Uncle Robert cleared his throat.

Delia winced. "I need to get back to work." She walked with them to the door. "I'll see you girls Wednesday."

"And don't forget your quilt. If my mama's there, she'll want to see it too." Sallie waggled her fingers.

Delia's heart sank. Just what she needed—not one, but two Parker women who would recognize that particular tie at a glance.

The quicker she could confess to Clarence, the better.

~

At one o'clock Wednesday, Delia, sewing bag in hand, climbed the steps of the Parker's four-square house. One more day she hadn't told Clarence about the necktie. Not that she hadn't had an opportunity, with the hardware shop within a short distance of the dry goods store.

Sallie opened the door wide. "I'm glad you're here. I can't wait to see the quilt. Come on back to the garden."

As Delia followed, Sallie spoke over her shoulder. "We've got the place all to ourselves. Mama's out visiting. You should see her garden. It's a feast of autumn color."

One less pair of sharp eyes and sharper questions if the tie was detected. "And your father? Is he here?"

"No, thankfully."

Delia frowned when her friend didn't elaborate. Sallie held the back door and motioned her through. Delia halted just beyond the threshold with a gasp. "How beautiful."

Beyond the small back porch, an array of brilliant yellows and reds and purples peppered the small, enclosed yard. She breathed in the aroma of the foliage. "It's amazing."

Sallie nodded, cheeks flushed. "We spend a lot of time out here. It's peaceful to dig in the dirt."

"I've never seen anything so wonderful."

This was nothing like the formal gardens at Gert's home. The organization was logical, but not fussy. Here and there, tiny weeds peeked through the clumps of coleus or chrysanthemums.

In the center, a small round table with three chairs awaited them. Lucy sprang to her feet. "Come here and sit."

Delia grinned as Sallie made an elaborate show of seating

her. They sat in comfortable silence as they dined on tea sandwiches, potato salad, and lemonade. Tall spiky blooms of white and orange swayed in the breeze, and every so often, a bee buzzed nearby. Conscious of the tension ebbing from her neck and shoulders, she took a long sip of her drink. "This is like a little oasis. I'll bet your family loves it out here."

"It's just Mama's hobby. Not that we don't enjoy it, of course." Sallie lifted her shoulders.

Lucy grinned. "Well, I have a bit of news. Thomas has arranged a meeting with my daddy." She looked from Delia to Sallie. "I'm just sure he will ask to court me."

Delia choked down her drink. "What?" Why hadn't Thomas said anything?

"Haven't you seen them? They're as moony as you and Clarence."

"B-but when did this happen?" Had she been so myopic as to not notice anyone except Clarence?

Sallie and Lucy exchanged a knowing look. "Don't you remember how Thomas made a show for Lucy's basket at the picnic?"

"Of course." But why hadn't she been in on the building relationship? She picked up her fork and took a bite of potato salad, though she barely tasted it.

As she fought against giving into feelings of isolation, she listened to their easy banter. They giggled and chatted about the budding romances around town.

"I just wish he noticed me, you know, as a woman."

Lucy waved off Sallie's wistfulness. "He will."

Delia looked between the two as if they spoke a language she hadn't learned. "Who?"

"Rabb, of course. I told you." The words held a hint of accusation and hurt.

"I'm sorry. I didn't realize you still had feelings for him."

Sallie's cheeks reddened. "It sounds pathetic, doesn't it, holding out hope for the man every girl wants."

Delia bit her lip. How insensitive she'd been. She knew little of their lives, yet they'd celebrated her accomplishment with this garden party. "I'm sorry. I've just been so busy ..." Her words trailed away in the awkward silence. She swallowed. "I'd love to hear all I've missed."

Lucy tsked. "This is all about you. Now, tell us everything."

Delia shrugged. "You know about my job at Truitt's. I've been able to contribute a little to my family's saving jar. And Mother will have the baby in a few weeks, at the beginning of October. Papa's building a crib, and I've made a few gowns." She looked at both friends. "Speaking of sewing, I've made a fine friend out of Eleanor Baskin, the woman we helped at the parade. She's a very kind woman."

Sallie's eyes grew big. "Delia, how can you befriend a woman like her?"

"How can I not? Oh, I know, she's the wife of an outlaw. But have you heard the real story? She wants nothing to do with him. There's more to Eleanor than her alliance to Big Jake. Have you ever taken the time to speak with her?" She let the question lay in the small space between them, waiting for their resolute expressions to soften before continuing. "I have sympathy for the poor woman. She has fewer clients by the day, just because of rumors."

"And the newspapers." Lucy's voice was quiet. "They haven't been kind to her. I'm not surprised her business is dwindling. You must admit, it's daunting to think of that woman being Big Jake Baskin's wife."

Sallie's expression was apologetic. "You can't blame us for being cautious, Delia. We're only human."

Delia looked from one to another, incredulous. "You are good Christian women, are you not? What happened to

157

charity? Eleanor is a wonderful woman who's suffered at the hands of gossips. The least you can do is show her the grace that has been granted you."

After a tense moment, Sallie sat back. "You're right. We are Christians. I hate the thought of anyone feeling like I've done them wrong. Why don't you introduce us to her?"

"But I don't have to. She already knows who you are. She thinks the three of us are angels for helping her to the doctor back in July."

Lucy lifted her shoulders. "Then take us with you next time you visit with her. Maybe we can get to know her for ourselves."

Delia's spirits lifted and she smiled her agreement before sipping the last of her lemonade. Maybe, if the three of them openly accepted Eleanor, the town would come around.

Chapter 14

*Such a woman was it who fell a victim to that "crazy quilt"
mania which is now insidiously undermining the moral and
intellectual character of the females in all ranks of life
throughout this whole country.—Chicago Tribune (Chicago,
Illinois) Saturday, April 5, 1884.*

Around the little table in the Parker garden, the conversation turned to lighter subjects when Lucy served them generous wedges of chocolate cake. Delia took her time with every bite. Now that they had settled into easy rapport, she didn't want to ruin it by bringing out the quilt. But she couldn't stall forever. Long after her friends were finished, Delia had half a slice remaining on her plate.

Lucy threw up her hands. "Why are you eating so slowly? I'm beginning to think you don't want us to see your quilt."

"I'm almost finished."

Lucy's finger tapped the table. Then, all at once, she leaned toward Sallie. "I heard the most delicious gossip, and it concerns your brother, Sallie."

Delia's chewing stilled. Gossip regarding Clarence?

Sallie groaned and rubbed her smudged lenses with her green calico skirt. "If I've heard it once, I've heard it a thousand times. And the answer is yes."

"But you don't know what I'm going to tell you."

"Is it about the paper?"

Lucy's shoulders slumped. "So, you've heard."

"About a thousand people have asked me about the advertisement in the classifieds. Yes, Clarence placed it. Who else could it have been? He's the only one I know on a mad hunt for a stolen necktie." She placed her spectacles on her nose. "To tell you the truth, it was smart. Now everyone knows to look out for it."

Delia smashed a crumb on her fork. He'd placed an ad in the paper.

Lucy laughed. "Perhaps he should ask the sheriff to put out posters too. Wanted, Dead or Alive: Tie Thief."

"Don't laugh. That tie meant a lot to him."

"It's a necktie."

"It was our brother's." Sallie's voice faltered. "After he died, his wife gave us things to help remember Joe. I got his monogrammed handkerchief, and Clarence got the tie he wore at his wedding."

Delia rubbed her forehead. This was awful. She must return that necktie to Clarence. Or at least, what little was left of it. Her entering the fair was of little consequence. She had to go home, get her embroidery scissors, and snip that silk out of the central design.

Because she couldn't live with herself if she kept such a dear possession for her own gain.

She pushed away from the table. "I have to go."

Lucy's jaw dropped. "What? No, you can't leave. You haven't shown us the quilt."

Her eyes roamed the remains of the luncheon they'd prepared for her. They'd gone to such effort just to celebrate her quilt.

"All right." Delia crossed to where she'd left her bag. She'd have to tell them the whole story. So be it.

They gathered around her as she slowly unfolded the quilt. She couldn't bear to look at their faces as she stretched it out before them. They murmured every expression of awe she'd dreamed of hearing. But the admiration failed to make her proud.

She dared to look at Sallie just when her friend pushed up her glasses and rested a troubled gaze on Delia. "Is that ...?"

Pressing her eyelids shut, she nodded. "I'm sorry."

Lucy said, "What are you looking at? Show me."

Delia gulped. "It's not what you think."

The shock and hurt on Sallie's face gutted Delia. "You knew he was frantic."

"I had no way of knowing that." Not until the other day, anyway.

Sallie crossed her arms. Lucy looked from one to the other. Then she gasped. "Wait—*you* are the one who stole Clarence's tie?"

"No!"

"Then how do you explain this?" Sallie pointed to the wedge-shaped silk.

"Well, yes, it's his tie, but I didn't steal it. He left it at the store when he bought another one, so I took it. I sewed it into the quilt before I knew he was searching for it."

"Why didn't you tell him?"

Delia sighed. "I tried to, but I don't think he understood." Evidenced by the ad in the newspaper.

For a moment, the silence lay between the three. "I didn't know anything about Joe or the tie being special. He left it on

161

the counter in Truitt's, and I thought he didn't want it anymore. It was so worn."

Sallie scoffed. "Yet good enough to use in your quilt."

"No." How could she explain without sounding like a self-serving person? "I found the tie all wadded up on the counter. I almost threw it away." And if Uncle Robert had his way, she would have. "But then I recognized it as his. It seemed right to keep it." Her cheeks flamed, remembering how she'd inhaled its scent. "I consulted Eleanor, and she thought it was the answer for my torn quilt."

Sallie scoffed. "Eleanor? Of course you'd do what she tells you. That just proves she's a bad influence on you. You're a thief."

Delia reared back. Of all people, gentle, patient Sallie, hissing such a hurtful accusation. Tears coated Delia's eyes. She swept up the quilt and held it against her chest. "I am not a thief! You know how this whole predicament upsets me."

"How would I? You didn't tell me. Or Lucy. But you certainly told your friend, Eleanor."

"What is that supposed to mean?"

"That you've replaced us with an outlaw's wife, that's what." Sallie stood with her arms crossed as if they were a shield.

"If you must know, I didn't tell because you're his sister, and you,"—she turned to Lucy—"talk too much."

Lucy gasped. "Are you calling me a gossip?"

Delia wilted. She'd gone too far. "Please, can't we just talk without name-calling?"

Sallie shook her head. "You've made a fool out of my brother, so don't blame me for being angry. If you really cared about him, you would tell him."

The words took on a life of their own inside Delia's head. How had one simple act snowballed into an enormous mistake?

This was truth, raw and scary. Minutes ago, she'd wanted to cut the tie out and give it back. But would he take it? Or would he turn his back on her?

She sagged into a chair. "I will tell him. But I'm scared he will jump to the wrong conclusion." As Sallie had.

Delia traced the symmetrical stitches on her quilt. The thought of the tie being the providential gift she needed now seemed preposterous. What had she been thinking?

"I guess I got caught up in perfecting my quilt and competing with Gert at the fair."

Lucy crouched next to her. "Aren't you afraid he'll be angry?"

Delia nodded, miserable. "I can't stand the thought."

They didn't respond, but she could guess what they were thinking, that she'd prioritized the fair entry over her relationship with Clarence. Because in the end, she'd done exactly that.

Sallie's tight expression softened. "Look, if he doesn't hear that from you, how do you think he'll react when he spots his tie in your quilt?"

"I'd do anything to keep that from happening. I've even considered cutting it out of the quilt."

Lucy looked shocked. "You can't do that. This is your one chance to prove yourself and win that fifty-dollar prize."

"I have to confess the tie is in my possession." She shook out the quilt and folded it neatly before placing it in her bag.

Sallie nodded. "It's the least you can do. I just hope it's not too late. He's awfully upset about losing it."

"Don't tell her that." Lucy squeezed Delia's shoulder. "We'll pray everything works out."

Delia tried to smile. The three stood and prepared to leave, the mood now heavy.

Lucy's mouth twitched as she caught Delia's eye. "You

know what this makes you?" She paused. "The Tie Thief of Blooming Grove."

Lucy dissolved into giggles. Her musical laughter lifted on the air.

"It's not funny."

"Come on, Sallie. Don't be so serious. Let's make up some headlines for our robber friend here. How's this—*Beware of the five-foot bandit!*" Lucy lifted her hands as if casting her words against the blue-sky backdrop. "*Men, hold on to your neckties. The Tie Thief of Blooming Grove looms large.*"

Delia giggled, then clamped her hand over her mouth.

Sallie's lips pursed. She picked up their dirty dishes and made her way into the house without a word, letting the screen slam behind her.

Lucy's laughter dissolved. "Don't worry about her. She'll get over it."

Delia wasn't so sure.

Clarence folded his arms in satisfaction and looked around the store. His store.

Spying Hardy, he strode to his former boss. "You going to let me take you and your wife to dinner?"

Hardy's face split in a rueful smile. "You keep talking about that. But I tell you what, son, why don't you take that little gal you been courting. I've got a tasty meal at home, and a fine woman who cooked it. And that sounds mighty good to me."

"You sure? I owe you so much. I just want to thank you."

Hardy bobbed his head. "I'm the one ought to be thanking you. My mind's easy with you taking over. This old store, she's been a blessing and a noose. Been in business since the town pulled up stakes in 1888, and moved a mile north so's we could be on the Cotton Belt rail line. Them was some exciting times, but this old man's done had his turn. So, I'm giving it over to you, son, and trust you'll take it forward into the 1900s."

Clarence's eyes stung as he embraced the man who'd accepted him as a newcomer and groomed him for business ownership. A wave of nostalgia swept over him as he watched Hardy hobble out the door.

He shook himself out of his reflections and entered the office. Now that the business was all his, Clarence would resist succumbing to the blanket of stress that threatened to overwhelm him.

He sat in the squeaky desk chair and gazed at the chaos that lay willy-nilly on the desk. So many loose ends. How would he ever make sense of this?

Sensing a presence in the doorway, he glanced up and almost toppled his chair in an attempt to welcome his father. "Pa!"

He hadn't seen him in weeks. Every time he'd dropped in on Ma and Sallie, Pa was out working. It hadn't surprised him. Hadn't the man always been absent? Always tinkering with something in the barn or plowing the field. It always seemed to Clarence that Pa hated being with the family. His father's grouchiness backed that belief at holiday meals, when he was forced to be inside and part of the celebration. If it could be called that.

Now, the very man who'd avoided being in the same room with his son took two halting steps inside the office. "Heard you bought this place."

"Yes, sir."

A decent father would praise his son. But Pa didn't offer congratulations or even a pat on the shoulder. Instead, he puckered his mouth and spit tobacco juice on the floor. Clarence swallowed, speechless.

Nodding at the cluttered desk, Pa said, "That how you run your store?"

Clarence glanced down at the desk, heat running up his neck. "Today's my first day, I was just—"

But Pa turned and walked away. Desperation clawed at Clarence. This was his one chance to impress his father. He hurried to follow him. "You need any nails? Paint? How about some gloves? It's on me, whatever you need."

Pa wheeled on him. "You think I need your handout? Well, I don't need it. Especially not a no-good like you. You may have this crowd fooled, but not me. I know you."

Shame coursed through Clarence. He knew better than to speak back, defend himself. From the corner of his eye, he saw one of his co-workers turn. No, not co-worker. Employee. An employee who just witnessed his boss being taken down by his old man. What kind of leader did that make him?

Uncertain of what to do, he shoved his hands in his trouser pockets and looked at the ground. It wasn't long before Pa walked away, and Clarence returned to his new office and the overrun desk. He sat down hard. Why'd his father have to come in here today, of all days? He'd worked here almost five years now, and the man never so much as looked this way. He made it known he gave his business to the competition.

Clarence leaned over, taking his head in his hands. *Lord, I've tried to love him, but he's a hard man. I need your help. I just can't do it on my own.*

For the millionth time, Clarence wished he wasn't the son of Joseph Parker. Why couldn't God have given him to another man? A man who was proud of his son's accomplishments, few as they were. A man who showed him how to be respectable without even saying a word. A man who loved him.

I'll never be like him.

"Clarence?"

He looked up. "Delia!" He stood and plastered a smile on his face, hurrying to greet her. All the while, he wondered if she'd heard any of the words between him and Pa.

"Come in and sit down. Sorry my desk's a mess. I haven't had an opportunity to sort things yet."

"So, the business is officially yours now?"

He sat in his chair behind the desk. "Sure is."

She nodded. "It's a very fine store." Her smile faded. "Clarence, was that your father talking to you like that?"

His stomach dipped. "You heard?"

She leaned forward, and the warmth of her hand on his arm both touched and humiliated him. "The way he spoke to you broke my heart."

He looked away. Her compassion made him want to cave to his sorrow. But he had to be strong.

"Don't be sad about it. I'm used to it. Life with Pa isn't easy." He attempted a smile, but failed.

"I'm so sorry."

He tried to shrug off her sympathy. "Yeah, well ... I'm just sorry Sallie has to live under his roof."

Shock widened her eyes. "Please tell me he doesn't hurt her?"

"No, no. I never would've left if I thought he'd hurt her or Ma." At least that was one good thing about Pa. He'd never lifted a hand to them.

"I want you to know, you're a fine man, Clarence Parker."

The words he'd always wanted to hear. Why didn't they make him whoop and holler inside?

"Come on, let me show you around. I'm glad you came in today." He crooked his arm, and she tucked her hand at his elbow.

"Yes, me too. But actually, I came here to tell you something."

He patted her hand. "Sure. But first, let's look around the place."

He needed to get Pa's bitter words out of his head.

Chapter 15

The crazy quilt mania allows no neck ties to accumulate on the hands of brother, husbands and lovers, while all of the triumvirate keep their best hats at the office to save the lining from spoilation.—Chester Times (Chester, Pennsylvania) March 14, 1884.

She was a coward. She should have admitted what she'd done. But after the way his father talked down to him, Delia didn't have the heart to tell him the bad news. She'd wait for a better day.

Only, several days had gone by, and each time she'd worked up her courage to admit she'd used the tie, she'd ended up taking the coward's way out.

Now, here it was, the day the entries were due to the fair. Time had run out. Delia found herself torn between confessing her deed to Clarence and offering him the quilt, or turning in her project without a word. Of course, she didn't have to be told the right thing to do. She just didn't want to risk their courtship crumbling like a dry cookie.

She gazed down at the colorful crazy quilt spread on her

bed. She was so proud of her work. She traced the tie's outline. Maybe she could show him before she handed it to her aunt, who was undertaking the fifteen-mile journey to the county seat to enter Blooming Grove's contribution to the fair.

He'll hate you.

"Is that your fair entry?"

Delia started, laying a hand over her heart. "You scared me."

Mother came to stand beside her. "Your stitching is precise. So interesting to look at." Mother traced the spot where the hole had been. "It looks like you found a solution. It's lovely."

Echoes of Mother's past comments rolled through Delia's mind. Too frivolous. Not practical. A waste of time. But lovely?

"I'm happy you approve, Mother."

"Approve? No. There's nothing at all practical about this. It's not big enough to be called a bed covering, and it's too fancy to be a baby's blanket. To say nothing of how you've allowed it to interfere with the running of our home. And by the looks of those dark circles under your eyes, it's affected your health as well. No, I do not approve of crazy quilting."

She should've known.

"But I'll grant you, this quilt is a thing of beauty."

Delia couldn't muster much enthusiasm in her voice. "Thanks."

Mother returned her hand to her lower back and grimaced.

It was a gesture she'd often witnessed, but not like this. "Are you feeling all right? Is there something I can get you?"

Mother shook her head, silent for a long moment. For every second that ticked by, Delia held her breath, waiting. Finally, the tension eased from her mother's face. "Just a little pain, nothing to worry about. Now, get this to Aunt Mary. I've asked Rabb to drive you there and right back. I need your help with laundry." Mother lumbered out of the room. Delia didn't miss the way she placed her hand again on her lower back, or how the damp tendrils of brown hair had escaped their pins.

Was it time for the baby?

She skittered after Mother. "I can stay here with you. Rabb can take the quilt." However, it would pain her to trust her carefree brother with such an enormous responsibility.

"Don't be silly. You'll rest easier if you deliver that package yourself. I know you well, remember."

The choice warred as she studied Mother's movement through the home. It was as if the pain had subsided. "If you're sure."

With a wave, Mother dismissed the subject, and Delia wandered back to her quilt. Either way, she'd regret her decision. Leaving and wondering if the birth was imminent, or staying, and hoping Rabb would do as bid before the deadline ran out.

It seemed she was always caught between two hard places these days.

Mother's words threaded her mind as she folded the quilt. She thought she'd learned to abide the criticism, but her disapproval stung. Why did everything have to be practical? Why couldn't she see the soul-filling nature of beauty?

A memory came to her over the miles and months, the image of Papa on the big porch in Georgia, his violin tucked under his chin, drawing the bow across the strings in a mournful melody to a captivated audience of friends and family. Then trading his fiddle for a guitar and leading them all to sing hymns or current songs.

She'd never connected her artistry with Papa's, but weren't they related? Music was art that was heard and sensed, soul deep. Crazy quilting, embroidery, even dressmaking were art experienced through sight and touch. Had she inherited Papa's artist's soul?

But when was the last time he'd played for them? How surprised she'd been when he strummed his guitar at the Fourth of July dance.

She would ask him to play, like they used to. Now it wouldn't be a great crowd on an elegant porch. And yet, the thought of him playing fiddle under the cover of the rustic breezeway seemed more appropriate. Maybe tonight.

Her spirits lifted as she wrapped brown paper around her treasured fair entry and tied it with string.

"Come on, Red, I don't got all day."

Rabb's panther-like energy breathed new life into the room. She hugged the paper-bound quilt to her chest and rushed after Rabb. "I don't, either."

Though her job at Truitt's had ended, due to the baby's imminent arrival, finishing the quilt had monopolized her time. Now, she'd have time to make the baby's layette. She'd purchased a lightweight cotton, and her fingers itched to get started.

Mother stood on the lawn beside a pile of laundry, hand braced on her lower back, watching the fire grow to yellow-orange tongues that licked the bottom of the cauldron. Perspiration dotted her porcelain forehead, the tendrils now damp and clinging to her face.

Delia slowed. "Mother, why don't you rest? Hazel and I can do the washing."

Mother tossed assorted clothes into the kettle. "Hazel is at school, dear."

"I meant after she comes home."

"I'll manage fine. Don't worry."

From the wagon, Rabb called, "Red, quit gabbing. Let's go."

Impulsively, Delia planted a kiss on Mother's cheek.

Mother touched her cheek, bemused. "What was that for?"

Delia ignored the question and squashed the niggle of

uncertainty blossoming in her chest. "Why don't you leave all this for me? I'm worried you'll overdo."

"A little wash won't send me into labor, Delia. But I'll look forward to your help."

Delia nodded, not at all sure this venture to town was the right thing to do. As if reading her mind, Mother waved her on. "Go on, I'll be fine. You're turning into a mother hen."

Delia joined Rabb on the wagon seat. "I'm worried about her."

He steered the wagon onto the dirt lane. "Who? Ma?"

"Yes."

Rabb shrugged and hunched over the loosely held reins. "Seems fine to me."

"Fine? Didn't you see the way she was holding herself? And earlier, I thought for sure the baby was coming. But there she is, doing the laundry as if it's any other day."

"Isn't it?"

Delia blew an impatient breath. "Of course, it's not. We can't take anything for granted this close to the birth. I probably shouldn't have left her just now. Mark my words, the way she's rubbing her back means the baby's coming, and we've got to make preparations."

He grimaced. "Don't talk about all that woman business. I don't wanna know nothing about birthing stuff."

It was no use talking to her thick-headed brother. They traveled in mutual silence the rest of the way to town.

When he pulled the mules to a halt in front of Truitt's, she hopped down with the quilt. "You won't go anywhere?"

"Nope."

The bell jingled as the door opened, and Aunt Mary looked up as she dusted the counters. Unlike the busy before-school rush, the store was empty.

"There you are, Delia. Ten minutes more and you would have missed me."

Aunt Mary swept over, skirts brushing the wooden floor, and reached for the parcel. Delia held onto it. "You'll be careful with it?"

"Of course, darling."

"And you'll make sure they spell my name correctly?"

Aunt Mary laughed. "Indeed. Now let go so we can get these entries turned in before the cut-off time."

Delia released the bundle and followed her aunt to the back of the store, where a half dozen other wrapped packages awaited. "Should I mark the category?"

"No need. I'll deliver it to the textile counter."

"Make sure it's placed with the quilts."

"I've done this before, you know." Aunt Mary delivered the words over her shoulder. "Now, run along. Your creation is safe with me. I will guard it with my life."

"Don't jest! It took months to finish. I started it back in Georgia."

"Yes, of course, dear. Now go home and help your mother." She lowered her voice. "Her ankles are a might swollen, you know. If she keeps up her rigorous pace, she will have that baby too soon."

Uncle Robert emerged from the curtained opening to the back room. He dipped his head with an embarrassed expression. "Propriety, dear."

"Worry not, dear husband. I'm the picture of propriety." She winked at Delia. "Now, run along and take care of your mother."

Chapter 16

A Janesville woman has worked on a crazy quilt an hour a day for thirteen years, and the quilt is not finished yet.—Indiana Progress (Indiana, Pennsylvania) November 1889.

Riding on the wagon seat beside Rabb was never dull, but his constant calling to people on the street plucked every nerve Delia possessed. As soon as they set out from Truitt's Dry Goods, an uneasy sensation curdled her stomach. If only they could go faster.

"Don't even think about stopping to chat."

Rabb snorted. "Men don't chat. We trade yarns. Howdy there, Mr. Perkins."

"Whatever you call it, do not slow down."

"Why're you nagging me for? I ain't done nothing."

True. He'd done nothing more than call out greetings. So why was she tense about such a little thing? "We need to get home. I just know Mother's going to overdo."

Rabb lifted one brow. "You ain't gonna talk her outta work, no matter what."

"I should've stayed. What if things go wrong, like last time? I'd never forgive myself ..."

A shadow passed over his face. Without a word, he urged the horse faster.

Finally, Rabb turned the wagon into the yard and pulled on the brake. Delia craned her neck to spot Mother. Delia groaned. "I knew it. Just look at her lifting all those wet clothes."

"Shoulda known she would."

Delia jumped down and hurried across the yard toward her mama. "Here, let me do that."

Without objection, Mother handed over a heavy, wet dress. On tiptoes, Delia pinned it to the clothesline before turning to assess her parent. She looked weary. "Why don't you go put your feet up while I finish up here?"

Perspiration rolled down Mother's cheek before she swiped it away with the back of her hand. "All right."

Mother trudged back to the dogtrot without a word of admonishment against wrinkling the wet clothes. Not at all like her exacting mother.

Delia flung the remaining laundry over the drying wire as fast as she could, anxious to get back to the house. Dousing the flame under the pot, she headed to the cabin.

But when she stuck her head in the living room, it was empty. A strange silence hung over the usually chaotic room. She crossed the breezeway and stilled just inside the door to the sleeping area, calling out. Nothing stirred.

Maybe she'd gone to the outhouse. She'd give it a few minutes before checking there.

The sound of hooves out on the road arrested her attention. She moved to the path that led to the road and inwardly groaned as Eleanor Baskin halted in front of the house.

What was she doing here? This was no time for a social

visit, especially when she couldn't locate her very expectant mother.

Delia tried to force a smile but failed as her gaze circled the yard beyond Eleanor's approaching form. "Eleanor. This is a surprise." She glanced at the package her friend offered. "What's this?"

"Just a little treat. You folks have been so kind to me, I thought I'd ride out here to offer some sweets." Eleanor stepped closer, her smile fading. "Something's wrong, isn't it? I knew it. This treat is just an excuse to come out here and check on you. The Lord compelled me to come at once."

A shiver raised the hairs on Delia's arms. Did this woman know something?

Behind them, an agonized cry rose.

"Mother!" Delia grabbed up her skirt, running through the breezeway to the area in back of the cabin. "Mother!"

Mother propped herself against the log wall, moaning, her hair partially hanging down her back. Delia rushed forward. "Eleanor, help me get her inside."

Together, they propped her up and got her inside. "Her waters broke," Eleanor murmured as they lowered her onto the bed, shifting her gaze to Mother's skirt.

Mother clutched Delia's arm. "Get the doctor."

Delia nodded, memories swirling. Sweat-soaked sheets. Mother, moaning in pain. Calls for help. *Please Lord, not again.*

Mother clawed her arm. "Delia! Do you hear me? Get the doctor!"

"Of-of course." Delia dashed outside. She couldn't go. One of the men should. Grasping the rope to the iron dinner bell, she pulled again and again, the clanging of the bell unmistakable in its urgent call. Time dragged before finally, Papa, Thomas, and Rabb appeared. She could weep with relief. "Get the doctor! Baby's coming!"

Thomas sprinted to the barn, and Papa ran into the house. Beside her, Rabb's eyes were wide. "Ma doing all right?"

"Oh, Rabb, pray with all your might. I can't bear the thought of it ending like last time."

"It won't."

Though his words sounded strong, fear shadowed his eyes.

Clarence didn't mind closing for the midday meal and heading to the diner, since there had been only a trickle of customers that morning.

"Bill, let's go eat. Lawrence can man the store."

Bill Graford, his new assistant manager, agreed, and the two ambled down Main Street, discussing the supply order. Ahead, a clatter of horse hooves snagged their attention. Clarence squinted at the man who pulled his horse to a stop in front of the doctor's office.

"What's Thomas in such a hurry for?"

"You know him?"

He nodded distractedly, watching Thomas jump from the saddle and sprint into the clinic. "Something's wrong. He's never in a hurry."

"Could've fooled me."

Exactly. "Tell you what, you go on. I'll be there directly." Clarence jogged in the direction of the doctor's office.

Before he could enter, Thomas barreled out and made a beeline for his horse.

Clarence raised his arm to catch Thomas's attention. "What's going on?"

"Ma's having her baby." He swung into the saddle, kicking the animal into action. "Pray!"

Clouds of dust rose behind him, hiding the horse and rider

from view. Pray? Though puzzled, he did so, turning when he heard the clinic door open behind him. Dr. Taggert, grasping a small black bag, strode toward the barn, nodding curtly as he passed.

Clarence caught up with the man. "Hey, doc." He rushed forward to help cinch the saddle. "What's going on with Mrs. Truitt? Everything ... all right?" Aw, crumb. It was obvious everything wasn't all right.

Dr. Taggert secured his bag and swung onto the horse. "Say a prayer, Clarence."

Taggert rode away in the direction of the Truitt farm, leaving Clarence puzzled. The physician's grim expression cast a pall over a usually joyful event. Was Mrs. Truitt in danger?

He walked down the road and entered the diner. Though his stomach growled at the aroma of roast beef and biscuits, his thoughts revolved around Delia and the situation at her home.

Clarence settled in a straight-backed chair across a small table from his assistant manager.

"What's going on?"

Clarence became aware of the silence around him. He glanced around the room. Every pair of eyes were trained on him. When he didn't answer Bill, the man prompted his response. "Well?"

Clarence hesitated. Of course he'd known small communities had rumor mills, but until now, it had seemed a harmless vice. But this was Delia's family. He sure wasn't going to divulge what Dr. Taggert said so the whole town could speculate.

But he didn't want to be rude, either. After all, surely most folks here had seen the very expectant Mrs. Truitt. It wouldn't be gossip to state the fact.

Ignoring the expectant silence that surrounded him, Clarence directed his words to Bill. "Reckon a baby's coming."

Delia stood as far from the bed as she could manage. She needed to calm down. She didn't want Mother to know how rattled she was. She had to pretend everything was fine, and not like that tragic day when her twin brothers never took a breath.

Memories assaulted her. Then, she'd been a curious seven-year-old, sneaking into the birthing room, hiding in the shadows as night fell. Concern lined her aunts' faces as minutes dragged into hours. Once her aunts discovered her presence, she'd been banished. *"This is no place for a child."*

Indeed, it hadn't been. Not when anticipation soured to grief.

At the cemetery, women murmured how close Mother had come to meeting the Lord right along with those precious babies.

It had been weeks before Mother resumed normal life. Delia, at seven, took little Hazel under her care. Watching over her toddling steps, helping her dress, cleaning her messes. She'd have done anything to make Mother happy again.

Just like now.

Delia jerked at another sharp cry from the bed. Eleanor looked up from wiping Mother's brow. "Delia, why don't you tell the family everything is fine in here."

Relief poured over her. She slipped out the door onto the breezeway and inhaled the fresh, cool air. Papa whirled. "What's happening?"

"Everything is fine. Mother's doing well."

Papa nodded, grabbing the back of his neck. "That what the doc said?"

She nodded.

"And he knows about last time?"

Again, she forced her head to move in an up and down motion. Dr. Taggert's concern was evident in his quiet movements.

For the millionth time, she shot an arrow prayer. *Lord, help her.*

She stepped off the breezeway and stood in the yard, shading her eyes from the hazy midafternoon glare. Outside the birth room, life continued in a blessedly routine manner. Birds whistled, and the breeze ruffled the still-green leaves, causing a couple to float to the ground.

"Red!"

She turned to see her brothers standing outside the barn and made her way to them. Thomas tipped back his hat with a concerned frown. "Well?"

She caught a whiff of manure as she approached the animal pen adjacent to the barn. "Fine." So far.

Thomas used his sleeve to wipe the sweat from his brow. "She's strong."

Rabb leaned on the fence he and Thomas had constructed when they first arrived. "Strong then, too, and younger. That was eleven years ago."

So, she wasn't the only one plagued by memories of that day. It had been easy to push the fears away in the everyday activities of farm life. After all, Mother had no visible anxiety over the baby's arrival. Why should they? Today, everything changed.

Rabb squinted at the house, a sprig of hay resting in his mouth. "Sure glad I ain't no gal."

Thomas grunted and disappeared into the shadows of the barn, leaving her alone with Rabb. From this distance, she could hear no shrieks or wails, and her shoulders relaxed in the reflective silence.

"You remember that night Pa told us we was coming here?"

Delia turned to Rabb with a frown. "That's what's you're thinking about? What about Mother—"

"Just hear me out, Red. I been thinking about something Ma told us that night."

"Lots of things were said that day." Though perhaps more were unsaid, like the fear of a new place with no guarantees.

Rabb shifted the hay sprig to the opposite corner of his mouth. "Ma said, 'Sometimes we must walk a hard road before we find joy.'" He paused. "You ever think about that?"

She lifted her shoulders and let them drop. At this moment, worry shut out all other thoughts.

"I do. All the time."

She studied his thoughtful expression. He rarely was circumspect. "What do you mean?"

His gaze looked beyond the farm. "This road we been walking, it's tough. I'm about ready for some joy."

Birds chirped in the trees that separated the road from the farm. Delia knotted her fingers. "Me too."

They stood in silence a few minutes longer. Then Delia pushed away from the wooden fence with a small sigh. "I should get back."

Rabb gave her shoulder a squeeze and retreated into the barn without a word.

Her steps back to the house were slow, and her mind filled with that last day in Georgia, when her mother had kneeled on the graves and wept. Would there be a tiny grave here in Texas? Mother might not survive the loss.

She quickened her steps. Today, she would stand beside her mother as a woman, ready to face whatever came.

Sometimes we must walk a hard road before we find joy.

And sometimes, hard roads must be walked, whether or not joy awaited.

Eleanor glanced at her with a relieved smile. "I wondered when you'd come back."

Delia closed the door behind her. "Why don't you take a little break? I'll be here."

Eleanor nodded. "The doctor is having coffee. Would you like me to bring a cup?"

Delia shook her head, and Eleanor slipped outside. Delia stood beside the bed. Exhaustion lined Mother's face, and her mussed hair spread around her pillow. "Oh, Mother. I forgot to braid your hair."

"Do it now. It mustn't get tangled."

Mother pushed herself up, leaving some room for Delia to work a brush through the matted tresses. She'd always been puzzled when women talked about the importance of braiding hair when labor first ensued. Now she understood. She quickly worked the strands into one long plait, for the first time noticing the gray that mingled with brown.

Mother stiffened. Perspiration beaded on her face until the contraction passed.

"Do you want a cool rag?" A paltry offering, but it was a start.

The slightest gesture in the affirmative and Delia skittered to serve her. She gently swabbed Mother's forehead, gratified to see the furrowed brow ease some.

"Thank you." Mother's voice was ragged. "You've been worried about me, haven't you?"

Delia started to deny it, then nodded. "I can't help it. This is so much harder than I thought it would be."

"It's worth it."

Delia looked at her, incredulous. "But last time ..."

Mother's eyes closed, and Delia hated herself for reminding her of the grief. Then she grasped Delia's hand. "A child is worth every bit of pain or grief or joy. Remember that, my sweet girl."

At once, Mother cried out and stiffened her grip with a moan. Though Delia's fingers throbbed, she wouldn't withdraw her hand.

"Get ... the doctor!"

Though she'd sworn not to leave her, Delia hastened to the door as Mother screamed in agony. Delia's heart thumped. *Help her, Lord!*

"Dr. Taggert! Come quick!"

He rushed past her, followed by Eleanor and Papa. Screams echoed in the stifling room. Delia pressed a hand to her mouth to smother the sobs that threatened. Mother grimaced, holding Papa's hands in a white-knuckled grip.

"Push!"

Again and again, Mother grimaced with effort, and then cried out before laying back on the bed. Until the next wave of horrific pains started the sequence all over again. Delia turned her head to the side and squeezed her eyes shut, praying.

The doctor said, "It's coming."

Delia held her breath, waiting, not daring to see for herself. *God, help.*

A baby's thin little cry pierced the air. Delia sagged, relief and joy bringing tears to her eyes. She stepped forward in time to see Dr. Taggert hand a tiny baby to Papa, who gazed long into dark, wide-open eyes.

His voiced filled with tenderness. "It's a girl, Esther. A healthy baby girl."

Small arms flailed, and Mother reached to catch a tiny fist. "My sweet little Imajean."

Dr. Taggert took the infant, and Papa dodged out to relay the joyous news to Thomas and Rabb.

Eleanor gave Delia's shoulders a quick squeeze. "God be praised."

Outside, muffled shouts of joy rose, but in the dim room, all was quiet except for the sound of the baby suckling. Delia slipped outside then, brushing away the wetness on her cheeks.

As Thomas and Rabb whooped, she rushed to Papa. His embrace was strong. She gave way to the sobs that had laid so near the surface throughout the day.

"Why're you crying? Be happy!"

"I'm just so relieved." She sniffled. "I'm glad you were with Mother." Who cared what other people thought about a father's place?

"You couldn't have kept me away. I wasn't there for her ... before." He paused, taking a breath.

High-pitched squalling sounded, and he chuckled. "Just listen to that healthy babe."

"When can we see her?"

Papa held up his finger to Thomas. "Let me make sure it's a good time first."

Rabb grunted with mock fierceness. "Another girl. Sounds just as ornery as Red."

Thomas groaned. "We're outnumbered."

Delia put her hands on her hips. "Oh, go on with your grumbling. I see your smiles. Y'all are as tickled as I am."

Running footsteps sounded just beyond the cabin, and Hazel appeared, rivulets of perspiration lining her red face. She dropped her books and collapsed on the step. "Did she have it? Is it a girl or boy?"

Delia fanned her with her hand. "Did you run all the way from town?"

Hazel nodded, panting. "What'd she have?"

Thomas brought the water dipper to her and waited until she gulped the contents.

Delia finger combed the straggles of Hazel's dark hair. "It's a girl. But how'd you know it was happening?"

"Your beau blabbed it all around town."

"Clarence? That doesn't sound like something he'd do."

"Got it from my teacher, who heard it from her sister, who heard it from Minnie at the diner." Hazel stood, palm thrust toward Rabb. "Pay up."

Grumbling, Rabb dug in his pocket. "Hold on."

Delia gaped, looking from one to the other. "You two placed a bet on the baby's gender?"

"That's right." Hazel shook her hand impatiently. "Hurry, before Papa comes."

Delia couldn't hide her astonished laugh. "Rabb Truitt, what kinds of awful things are you teaching our little sister?"

Rabb winced. "Wasn't my idea." He bobbed his chin at the grinning Hazel. "She's ten times as hardheaded as you." He slapped a coin into Hazel's hand. "Don't tell Ma about this, you hear?"

Chapter 17

*The girl with soft gray eyes and rippling brown hair, who walked
all over your poor fluttering heart at the charity ball, has just
finished a crazy quilt containing 1864 pieces of neckties and hat
linings, put together with 21,390 stitches. And her poor old
father fastens on his suspenders with a long nail, a piece of
twine, a sharp stick and one regularly ordained button. This,
also, is vanity.—Morning Oregonian (Portland, Oregon) April 5,
1888.*

"Can I count on you to take over the meal preparation
during my lying in?"

Mother stared up at Delia from her bed, where
Baby Imajean slept in her arms. The family lined the small
room to take in the sweet sight of their newest sibling.

A chorus of groans filled the room.

Delia shot them all an annoyed glance, though the thought
of cutting up a chicken or of figuring out the timing of baking
bread made perspiration sprout at the back of her neck. But she
mustn't upset Mother, not when she was in such a delicate
condition.

"Certainly." She swallowed. "For how long?"

"Dr. Taggert advises two weeks."

Hazel's mouth dropped. "Two whole weeks?"

Delia arched her eyebrows at Hazel. "Don't you worry, I'll do my utmost to keep the household running. And Hazel will help, won't you?"

The girl nodded.

Delia glanced at the males. "My first order of business is to get all of you out of here. Mother and Baby Imajean need their rest." Delia made a shooing motion with her hands. "You, too, Papa. Let's go."

As everyone filed from the room, her own gaze fell on Mother as she held little Imajean. Had she ever looked more peaceful? Though dark circles shadowed her eyes, she radiated happiness. The worried frown that had plagued Mother's face had disappeared.

Mother cupped sleeping Imajean's head. "I think this little one takes after Thomas, with this crown of dark hair."

Papa smiled as he trailed his finger along the infant's cheek. "She's much prettier."

From beyond the doorway, Thomas called, "I heard that."

Delia waited for the room to clear, then kissed Mother's cheek. "Is there anything I can bring you?"

Mother stifled a yawn. "If you'd just put her in the cradle, I'll take a nap while she does."

Delia gathered the delicate babe from her mother's arms. It wasn't the first time she'd held a tiny life, but somehow, this precious one held more significance than any other baby. She gently placed her in the cradle. Mother's closed eyelids and steady breathing indicated she'd already succumbed to sleep.

Emerging from the room onto the breezeway, Delia came upon a lively discussion in which her name was repeated. "Are y'all talking about me?"

Guilty looks passed between the three siblings. Even Papa looked contrite. "We were just talking about how we can help you out."

Rabb snorted. "Help ourselves, more like it. Shoot, why'd you have to go and tell Ma you'd do all the cooking?"

She put her hands on her hips. "Well, that's a fine thing! Here I volunteer to help and you're out here criticizing."

Thomas said, "Look, it ain't that we don't appreciate you and all."

She waited for him to finish. But his words seemed to drift away.

Hazel crossed her arms. "I'm not about to miss school."

"I said nothing about you missing school. As for cooking, you need to learn."

"With you as my teacher? You're hopeless in the kitchen."

No use trying to argue that one. "All the more reason for you to learn, then. And we'll begin right now. We're running low on butter."

"But I'm so tired! I've been working hard all day long."

Delia shook her head indulgently. "Yes, I'm sure a whole day sitting at a desk reading and writing has worn you out. Come with me, and we'll get you situated."

Hazel tromped behind her. "Fine. I'll read while I churn."

"You and your books." But whatever it took to sweeten the chore for her pouty sister, so be it. She chuckled to herself when Hazel settled on a chair in the breezeway, book in one hand while the other worked the butter churn.

A delicious aroma wafted to her from the kitchen, making Delia's mouth water. It was close to suppertime, but who was in the kitchen? Rounding a corner, she spied Eleanor clad in an apron, stirring a pot.

"I thought you'd gone home."

"I'm just whipping together some pork and dumplings,

189

rather humble fare for such an auspicious day. I hope you don't mind." She cast a timid glance Delia's way. "To be honest, your brothers asked me to return. Seems they have little confidence in your ability to provide a tasty meal for them."

Delia groaned. "I can't believe they did that." She could hug them.

Eleanor tapped her wooden spoon on the pot before laying it on the stovetop. "You know, I would be happy to cook for your family."

"But what about your shop?"

"Actually, I wondered if you might be interested in swapping places. Just for a while, of course. I wouldn't want to obligate you to anything."

"You mean, you would come here and cook, and I would sew all day?" What a delightful idea.

Eleanor nodded. "We'll talk to your father, of course."

Papa might jump at the idea.

"You know, Mother's confinement is two weeks."

"Yes."

"That's three meals a day. Fourteen days. That equals forty-two meals."

"Sounds like you've given it some thought."

It was the stuff of nightmares. "I'm quick with numbers."

"So, you would be willing to trade places if your father approves?"

Delia hesitated. She wanted to jump at the opportunity. How many times would she have occasion to see Clarence if she were in town? Her heart skipped. She could imagine looking up from sewing to see his tall, lanky form walking through the door. He'd ask her to supper, perhaps. Or maybe he'd insist they have every meal together, since she'd only be in town for two weeks.

But then, would he think less of her if he knew the reason

for taking over the seamstress's duties? Her failure in the kitchen would brand her as undesirable. After all, it was one thing to tell him she wasn't handy with food preparation. But to willingly assign a substitute cook? It just wasn't done.

Not that she made much of conventions. Riding her two-wheeled conveyance in a split skirt was proof. The bicycle amused Clarence. Cooking was another thing, though. He'd wonder about their future, the cook stove sitting cold and dormant until he made the meals.

Even she saw the folly in that.

If trading places with Eleanor cast a pall on her, she might lose Clarence. And she couldn't stand the thought.

"So, the idea pleases you?"

"What idea?" Hazel breezed into the kitchen and reached past them to grab an apple from the counter, bringing it to her mouth with a crunch.

"Where are your manners? We have a guest."

Hazel's cheeks reddened, almost matching the apple she gripped. "Pardon me, Miss Eleanor."

Watching Hazel retreat brought another consideration to Delia's mind. How would it affect her sister's domestic maturation if Delia abandoned her role as the household manager to a woman who was not related to them? Worse, what would Mother think of her, especially now that they'd become closer?

She let out her breath slowly, fingering the seam on a sack of flour. "I suppose I should stay here, with my family."

She sensed Eleanor's gaze scrutinizing her. Perhaps this was another hard road she had to journey before arriving at something wonderful. If she just made herself, surely she could conquer cooking. Every other woman could do it. It couldn't be tricky.

"Thank you, but I think this is something I need to do.

Honestly, at this point in my life, I need to take on the hard things like cooking for the family. I just think I need to prove myself by putting my mind to it and giving it my all." And forty-two meals was certainly giving it her all.

Eleanor nodded. "Ah. I think that's a very mature decision." She reached to untie her apron.

"But please don't stop what you're doing. It won't hurt if you cook this one meal."

The next morning, Delia dragged herself out of bed. Newborn cries during the night had awoken her, and her head ached. She tiptoed out of the room and entered the kitchen on unsteady legs. On this morning of all mornings, she longed for the aroma of freshly made coffee to fill the air.

But making coffee was her job now. And before anything, that venerable stove must be lit. She placed her fists on her hips and faced her enemy, the stove.

"It's me and you, every day for two weeks. Believe me, I don't like this any more than you do."

After checking the ash box and laying in fresh logs, she dragged a match against the matchbox. Nothing.

She scrunched her nose at the sulphureous odor. She struck it again, firmer this time. No flicker of flame. For crying out loud.

After six failed attempts, the match burst to life with a bright yellow dancing flame, and she yelped, almost extinguishing the fire. She forced herself to be calm and place the small blazing stick on the kindling. There! The kindling ignited with a small burst of brilliance, and the blaze traveled quickly toward the logs. Rocking back on her heels, she watched the fire spread to the logs, turning them orange and red as the yellow tongue frolicked across the top.

She stood. "I did it!"

The empty room gave no applause for her effort, so she brushed her hands together. That wasn't so bad.

Now for coffee, although she was certainly awake. Once it had percolated, she poured herself a cup and warily sipped. Not too watery, as Mother's coffee often was. She sipped again and sighed as she leaned back in her chair. Just right.

She had a second cup to celebrate her victory over one part of the breakfast. Maybe cooking wouldn't be so bad after all.

A half hour later, with a table full of skeptical onlookers waiting for breakfast, she wiped her forehead with her sleeve. She grabbed the serving bowl full of oatmeal and carried it to the table with mincing steps so as not to spill it on the floor. Only, it made no movement at all. Funny.

She smiled at Papa and Hazel and Thomas. "Here you go. Just like Mother makes it." She took a bowl and tried to ladle a portion. The oatmeal was more like cornbread than hot cereal. Not that it was hot. More like tepid.

"I don't think it's supposed to be stuck together like that."

Leave it to Thomas to state the obvious. She tried again, this time using the ladle as if it were a carving tool. The spoon sliced into the substance. But that was as far as it would cooperate. She tugged the handle, and with a strange slurping sound, the ladle came out.

"Ew." Hazel grimaced. "What'd you do to the oatmeal?"

Delia lifted her chin. "It's fine. Just pour some milk on it. Go on, pass it down." With lip-curling disgust, Hazel thrust the bowl toward Thomas.

The door opened, and Rabb paused on the threshold, scrunching his bronze face as he sniffed the air. "Something's burning."

Delia gasped. "The bacon!" She whirled back to the cookstove, where a smoky haze hovered over the black frying pan. She reached to move the pan from the heat. *Pop!* She cried out, hand over the tender flesh of her wrist.

She grabbed a towel and removed the pan from the fire. Faint sizzling bubbled around each charred, shriveled piece. Why, not a minute before, the bacon had been raw. Surely she hadn't turned her back long enough for this to happen. She would have tossed them out for the animals had it not been for her father's insistence that he loved crispy bacon.

"You do? It's awfully brittle."

He nodded. "Bring it on. Nothing wrong with it."

But when she served it, she couldn't help but notice the disappointment on Thomas and Rabb's faces.

Hazel shook her head. "I certainly hope you're taking something else to Mother."

Delia sank into her chair at the table. "I completely forgot."

If she could only wave a magic wand and change everything. Especially the part about doing all this again in a few hours for the midday meal.

She managed a decent enough dinner at noon, mostly because she served leftover pork and dumplings that Eleanor had prepared. She dreaded facing the kitchen in mere hours for another attempt at edible food.

Maybe she should give more consideration to Eleanor's offer.

That evening, Delia summoned her courage to face the impatiently waiting family with the supper of blackened biscuits, mushy boiled potatoes, and leathery beef slices.

She set the food on the table and backed away, hands clasped. "Please, just try it."

Thomas peered at the platter of meat. "What is it?"

"Beef steak."

Hazel stabbed one with her fork. When it didn't penetrate, she half stood and gave it a whack. "These are harder than rocks. Mother really doesn't need two whole weeks of confinement, does she?"

Thomas shook his head dolefully. "Aunt Mary told me she'd feed us whenever we liked. Wish now I'd taken her up on the offer."

Papa reached for the potatoes. "Let's not complain, you two. Your sister is trying."

How sweet of her father. "Oh, and I've got biscuits and gravy too."

She fetched the pan of gravy from the stove and set it on the table it with a heavy thud. After a long moment, Thomas reached for the gravy spoon and helped himself to brown lumps.

Thomas groaned. "You ever think about cooking lessons?"

"You think it's easy, making food you'll eat? Go ahead and try. We'll just see what you say then."

"Anything'd be better than this," Thomas muttered.

Papa reached for her hand. "I appreciate your effort."

She smiled his way as she slid into her seat. At least one person understood. Frowning at the empty chair beside her, she said, "Where is Rabb?"

Hazel sighed. "He went to Aunt Mary's. He said he needed nourishment, not a belly ache."

Thomas tossed his napkin on the table and stood. "That sounds mighty fine to me."

Delia gaped. "What? You're just going to leave, after all my work?"

Thomas slapped his hat on his head and opened the door. "Sorry, Delia. I just can't do it no more."

"But I've only made three meals. There's thirty-nine to go."

She couldn't imagine it. Judging by the way Papa and Hazel wouldn't meet her gaze, they shared her dismay.

Delia sighed. "I suppose y'all would rather dine at Aunt Mary's too?"

When they made no move to respond, she waved her hand. "Fine. Just go."

Relief washed over Papa's face as he scrambled to his feet, moving so fast his chair fell backward and clattered against the floor. He righted it with an apologetic smile. "Bless you! You really won't mind?"

Not waiting for Delia's response, he rushed to the door and donned his jacket. "Hurry now, Hazel."

Her sister skipped to the door, which a grinning Papa held open for her. He blew an exuberant kiss Delia's way. "Thank you, daughter. Thank you so very much." The door slammed behind him, leaving Delia sitting alone at the table.

Well, didn't that just beat all.

Suddenly, the door burst open. Delia's hopes skyrocketed. They'd changed their minds.

Papa stood with his hand on the knob. "And tell your mother I'm bringing her some good food." With a slam, he disappeared.

Good food indeed. She had a mind to lock that door. That'd show them all.

Folding her arms, she sat back and surveyed her culinary creation. All that effort, with nothing to show for it except food fit only for raccoons and mice. And to think, she'd turned down Eleanor's proposal to fulfill her responsibility here.

Well, that did it. Tomorrow morning, she'd go into town and tell her she would gladly trade places. And if she was lucky, maybe it wouldn't be a temporary move.

Delia sprang from her chair and threw open the door. "Wait for me!"

Chapter 18

*A Kenton young lady has received in response to a letter a piece
of Grover Cleveland's necktie for a crazy quilt. Mr. Cleveland
will find the demand too large for the supply if the style of
necktie suits the young ladies of Kenton.—The Marion Daily
Star (Marion, Ohio) January 19, 1885.*

Clarence drummed his fingers on the glass counter. How early could he visit Delia? His ma would tell him any time before noon was rude.

But this was different. He needed to see for himself that everything was fine, especially after seeing Thomas in such an all-fired hurry to summon the doc. Wouldn't his sweetheart have been in the midst of the birthing? He grimaced. Good thing men weren't permitted to know much about the mysteries of childbirth.

At least the news of the blessed event had reached him, courtesy of his nosy landlady. "The Truitts have a baby girl, fine and healthy. Name's Imajean Alice."

No inquiry into just how she'd learned this information had been necessary. The gossip chain, no doubt. Of course, he'd been a link in that chain. Why couldn't folks in this town keep to themselves and mind their own business?

But in the end, a healthy baby girl now thrived, thank the Lord. Someday, he'd await news of his children's births. Delia's image drifted through his thoughts. That beautiful hair and creamy skin beckoned him. Those full lips ...

"I thought I told you never to do that again!"

With a jerk, Clarence shook himself free of his daydream and turned to see the owner of the raspy voice, a haggard-looking woman shaking her finger in the sullen face of an adolescent boy, who stood a head taller than her. Her son, surely.

He approached them with caution. "Welcome to Parker's Hardware and Carriages. May I help you with something, ma'am?"

"You could teach this boy of mine some manners."

The woman's eyes narrowed, causing the boy to fold his arms across his chest and return her glare.

"See there? Get that look off your face, boy. Taking something that don't belong to you's against the law."

"I didn't."

"You'd best not tell an untruth, young man. I saw you eyeing that tomato. You's about to steal it if I hadn't come along first."

"You don't gotta shout. The whole store can hear you."

Clarence cleared his throat. "What can I do for you today?" Besides guard against sticky fingers.

With a huff, the woman told him they needed a box of nails. "Right this way. We just got a shipment in."

Retrieving it from the row of neatly stacked boxes, an idea came to him. As he waited for the mother to look at the nails, he studied the teenager. Those warring emotions of youth came back to him in a rush, the need for freedom wedged against necessary dependence. Only, back then, he'd gone off the right path. Pa and Joe had been immersed in farming, and Ma busy raising Sallie. Left out and lonely, he'd coped by rebelling. If only he'd had someone to guide him in the right direction when he was this boy's age. Someone to believe in him.

Before he thought better of it, he said, "What's your name, son?"

Scowling, the boy said, "Joe."

Clarence swallowed. Mentally shaking himself, he continued. "Joe's a fine name, same's my brother's. Say, I could use a strong boy like yourself to help out around here."

"Doing what?"

If the boy had wanted to hide his interest behind a doubtful façade, he was too late. Clarence gestured to the stack of crates further down on the counter. "Sure could use someone who's not afraid of lifting heavy boxes and sweating. Pays a bit too."

The sullen expression dissolved into a hopeful smile. "Honest, mister, you'd pay me money? Sure!"

His mother narrowed her eyes. "Joseph Carruthers, you'd best be minding your chores around our home, not doing this man's bidding."

The scowl was back. "I'm a man, not a boy."

No sooner had he said that than the woman grabbed Joe's ear and twisted, making the boy howl. "I'll show you who's the boss. Come on."

Yelping all the way to the door, Joe and the woman left.

Clarence scooped the nails back into the box and slid them back in their place, shaking his head. The kid was far from manhood, but Clarence doubted he'd find it easily with such a haranguing woman.

Opening one of the crates, he replayed his offer in his mind. Maybe he'd been a bit rash. He hadn't worked the figures out to hire somebody.

But the thought of helping another kid overrode his common sense. It probably worked out the way it should have. He couldn't hire on every unhappy kid. He had a business to run.

This morning, Papa was in a jolly mood. Whether it was Aunt Mary's wonderful meal the night before, or his delight over Little Imajean, who now slept peacefully in the crook of his arm, Delia didn't know. But she intended to take advantage of his lighter heart and discuss a few things.

"Here you go, Papa. Coffee just the way you like it."

His pleasant expression faded, and he waved his free hand. "That's all right. I don't need coffee this morning."

Who was he joshing? He had upwards of three cups a day. "Just give it a try. Who knows? You might like it."

He straightened, lifting the baby a bit. Delia placed her hands under the tiny body and the head and carefully placed her against her chest. So tiny. She gingerly kissed the fine dark hair on top of Imajean's little head and nuzzled her.

Papa smacked his lips. "Coffee's good." He laughed. "It's actually good."

"Don't sound so surprised." She grabbed the bowl of oatmeal she'd prepared for him and laid it on the table in front of him. "Now, try that."

She lifted her chin and waited expectantly. He scooped the oatmeal with his spoon and brought a bite to his mouth. He made a little choking sound and his head moved vigorously from side to side before gulping hot coffee.

She slid into a chair, careful not to jar the baby. "I'm sorry."

Papa wiped his mouth. "I appreciate the ... effort."

"That brings up an excellent point, Papa. You know I'm

hopeless in the kitchen. No, don't deny it. I know the food yesterday was barely edible."

"The midday meal was all right."

"Only because I used the leftovers that Eleanor prepared the night before." Butterflies took flight in her stomach. Her words came out in a rush. "She's a wonderful cook and she was such a help with Mother when I knew nothing to do but she did and we all need sustenance so I think she and I should trade places."

There.

A concerned frown creased his face, and he reached for Imajean. "Here, why don't you give her to me?"

Was he even listening? They made the transfer, and she sat back in her chair. "Do you understand what I'm asking?"

"Not one word. You must be tired."

More than that, she wanted this trade so much it physically hurt. "What I'm trying to say is that Eleanor and I want to work out an exchange of services for the next two weeks of Mother's confinement. She would come here to take care of the household and watch after Mother, and I would go to town and look after her shop."

She held her breath. After a moment's silence, she said, "What do you think?"

"You already have a job at the store."

"Remember, Uncle Robert let me go so I could be with Mother once the baby came along. Besides, they aren't very busy these days and won't be until December."

Papa considered her words, nodding. "Yes, but I don't care much for the idea of you staying up there in town all by yourself."

Her shoulders fell. "Are you worried about my safety? That gang went somewhere else, remember? Besides, what can happen in Blooming Grove, Texas?"

He held up his palm. "A young lady has no business staying alone."

"But Papa—"

His right eyebrow hitched, the sign she should stop arguing. They sat in silence as Papa finished his coffee.

"I gotta say, I like the idea of Mrs. Baskin cooking for us, taking care of your mother and all." His eyes landed on the stiff oatmeal. "I like it right well."

With a gasp, Delia sprang to her feet. "Oh, thank you, Papa. Do you mind if I tell her the news?"

"Now, hold on and let me finish. Even though you have my permission to work in town, you have to spend your nights here."

She let out her breath and reigned in the mental image of her own apartment. "As long as I can work as a seamstress in Eleanor's shop, I'm happy."

When Papa started to rise, she placed a hand on his arm. "One more thing."

He glanced at the slumbering infant in his arms and settled back down upon the chair, mumbling, "There always is."

She ignored the comment. "The fair opens in a couple of days. I'd like to be there on Friday when they announce the winners."

Please, please, please.

His spoon clinked against the empty cup, and he eased back. "Reckon you should."

Her jaw dropped.

The baby squeaked in her sleep, and they stilled, watching her little face shift expressions from sadness to joy, ending with a pout before relaxing back into sleep. The ghost smiles and fleeting expressions were the cutest things Delia had ever seen.

"I know how much it means to see that quilt hang in the fair. One of your brothers can drive you."

"Really?"

His smile was warm. "You worked hard on your little quilt. Go see how it fared." He chuckled. "Get it? Fared, at the fair?"

"Oh, Papa." She jumped out of her chair and planted a kiss on his forehead. "Thank you." She hurried from the room before he could rethink his offer. The breakfast dishes could wait. She had to get to town and talk to Eleanor, then get home to pick out her outfit for the fair.

Delia rode her bicycle to town, adrenaline pumping. Her dream came true, even in the most unlikely way. She leaned her bike against the outer wall of Eleanor's shop and burst through the door. "Eleanor, guess what?"

Eleanor clapped a hand over her heart. "Delia! You just about gave me a heart attack."

"I'm sorry. I couldn't wait to talk to you."

"Everything's all right, then?"

Delia bounced on her toes. "I'd say so. That trade we discussed?"

Eleanor nodded.

"After talking about it, my parents think it is a fine idea. They suggested we start tomorrow."

Surprise lifted Eleanor's eyebrows, and she sat back as if stunned. Then she recovered and chuckled softly. "Yes, Lord, I will follow." She reached for a handkerchief and dabbed her eyes.

"I-I beg your pardon?"

"I suppose it sounds a bit strange, talking directly to the Father, especially to one so young as you. But when you've walked this earth as long as I have and experienced both

203

happiness and heartbreak, you learn when God changes your path, He has something in mind."

"You're not saying there's some divine purpose in cooking or sewing, are you?"

Again, Eleanor chuckled. "Sounds too simple, doesn't it? But trust me. There's joy in following the path he's laid before us. God uses willing people, no matter what the task. He'll put my talent to use, no matter where He sends me."

Delia shifted her feet. "So, yes?"

"Delia, God put you in this little shop for a purpose. With your youth and energy, there's no telling what you can do here."

Delia let her eyes roam. The shop, though cozy, could use freshening. "I might change out the little curtains on the shelves. That is, if you don't mind."

"Mind? Honey, you do whatever you hear the Lord telling you to do. Curtains, shelves, what have you. I'm just tickled to be cooking for such a loving family."

A rush of compassion filled Delia for this woman who traveled through most days without the communion of friends or family. This could be the beginning of a new existence for her, one which hopefully would mirror the love and acceptance she craved. Though Delia had at first taken this trade as a favor, now she recognized how deeply Eleanor yearned to be included. She needed the Truitts as much as they needed her. And according to Eleanor, God had arranged it all.

Ten minutes later, Delia walked out, knowing she had two stops to make while in town.

It didn't take long to stop in at Truitt's Dry Goods and let them know why they might see her in the seamstress shop.

Aunt Mary huffed. "Need I remind you of that woman's connection to an outlaw? I don't care if he's dead and buried, you still shouldn't trust Eleanor Baskin."

"I do trust her. You don't realize what a kind woman she is. She was so helpful during Imajean's birth. I'm grateful she wants to help take care of Mother and the baby."

Aunt Mary lifted one shoulder. "Suit yourself. But if I were you, I'd tell Hazel to count the silver every day."

Delia suppressed a grin. "A difficult task, since all the silver was auctioned off back in Georgia."

Aunt Mary's cheeks tinged pink. "Don't be impertinent. As for you working in that rundown seamstress shop, be my guest. But I'll wager you come back here if it's money you want to earn instead of charity."

Delia dug her fingernails into her palms. If it took everything within her, she would not set foot back in this store. More than anything, she wanted Eleanor's shop to be successful.

She forced herself to thank Aunt Mary and Uncle Robert before setting out for her second errand.

In her mind, she heard Eleanor's words: *Honey, you do whatever you hear the Lord telling you to do.*

Handlebars in her grasp, she rolled the bicycle along Main Street until she stood before the hardware store. She'd avoided this place. With a start, she realized the last time she'd walked inside the building was the day she'd overheard Clarence's father berating him.

What a shock that had been. Papa would never talk to any of them in such a way. His pride in his offspring lived in every smile or pat on the back. He might not say, *I love you,* but she knew he did. Never, though, had he spoken with contempt, like Mr. Parker had. Her heart swelled at the dignity he'd displayed that day. Clarence was a very fine man.

Propping her bicycle against the outer wall, her heart pounded as she pulled the door open and stepped inside. Men filled the room. Delia shrank back, eager to flee. Like every time she'd wanted to spill the truth of the tie.

But not this time. She forced herself to step into the melee of farmers and ranchers wanting tools, ropes, saddles, and other things she never cared a whit about. If Clarence cared about garden spades and saddlebags and big round sturdy-looking buggy wheels, then she'd learn about them. He deserved it.

For too long, she'd put this off. Good men prided themselves on honesty. Kindness. Respect. What had she given him in return? Lies, secrets, and pride. Sorrow pricked her heart. Tears blurred her vision, and she blinked lest these men surrounding her grew concerned.

She spotted him in the middle of the crowd, and for a moment, she studied him. His slicked hair was mussed, shirtsleeves rolled up with one higher than the other, and tie loosened. Even in his disheveled state at the height of business, he took her breath away. Her heart flipped. Here he was different. She'd never witnessed this side of Clarence—fast-talking, full of pent-up energy, eyes sharp as he replied to one man after another. He was happy. Confident. Tough. Masculine.

Her beau.

Their gaze connected, and his face lit. He waved her closer. The words she'd rehearsed vanished. Courage flagged. Now. It was her last chance. She forced herself forward, weaving through the bodies until she stood before him. The odor of unwashed bodies combined with leather and nicotine couldn't force her from this place.

She pressed close and cupped her hand around her mouth to be heard above the racket. "Hello, Clarence. May I speak with you?"

Delight played over the features of his face, and only when he glanced at the man next to her did she realize she'd interrupted his conversation. Covering her mouth, she turned, wide-eyed, intending to apologize.

Mayor Clive Waldrop flicked ash from the cigar he held and narrowed his gaze at her. "Miss Truitt, I suggest you run along. We're talking business." Turning back to Clarence, he said, "Parker, I'm a busy man. Can you sell me a rig or not?"

Delia's lips parted. With the political mask gone, the mayor behaved every bit as rudely as his daughter. Even as her anger seared her middle, she tried to smile up at Clarence. "That's fine. I'll wait. You go ahead."

"Mayor, I'll be right back."

Clive Waldrop narrowed his gaze. "You walk away from this sale, and I'll take my business down the road."

Clarence looked unimpressed. "If you want the best quality rig, you'll wait."

He took her elbow and guided her to the door. With his lips close enough to her ear to raise gooseflesh, he said, "Wish I could take a minute to chat, but I need to tend to the mayor. He's about to order a carriage that we'll design and make right here in the carriage shop. Big sale. Maybe we can talk Saturday evening?" Clarence's gaze met hers, then his step hitched. "Wait—is this about the baby? I meant to get out to see you all earlier today, but then the mayor came in."

It took a moment before understanding he meant little Imajean. "The baby's fine. But if you can just give me one minute ... I have something I need to tell you."

But he shook his head, hand on her back as he walked her through the doors. "Wish I could but seems like everyone wants a minute of my time. Can you believe all those customers?" He laughed, an expression of disbelief on his face. "I never dreamed the store would have this much business." He lifted one of her hands and pressed a quick, preoccupied kiss upon it before vanishing inside.

Delia rubbed her temples. Well, she couldn't leave. Not without making her confession. She'd waited this long, another ten minutes wouldn't hurt. After twenty minutes of pacing up and down the boardwalk, Delia entered the hardware store. No sign of Clarence. The busy workers ignored her as she headed to his office.

Her gaze fell on his littered desk. The least she could do was bring some order to the chaos. She pushed his chair out of her way and surveyed the receipts, scribbled notes, and official-looking documents. She sorted the clutter into logical piles. At the bottom of the mess, paper money spread haphazardly. She couldn't imagine leaving dollar bills scattered like this. She stacked them neatly, trying not to mentally tick off the sum. Perhaps her family's misfortune had made her a better steward of her earnings.

When Clarence finally entered the tiny office, surprise lifted his eyebrows. "I thought you'd gone."

She stood and twisted her fingers one by one. "Clarence, I have your tie."

His jaw dropped. "Y-you have my brother's necktie?"

She rushed around the desk and stood with hands clasped, talking lightning fast so nothing would interrupt them. "I'm so sorry. I didn't mean to take it. Please don't hate me. I wouldn't have picked it up unless—that is, I thought it meant nothing to you, it was so worn and all, but it suited me—well, in fact, it provided the perfect remedy, you see. I realize it appears selfish on my part, and perhaps it was, just a teeny tiny bit, but I assure you, I never meant to cause you grief."

Delia gulped, ready to keep spinning the words as fast as she could. Except Clarence wasn't angry. Quite the opposite, in fact. He took her into his arms and swung her once around. "That's the best news I've heard all day."

He was happy?

"You are the sweetest girl, waiting all this time to tell me that. I sure wish I could stick around, but I've got to write up a bill of sale." With the same farewell gesture he'd used an hour before, Clarence kissed her fingers.

His gaze caught on the once-messy desk. "What happened here?"

"I just straightened it a little. I hope that's all right."

"All right? First you tell me you've got my tie, then you straighten my chaotic desk. What did I do to deserve you?" He gave her an exuberant hug. "You're amazing." He pulled out a drawer, then stopped, as if just remembering. "Are you going to the fair tomorrow?"

"Yes. But Clarence, you do understand about the tie—"

Rummaging through another drawer, he didn't seem to hear as he continued. "I'm hoping to get away so I can be there for the awards ceremony. Ah! Here it is." He waved a pencil and dashed out the office door. His words floated back to her. "I'm rooting for you to win!"

Chapter 19

A young lady at Heyworth, Ill., has made a crazy-quilt with 28,062 pieces in it, and its dollars to doughnuts that her husband—if she ever has one—will have to pin his coat-tails to his trousers for want of a single patch.—Morning Oregonian (Portland, Oregon) March 7, 1888.

Delia replayed the scene in Clarence's office when she'd confessed and he'd rejoiced. His response didn't make sense. Shouldn't he at least have been surprised? Asked where she'd found it, or when? It was odd. Like when she plucked a string on Papa's fiddle, expecting a note but getting a twang.

It brought her to the same conclusion every time she pondered it—Clarence didn't know his tie was sewn into the crazy quilt. And when he learned where it was, how would he react?

Delia's nerves hummed as Rabb drove her to the site of the fair. Eleanor had packed them apples and sandwiches for the two-hour journey, but she turned her nose up at the sight of food.

Rabb whistled the whole way, and by the time they arrived, she'd had her fill of his cheerfulness. She took Rabb's proffered hand and jumped to the ground, beating the hay and dust from her skirt.

"If you whistle one more tune, I'll scream."

He grinned. "Like this, you mean?" His eyes danced as he gave her a sample.

"I mean it. No whistling. No joking. No clowning."

He fell into step beside her. "You nervous or something?"

If he only knew. "Of course not. Now, let's go before we miss the whole thing."

Butterflies looped in her stomach as they joined the throng of people headed for the big tent. What a crowd. The whole county must have turned out.

Passing a stand labeled Taffy, she choked back a gag at the sickeningly sweet aroma. Who could eat at a time like this? Her palm skittered across her uneasy stomach. At this rate, she might not eat again for days.

Shoulder to shoulder with other fairgoers, they entered the opening of the big tent. Delia's step hitched. So much to study, it almost hurt her eyes to take it all in. Even as other fair patrons bumped and jostled her, she gazed in amazement at the seed exhibit, arranged in a pyramid of flower seed containers. Beyond, jars of okra, peaches, green beans, apples, and other canned produce lined the shelves. The colors alone were a beautiful combination, bringing solace to her agitated state.

Rabb took her elbow and led her to the raised platform where a crowd gathered. They wove between clusters to get to the front.

Moisture sprouted on the palms of her hands. A rainbow of prize ribbons lay arranged in a precisely shaped arch. Would she receive one of those?

Rabb gestured to the stage, where a distinguished man smiled at the audience. "Looks like we got here in time."

She nodded, listening to the announcer. "Ladies and gentlemen, welcome to the Textile division awards ceremony. We are so pleased to have with us ..."

Delia tapped her thumb against her leg as the man delivered his recognitions in monotone. She blew out the breath she'd been holding and scanned the crowd for familiar faces.

Her gaze collided with Gert Waldrop's icy stare. A frisson of dread danced up her spine. She could do nothing but watch helplessly as her rival maneuvered to stand beside her. Aside from the characteristic smirk on her face, she looked fresh and crisp in her dark green suit and smart sailor hat. Gert Waldrop embodied style and confidence. Something Delia, in her out-of-season pastel dress, did not.

"Good luck, Delia." A nice sentiment, even if it reeked of insincerity.

"To you, as well." Delia managed to lift the corners of her lips in a semblance of goodwill.

Up on the stage, the official droned on. "You will find our fair has a fine assortment of jellies, cakes, and pies, which we will auction at the conclusion of the fair."

Rabb leaned closer to Delia. "You ain't gonna sell your quilt, are ya?"

"Of course not." She wouldn't dream of parting with something so precious to her.

Rabb pointed at the platform, where three women stood beside the mayor.

"May I present to you Mrs. O'Donnell, who will announce the winners from the various categories."

The crowd applauded, and the woman called Mrs. O'Donnell stepped to the center.

Gert clucked her tongue. "I don't know why they picked her to announce the winners. Her voice won't carry two feet, if that." Sure enough, the woman's timid presence caused the crowd to murmur with impatience. Finally, a male officiant whispered to the woman and took the paper out of her trembling hand. The man stepped forward and signaled for the crowd to hush. "The first category is Quilts."

Gert's chin lifted. "At last." There was no mistaking the triumph in her words.

Delia folded her arms. "May the best woman win."

The gentleman paused as he eyed the crowd. Wonderful, a man who loved suspense. "In fourth place, Mrs. Emily Watkins."

The crowd applauded as a woman made her way to the stage to accept her certificate and shake the official's hand. Delia pressed her stomach. She was going to be sick.

"Next, we have in third place, Miss Caroline Krauss."

The crowd responded as they had for the first woman, only this time the winner was not present, a fact obvious after the fourth time to call her name. Delia pressed her eyelids shut and tried to regulate her breathing.

"Of course, we will hold the third-place certificate for Miss Caroline Krauss. Now for the runner-up in the Quilting category."

Delia swallowed.

"Second place—well, this is a surprise." He paused. "Miss Gert Waldrop."

Beside her, Gert narrowed her eyes at the announcer and hissed, "Second place?"

Though her words were aimed only at the red-faced man on the stage, they were loud enough for all to hear. Uncomfortable murmurs and hushed whispers rolled through the crowd.

Delia touched her arm. "Go get your ribbon."

Gert jerked out of reach. "I deserve the blue ribbon, and I won't rest until I get it."

An audible gasp lifted around them. Gert stormed up the steps, grabbed the paper, and stomped down again, parting the crowd like the Red Sea as she stalked toward the exit.

Rabb shook his head. "She's got no manners."

Delia gazed after her. "I can't blame her for being disappointed. Her quilt is beautiful." Though down deep, she was satisfied that Gert hadn't earned the top prize. But who had? Could she hope hers had placed first? The waiting was unbearable.

"I can't watch."

She bowed her head against Rabb's arm. But he jostled free of her and pointed to the stage. "Look up there. Ain't that one yours?"

She held her breath as two women held aloft her crazy quilt. The announcer read the judges' comments so fast she only caught words like unusual ... kaleidoscope of colors...artful stitching."

Then he lifted a blue ribbon for all to see, the meaning clear. Delia covered her mouth.

"First Place and the fifty-dollar prize money goes to Miss Delia Truitt."

Rabb whooped and took Delia into his arms, squeezing her tight. "That's my sister!"

Laughing, she batted his arm. She'd won. She wiped her cheeks as she stepped to the stage. Fingers trembling, she accepted the certificate from the announcer. Could this be real? Her heart might burst with joy.

"Congratulations and well done, Miss Truitt. This crazy quilt will be displayed for all to see."

He thrust an envelope in her hand. She stared in

215

amazement at the envelope that held not only the fifty-dollar prize, but her family's future with it. With only a couple months before they had to leave the farm, this would assure a new home for them. She stood beside her quilt, applause thunderous. Her cheeks hurt from the intensity of her smile.

Her gaze alighted on a handsome man at the back of the crowd, clapping his hands with gusto. Clarence.

Her smile faded. Moments from now, he'd see the truth in her quilt. No more holding back, no more convoluted words to get her meaning across. No, words couldn't help either of them now.

As if in a dream she couldn't escape, she watched Clarence weave his way toward the front. Beside her, Rabb gestured to leave the stage. "Let's go see where they're hanging it."

With plodding steps, she allowed herself to be propelled forward with the crowd, barely acknowledging the pats on her back and congratulations doled upon her. All she could see were the glances over her shoulder that marked his progress toward her. To the quilt and the tie.

"Delia." Clarence embraced her, squishing her face into the front of his shirt. "Congratulations!" He released her, laughing. "How does it feel to be the best of all the quilters?"

"Clarence, you've got to listen to me."

He pulled her to him for another quick embrace. "I'm so proud of you."

Grasping his jacket lapel, she said, "Let's go somewhere we can talk."

"Sure. Here, let me clear the way."

Then he stopped and gestured. "Wait, they're hanging it up. Come on, maybe they'll take your photograph."

She grabbed his arm to stop his forward motion, panic building inside her. Either he ignored her protests or didn't hear her, because she found herself hurrying after him, toward the display of quilts. He planted himself before her prize winner and whistled. "It's a beauty. All those colors and shapes and all."

Delia sensed a presence beside her.

"My, my. Look who won first prize." Gert.

What did she want? "I thought you'd gone."

"I couldn't leave without seeing who stole first place from me. Imagine my surprise to see it was you, Delia. But then, you took extreme measures to ensure your win."

An icy chill lifted the hair on the back of Delia's neck. Their gazes clashed. And Delia knew with heavy certainty that everything was about to change.

"Now look here, don't spoil Delia's happiness. She won fair and square." Clarence lifted his palms in a show of reasonableness.

"Funny you should say that." Turning her gaze on Delia, she said, "He must not know how you repaired that ghastly rip."

"How did you ..."

"I'm aware of everything that happens in this town. Don't you know that by now?"

Delia sensed Clarence's gaze shift from Gert to her. *Oh, Lord, don't let this happen.* Not here. Not now.

She tugged at Clarence's jacket sleeve. "Let's go."

But Gert stepped in front of them, blocking their escape. "The way I hear it, a terrible accident happened, and you were left to repair a jagged tear."

Delia said, "Was it an accident? You seem to know a lot about it."

Gert widened her eyes. "Are you accusing me?"

Delia's anger spiked. "It *was* you. No one else here had a reason to destroy my chances at the fair except you."

Clarence looked between them. "What are you talking about?"

Unperturbed, Gert moved closer to the crazy quilt. "Oh, there it is, right in the middle, where that attractive appliqué of a fan is." Her mouth formed an *O* as she gasped. "How fortunate you were able to repair it, dear. Tell me, where did you get that fabric there? It looks familiar."

Clarence's jaw pulsed. "You need to leave. You're upsetting Delia. This is her victory. Don't ruin it."

Gert laughed, a cruel sound. "What if I told you Delia used your necktie to win the competition?"

"That's ridiculous."

"Is it? See the little blue stitching?" Gert turned her icy gaze on him. "I'd know it anywhere, as much as you wore that tie."

Delia couldn't breathe. She watched as Clarence stepped closer to the crazy quilt.

The moment his eyes stopped roaming the fabric and homed in on the tie—his brother's tie—her heart crashed.

"Is that ..." He turned to her with a confused frown. "But you said you had it."

Gert's laugh was harsh. "It appears the tie you've searched for all these weeks was right there in your sweetheart's quilt the whole time."

Clarence stared at Delia, barely hearing Gert's syrupy words before she stepped away. The Delia he knew would never deceive him. But one look at those brown eyes brimming with tears and he felt like he'd been gut punched. The proof was within reach, pinned with a big blue First Place ribbon.

"How could you do that to me?"

"I'm so sorry. I tried to tell you."

"Over a month, that's how long it's been. You couldn't tell me about this in all that time?"

"I'm so sorry—"

"You knew. All the stuff about Joe. I even took out an ad."

"Clarence, please—"

"You had it the whole time? You just let me worry?"

Her face crumpled. "I'm sorry. I never wanted to hurt you ..." Sobs hiccupped between words.

He held up his palms and backed away. He needed space. Maybe he'd been wrong about her all along.

Between gulping spasms of sorrow, Delia called after Clarence, to no avail.

Gert returned, sneering. "Do you really think he'll come back to you? You're more pathetic than I thought."

Fists clenched, Delia narrowed her watery gaze. "This is none of your business."

"It *is* my business. You stole first place from me, just like you stole Clarence's tie to sew into your quilt." Gert stepped close, reminding Delia of a hooded snake ready to strike. "You may think you got away with it, but I'll stop at nothing to see you disqualified."

"Haven't you done enough?"

A spark ignited something in Gert's eyes. "Nobody ever wins over me. Especially a cheater. I'm going to the judges. We'll just see who's the real winner."

Gert marched away, leaving Delia alone. Alone, that is, alongside at least ten bug-eyed, slack-jawed women. Wonderful. A host of witnesses.

Clarence sought refuge on a wooden bench situated away from the excited fair attendees. He sank down and leaned forward, elbows jabbing his thighs.

A mental collage bumped in the corners of his mind. The white tie around his brother's neck at his wedding. Accepting the limp remembrance from his widow. The countless times he'd looped it around his neck, trying in vain to live up to Joe's legacy.

He huffed an ironic chuckle, the mystery solved at last. Since Delia had it, he'd undoubtedly left it on the counter of Truitt's Dry Goods. She'd probably had it all along.

He'd demand it back from her. She owed him that much.

A familiar voice grabbed his attention, and he looked up into a face he never wanted to see again. He groaned. "Haven't you done enough?"

Chapter 20

*Mrs. Chugwater looking up from her paper—"Josiah, what is an
'insane bureau'?" Mr. Chugwater—"It's a piece of furniture they
keep crazy quilts in. Haven't you any reasoning powers?"—
Daily Advocate (Victoria, Texas), December 19, 1903.*

Delia's vision blurred as a waterfall of tears flowed
down her face. The nightmare had come true.

A hand landed on her shoulder, stopping her
progress across the grounds. She wrenched away, only to find it
was Rabb.

"Hey, I didn't do nothing. Unless you count getting myself
pigeon-holed by some little girl who wanted to show me the
dolly she made." He rolled his eyes. "I didn't even get a good
look at your prize-winner. How come you went running out the
door?" His eyes widened. "You been crying?"

She brushed at a telltale tear. "It's rather obvious, don't you
think?" Her gaze traveled past him, to the women staring and
whispering. Rabb must have noticed, too, judging by the grunt
of frustration as he led her to an out-of-the-way spot where they
could sit and talk.

"Now, what's all this? I leave your side for two minutes and everything falls apart. Thought you'd be happy about that blue ribbon."

"I never want to see it again. Take me home."

"What happened?"

She tried to shrug in answer, but he kept after her until finally she said, "Oh, Rabb, I did something awful, and I don't know if I can ever repair the damage I've done."

"Hold on, Red. Start at the beginning."

She told the whole sordid story to him. "I told him I had his tie, but he thought ... he didn't realize it was a tiny part of my crazy quilt."

"Why didn't you just show him? He's been looking all over for that thing."

Her heart squeezed, spilling fresh tears onto her wet face. "Can we just go?"

He ran a hand over his face. "I feel kinda sorry for you. I get in scrapes all the time. Not you."

She hugged herself, shame washing over her. "Oh, Rabb, what should I do?"

"Reckon you oughta apologize."

"I did. I don't think it mattered, though."

"Answer me something." He waited until she met his clear, brown-eyed gaze. "You care for Clarence?"

She pressed her eyelids shut. "Yes." So much.

The way her heart ached, like it would rather die than keep beating, made her wonder if this was what love was like. It was awful.

"Well, then, the answer's simple. Tell him you was plum crazy and you're sorry."

Delia massaged the ache in her shoulder. "But what if he doesn't listen?"

He shrugged. "Keep talking until he does."

Images of Clarence's grim expression ran through her mind, making her shrink inside. How could he stare at her with such disgust? She couldn't face him. Not alone, anyway. "Will you go with me?"

Rabb reluctantly agreed, and they walked side by side along the grounds, searching for Clarence.

"I gotta say, Red, I'm surprised at you. When he was talking about losing his brother's tie, you was lapping up every word, looking all moony-eyed. But you had it all along." He whistled, the sound low and full of amazement. "I never reckoned you for a liar."

"Me, either."

The crisp fall air caressed her skin, settling her nerves and strengthening her resolve. Standing on the solid dirt of the field, she breathed a prayer. If he turned away and refused to grant her forgiveness, she'd have to live with the biggest mistake of her life.

"There he is, over yonder."

Delia adjusted her gaze to follow Rabb's gesture, to a spot closer to the big tent. Her pulse skittered. Gert had gotten to him first. How much more could she poison his opinion of her?

"Go away."

Though Clarence's harsh words would have made any other woman weep, it had little effect on Gert.

"You deserve better than Delia Truitt."

"She's none of your business. Excuse me while I clear my head. And don't follow me." When she waved his words away, he pointed at her sternly. "I mean it."

He set out for somewhere, anywhere, that the troublemaker wouldn't follow. All around him, children shrieked and laughed and darted in and out of his path. Lucky for them, they weren't old enough to deal with women.

When he was far enough away, he sank onto a bench, sharing it with an older woman whose widened eyes followed his movements. Let her stare. Let her talk. Nothing mattered anymore.

He slid his hat from his head and mindlessly worked the brim round and round with his fingers. He wasn't used to deception. His sister Sallie was simple and honest. The way all women should be. But not Delia.

You're an idiot, Parker.

A long, slow breath whooshed from his lungs. He never would've thought his sweetheart capable of stealing his tie so she could fix that gash in her quilt. She wanted to win, and apparently, she'd let nothing stand in her way.

Good thing he'd found out before it was too late.

A dull ache spread in his chest. People talked about betrayal, but he'd never thought it could hurt like this.

She was clever, he'd give her that. He'd never been a pushover, until she came along, with her big brown eyes and soft curves and silky voice.

It'd be a cold day in July before he'd be anybody's fool again.

Just outside the tent, a young man intercepted her. "Are you Delia Truitt?"

She nodded.

"You've been summoned by the judges."

She gasped and reached for her brother's arm. Heart thundering, she barely heard Rabb's demand to know the reason they wanted to see her. But she knew. This was the time of her reckoning.

Rabb laid his hand over hers. "Come on. I'll be right there with you."

Her breath came unevenly, and she kept her gaze to the ground. Nausea made her stomach clench. She clung to her brother's arm and followed the man back to a curtained-off area within the textile division. Inside the small area, two men stood holding her crazy quilt between them. The ribbon now lay on a small table.

Delia's knees trembled. These were the distinguished judges who'd granted her award. Mr. Davis and Mr. Fields ignored her brother and zeroed in on her.

"Ah, Miss Truitt. We have a few questions about your entry."

Rabb gestured to the ribbon. "You're pretty quick to take away her ribbon."

"And you are?"

Rabb identified himself. "What you say to my sister, you can say to me."

Mr. Davis nodded curtly and returned his narrowed gaze to Delia. "You've been accused of using illicit methods in order to win first place. Can you confirm this, Miss Truitt?"

She blinked. Illicit methods? Mr. Fields stepped forward. "Does your quilt contain stolen fabric?"

She swallowed. "I would never steal anything, sir."

Mr. Davis narrowed his eyes. "Are you saying the accusation has no merit? I must tell you, the complaint was lodged by a young lady with a stellar reputation."

Rabb responded, "You mean Gert Waldrop? *Pffff.*"

Delia twisted her hands. "I-I meant no harm."

"You stole a man's tie, thinking you would not do harm?"

"I thought he'd appreciate my saving it for posterity."

Mr. Fields snorted. "Young lady, I don't know who you're trying to fool by twisting words, but unless you want your quilt disqualified immediately, you will issue a forthright answer. Did you or did you not steal any portion of this entry?"

"Looking for Clarence Parker."

Clarence turned from the liveryman and frowned. Now what? All he wanted to do was get his horse and ride out of there. "That's me."

The boy gulped air before saying, "They need you back in the tent."

"Who? What do they want?"

The kid shrugged. "Mr. Davis told me to fetch you. Said it's important, that I should take you there."

The boy looked ready to bolt. But Clarence wasn't about to give in so fast. "Are you sure Mr. Davis meant me?"

"He said Clarence Parker. You coming?"

Clarence's shoulders sagged. He came so close to getting away.

"Fine." He ground his teeth with every step back to that miserable tent. Whatever this was, he'd get it done quick. Then he'd leave and never look back.

Inside, the kid led him to the curtained-off space behind the quilt display before sprinting away. Behind him, Gert Waldrop called, "I told those men what she did to you. I hope she pays the price for your humiliation."

He wheeled in time to see her dab a crisp white hanky to her dry eyes. This was too much. "I told you to stop following me." Clarence moved toward the makeshift room.

"You didn't mean it, though. But don't worry, I'll be waiting, right here."

Of course she would. This day just wouldn't end.

Inside the curtained space, two men stood on either side of Delia, pelting her with questions. On instinct, Clarence stepped up as if to protect her, then remembered why he was there. Still, she looked defenseless, standing before powerful men, even with Rabb nearby.

He recognized these two judges from his carriage deliveries. Jack Davis, a prominent attorney in the area, appeared to be in charge. With his barrel chest and bushy mustache, he resembled that brash politician, Theodore Roosevelt. Davis would ferret out the truth, but at what price?

"Excuse me, Mr. Davis." He nodded to the other gentleman, a tall, angular man. "Mr. Fields. You wanted me?"

He tried not to flinch when Delia sniffed. These men had cornered her as if they were cats chasing a mouse.

Davis peered over his eyeglasses. "We're told that this young woman has stolen a valuable item from you, Mr. Parker. Can you confirm that?"

Mr. Fields stepped closer. "Miss Gertrude Waldrop alleges that Miss Truitt is concealing stolen goods within her entry, one of those insane quilts. Is that true?"

"C-crazy quilt."

The men ignored Delia's comment. Gray ash dripped to the floor from the fat cigar Davis held. "Are the allegations true, Mr. Parker?"

He looked from one man to another, swallowing. "Can you be more specific, sir?"

Davis narrowed his eyes as he puffed the cigar. The odorous smoke filled the small space. "Necktie."

Delia coughed delicately as whirls of offending smoke billowed around them.

What could he say? Of course, she'd taken Joe's tie. But a small voice inside prompted caution. He might be angry at her, but did he really want to expose her sin for all to see? "I thought it might have been the tie I'd misplaced, but ..." he swallowed. "I was mistaken."

Delia's jaw dropped, Rabb's eyes narrowed, and the men exchanged puzzled glances while fury squealed just beyond the curtain's border, sounding much like Gert.

He cleared his throat. "Gentleman, if that's all you need, I'll be on my way."

Davis and Fields exchanged a look. Davis said, "Then we have nothing further. The blue ribbon remains with Miss Truitt's quilt, and the prize money should not be returned."

Clarence ducked away from the enclosed space and took a deep breath. Gert stood with folded arms and speared him with her furious glare.

From behind him, Delia called. "Clarence, please wait."

His step faltered. Much as he wanted to keep walking, he turned. Despite his disgust, he couldn't ignore her. Delia whispered something to Rabb, and with a nod to her, he left them, clapping Clarence's shoulder as he passed.

She came to stand before him, hands clasped as if praying. "Thank you."

"Don't thank me. Nothing's changed, Delia."

"But ... back there, I thought—"

"I did what any gentleman would do, which is more than you deserve."

Her face went slack. For one instant, something inside his gut dipped. Then he remembered the way she let him hunt high and low like a crazed man, when all along she not only knew where the tie was, she hid it from him and everyone else.

He'd given her his heart. Now he was taking it back.

Chapter 21

*Motto for crazy quilt manufacturers: "Blessed are the peace-
makers."—Chicago Sun—Delta Herald & Times (Delta
Pennsylvania) December 5, 1884.*

When Sunday dawned, Delia lay in bed and
pretended to sleep, despite the fact she hadn't
slept all night. Or the night before, after the
disastrous day at the fair. Images of her beloved's face
when he discovered the tie embedded in her quilt were the
stuff of her nightmares, waking or sleeping.

Hazel stood beside the bed. "Get up or we'll be late to
church."

"I'm not going."

"Come on. I've been up for an hour."

Delia burrowed deeper under the comforter. "I can't face
everyone, after what I've done."

"I don't think you've done anything to be ashamed of."

Delia rolled over and peered, one-eyed, at her sister. "I told
you—"

"I know what you told me." Hazel sat on the bed, making the bed squeak. "And frankly, I think the whole thing is stupid."

"It might appear that way to a fourteen-year-old."

"I beg your pardon, I'm fifteen now."

"That changes everything, then."

Hazel ignored the comment and lifted her index finger. "You are making too much of all this. First of all, you found that stupid tie. You did not steal it. Right?"

"Yes."

"Second, you rejuvenated that worn out rag Clarence called a necktie. That alone should have earned you a blue ribbon. Me? I would've tossed it in the rubbish bin."

Delia sighed and propped herself up on an elbow. "I'd have never thrown it away."

"Anyhow, my third point is you made something beautiful out of nothing, and you entered it in the fair in good conscience."

Beauty for ashes? Clarence likely wouldn't agree. "But you forget. I knew full well he was frantic. I should've told him."

"True. But still, you never meant to cheat. Or whatever it was those dumb judges said you did."

"He defended me, you know."

"Nobody had to stand up for you. Not Clarence, not Papa, nobody. Aside from not telling him you had it, you did absolutely nothing wrong."

Delia rubbed her face and sighed. "Well, that's not how Gert told it."

"But it's the truth."

"The whole town probably thinks I'm a terrible person."

Hazel opened her mouth to speak once more, then snapped it shut.

Delia gestured for her to continue. "Don't stop now. Say it."

"Miss Eleanor."

Delia frowned. "What?"

"People turned their backs on her and practically put her out of business. Is that what you're afraid of? Being ostracized?"

Was it? Delia bit her lip. "Maybe."

"But don't you see? You've been championing her right to be judged fairly. But when it comes to standing up for yourself in the same way, I find you ducking under the bedcovers."

"It's not that easy. I don't want to lose the friends I've made."

"I understand. Especially after we had to say goodbye forever to our loved ones back home. But if Lucy and Sallie are true friends, they'll stick by your side."

Delia blew out a breath as she looped her arms around her bent legs. "Sallie's plenty mad at me. When it comes to Clarence, blood comes before friendship."

"So let her be mad. But don't you think she'll forgive you?"

Delia bit her nail, considering Sallie's gentle nature versus her allegiance to her brother. "If she's talked to Clarence, I'm not sure she will."

"Well, then, talk to her. Just don't mope. The big sister I know can slay dragons."

She looked at Hazel with dull eyes. Her sister's confidence was enviable, but misplaced. "You're sweet, but I'm not like one of those heroines from your books. I'm a terribly selfish woman who's messed things up in a big way."

Hazel slid off the bed with a note of finality. "Get up and get dressed. And while you're at it, put on some strength and courage. I want to see you stand up to those gossips, like you've done for Eleanor."

Delia watched her sister march to the wall where her few

dresses hung from pegs and return with her blue dress with puffed sleeves. "Come on. You put on this pretty frock, and if you're quick, I'll fix your hair."

Delia swung her legs to the side of the bed and allowed her little sister to help her dress. What a role reversal. Most Sundays, it was Delia who did the persuading. She squeezed Hazel's hand. "How did you get to be so grown up, taking charge like that?"

Without a pause, Hazel said, "It's from reading *Little Women*. I love Jo."

Delia's mouth fell open with a puff of humor. "You could have at least hinted that *I* had some influence on your budding wisdom."

Hazel shrugged. "I'm just being honest."

Something Delia should learn from her younger sibling.

Approaching the church, Delia couldn't help but pin her hopes on seeing Clarence waiting outside the building for her, misdeeds forgotten in light of his true love. But no one stood there. As she proceeded to the seat at the front, her eyes betrayed the effort to keep her gaze forward and wandered to the Parkers' pew.

There he was, flanked between Sallie and their mother in the center of the congregation. She tried to catch his eye, but his granite jaw and stony forward gaze said it all. Her heart plunged.

Sitting through the sermon was agony. The pastor's words droned as she fidgeted throughout the interminably long service. Her insides quivered as she exited the building, one of the last. Along the way, women murmured their congratulations on her blue-ribbon win at the fair.

Outside, the group of single men and women she'd become so fond of now caused her stomach to lurch, especially when Gert stood at Clarence's side. How Delia longed to flee. Instead, she feigned confidence as she joined the circle beside Lucy, who squeezed her shoulder. But the hush that landed over the group told her no amount of confidence could overcome the gossip sure to have twisted through the gathering. By the looks of some guilty faces, it would seem they'd been discussing her dubious win at the fair.

"Delia, I'm surprised to see you at church." Gert had a triumphant look, like the cat who cornered the mouse.

Delia's knees shook. "I'm here every Sunday."

The shrill, humorless laugh grated against Delia's nerves. "I suppose they'll let anyone through the doors. Some would wonder if you've learned your lesson after cheating at the fair."

Lucy's voice was stern. "Stop it. Delia won that blue ribbon. Don't be a sore loser."

The group shifted, darting glances at one another. Heat crept up Delia's neck. This was so uncomfortable. Would she face this kind of conjecture everywhere she went?

Without a word, Sallie fell into place by Delia's side. Her support was clear, even though she wasn't her usual amiable self. With Lucy to her right and Sallie to her left, Delia breathed easier.

Clarence spoke. "Delia didn't steal the tie. She deserves the blue ribbon." He turned to Gert. "The ruckus you raised was uncalled for. I think you owe Delia an apology."

A quick intake of air snaked through the group, and everyone seemed to wait anxiously for Gert's response. She arched an eyebrow. "Well, poor Clarence can't see the truth if it hit him broadside. We'll see how it hits you in black and white." She stormed away.

Milly looked at the group. "What's she talking about, in black and white?"

Lucy rolled her eyes. "Who knows."

Delia watched Clarence move toward the street. The urge to speak to him overtook good sense. She hurried to catch up. "Clarence, wait."

She came even with him, a little breathless. "Thank you for what you said to the group. You saved my reputation, you know. That was kind."

"I don't believe you stole that from me. I also respect your talent, and I'm glad you got what you wanted." His eyes scanned the landscape behind her. He wouldn't meet her gaze, which made her heart squeeze with sorrow.

Seconds ticked by with no words. Desperation clawed at her. She just wanted him to look at her the way he used to. It was as if he viewed her as no more than an acquaintance now.

"Clarence." Her voice broke. "I'm sorry. So very sorry. I should have come to you when I found the tie."

"Why didn't you?"

It was what she'd asked herself over and over. Delia looked away. She sensed his gaze on her.

"Did you keep it so you could win over Gert?"

She looked up sharply. "No, of course not. I'd never do something like that."

His gray-green eyes held sorrow. "Part of me wants to believe you."

She swallowed. "And the other?"

He rubbed the back of his neck. "Honestly, I don't know. I want to think you wouldn't use me to win, but on the other hand, you told me crazy quilting is who you are. Maybe it proved more important than me."

The words slapped her. "No, not at all."

He took a deep breath. "I think it's best if we don't continue our courtship. I wish you well, Delia."

He turned and walked away.

She'd lost him.

The emotion she'd banked burst. She covered her face as sobs shook her. She'd ruined everything. *God, don't let this happen. Please don't let him walk away from me.*

But he continued down the road until he rounded a corner and disappeared from sight.

In the privacy of his rented room, Clarence stripped off his jacket and tossed it on the bed.

He should've skipped church.

One by one, he pushed the buttons of his vest through the buttonholes and shrugged it onto the floor. He'd done some hard things in his life, but telling her goodbye was one of the worst.

He tugged the necktie loose and flung it on his dressing table. It was the right thing, cutting it off.

He peeled off his stiff collar and rolled his sleeves to just below his elbows. He strode to the window and lifted the sash, craving the autumn breeze. But nothing helped, not even the refreshing air.

He scooped the strewn clothes and set them on the straight-back wooden chair, then sank onto the bed, willing sleep to overtake him. His stomach growled at the wafting aroma of beef from downstairs. But no amount of food was worth sitting around a table with other men and acting like nothing was wrong. His world had just tilted.

Sallie and Lucy were waiting for her when she returned to the churchyard. Wordlessly, Lucy rubbed her arm in sympathy.

"Thank you." Delia could only manage a whisper. She looked at Sallie. "I never meant to hurt him."

Sallie pushed her spectacles up on the bridge of her nose. "You're my friend, and I know in time I'll forget all this. But he's my brother, and when he hurts, I hurt."

A tear spilled over the rim of her watery eyes. Delia nodded. "I understand."

With an apologetic smile, Sallie waved her hand before joining her mother, leaving Lucy and Delia looking after her.

"I've ruined everything."

"You made a mistake. Just give Sallie a little time."

"And what about Clarence?"

Lucy hesitated. "Maybe he isn't the man you're supposed to marry."

Emptiness sat heavy in her chest. "He deserves better than me."

Lucy gave her shoulders a shake. "Now that's enough. You are a fine person. Live your life. If you and Clarence are meant for each other, everything will work out in the end."

Delia drew out her damp handkerchief and blew her nose. She was sick of crying.

She hugged Lucy and walked to the wagon. Her father sat beside Thomas, loosely holding the reins. Once all the siblings were there, they rode home.

"Can't wait to taste what Eleanor's made." Rabb adjusted his hat. "Thought I heard her say something about pie."

Hazel leaned toward Delia. "I heard Clarence eradicated you."

Delia drew back in confusion. Hazel and her big words. "Are you saying he destroyed me?"

"Of course not. He said you weren't guilty."

Thomas looked over his shoulder. "The word you mean is exonerated."

Wasn't he the smart one.

"Yes, that's it. Exonerated."

Delia stared at her hands. Hazel had the right word, all right. Clarence had stamped out all that remained of their relationship.

Chapter 22

A Laporte (Ind), woman spent 25 years making a quilt, so quite naturally it's a crazy quilt.—The Bridgeport Telegram (Bridgeport, Connecticut) February 8, 1923.

Because of her trade with Eleanor, Delia sat in the seamstress shop each day, smiling and thanking each person who stopped in to congratulate her on her blue-ribbon victory. It was like heaping ashes upon her head.

The week-long county fair was the social event of the region, gathering folks from near and far to celebrate livestock, harvest, and general domesticity. The praise she'd once craved did nothing to satisfy her sadness. Worse, none of the people who dropped by placed an order. She tried to busy herself with organizing bobbins of thread and sweeping the shop floor. Anything to keep her thoughts from Clarence.

It might help if Clarence had shouted at her. But he'd been a gentleman, as always. Sure, he'd been frustrated that first day. But he'd cleared her name. It made her heart all the heavier.

Rabb's silent pats on the back made her feel even worse.

She just wanted to get on with life and cast off the cloud of sorrow that wouldn't go away.

The night before the fair ended, Thomas stood beside her as she dried the supper dishes. "Fair ends tomorrow. I'll take you to get your quilt."

She set a fork on the counter with more force than necessary. "I'm not setting foot back in that place."

His dark eyes narrowed. "Why? You afraid of what folks will say?"

She lifted her chin. "No." She just didn't want to return to the scene of her greatest failure.

"What's done is done. You apologized, now get beyond it." Thomas tapped the counter. "We'll leave out at daybreak."

"Why so early?"

"We gotta get there in time for—" He snapped his mouth shut.

She paused, wet plate in hand. "For what?"

The tips of his ears blazed red. "Uh, just something I wanted to see."

Knowing him, one of the farming exhibits had caught his imagination. She turned back to her task before setting the dry plate on the shelf. Thomas had become more single-minded since they'd moved here. More often than not, he carried a notebook and pencil with him as he made his rounds, jotting notes that had meaning to him alone. She'd peeked once, but the columns of abbreviated terms and amounts might as well have been Greek. No surprise, then, if he wished to congregate with other farmers to discuss the right way to plant or run the plow. Bless 'his heart, the science of farming consumed his every thought.

Maybe if she allowed herself, she could see the fair from Thomas's viewpoint. Stroll along the livestock pens and try to make sense of animal husbandry. Undoubtedly, there was much to see besides the Textiles department. The change would be refreshing.

The next day, she trailed her brother and soaked up the smells of sweet hay and roasted corn, chuckled at the antics of a couple of clowns, and bit into a juicy, tart apple coated in creamy caramel. Outside the main tent, the livestock arena boasted hearty bulls, pink pigs, and cottony sheep. Farmers bragged. Newcomers and old timers greeted each other.

After an hour, she begged off and arranged to meet Thomas inside the tent when he finished. She avoided the quilt display and took her time in the food exhibit with its savory aromas. She strolled before the lovely glass jars of amber peach preserves, the green pickled okra, the bright yellow ears of corn, accepting tasty morsels of fresh fruit or jam on crackers whenever offered. The sweetness of fudge and spice cake perfumed the cool air and mixed with the aroma of damp hay and popcorn.

There was no place like the fair.

As she walked the exhibits, sampling chocolate confections and spiced pecans, Delia glanced toward the Textiles area with a mixture of pride and guilt. She longed to gaze up at her prize-winning creation with a clear conscience, but the hurt she'd inflicted on Clarence made that impossible.

Yet she was drawn to it. In spite of everything, it was a beauty. Next to her, two women discussed the merits of her crazy quilt. What would those women say if they knew the story behind the blue-ribbon win? She couldn't help but think it would diminish their praise.

Thomas strode up to her. "I've been looking everywhere for you. Come on, I need to get to the auction."

She wrinkled her nose. Farm implements, no doubt. "You go on. I'm fine here."

When he gave no argument, merely walked in the opposite

direction, the fear of missing something important made her call out to him. "Thomas, wait."

Whether or not he heard her, he stopped to watch the crowd collecting in front of the raised platform. Wonderful. Just what she wanted to do, stand in the very same place where her life had taken a turn for the better and for the worse.

"Isn't the auction outside?"

He didn't respond, only stared in the direction of the platform, where a gentleman raised his arms to hush the crowd, just like that disastrous day a week and a lifetime ago. She lowered her voice. "If you take too long, you might not get the tools you want."

His face wrinkled as if he sucked a lemon. "Huh?"

The announcer's voice boomed. "Ladies and gents, here we have award-winning jams and jellies. We'll start the bidding for this delicious apple butter by Mrs. Mabel Smith. Who will give me ten cents?"

Thomas pushed closer into the crowd, gesturing for her to follow.

"You're not going to buy jams and jellies, are you?" She lowered her voice when a few people gave her scathing looks. "That'd be insulting to Mother's canned goods."

He ignored her, so she tugged on his shirt sleeve. "Thomas, please. Let's go."

But her usually amenable brother shook his head resolutely, arms folded across his chest as if to shield himself from her arguments. She blew out a breath and mimicked his posture, waiting for this normally sensible man to come to his senses and head to the part of the fair he knew best.

After several canned goods found new owners, the auctioneer announced the start of bidding on baked goods. The crowd stirred. Thomas looked at her. "Follow me."

He shouldered his way across the sea of people, leaving

Delia to murmur apologetically as she followed suit to the side of the platform. Lucy Grant stood in a line of women yet to be summoned onstage, a plate in her hands.

Obviously, Thomas wanted to purchase whatever it was Lucy had prepared. Delia gritted her teeth. She loved them both, but the last thing she needed was to be front and center for someone else's love story, especially when her own affections had been spurned. Watching Lucy bat her eyelashes at Thomas was akin to a knife in the heart.

She couldn't hear their exchange, but Thomas must have said something funny, for Lucy's tinkling giggle burst forth. Envy sliced through Delia's chest.

Delia swallowed her pain and smiled at her starry-eyed friend. "Hello, there." She looked between the two.

"Delia. I'm delighted to see you." Lucy's dimples flashed as she gazed up at Thomas. "I was just telling your brother my chocolate cake is about to be auctioned. I certainly hope y'all will stay."

Thomas gazed down into Lucy's smiling face. "Sure. I have all the time in the world, especially when it comes to fine chocolate cakes."

Oh, no. They had all the symptoms of two lovesick fools. Well, she wouldn't stick around. "I'll be over there."

Neither of them responded as they continued to smile at each other. She was happy for them. Mostly.

She pushed her way to the outskirts of the crowd, where she inhaled deeply. Now to get her quilt.

She blew out a sigh, headed back to the textile area, and dug her claim check out of her handbag. The woman working the exhibit peered at it with squinted eyes.

"Hmm, oh, yes. Our first-place winner. Let me get that for you."

Delia scanned the crowd as she waited. If she looked hard

enough, would she spy Clarence? He'd have no reason to return. How she wished he would, though.

She glanced back in the direction of the stage, only mildly interested in the activity there. The mayor held aloft a white frosted cake for all to see. Then the loud auctioneer volleyed with the crowd, and though she couldn't make out the prices, she saw several hands in the air.

"Here you go, Miss Truitt." The woman handed Delia the neatly folded crazy quilt. Her gaze flickered past her. "The auction is always lively, isn't it?"

"Actually, this is my first time to participate."

The woman looked surprised. "Well, then, you should be quite proud of yourself, getting a first-place ribbon. We had scads of entries, you know." She looked around and lowered her voice. "And I have it on good authority that yours was the talk of the fair."

Delia flushed. She could imagine how fast the rumors traveled when the judges called a piece into question. "Thank you. I put a lot of work into this." And lost her beau.

"Yes, indeed. Your stitches were nice and even, and your choice of fabrics are gorgeous. That rose-colored satin is quite unusual."

Delia slid her finger over the swatch, brushing the tie as well as the rose satin. What she wouldn't give to see Clarence now. Beg his forgiveness once more. Present him with this quilt, the forever home to his brother's heirloom.

"Well, I hope you've started on next year's entry. I have a feeling that the competition will be quite something after seeing your entry."

The thought of creating another crazy quilt made bile rise in her throat. The win had come with too dear a price. She'd put this quilt and its blue ribbon deep inside her trunk and never think about it again. Delia forced a polite acknowledgment of the woman's admiration and fled the area. If one more person praised her work, she'd lose all composure.

Voices rose from the auction. A lively bidding war was in progress and had heads turning from one side to the other, reminding her of the auction for box lunches months ago.

Her attention sharpened on two familiar voices, raising the price. Was that Rabb who bid against Thomas? When had he arrived, and how? The dreadful sight of brother against brother reminded her of the box lunch picnic months earlier. Only this time, Lucy looked none too happy about it as she stood uncertainly on the raised platform, grasping her chocolate cake.

"I've got a dollar on that cake." Thomas's bellow rang out with confidence from one side of the audience.

Rabb's answer belted from the opposite side of the crowd. "I'll give you two dollars."

Her stomach clenched as the two brothers exchanged a steely gaze over the many bodies that separated them. Murmurs rose like summer locusts as her brothers persisted, volleying rapid-fire until she couldn't distinguish one voice from the other.

"Two dollars ten cents."

"Make that two-fifty."

"Three dollars."

"Three-fifty."

Panic surged within her. Where did they get that kind of money? Mother would be mortified. What a spectacle they made, brother bidding against brother, and for what? A chocolate cake and the affections of its creator. Holding her quilt tightly against her chest, Delia wove through the crowd until she reached Rabb, clutching his coat sleeve to keep him from raising his bid. "Stop this at once!"

Rabb pulled away from her grip. "Five dollars and ten cents."

From across the sea of amused faces, Thomas hollered his answer. "Six dollars."

A gasp rose, her own with them. But Rabb wasted no time. "Six-fifty."

The delighted auctioneer barked, "Do I hear seven? Anyone?"

Thomas responded with the kind of confidence that boasted a hearty roll of dollars. But Rabb was not to be undone. Back and forth they fought, exchanging glares as they went.

On the platform, Lucy's countenance no longer reflected uncertainty as she made a show of lifting the cake invitingly for all to see. No doubt she loved the spotlight. For a moment, jealousy laced Delia. How nice to be fought over. But as she studied her friend, she noticed Lucy wasn't just grinning because she was the object of a bidding war. It was Thomas. Every time he raised the bid, she looked at him with an endearing smile. A woman in love.

Thomas's head swiveled. At first, she thought he was looking at her. But when he lifted his chin and Rabb silenced, she understood. She looked up at him as the auctioneer counted down. Rabb plunged both hands into his trouser pockets.

"Going once. Twice. SOLD for ten whole dollars, to Thomas Truitt."

Thomas raised his hands in victory. "Ten dollars for the finest chocolate cake this side of the Mississippi."

A cacophony of laughter and applause filled the air. On the platform, Lucy beamed as Thomas paid, then reached to take the cake from her. Whistles and teasing lifted, but the pair gave no notice as he helped her down.

Delia turned to Rabb, but he was gone. She searched the crowd and spotted him making his way toward the exit. She hurried to catch up.

"Rabb, stop. What was that about?"

When he turned, his face held no trace of bitterness at losing. Instead, his mouth twitched with amusement.

"You know he's sweet on her, yet you bid against him anyway."

Crinkles formed at the corner of his brown eyes. "Pretty good, huh?"

She blinked. "Actually, I find it disgusting that you would take pleasure in driving up the price of Lucy's cake. Despicable."

Bending to speak into her ear, he said, "Thomas and me, we had it worked out. I'd bid against him until he gave me the high sign. Paid me fifty cents too."

She narrowed her eyes. "That's ridiculous. Why would he need to do that? He's barely got two pennies to rub together."

Rabb grinned. "Our big brother's got plenty, with all the extra chores he's doing for Uncle Robert. He's been planning for this big show for Lucy. Calls it his grand gesture. She likes that kinda thing, you know."

With dagger-like clarity, she thought of Clarence's foolish and thrilling bid on her sad little box of food. It had been his grand gesture.

One he'd never repeat.

Chapter 23

An Oregon, Ill., young woman is making a crazy quilt of silk ties which have been given her by her devoted admirers. Her pillows are to be stuffed with their love letters.—Davenport Daily Leader (Davenport, Iowa) September 20, 1893.

Almost three weeks dragged by with no communication from Clarence. The few times they'd come face to face at church, he'd avoided her gaze. How badly she wanted to toss her head and proclaim herself free of any feelings for Clarence Parker. But her heart was too heavy for feigned indifference.

With Eleanor helping with Mother and the baby, and furnishing her family with delicious food, Delia had plenty of solitary hours in the seamstress shop. The buzz from her fair win had died down, leaving her alone to gaze out the window as women passed without a glance her way.

Did the ladies in this town cross the street in order not to come near the infamous former wife of Big Jake Baskin? They had only to glance through the window to know the proprietress didn't sit at the Singer.

Poor Eleanor had lived this life, but unlike Delia, she had no friendly faces to quell her loneliness in the evening. More and more, this isolated little shop caused Delia to question her dreams.

One thing she took pleasure in was taking one of Mother's dresses apart to make it over for Hazel. She'd brought the dress here to work on it, at Mother's insistence.

"I'll never wear this again, I'm sure. Your sister is growing taller by the day, and she needs something presentable to wear to school."

It had been a relief to work on something so needed. She spread the skirt on the table and with her smallest scissors, began ripping out the seams. With a few clever changes, this dark green wool would make Hazel a fine winter outfit. When she turned sixteen next year, she'd need to let out the hem so that it might fall to her ankles.

After a few minutes, her mind filled again with images of her former beau and the pervasive *"Now, what?"* question. Should she offer to cut the necktie out of her quilt, or at least what remained of his brother's gift? The prospect caused a shudder to run through her, especially now that her prize-winning entry hung in the window. But if there was any chance of bridging the chasm between them, of proving her many apologies were sincere, she would take the scissors to it.

She glanced up as footsteps sounded on the boardwalk outside. Aunt Mary pushed through the door, with a newspaper in her grasp. The chill October wind made Delia shudder and hurry forth to shut the door.

Without a word of greeting, the woman rattled the newspaper between them. "You'll never believe what I just read!"

Delia quirked a brow. "Good afternoon, Aunt Mary. Would you like a cup of tea?"

"I don't have time, dearie. Don't you want to hear the news?"

"Not particularly." No telling what had her in a tizzy, and she didn't want to find out. Drama encircled her aunt like a Texas dust devil, and right now, Delia wanted nothing to do with it.

"Well, that's a fine how do you do, considering that I bring you news of the best kind."

Delia smothered a sigh as she sat at the table. "Fine, tell me if you must."

With a flare, Aunt Mary unfolded the paper. In her trumpeting voice, she read.

A Crazy Quilt Romance

A romance growing out of a local quilt show has come to light in Blooming Grove, Texas, involving a prominent business owner and a girl fresh from Georgia. Last summer, handsome bachelor Clarence Parker went to a local dry goods store and purchased a necktie, leaving his old one on the counter. The clerk, beautiful seamstress Delia Truitt, ignored her uncle's advice to toss it, and placed the silk in her crazy quilt. Weeks later, the young lady was awarded a blue ribbon for her creation, and during the award ceremony, Clarence Parker spied his missing tie within the intricacies of her design. Fireworks lit between the two when he demanded his tie, and she refused to remove it. The sparks set off at a county fair turned to a romantic nature, as the two were observed kissing under Lover's Oak. So, it seems that the purloined silk ascot ties the young lovers together forever, as they plan to join in matrimony in a festive December wedding at the home of the bride. Custody of the prize-winning quilt will be shared by the happy couple at their love nest at 219 Oak Road, but for now, it remains on display at the seamstress' shop in Blooming Grove, Texas. If you make haste, esteemed Reader, you, too, can witness the insane phenomenon that unites two lost souls!

"What?" Delia sprang from her chair and snatched the paper. Her horrified gaze moved across the newsprint. "This isn't true!"

Aunt Mary tugged the paper from Delia's trembling fingers. "What does truth matter? My dear, this is worth gold. The story has gone out to dozens of communities, even big cities. Just think of all the business that will come your way."

Delia pressed her temples. "But what will Mother and Papa say when they read about me kissing Clarence in plain view of the world? Oh, this is awful."

Aunt Mary bobbed her head side to side, as if weighing that possibility against the gain. "You can tell them it's not true."

Delia uttered a frustrated moan. "Certainly, I will, because it's not. Papa will be so mad at Clarence. I can't imagine what he would do. And Clarence. What will he think when he reads this?"

He'd think she planted that article to get business. This was worse than anything she'd imagined. If there had been a sliver of a chance she'd get back together with the man she loved, all hope shattered with the appearance of that article.

"If he's a smart businessman, he'll recognize the opportunity. My only regret is that Truitt's isn't named specifically. You can bet Neil Logan will be claiming the deed happened at their business, mark my words." She folded the paper and shoved it under her arm. "And that's exactly why I'm buying multiple copies and delivering them to our fellow store owners, explaining that this happened in our store."

"Please don't. Clarence will be so embarrassed."

"Nonsense. He's my first stop."

Delia gasped as she grabbed her aunt by the arms. "I beg you, don't give this to him. Please."

But Aunt Mary only shrugged off her grasp and walked to the door. Turning back, she smiled as if she held the future in her fingers. "Someday you'll thank me for this."

Aunt Mary left, and Delia sank her head into her hands.

Clarence shook the mayor's hand. "I sure appreciate your business."

He stood at the opening of the carriage house and watched as the buggy rolled down the street. It was the first he'd stamped his brand onto, a true beauty. Sleek, lightweight. Just right for handling the traffic of a bigger town, like Corsicana or Dallas. His heart pumped with pride. Give him five years, and the name Clarence Parker would stand for fine carriages and quality hardware.

Just as he turned, he heard his name from down the road. He cupped his hand over his eyes. Aw, crumb. Just what he didn't need today or any other day. Mary Truitt, barreling down the street waving something over her head. He rocked with a wild impulse to dash into the building and lock the doors.

Instead, he settled his hands at his hips and pinned his most ferocious frown in place.

Everything about Mary Truitt grated on his nerves. Her high-pitched squeal, her domineering presence, and the way she called him out. Like now.

"Well, well, well. So, the great Clarence Parker is alive. You haven't darkened our door for several weeks."

He'd thought she was overbearing when he was courting Delia. Now they'd broken off their relationship, and the woman had the fierceness of a grizzly bear.

"What can I do for you, Mrs. Truitt?"

Her eyebrows arched. A knowing smile creased her face. "Oh, no, Mr. Parker. It's what *I* can do for *you*."

She thrust the newspaper against his chest and smirked. "Congratulations. You made the front page of the *Blooming Grove Gazette*." She waved her finger. "Front page, just under the fold, right side."

Frowning, he searched the dense text. "I don't see anything."

She grabbed the paper and rapped a small article. "Plain as day, Mr. Parker. This one, entitled, 'A Crazy Quilt Romance.'"

His jaw sagged as he took the paper from her. Dread grew as he read the lines, then re-read them two more times, anger shooting through his veins.

He threw the paper to the ground. "Who's responsible for this?"

"Temper, Mr. Parker." She stooped to retrieve the newspaper as crinkled pages lifted in the breeze.

"Boss?" Over his shoulder, he saw a group of his workers standing only feet away with bewildered expressions.

Clarence waved. "You boys go on inside. I'll be there in a minute." Clarence raked his fingers through his hair, pacing. "Your niece did this?"

"You are wrong, Mr. Parker. She was just as astonished as you."

He glared at her. "Or maybe she fooled you." She'd sure fooled him.

Her eyes hooded as traces of humor drained from her face.

"You're mistaken to think so little of her. Delia would never solicit this kind of attention for either of you."

He used his sleeve to wipe the sweat from his brow. "I'm sure you think so."

She sighed and smoothed the rumpled pages before handing it back. "Keep this. Someday you might view this article with a different eye. For now, though, enjoy the attention it brings."

He stared after the woman as she marched down the street. He didn't need this kind of attention. After this, he'd be lucky if any man worth his salt would buy a carriage from him. Or tools.

He shook his head as he stomped inside. Laughingstock, that's what the article branded him. Fine. He'd just keep his head down and mind his own business.

He still couldn't believe Delia sank so low as to feed a false story to the press. Thank the Lord, he didn't marry her. Like the proverb said, it was better to dwell in the wilderness than live with a contentious woman.

He slumped into his office chair and rubbed his face with his hands. Thing was, he'd never pictured Delia Truitt as that kind of woman.

Guess he had a lot to learn about women.

Delia pulled the window shade down, though it did nothing to silence the laughter and chatter on the other side of the glass. It sounded like a hundred elephants tromped on the boardwalk. She'd tried to ignore the clusters of people who pointed and waved their copy of the paper. But when an unsavory fellow who reeked of whiskey burst in and demanded a kiss, she'd pushed him out and locked the door. What had that article caused? No good, that was for sure.

She longed to go home, where routine delivered the comfort she needed after hours of unwanted attention. She could sneak out the back, ride her bicycle far away from here, and nobody out front would be the wiser.

The tapping on both door and window reached a frenzied pace. Fine. She'd face her hecklers. Gert Waldrop was no doubt first in line to taunt her.

Crossing to the window, she snapped the shade, sending it flying around and around the rod at the top. She gasped. There must be a dozen women peering at her.

"Open up, Delia." Milly pointed at the door. "Won't you please let us in?"

Voices echoed the plea. Delia shook her head in amazement. Didn't these women have anything better to do than give her a hard time?

Lucy shouldered her way to the glass and lifted a newspaper. "Dear friend, you are famous."

Delia groaned. That article. Reluctantly, she unlocked the door for Lucy, who kissed her cheek. "Have you seen this? It's wonderful!"

"It's slanderous."

A stream of chattering women nudged past the two, filling the shop within minutes. Someone waved the paper in her face. "Delia! Won't you autograph my newspaper?"

"I was here first, Betsey."

"Oh, Nelly, you'll get your turn."

"Delia, won't you tell us all about stealing the tie?"

"There's nothing to tell," Delia protested, but nodding heads and echoes of, "Please do tell," overrode her.

But speaking above all the titters and feminine exclamations was impossible, until a shrill whistle rent the air and all movement ceased. "Excuse my rude behavior, ladies, but if you'd like an eyewitness account from our dear friend, you must be silent."

Lucy?

Before Delia could locate her friend, all at once she popped up on top of the worktable. She hoped there were no shoeprints on Hazel's made-over skirt.

Lucy's face was tomato red from laughing, and she gestured for the women to quiet.

"I happen to know"—she winked at Delia—"that Miss Truitt did indeed take Clarence Parker's tie to use in her crazy quilt. However, the story in the newspaper isn't the most accurate. Perhaps we can persuade her to come up here on our little stage"—another wink—"and tell us the truth behind the fiction. What say all of you?"

Cheers erupted, and before she knew it, Delia was pushed to the front and helped up onto the table beside Lucy. "I certainly hope this table can hold us both."

Laughter rippled throughout the room. She added, "This is the most ridiculous thing I've ever done. Including taking my beau's tie."

A woman called, "Why'd you do it?"

"First, you all need to understand that I in no way stole Clarence's tie. It was lying on the counter at Truitt's, and I assumed he didn't want it. I needed silk for my fair entry, and the necktie seemed like a gift from above. And it reminded me of him." The last words slipped out without thought.

All around her, women sighed and giggled. Phrases like "That's so romantic" and "I wish I could find a handsome man's necktie" wafted around the shop. Delia looked down, embarrassed. There was nothing starry-eyed about the stiff reserve that existed between her and Clarence these days.

From behind her, a voice dripped cynicism. "Oh, please."

Gert Waldrop narrowed her eyes. "You seized the opportunity to win, that's all there was to it."

A hush settled over the room as women exchanged wide-eyed glances. There was nothing to do but stand up to the bully in her doorway. Which was fine. She was ready to meet Gert word for word.

"Opportunity to win, something you would know well." Delia arched her eyebrows. "Like the way that horrible rip appeared in my crazy quilt just after your sewing bee."

Splotches of red tinged Gert's cheeks as she stood to her full height. "You can't prove I did that."

"Perhaps not. But what a coincidence that I was unable to repair the damage after you and your mother bought all the silk in town."

Gert blinked in feigned innocence. "My dear, it's a free country. It's called capitalism, in case you've not heard of it."

Lucy held up her hands. "Enough. Gert, we are here to rejoice over our dear friend's fame, in case you haven't read the article. You are welcome to stay and help us celebrate." She leveled a look at Gert, who scoffed.

"Celebrate? I should think console is a better word. The article sheds a poor light on Delia, and I hope you ladies take caution to never do business with someone who steals." Gert cut her eyes at Delia. "Curious, isn't it, what the news wrote about pending nuptials when it's the opposite. Clarence wants nothing to do with you. Far from wedding bells." She waggled her fingers at the women in the shop. "You girls have fun. I have better things to do."

A few beats of silence followed Gert's exit. Delia exchanged looks with Lucy, who rolled her eyes. "Don't pay her any mind. These ladies want the love story. Go ahead."

The love story. If only she were still living it.

Thoughts swirled and refused to focus. *Clarence wants*

nothing to do with you echoed in her ears. The words pierced her.

"That's all." Her heart was too heavy. Looking for some escape from the tabletop, she reached for hands to help her climb down. A few groans made her glance at the women, and their crestfallen expressions gave her pause.

Lucy touched her arm. "Tell them."

Delia blew out a breath as she waited for the sadness to ebb. "His tie fit perfectly. I thought it was meant to be." Swallowing, she tried to utter the next words without emotion. "But Clarence disagreed. You see, I wasn't honest with him when I realized he left it on the counter by accident. I should have told him what I did. Instead, I allowed him to think it was lost. So, naturally, he had second-thoughts about me. I'm afraid we are not destined for matrimony."

And there it was, the ugly truth. Tears stung her eyes. She turned and took helpful hands that guided her down from the makeshift pedestal. As conversation bubbled, the same shrill whistle arrested their attention. Lucy again.

"Now that we've heard the unfortunate story behind the tie in the crazy quilt, I beg you to take pity on our dear friend. After all, who among us hasn't told a tiny fib to the men we love?" She paused to allow the small, embarrassed nods to ripple through the room. "Though we aren't promoting it, we can appreciate a woman's struggle to tell the whole truth. Friends, let's unite as women around our dear sister-in-arms. The beautiful creation hanging in the window proves her finesse with a needle. Won't you please consider hiring her for your dress needs this winter?"

Delia's lips parted in amazement as women fought for a chance to speak to her. Questions flew at her, too many to keep up with.

"I want you to make my Christmas dress."

"Do you make lace?"

"May I purchase your crazy quilt?"

Delia chuckled softly at the teenaged girl before her, who undoubtedly had no clue as to the high price crazy quilts went for. "No, that one isn't for sale, but I'd be glad to make one for you, as long as we can agree on a fair price." Then, at her disappointed expression, she added, "Or I could teach you how to make one yourself."

The girl's eyes grew wide. "You would do that?"

Delia squeezed the girl's arm, whose name, she later learned, was Avanell. "As long as you promise to pass along what I teach you."

By the time the shop emptied, Delia had set appointments with thirty-eight women. Lucy, who'd stayed behind to help restore order to the shop, clasped her hands.

"Congratulations. You are the best-known seamstress west of the Mississippi River. And you know why?"

Delia shook her head, shaking the rumples from the wool she'd been making over.

"Because you accepted responsibility for what happened with Clarence. You could have made it sound like you had no culpability in the matter. And because you admitted your wrong, these women trust you."

Delia shrugged. "Seems a small thing to do." She moved to flip the *Closed* sign on the door before facing Lucy. "How can I thank you?" Her heart swelled as she wrapped her friend in a quick embrace. "Because of all these appointments and the generous commissions I received for crazy quilts, I might have a chance to buy this shop from Eleanor if she's willing."

Lucy said, "Let's not get the cart before the horse. But I'd say you're off to a grand start, my friend."

As they did the last bit of straightening, Delia replayed the last hour. Finally, an end to her gloomy existence. Beauty from ashes, indeed.

As long as Gert didn't try to wreck her newfound joy.

Chapter 24

Mrs. Charley Grimm plans to spend the winter making a crazy quilt from the ties and shirts the Cubs ripped off one another during their pennant-winning celebration. That should be an appropriate memento of a crazy season...—Walla Walla Union Bulletin (Walla Walla, Washington) October 3, 1945.

Delia relayed the events of the day to her mother and Eleanor that night.

"Thirty-eight women want to consult with me about dressmaking. That's at least that many dresses, maybe more. One woman wants a crazy quilt for each of her daughters, and another woman commissioned one to commemorate her parents' lives." She grinned, digging in her bag and hiding her hand behind her back. "Best of all? She paid me, up front." She flashed the bills in front of Mother and Eleanor. Eyes stinging, she said, "And now, I think I have enough for a down payment on the business, Eleanor. That is, if you still want to sell."

"I can't think of anyone I'd rather sell to."

Mother smiled at her as she nursed baby Imajean. "God's

plan always surprises me. When you first told us what happened at the fair, I worried you'd made yourself a bad reputation. But look how the Lord has turned it around for the good."

Eleanor clasped Delia's hands. "You see? Prayer works."

Delia pressed her eyelids shut, then gazed at both women. "This has been an amazing day, everything I've dreamed of." She sobered. "But I wonder if it's worth sacrificing love."

Her heart squeezed in that familiar way since Clarence had walked away. If she'd done things differently, would they still be courting? Planning a future together?

Eleanor shook her head. "I've no doubt of your heartache. But difficult roads make us stronger, if we allow ourselves to grow from the experience." Her smile sagged. "After I found out about Jake's criminal activities, I asked myself if I was the kind of woman who'd turn a blind eye to crime. If not, was I strong enough to walk away? God made the answer clear. It hasn't been an easy path, but it was the right one."

Delia knew it was true. But she didn't want to go through hard times. She thought about Gert's life and how easy it seemed. Why couldn't Delia have it easy?

Beauty from ashes.

And why did those words keep floating through her head?

She watched her mother with Imajean. Having finished nursing, she gently brought the babe to her shoulder and jiggled a burp from the infant. Delia moved to take her sister from her mother. She looked down at the tiny miracle of life.

"Are you soaking up all this womanly wisdom, little sweetie?"

Imajean nuzzled against her blouse with little squeaking sounds, closing and opening her dark eyes as if fighting sleep. When she focused on Delia's face, the depths of the baby's gaze caused Delia's heart to quiver, stirring longing. Would this ever be her future? Or had she lost any chance at a family when Clarence walked away?

She placed Imajean in her cradle and murmured an excuse to leave the room.

"Dinner will be served in a half hour," Eleanor called after her.

Good. She needed time to think. She wandered outside into the bracing wind. She rubbed her arms and walked to the barn. The acrid odor of manure didn't turn her off as it once had. Now it blended with the fresh air, the lowing of the cows, and the slightly sulphureous odor coming from the well. She walked slowly to the edge of their place, close to the lonely road, and faced the house, where a ribbon of smoke rose from the chimney, perfuming the air with the woodsy tang that characterized autumn.

This was home.

The dogtrot cabin, now rosy tinged with the ebbing of the sun, held a coziness that drew her. Funny, the things that created a sense of belonging. Had she ever experienced a connection to their former home, a big rambling house full of large rooms and plush furnishings? But somehow, in the last few months of complaining about what they didn't have, she'd come to appreciate what this downtrodden farm had given them. A sense of belonging. Of family.

She let her head fall back. The dimming sky was so vast. "Lord, I've messed things up, and yet You've blessed me. I don't deserve Your mercy."

A noise startled her, breaking the sacred moment, and she jerked her gaze forward. A black crow sailed from the barn roof to a nearby oak tree. Slow clip-clops on the road behind her made her whirl. A rider on horseback.

He dismounted and lifted his hat in greeting. "Evening, miss."

Unease niggled. This was no neighbor. Fortyish, with a straggly beard and dirt-encrusted clothing, he grinned, showing tobacco-stained teeth. The same man who'd been watching her ride her bicycle into town. She glanced uncertainly at the cabin.

"Do you need something?"

"Well, now, I got me a hankering for a nice, cool drink of water."

She swallowed. The way he looked her up and down suggested he wanted something else.

He stepped closer. "See, I been riding awhile, and need to wet my whistle." His stench covered the distance between them.

"There's a town just up the road." She gestured, but his eyes were trained on her. "There's a hotel, wagon yard, and a cafe."

Though he smiled, his eyes remained cold. She stepped back, signaling an end to the conversation, but he closed the distance. "I'm looking for a friend of mine. Maybe you've seen her."

She swallowed, mentally calculating how far she could get before he overtook her.

"Name's Ellie Baskin. You know her?"

Cold sweat broke out on the back of her neck. What would this stranger need with Eleanor? He narrowed his eyes.

She attempted to steady her breathing. Was this one of the gang members?

His bearded mouth tipped up in a grin, like a cat studying a mouse. "You know her." He stepped closer, placing her within grabbing distance. "She's here, ain't she?"

She shook her head, almost gagging on his body odor. "I don't know what you're talking about."

"I seen you in town. You're that gal been doing Ellie's

sewing while she hides out." His tone was triumphant, and Delia knew this man was no friend of Eleanor.

"I d-don't know what you're talking about," she repeated. Should she scream? But if she did, would Eleanor herself come running? Fear paralyzed her.

Behind her, a twig snapped. "Red, you all right?"

Relief made her knees weak. Rabb walked to her side, his gaze on the stranger. "Why're you here?"

His question sounded strange, almost like he knew this man.

The man took a step toward the road. "Might ask you the same."

Rabb narrowed his eyes. "You looking for me?"

The man lifted a shoulder and let it fall. "Mebbe. Or mebbe looking for my old friend Ellie."

Rabb didn't take his eyes off the man when he told Delia, "Get in the house."

Her lips parted in surprise. "But—"

"Let me handle this."

She hesitated, then turned, and dashed back to the dogtrot, where Thomas sat whittling on the breezeway. "Where's Papa?"

Thomas stood, wood shavings drifting from his lap like snowflakes. "What's wrong?"

"There's a man on the road, asking about Eleanor. Rabb told me to get inside. I think he's a bad man."

Eleanor stood in the open doorway, face pale. "A man wants to see me?"

Delia pumped her head. "He called you Ellie. Says he's an old friend." She stopped before saying surely, he was no friend. But doubt muted her.

"Oh, no." Eleanor grasped the doorframe.

Dread curled within Delia's stomach as Thomas gently but

firmly moved Eleanor out of the way. He reached for the shotgun fastened above the door.

"Pa's with Mother. Tell him to catch up."

Before Thomas could go through the door, Rabb appeared. "No need. The varmint's gone." His gaze zeroed in on Eleanor. "How do you know that fella?"

Eleanor looked ready to faint. Delia stepped between them. "Rabb, do you know that man?"

"We crossed paths. He's a mean cuss." He pointed to Eleanor. "She needs to tell us why he's looking for her."

Eleanor wrung her hands. "It's likely someone who ran with Jake. I never should've come to your home."

"So, you do know him." Thomas still held the gun with both hands. His eyes were sharp as he waited for a reply.

Sympathy warred with caution. Eleanor's strength seemed to have left her, reminding Delia of the bird-like creature who'd been hurt at the parade. "Come and sit, then tell us." Delia led Eleanor to a chair and kneeled beside it.

Mrs. Baskin rubbed her temple. "Awhile back, I saw some men in town. They looked like people my husband associated with."

Thomas stepped closer. "His gang?"

Looking up at him, she nodded. "Ever since I left him, I was terrified Jake would hunt me down. I have something he wants. But then, he went to jail, and I felt I could let my guard down. I hoped so, especially after the reports of his death."

"You say you've got something he wants—or rather, wanted. Is it the loot?"

Eleanor shook her head with a vehemence Delia'd never seen. "No!"

Rabb stood beside Thomas with his hands propped on his hips. "That's what folks say."

"I'm not in cahoots with them. When I found out what he

and his friends were doing, I tried to get away. But each time I ran, he found me." She pulled her hanky from her sleeve and wiped away tears. "He has friends all over. When I finally got out of his clutches, I turned him in. Only when they arrested him did I experience freedom."

Until the gang broke out of jail. Delia swallowed.

She touched her arm. "Eleanor, why would they want to find you?"

The woman squeezed her eyes shut. "I found their money in the false bottom of my trunk. I turned it over to the sheriff."

Thomas's grip tightened on the shotgun resting in the crook of his arm. "But they don't know that?"

Eleanor shook her head. She put her trembling hand to her throat. "I hoped this nightmare was over. But I don't guess it ever will be. I've put you all in jeopardy. I must leave."

The door opened, making all in the room alert until Mother and Baby Imajean entered, with Papa shutting the door behind them. "What's going on?"

Rabb came forward. "We got trouble. I'm going for the sheriff."

Clarence sat at his desk, but his thoughts were anywhere but on the sales receipts before him. He got up and went to the trash bin, where he'd tossed the newspaper. He reached for it, shaking off an apple core that stuck to the pages.

Who else could've done this but Delia?

He wouldn't have thought she'd go so far to get his attention. She, of all people, knew how he regarded his reputation. And this? It made a mockery of his attempt to live as an honest businessman. He looked like a fool.

He dropped it on the desk and rubbed his eyes. It'd been a

busy day, especially for a Monday. Even stingy Mitchell Dean let go of his coins today.

He shuffled the papers into a pile. The numbers would make more sense to him tomorrow. He was too tired to keep at it tonight. He needed a hearty meal and some rest. And maybe another chance to read that write-up.

He secured the building and tucked the newspaper under his arm for the walk to Minnie's Diner. Mondays meant roast beef.

No sooner had he entered the restaurant than a hush settled over the dining room. A quick glance around the room proved he was the object of a dozen different stares. Did he spill something on his jacket? Puzzled, he scanned his attire. A little rumpled, but nothing to garner the attention of every diner in the place.

"The man of the hour," one man called with a grin.

"New tie?" Another said.

"You're famous now!"

The comments came from all directions. Clarence scowled. Yet, all these faces held mirth, not malice. Maybe he was a little sensitive.

He lifted a hand. "Evening. How's the roast beef?"

That got a response. Soon, he was chatting with those who sat around him. Naturally, they inquired about the article. He played it off as best he could.

By the end of his meal, his back had been clapped more times than he could count. He was one of the last customers, and as he prepared to leave coins to cover his meal, the cashier, Dickie Pendergrass, approached.

"Your meal's been paid for."

Stunned, Clarence stuffed the coins into his pocket. "By who?"

Dickie's smile broadened. "You got friends around here.

Consider yourself a lucky man, Clarence." The man grasped his arm, the same as many others had done. "By the way, I'm gonna mosey down to your store this week. Take a gander at a new stove."

Clarence pumped his hand. "I'll give you a special friends-and-family rate."

He said good night and stood for a moment, staring up at the stars. He'd never received that kind of warmth before. He buttoned his jacket, walking slowly down the street. All that attention, because of a lousy newspaper article? He wouldn't give credit to Delia. Still ...

He slowed in front of the seamstress shop. Something was odd. He'd walked this way every day and never taken note of the gleam of those windows. Maybe the moon was brighter tonight.

He moved closer to investigate. His jaw sagged. The glass door was broken, and just beyond, movement and crashing made anger surge. Somebody was destroying Delia's shop.

"Hey! What are you doing in there?"

The figures froze. Then the unmistakable cock of a gun cracked the silence. Clarence threw himself against the wall as bullets whizzed through the air. Heart pounding, he tensed for more. Pinned as he was, he could only hope they wouldn't come looking for him. He'd be easy prey.

He held his breath. No sound. He crawled just far enough to peer inside. No sign of movement.

"Who's there?"

Sheriff Akin and his deputy ran toward him. Clarence scrambled to his feet, fighting past a strange wave of dizziness.

The sheriff whipped out his revolver. "Don't move! Get your hands in the air."

Clarence slowly lifted his hands. "It's Clarence Parker."

The sheriff looked at him a long minute before holstering his gun. "Parker, what's going on here?"

He lowered his hands and pointed to the shattered door. "Two men were in there. Shot at me. They got away out back."

Sheriff Akin gestured for his deputy to go to the back. He stepped up on the boardwalk next to Clarence. "Did you get a look at them?"

"Too dark. But there were two men."

The sheriff muttered under his breath.

The adrenaline surge that filled Clarence with boldness and agility earlier now made his whole body tremble. He gripped the wooden post to steady himself.

The sheriff eyed him warily. "You're bleeding."

Clarence started to protest, then became aware of a growing burning sensation in his right shoulder. He touched the spot, and his fingers came away coated with blood. His blood.

The street swirled and his legs gave way. Hands hooked his underarms, and men shouted before everything went dark.

Chapter 25

A once popular and pretty young lady of Newark has just completed a crazy-quilt composed entirely of silk neckties contributed by gentlemen friends. It is, perhaps, safe to say they are no longer friends.—The Daily Gazette (Fort Wayne, Indiana) April 7, 1885.

Finding she could no longer bear to stay in bed, Delia rose. Images of that horrible man on the road had kept her awake, especially after Rabb couldn't locate the sheriff. She'd started at every hoot or bump in the night. When the baby cried, Delia sat up, alert, until she realized it was only a routine feeding time. No use trying to sleep when her mind pinged with questions.

Darkness held the outside captive, and she slipped across the breezeway to seek relief in the living area. She was surprised to find it already lit. Papa looked over his shoulder, caught in the act of spooning coffee grounds into the pot.

"You're up early."

"So are you. Can I finish that for you?"

He set the spoon down. "All done. Eleanor's out gathering

eggs." He lifted his chin in the direction of the stove. "Biscuits are baking."

Delia blinked. "You let her go out alone?"

"Couldn't stop her." Papa pointed at the table, and she lowered herself to a seat beside him. "Besides, your brothers are walking the place. Now, tell me again what happened last night."

She wilted. "I told you three times."

"Things come to mind after a long night's sleep."

"I hardly know what a long night's sleep is these days." She quickly recounted the meeting with the man. If she told it fast, maybe that image wouldn't float to the surface of her mind.

Papa said, "You're sure you're not leaving out anything?"

"I'm sure."

She rose to fill two coffee cups and placed his in front of him before returning to her seat. The aromatic steam she inhaled comforted her. Looking at him over the rim of the cup, she voiced the question running through her brain. "Do you think he'll come back here?"

Papa rubbed his face. "I'm headed to the sheriff's in a bit. Not taking any chances."

The door opened and Eleanor entered, a basket on her arm. "I'm sorry to keep you folks waiting." She lifted the basket. "The hens were a little miserly. There's only four."

Delia left the table to relieve Eleanor of the basket. "Do me a favor and don't go out alone next time."

Eleanor hung her cape on a peg. "I must admit, my mind played tricks on me out in the henhouse. I jumped at every shadow."

They lapsed into silence, broken only by the scrape of Papa's chair when he refilled his cup. Delia wished she'd brought something with her from the shop to keep her fingers busy. Even the mending basket was empty. Eleanor's short presence in their home had brought a peace and order to the place that Delia hadn't been able to achieve.

The woman laid the plates of food on the table just as Thomas and Rabb walked through the door. They both nodded to Eleanor with a courtesy and deference Delia had not witnessed before now.

The group ate in silence, broken only when Eleanor cleared her throat. "Mr. Truitt, have you considered what I told you last night?"

All movement ceased, causing the words to almost float amongst them. Papa nodded. "I understand you wanting to get out of here. But I'd like you to think about staying."

Thomas said, "We need you. Besides that, I think we can help."

Delia beamed at her oldest brother.

Eleanor's eyes reddened before she dabbed her mouth. "We shall see. I prayed on it last night, and the Lord's answer seems to be stay. But I don't want to bring my problems into your family." Before anyone could object, she rose. "I should take Mrs. Truitt her breakfast and see if she needs help with the baby."

After she left, Papa thumped the table. "You boys see anything this morning?"

Thomas shook his head solemnly. "Nothing missing."

Rabb plucked a biscuit from the emptying platter. "Reckon everything looked fine. But I don't trust the crook, even after I threatened him. Bet he'll be back today."

Delia blinked. "Rabb, what's his name?"

"He goes by Poe. Shady character. He's been showing up to that land where me and my friends practice shooting."

Thomas huffed, as if he knew there was more to this story than Rabb let on. She glanced between her brothers. Maybe she didn't want to know. She'd had too little sleep and too many worries to dig the truth from them.

Papa went to the window and cast aside the curtain. Beyond, the navy sky had lightened to gray. "Almost dawn. I'll be headed into town directly. I'll take the shotgun. You boys keep your rifles with you at all times."

Alarm coursed through her. Papa reached for the shotgun in the corner. He broke it open, then snapped it back together. It rested in the crook of his arm as he went out the door.

A frisson of fear traveled up her spine. *Oh, Lord, protect us all.* "Do you think he'll be all right out there alone? Should one of you go with him?"

Rabb continued eating. "Naw."

She looked to Thomas, who said, "Pa's a fine shot."

"You think it will come to that?"

"If that no-good comes slinking around here again."

Her stomach churned. Who knew what would happen? He'd been so threatening. So sure of himself.

A half hour later, Delia and Eleanor dried the last of the dishes and were putting them away when heavy footsteps preceded the opening of the door. Papa entered, and to her surprise, the sheriff was on his heels, hat in hand. Finally. Where had he been last night when Rabb tried to fetch him?

"Eleanor, Sheriff Akin has some questions for you."

Delia wadded the towel she held as she observed the sheriff's grim expression. Eleanor's smile wobbled as she offered him coffee. When she poured it, her hands trembled. She was so shaky she might drop the cup.

Delia gently took it from her. "Go on, I'll get this."

Eleanor removed her apron and placed it on the counter before standing before the sheriff. How small she looked, across from Papa and Sheriff Akin, almost as if she were a child awaiting a punishment.

The sheriff glanced at Delia before taking the cup and sipping gratefully. "Thank you kindly. Been a long night. Miss Delia, I reckon you need to hear this too."

"Me?" She put her hand to her throat, watching the man gulp the entire cup of hot coffee before he set it on the table.

"Mrs. Baskin, you heard anything from your husband's gang?"

Eleanor's eyes bulged. "No."

Tension held the room still, while in the distance, snatches of Mother's lullaby wafted to them from across the breezeway.

Papa shifted his stance. "Sheriff, yesterday a no-account man came along. Eleanor here thought he might be someone who knew her husband."

Sheriff Akin's brows lifted. He looked at Eleanor. "That right?"

She nodded.

"What's the name?"

The woman's eyelashes fluttered. Was she about to faint?

Delia leaned forward. "Rabb said he goes by Poe."

Tears trailed Eleanor's weathered face. "I don't know if that's his given name. It's what my husband called him. There are others, as well." She took a shaky breath and ticked off the names on her arthritic fingers. "One was Junior, then there was Clem, Howard, Royce. They worked on our farm for years. Since before we married. But there were two younger ones to come along. Eugene and Virgil."

Delia frowned. She'd heard those names coupled together before.

The sheriff wrote the names on a piece of paper.

"I tried to convince myself I was imagining when I saw a man who looked familiar. Until I heard my husband broke out of jail."

He tucked the list in his pocket and sighed. "Virgil Mason,

he's the head of the gang now. Meaner than Big Jake ever was. The gang's after something. Know anything about that, ma'am?"

Eleanor paled. "I handed over everything I found five years ago, when I turned them in."

He nodded. "I believe you. But last night, your shop was broken into. What do you think they wanted?"

Eleanor shut her eyes. "There's nothing."

Sheriff Akin cleared his throat. "Reckon that don't matter, if the gang thinks you're hiding something. They've gotten bold, even shot a citizen of our town."

It was the way the sheriff turned his gaze on Delia that made dread climb up her spine. "It was Clarence Parker."

Terror struck Delia like a hot knife. "Is he ...?"

Sheriff Akin shook his head. "He's hanging on, though he lost a lot of blood. I'm going to see him at the clinic."

She sprang to her feet. "I'm going with you."

The lawman stood. "Nope, you're staying right here."

His gaze circled the room. "That goes for the rest of you too. Can't have y'all taking a chance out there before we get these yahoos."

Delia hurried after him. "You can't leave me here. I must see Clarence."

Papa called after her, but she continued on without looking back. "Sheriff, please."

Clarence opened his eyes to a distant familiar voice. Delia. Where was she? For that matter, where was he? He lifted his head from the pillow and groaned. His whole body screamed, especially his left side. He gingerly touched his left arm. Gauze encircled the upper portion. What happened? Here he lay, chest bared, on some kind of cot in a room so dim he could barely make out a chair and the door.

Delia's wasn't the only far-off voice. A deeper one demanded she get away from the door. Just as cottony sleep threatened to overtake him, the door to his room burst open, causing him to startle, fully awake now. There she stood, pausing on the threshold, a tender smile on her lips. Best sight he'd ever seen.

Behind her, Dr. Taggert appeared. "Miss Truitt! I told you not to come in here. You need to leave at once."

"Not until I make sure he's all right."

The doctor's voice grew edgy. "This is my clinic. Leave."

"I won't stay long."

Clarence extended the arm that worked. "Delia."

In seconds, she kneeled beside him, smelling like the flowers in his mother's garden. He grimaced as she grabbed his hand.

She released it as if it were a hot coal. "I'm sorry. I don't want to hurt you."

He managed a nod and spoke through gritted teeth. "I'm fine."

"I only just heard. Clarence, what were you doing at the shop? Does it hurt where they shot you?"

He frowned. The hazy picture in his mind grew clearer with her words. "Shot?"

Her gaze drifted to the arm with the bandage. "That's what the sheriff said. Someone broke into the seamstress shop, and you tried to stop them. At least, that's the story."

The clearing of a throat reminded them of the ever-present Dr. Taggert. Clarence's vision was clearing, along with his memory of the night before.

"Let her stay."

The doctor came closer. "Clarence, I had to operate on you

to get that bullet out. I've given you two more time than I should, and now it's time for Miss Truitt to leave."

Delia jerked her head up. "I'll be as quiet as a mouse. You'll never know I was here."

"No matter how quiet you are, Clarence won't get any rest if you're around, judging by the hunger in his eyes. Come on, Miss Truitt. If you want the best for him, you'll leave at once."

Reluctantly, she got to her feet, face full of remorse. He couldn't let her go so quickly. Not after all this time apart. They'd bridged the gap their mistakes had cratered.

He reached for her with his good arm. "Don't go."

Delia's heart leaped at his words, ragged as they were. His eyelids blinked slowly. She bent and cupped his cheek.

"Sleep, dear sweet Clarence. I won't go far." If the doctor would allow her at least that much.

His eyelids closed and breathing regulated. She took a moment to study his strong jawline and hollowed cheeks. His pallor made her glad the doctor admonished rest. Just how badly did that bullet wound him, anyway? He'd had surgery, but she hadn't imagined it would drain him of all energy.

"Miss Truitt, come with me."

This time, she nodded. One more long look at Clarence before leaning down to kiss his cool forehead, then she turned to follow the physician to the small hallway outside the room. He stood in the shadows, hands on hips. "If I can't trust you to do as I say, I'll escort you out of my clinic. Are we clear?"

Her gaze fell to the floor. "Yes."

Apparently satisfied with her answer, he gestured curtly to his office, where he shut the door behind her.

"Won't you please leave it open so I can hear him if he calls me?"

"I'll do no such thing. Or do you think you can do my job better than me?"

Delia snapped her mouth shut as he continued, leaving the office door closed. "That man has lost a lot of blood. It took me a while to dig that bullet out of his arm, and he needs rest now."

Her heart dropped. "Is he going to be okay?"

"A good question. One you should have asked before you went bounding into his room."

"I had to see him."

"From now on, you'll see him with my permission and no other time. Do you understand?"

"Fine, of course. Whatever you say. I just need to be close by."

Dr. Taggert's face creased with incredulity. "And I'll remind you yet again, I am his doctor."

Delia inhaled deeply, trying to collect her wits. Her words were slow and deliberate. "I hear and understand, Dr. Taggert. But I promised to remain close by."

"A promise you had no right to make."

"But—"

Dr. Taggert shook his head. "That's final. You'll leave my clinic and come back only at my invitation."

Anger flared. "You cannot force me to leave."

The doctor flung open the door. "Sheriff?"

Heavy footsteps reverberated on the wood floor and Sheriff Akin appeared. Dr. Taggert quickly apprised him of the situation, and Sheriff Akin looked at her with weary eyes. "Just come on with me, Delia. Don't be bothering the doc."

She looked between both men. "I'm not leaving."

Mumbling something like "stubborn woman," he gripped her elbow and pulled her along with him through the doorway.

Outside, she tried to wrench free, but the man's hold was firm. Angry tears blurred her vision as she glared up at him. "Fine, I'll cooperate. Just let go of me."

He narrowed his eyes at her. "So you can run right back in there? Uh-uh." He lifted his chin to someone behind her. "Take this woman home, will you, Rabb?"

Rabb strode forward, and she blanched when he took hold of her. "Why are you here? Get your hands off me."

His grip was even tighter on her arm. Trying to get free would be useless, and she gave in to his quick step toward the waiting horse. "I don't understand why y'all think I'll be in the way."

"Sir, I'll make sure she don't come back."

He mounted and put his arm out to her to help her up, his scowl the only answer he offered her. She hesitated, looking over her shoulder at the closed door of the clinic. The sheriff had moved on down the street. Maybe she could dash through that door and into Clarence's room.

"Don't even try."

She blanched at Rabb's words, fiery anger shooting through her. "Don't tell me what to do." She swatted his proffered arm. "I'm walking."

Rabb uttered a curse. "Why you gotta be so stubborn? I'm trying to do you a favor."

She folded her arms. "So now you're cursing at me. Why don't you go your way and I'll go mine." She started walking toward home. Behind her, Rabb grunted and clicked his horse into a walk. He traveled beside her without comment, all the way down Main Street. When they'd gone the length of it, with only a lonely country lane ahead, he signaled the horse to stop.

"I ain't got time for this. You forget about them outlaws prowling around? Get on up here."

This time, she took his arm and mounted behind him,

wincing at the sight of her stockinged legs as she sat astride. She squealed as Rabb urged the animal into a lope, grabbing him around the waist to keep from falling off. "What are you trying to do?"

"Sorry."

He was no more sorry than she'd been rushing into Clarence's room at the clinic. The memory of him looking so weak and vulnerable made her heart constrict. Her mind replayed the sheriff's account of what happened the night before. Clarence had seen the broken window in the shop and gone to investigate. If only he hadn't been so noble. She'd much rather him take precautions instead of walking straight into danger. What if he'd been shot in the chest or belly? Things would be much worse.

He needed her. He'd as much as said those words. Nothing would stand between them.

But when she returned the next day, his mother was surprisingly fierce. "I would think after all the hurt you've brought my son, you'd leave him be."

The same thing occurred the next day, and the next. Maybe one day, Mrs. Parker would agree to let her see Clarence. Meanwhile, she would sit on the clinic porch and pray for Clarence as she sewed.

Chapter 26

No more "obnoxious" remarks, if you please, Mr. Parson, about that "crazy" bed quilt. —Vermont Phoenix (Brattleboro, Vermont) Friday, June 10, 1881.

Three weeks in this sling was more than Clarence could stand. The cloth might as well have been a calling card for every person he passed on the sidewalk.

"Hey, Clarence, you doing all right? Heard about the shooting. Been praying for you."

"Mr. Parker, you're taking it easy, aren't you? No use in breaking that wound open."

He'd wearied of his loss of privacy. He couldn't walk down the street without someone or three stopping him.

It was sweet. Kind, even. But he didn't want to dwell on the bullet wound and how an inch or two would have changed everything. After three weeks, the pain had settled down some. Still, he wished his full range of movement would return, as well as his stamina.

One good thing was his landlady's extra helpings on his

breakfast plate, and the fact that she'd hold his dinner warm in the oven until he returned home from work, no matter the time. Though he'd had few late nights this week. His manager was an upstanding man, a fine stand-in for when he'd been out or had to leave early.

Now, as Clarence walked down the street on his way to the town meeting, the seamstress shop stood just ahead in its desolate manner. Boards covered the windows where glass had once been. His thoughts darted to the last time he saw Delia. The memory of her kneeling beside his bed circled his dreams.

But that'd been the only time she'd come. Each lonely day she stayed away, his disappointment grew. He tried not to think about it. It hurt too much. Instead, he'd concentrate on getting back to normal.

If he even knew what normal was. Everyday life had taken on a melancholy tone. The others in town must sense it. They had to. There had been multiple town meetings since the break-in and shooting. The first two he'd missed, thanks to being laid up. But he headed now to the third, to be held in the Kerr Street Church.

He took off his hat when he walked through the doors and tried to smile politely when folks inquired about his health. All around him, people filed into the sanctuary, which was twice the size of his church. But with practically the whole town streaming into the building, latecomers would be relegated to standing along the walls.

He slipped into a pew and took the end seat, where he could shield his arm from bumps and jostles. Of course, that meant he'd have to stand every few minutes to allow people to pass to a place on the pew. So, when a light touch and a soft voice prompted him to stand again, his heart lurched to find himself face to face with Delia Truitt.

How long they stood there without speaking, he couldn't

say. Long enough to make his pulse ratchet and palms sweat. Long enough to want to reach out and gather her in his arms. Long enough to rein in that double-crossing impulse. She'd promised to return to the clinic. Only, she hadn't.

Chill filled his words. "Evening, Miss Truitt."

The hopeful expression in her brown eyes shuttered as if she'd pulled down a shade, making him regret his aloofness. She matched his tone. "Good evening, Mr. Parker. I just need to find a seat ... well, never mind." Her gaze wavered, and she stepped around him.

"There's room here, if you wouldn't mind sitting near me."

She turned back, clearly uncertain. He shouldn't have said anything. It was obvious she didn't want to see him. But she surprised him when her lips tipped in a brief smile. "Thank you."

In the crowded room, tobacco, sweat, and unbathed odors combined, making Delia's light floral scent refreshing as she passed him to enter the row. Longing took him by surprise. He averted his eyes as she sat two people down from him. He returned to his spot, but like a fly drawn to honey, he couldn't resist looking at her one more time. As if by agreement, she glanced his way. Their gazes locked.

A bell jangled, jarring their silent communication, and Clarence reluctantly turned his attention to Mayor Clive Waldrop on the raised platform where the minister typically stood. That man was a far cry from a preacher.

"Citizens of Blooming Grove, find a seat so we can get started."

The sanctuary hushed in anticipation. Clarence glanced over his shoulder at the doorway. People still filed in, though the steady stream had slowed to a trickle. Latecomers stood shoulder to shoulder along the perimeter of the room.

"I've called this town meeting because there's been a development the sheriff would like to tell you about."

Sheriff Akin stepped onto the platform. Without his ever-present wide-brimmed Stetson, his thick white hair and bags underneath his deep-set eyes harkened to the mounting strain of his role. Clarence had heard rumors of the man not seeking re-election. The job, especially these last tense weeks, had taken a physical toll on him.

"I have news."

An upstart from somewhere in the back shouted, "You made any arrests, Sheriff?"

The lawman grinned. "I did indeed, Dooley. Matter of fact, I got two men sitting in a cell, waiting on the next train to the county seat. They'll stand before the judge, charged with vandalism and attempted murder."

Clarence's face heated as heads swiveled his direction. He kept his eyes focused on the sheriff as he laid out the case.

"The men I arrested are members of Jake Baskin's gang."

"Thought he was killed?"

Sheriff Akin lifted a hand. "Dooley, if you'll give me a chance, I'll tell you all of it."

Chuckles traveled through the crowd.

Sheriff Akin cleared his throat, and the laughter died. "I've had my men on the lookout. Y'all been watching, too, since we hung the Wanted posters around town. After one of you told us about seeing a couple fellas skulking around outside the city limits, my deputies rounded them up and brought them in for questioning."

Clarence leaned forward. No names had been given. Could it have been his old pals, Eugene and Virgil? Rumors circulated that Eleanor Baskin had identified some of the gang members. Clarence wasn't sure they'd kept their membership in the gang, but it wouldn't surprise him if they had.

He'd seen the Wanted posters. Virgil's image wasn't right, though Eugene's was strikingly similar to reality. He wasn't sure which of them had put a bullet in his brother. Not that it mattered. As far as he was concerned, they were both guilty of murder.

"... so you all can stop your fretting. Go on about your lives without worrying one of these criminals will appear. I am certain these no-accounts were the only two in our vicinity. Once they've boarded the train for Corsicana and a trial, they'll be gone forever. Blooming Grove will return to the safe, friendly town it's always been before these two did their damage."

"Hey, Sheriff, what about that seamstress woman? I heared she was in on it. That true? She got some loot stowed?"

The audience murmured. This time, the sheriff didn't wait for the crowd to quiet before he answered. "I ain't talking about Mrs. Baskin or anything else pertaining to the case. Not before the trial. I reckon you know that, Dooley, since your daddy's a lawyer. But I'm gonna say one thing—this town might oughta think about showing that woman a little kindness."

This put a stop to further comments. Within minutes, the meeting adjourned and everyone filed from the church. Outside, dusk softened the landscape into hues of lavender and gray, and the November chill made Clarence button his coat. As before, people stopped Clarence to converse. Their chatter didn't register with him as he kept one eye out for Delia.

She was one of the last to emerge from the building, walking beside Lucy. She glanced at the different clusters of people. Was she looking for him? Their gazes met, and hope rose within him when she walked his direction. Her beauty struck him anew the closer she got. The pulse in his neck throbbed, and he murmured a quick apology before breaking away to meet her.

Standing before her, his words vanished. She seemed guarded, giving him only a polite smile, as if he were a stranger. They were back to this.

"I wanted to inquire about your health."

He winced at her formality. Had she given up on them? But he squelched the rising desire to take her in his arms. An impulse he didn't care to visit. He returned her manner as he nodded. "I'm doing well, thank you. And yourself?"

She looked down, fidgeting with the small bag she carried. The brim of her straw hat hid her face from him, and he wanted to tip her chin so he could gaze at her.

"I am quite well, now that the sheriff has arrested those men."

He swallowed, words refusing to come. Aw, crumb. This was all kinds of awkward.

Her gaze flickered over the dispersing crowd, brows drawn. "I hope they are all gone now."

"Gang members?"

"I suppose I'm just a worrywart. I'm sure everything is fine." But the furrow between her eyebrows only deepened.

Before he could comment, she changed the topic. "I guess you heard I'm buying Eleanor's business."

He rocked back on his heels. "The seamstress shop?"

She nodded. "I have an appointment with the bank to make the necessary arrangements. Papa and my brothers will make the repairs needed after those awful men vandalized it. After that, I'll be open for business."

A regular businesswoman. "Reckon you're proud of yourself."

"It's been my dream, you know."

"I know." Only too well.

Her cheeks pinked. "That silly news article about us, remember the one? Well, despite the horrible damage in the shop, I keep getting orders for dresses. Three women came all the way from Dallas, wanting to commission crazy quilts. They offered more money than I thought possible."

Ah. And there it was. "Guess you got everything you wanted."

Her glib expression cracked as she met his gaze. "Not everything."

Couldn't he read between the lines? Here she was, practically throwing herself at him, and he just stood there with his mouth open. Well, fine. She'd spell it out, plain and clear.

"The only thing missing is you."

The pulse in her neck raced. She'd taken a bold step, and she held her breath for his response.

He blinked and stepped back from her. A frisson of dread snaked through her belly. "Well, there's a surprise."

Her heart plunged at the steel in his voice. "W-why?"

His chuckle held no mirth. "Maybe because you say one thing and do the opposite."

Her breath caught. "What do you mean?"

"I need to go." He turned, but she caught his arm.

"You're mad at me?"

A couple of women walking by slowed, exchanging glances with each other. Clarence took her arm and guided her to a more out-of-the-way spot for their conversation.

Splaying her hands, she said, "Well, are you?"

His shoulders lifted. "Not mad. Just wise. Guess I've learned a thing or two about how you do things."

"What a hurtful thing to say."

"Experience is the best teacher."

She crossed her arms. "You're referring to the tie, once

more? I can't count all the times I've apologized to you, Clarence. You resent me instead of letting go of your anger."

"What are you talking about?"

She folded her arms against the heat rising within her core. "You can't tolerate anyone who does something wrong. Instead of forgiving, you hold a grudge."

"I don't do that."

"Let's see, there's me, of course. Then your father—"

"What?"

"And the death of your brother."

"You expect me to forget Joe was murdered?"

She pressed her hand to her throat. Perhaps she'd overstepped, but the words had to be spoken. "I'm not talking about the killers. I'm talking about *you*."

He stared at her. A muscle ticked in his jaw.

She took a breath and softened her tone. "Clarence, the reason you can't forgive others is because you can't forgive yourself for Joe's death."

"Don't."

Tears burned her eyes. "Do you hear yourself? You're angry. Defensive. It's affecting everyone you love."

"I don't want to talk about this."

"You know it's true. How will you ever find happiness if you don't learn to forgive?"

His eyes smoldered. "I might not forgive, but at least I don't lie."

"What?"

He shook his head. "Don't deny it. What about that day at the doc's when you promised to come back? You lied. You never intended to come back, did you? Fool that I was, I believed you."

She rocked back. "You think I didn't try?"

"Guess you had better things to do than be with me while I

mended from the gunshot wound. Maybe you had few commissions to make."

Shock silenced her reply. Her heart ached at the venomous words. Maybe this was it, the thing from which they could never recover.

"Your mother wouldn't let me visit you."

He set his hands on his hips and studied the ground. Seconds slipped by, and the longer the silence grew, her confidence faded.

Deep in her soul, a message resonated, as if someone murmured straight into her heart. *See him.*

She stepped back. What did that mean?

The words came to her again. *See him.*

Swallowing hard, she looked at Clarence once more. But this time, it was as if a film of dirt lifted, allowing her to imagine him differently. A troubled youth, looking for acceptance. A desperate runaway whose guilt drove him far from home until, at last, he found the one thing that filled his wounded soul. Jesus.

The hands that rested at his hips trembled. Her heart squeezed. This wasn't just a man who'd rejected her. Clarence was the culmination of everything good and bad that had happened to him over the years, just like her.

She touched his sleeve. "I don't want to argue. I care about you."

A muscle in his jaw worked as he stared at her, not speaking. Finally, he jerked his head once. "Look, I'm not saying I don't care. I just need a little time. All right?"

Chapter 27

As illustrating the feminine idea of business, a Belle Plain (Kas.)
woman cut up $250 worth of silk and velvet to make a crazy
quilt.—Lorain County Reporter (Elyria, Ohio) July 2, 1892.

In the days after the town meeting, Delia threw herself into plans for her shop. It seemed to help whenever she considered how uncertain things were with Clarence. Now, she was about to take a significant step, and she needed her wits about her. Nerves caused her stomach to roll when she, Eleanor, and Papa walked through the door of the bank to speak with Clive Waldrop.

"Remember, I'll do the talking," Papa said, looking at Delia. She wasn't surprised, but it rankled. After all, he had to sign for her, since women weren't granted bank loans.

Mr. Waldrop rose when his secretary ushered them into his private office. He bade them to be seated in the chairs in front of his mahogany desk. The man treated Eleanor with distrust, making Delia's hackles rise. Papa must have sensed her indignation, for he shook his head almost imperceptibly. She bit her lip to keep the words silent.

The banker studied Papa. "I must say, Will, I had my doubts about issuing a loan in your name after your financial troubles in Georgia."

Papa's face was stony, though his ears turned crimson. "My brother can vouch for me."

Mr. Waldrop sighed. "And so he has. You're lucky, you know, having Robert in your corner. He's one of my best customers."

Delia looked at the floor, ashamed to witness her father's embarrassment. Had he feared being turned down for the loan in front of his daughter?

She snuck a glance at him. The redness in his face had drained, leaving no sign of embarrassment as he answered questions pertaining to the financial agreement. Papa had risked his own humiliation to help her. Her vision blurred, and she pressed her lips together to keep emotion at bay.

The men used unfamiliar terms as they discussed the loan. She fought the insecurity that overwhelmed her as she watched the business dealings as if she were a spectator. But this was her shop they were talking about. Payments she would make. Questions circled her mind. What if she missed a payment? What if her customers changed their loyalty to some other dressmaker? They'd already proven a fickle lot. She'd have to be wise in her dealings, gathering new clients while managing the old. Purchase materials and supplies in a thrifty manner. It both excited and worried her. But in this office, she might as well be a decoration on a mantle for all the input she gave.

Maybe when it came time to sign papers, she'd be included. But Mr. Waldrop handed the pen to Papa without a glance at her.

She leaned forward, her voice squeaking. "May I?"

A flash of annoyance creased Mr. Waldrop's brow. He

glanced at Papa and chuckled with condescension. "No need, Miss Truitt. Your father and I are taking care of all the details."

He gestured for Papa to proceed. Delia put a hand on the desk. "And what about Eleanor? She's the seller, shouldn't she—"

Clive Waldrop held up a hand, his tone firm. "Your father will sign for her as well, since her husband is deceased. Really, Miss Truitt. Leave this to the men."

Even Papa frowned. "Delia, you must let us continue without interruption."

"But—"

Eleanor caught her attention and shook her head slightly. Delia schooled her breathing. What she wouldn't give to grab those papers and scrawl her name in big, bold letters. Frustrating as this was, though, she must abide by convention. No use in pitching a fit and proving herself too immature for this endeavor.

But the longer she sat without speaking, the more her anger grew. When the men finally stood and shook hands, she couldn't stand by any longer. She stormed out of the bank, pacing on the boardwalk as she waited for the others.

Papa helped Eleanor onto the wagon seat. He turned to Delia, but she shook her head, fury seeping from every pore.

"Papa, I'm grateful you went there with us, but why didn't you insist I take part in the discussion? At least write my own name, promising to make timely payments. It's my business, yet you men ignored me. So unfair." Without aid, Delia climbed onto the seat and sat heavily on the wagon bench beside Eleanor. "Women have just as much right to discuss finances as men do."

Eleanor inclined her head. "It's just one of those little injustices we women must put up with."

"But I don't want to put up with it. I want to be treated with respect."

Papa settled beside her and sat a moment, reins slack in his loose hold. "I agree to a point. However, daughter, respect is earned." His gaze landed on her tightly crossed arms. "To do that, you must be even-tempered."

She huffed.

Eleanor spoke softly. "If you want things to change, take it to the Lord in prayer."

Papa slipped the loan papers from his coat pocket. "But don't allow your sense of justice to overshadow the celebration." He offered them to Delia. "Congratulations. You are now a business owner."

Her breath caught as she clasped the agreement. This was it, the making of her dreams, even if the document didn't bear her signature. She swallowed. "I appreciate you making this possible, Papa."

He paused, seeming to weigh his words. "I've no doubt you can do anything you set your mind to, Delia. I-I'm proud of you." He clicked the horse into action.

Warmth filled her. When had he ever said those words to her?

They drove through town in silence, but when they'd cleared the town limits, Papa turned his head so both women could hear above the horse's hooves on the packed dirt road. "I appreciate you both remaining silent. Clive Waldrop wields a lot of power in this town and could have made things difficult."

"He's unbearable."

"I couldn't agree more." Papa harrumphed to punctuate the sentiment.

Delia let her gaze roam beyond the wagon to the endless pastures around them. When she'd first arrived, she'd considered this place a desert. Now, it appeared almost lush, even as autumn crested. Though she'd miss living in the quiet of the country, she needed to live in town, in the apartment over the shop. Her parents wouldn't welcome the idea.

Might as well begin the discussion now. "Papa, now that I have a business with a banknote to pay, I think I should live in town."

He said nothing, but a muscle in his jaw ticked.

Eleanor nodded, apparently oblivious to the tension hanging in the air. "The apartment over the shop should suit you just fine. It's very cozy, you know. I'll need to move the rest of my things out, to free up space for you." She flashed a smile at Delia.

Papa cleared his throat. "An unmarried young lady living alone is not appropriate."

Delia let her head fall back in frustration. Exactly as she predicted. "I'm not an unmarried young lady, I'm a businessowner. You just said it yourself. Besides, the apartment over the shop is in a well-populated section of the town. Perfectly safe. Tell him, Eleanor."

"Oh, don't involve me in this."

"But you're already in the middle of it. You lived there all by yourself. Please, help me convince him."

Papa's ears reddened, just as they had in the bank. She might as well not push, lest she ruin all chances of living in town.

Over the next few days, she reminded him of the living space above the shop, and how convenient it would be to reside there. Persistence paid off when she brought up the subject a final time one evening after supper and Papa said yes. With one condition.

"You cannot live alone."

She gaped. "You mean a roommate? But who?"

Mother spoke up from the rocking chair, where she jostled

a fussy Baby Imajean on her shoulder. "Another unmarried lady of high moral character."

Papa perched on a chair, fiddle in hand, and plucked a few strings before adding, "If you can't find anyone, you'll remain living under our roof."

He lifted the instrument to his chin and coaxed a lullaby from it. Delia slipped from the room, drawing her shawl close against the crisp breeze. The fiddle's melody faded behind her, and she lifted her face to the gray sky, considering who she might seek to live with her. Women her age either lived with their parents or they lived in a home shared with a husband.

After church, she tugged Lucy away from their group of friends. "Would you like to move in with me?"

"Of course, I want to. But I have my little brothers to care for when my parents are at the wagon yard. How about Sallie?"

Delia chewed her lip, considering. "It's not been the same between us since ..."

Lucy nodded. "The tie. But you never know until you ask."

She wasn't ready to face her friend. She wasn't sure how she felt about Clarence's sister living with her. But after talking with several single young women and reaching a dead end, she decided she might as well ask Sallie. She caught her before she left for home, and said the words fast. "You ought to know, I've asked others before you, because ... well, we're not close anymore. In fact, forget I said anything."

Sallie adjusted her glasses. "You're moving out of your parents' home?"

"Well, only if I can find an unmarried woman of high morals, as Mother says. And, of course, you fit that description. You probably don't want to live in a cramped little space with me, though." Delia shrugged as if this awkward conversation didn't make her heart heavy.

After a few seconds of silence, Delia nodded. "It's fine, I'll find someone else."

"No. I'll do it." Sallie looked toward the wagon where her parents waited.

"Are you sure?"

Sallie's lips pinched as she nodded. "I should go."

Delia blinked. This was almost too easy. "Wait—you do understand that you'll be rooming with me?"

Sallie sighed. "Delia, I forgave you a long time ago. I just don't like what you did."

"Me, either." The words were soft.

"I'll have to make arrangements." Mr. Parker called her name, and Sallie walked toward the wagon where her parents waited.

Delia called after her. "How about Wednesday?"

"The sooner the better. Anything for some peace and quiet."

"I'm not sure how quiet an apartment on Main Street will be, especially with the train tracks so close."

"Believe me, anything is better than listening to my parents quarrel."

It was the first mention of the Parkers' discontent, but Delia wasn't surprised. Mr. Parker was a gruff man. As she stood watching the Parkers drive away from the church, Clarence called out and jogged to their wagon. A pang of longing shot through Delia's heart. Earlier, when she'd talked to friends, she'd purposely avoided him. Now, she couldn't rip her gaze away from where he spoke to his family. As if he knew she watched, he looked over. Her pulse jumped as their gazes held across the churchyard. Finally, he turned away, leaving her empty inside.

Thankfully, Delia was too busy to think about Clarence. Between packing her trunk and making sure her bicycle was loaded in the wagon, she barely had time to kiss the top of Baby Imajean's sweet little head.

Eleanor stood at the door to the living room and thrust a parcel into Delia's hands. "Goodies for you girls to snack on."

"Thank you. You're so generous."

"You're the one giving me a gift. Long ago, I sensed the Lord urging me to give up the shop, that He had something better in mind. Just look at how it's turned out. You are the perfect woman to take it over, though I still wish you would have allowed me to give it to you."

But then it wouldn't really be hers. "I needed to purchase it myself."

The woman made a shooing motion. "Now get to that wagon, or your brother might leave without you."

Outside, Mother waited on the covered porch and walked with Delia.

"My first baby bird is leaving the nest. I admit, I didn't think it would be you. Not this way. I so wish you wouldn't move into town."

Delia dipped her head. Guilt warred with anticipation. "Mother, I know you wanted me to be like other women and wait until I'm married to leave home. But that's just not who I am."

Mother's laugh held no humor. "Yes, I know."

Delia prickled. "Just because I'm different doesn't mean I'm wrong."

"I just never dreamed my daughter would be so unconventional."

Delia tried another tactic. "Sewing isn't the most progressive job, but at least I'm able to contribute to our family. Did you know I received five new dress orders this week? I'll have to work into the night to keep up with the demand." She touched Mother's arm. "That apartment over the shop will be a blessing to me. And eventually, to all of us."

Mother rubbed her fingers as they walked. "That big window puts you in full view of whoever walks by."

Delia smothered a sigh. "Folks will see me working hard. That's good for business."

"But not all people are well-intentioned, Delia, like those horrible men who tore the shop apart."

"The sheriff said they're gone. Please don't worry about me. I'll be fine."

"Still, I worry ..."

Delia responded with an indulgent smile. "If it will make you happy, I'll sew curtains to cover that window." Though when she'd find time was the question.

At the end of the drive, Thomas and Rabb loaded Delia's few possessions and climbed aboard the wagon. Delia kissed her mother's cheek. "This is a good thing, Mother. Remember, I'm making money so we can have a better life."

Her mother shook her head and pulled her shawl tighter. "Keep your money. God provides all our needs."

She squeezed Mother's hand, then took Thomas's hand to clamber aboard. As Rabb flicked the reins, Delia blew a kiss to her family and the homey little dogtrot.

A new life awaited, just around the bend.

Chapter 28

*"A piece of Miss Alcott's best gown" was the written
endorsement that came with a scrap of black velvet, which is
embroidered with a large A in blue silk, illuminated with
carnation pinks.—Herald & Torch Light (Hagerstown,
Maryland) October 8, 1885.*

From his perch on the wagon seat parked adjacent to the seamstress shop, Clarence peered at the spot where his life came to a crossroads. The hair on the back of his neck rose. Gunshots ricocheted in his memory. Blood had flowed to the boardwalk. His blood. Now it would be no more than a stain on the planks. He looked away. Nightmares still jolted him awake, drenched in sweat and panting like he'd run a footrace.

The shop hadn't changed much since that terrible night, except for the new window with fancy gold letters that spelled out *Dressmaker*. The brick storefront was deceptively peaceful.

"Hmm." Sallie peered at the watch on her necklace. "We are a little early."

Good. He wanted a chance to talk to her. "I'm still confused about why you're moving in with Delia."

Sallie picked invisible dirt from underneath her nails. "I don't know."

He gave her shoulder a gentle bump with his own. "You can tell me."

Her hands sagged. He'd been right. Something created that wrinkle between her eyebrows.

"Mama and Pa fight a lot."

"He's not hitting her, is he?"

She shook her head. "No."

"You?"

"Pa barely acknowledges me."

How well he understood. "Then, what?"

In the silence, she twisted her fingers. "They fight about you."

"Me?"

Tears spilled from her eyes. "When you got shot, she tried to go right then and be with you, but Pa wouldn't let her." She hiccupped with emotion. "Mama cried all night."

It wasn't a surprise, exactly. But this was a new low, even for Pa. What kind of man would prevent his wife from going to the aid of her injured son?

"Aw, Sallie." He brought her close, and she buried her head on his shoulder.

At least now he knew why his mother hadn't come running that first night. But she'd stayed by his side all the days following. Unlike Delia.

"Sis, can I ask you something?"

Sallie nodded. He said, "Remember when I was in the clinic?"

"Of course."

"Did ... anyone try to visit?"

"What do you mean? Lots of folks asked after you."

He twisted his mouth. He'd have to just say it. "Delia said Ma turned her away, said she tried to see me."

Sallie straightened and removed her spectacles, rubbing them on her hem. "That's so."

He almost fell off the wagon seat. "You mean, she really did try to visit?"

She folded the specs and tucked them into her pocket, whisking residual moisture from her face. "She did."

He settled back against the seat. "Well, what do you know."

Behind them, the jingle of an approaching wagon drew their attention. Sallie peered over her shoulder, then gasped as she patted her upswept hair. "Am I presentable?"

He looked at her swollen eyes and blotched face. She looked terrible. But he wouldn't tell her. Instead, he hugged her. "If you can't be yourself with your best friend, that's pretty sorry."

"I'm not talking about Delia. I can't let Rabb see me like this."

"Rabb Truitt?" He was the last man Clarence would've chosen for his sister. "He's a womanizer."

She lifted a finger to her lips. "Shh. He might hear you."

Clarence grunted. Keeping his opinion to himself on the matter of Rabb Truitt was next to impossible. Oh, sure, he liked the fella just fine. But not for his sister.

"Come on." Sallie climbed down.

Before he considered his actions, Clarence jumped to the ground. He hissed as pain radiated through his arm with the jarring movement. He rubbed his healing arm.

"Hey, we'll get your load, buddy."

Clarence nodded his thanks. He'd be glad when all traces of that bullet wound disappeared. Downright tiresome not to be at full strength.

Rabb tipped his hat to Sallie. "How do, Miss Sallie."

Clarence stepped closer. He'd best treat her like a lady, not like some of those floosies he attracted. He opened his mouth to say something but stopped short when he caught the smile on Sallie's face. In the span of two minutes, she'd gone from distraught to dreamy. And all for a man like Rabb Truitt.

She peeked around him and giggled. "Oh, Rabb, it's so nice to see you."

Clarence ground his teeth. Sallie, giggling? He needed to stop this nonsense before she ended up hurt.

Delia emerged from the train depot where she'd insisted her brothers drop her. To her delight, a package awaited her with a Dallas return address. Fabric from the woman who placed an order for a crazy quilt, no doubt. She hurried toward the shop, but her footsteps faltered when she spotted Clarence. Everything within her froze. What was he doing there?

Of course. He was helping Sallie move in. Her heart flipped as she stood watching him. If only things could be different between them. Things were so awkward between them now. Every time she spotted him, she couldn't stop tracking his movements. If only she could forget him. But there wasn't much chance of putting him out of her mind now that Sallie would be living with her.

She resumed her walk to the shop, only now she made sure her steps were unhurried. Wouldn't want the man to think she was eager to be with him. The closer she came to him, the harder her heart pounded. What should she say? All wit and wisdom evaporated, leaving her tongue-tied.

She had to speak to him. Snubbing him was out of the question. Wasn't it? Yes, of course. She couldn't be rude.

Hello. That was all she needed to say. Just hello. Maybe hello, then inquire as to his health. Or, she could say hello, inquire as to his health, and then comment on the fine weather they were having. Yes, that was a good plan. She took three more steps and opened her mouth to recite the mental script. But when she glanced down at the dark red spot on the boardwalk, she blanched. His blood. Her mouth dried. Though she'd stared at that horrific reminder before, this was different. Her knees shook, seeing Clarence against the backdrop of his spilled blood. What a terribly close brush with death. How could she pretend she didn't care about him? The thought of his near death made her nauseous.

Delia's horror-filled expression made him step closer, concerned. "May I take that for you?"

When she hesitated, Clarence added, "That parcel looks light enough for me."

A joke, at his own expense. But instead of laughing, she paled. He scooped the package from her, wincing when pain radiated from his bum arm. No way would he give an indication that he couldn't hold onto a parcel.

She stared beyond him, that strange expression still there.

"Are you all right? Need to sit down?"

She shook her head with a frown.

He adjusted the package so he could take her elbow. "How about I open the store for you?"

Wordlessly, she fumbled through her tiny bag.

He shifted his feet. How hard could it be to find a key? "Need me to look?"

She shook her head, finally producing the key. Adjusting

the package to lodge under his bad arm, he turned the key in the lock and gestured for her to enter.

But she just stared at him with that dazed expression. He glanced back at the wagon, where Sallie chatted with Delia's brothers. "Uh, don't you wanna go in?"

Delia didn't move, but stared up at him as if searching for answers. "How are you?"

"Fine." The word stretched with uncertainty. What was wrong with her? "Business keeps me plenty busy." He offered her the key and noticed the tremble in her fingers when she accepted it. He purposely made his tone light. "Some nights, I have to force people to leave."

Once again, he held out his arm for her to precede him into the building. This time, she did, with sure steps. Relieved, he followed, glad to see her normal coloring return to her face. Whatever caused her to be woozy must have passed. If he lived to be one hundred, he'd never figure her out.

She blinked rapidly, then smiled, and she seemed back to her normal self. "The article brought us both prosperity. I wish we knew who to thank."

"Or strangle."

She laughed softly. "Perhaps that too. Still, this shop was dying a swift death. Now I have an avalanche of new business." She laid her hand on his sleeve. "Clarence, thank you for what you did that night."

He stared at her fingers resting on his arm. Heat crawled up his neck. He forced his gaze to meet hers. "No need to thank me." He lifted the postal box. "Where do you want me to put this?"

Surprise and something like disappointment played over her face. "I'd appreciate your running it upstairs."

To her living quarters?

He climbed the stairs and laid the package on a small table

just inside the bedroom. He rushed back down to the first floor. No way he'd let her brothers catch him up there.

Delia took charge of the move in, pointing to the places where items should settle. Rabb, Thomas, and Sallie carried items inside while he stood useless.

Delia crooked her finger. "I have just the job for you." She placed a wooden bowl of spools in his hands.

"What's this?"

"Would you load these spools into the sewing cabinet?" She demonstrated by pulling out each of the four wooden drawers on the Singer sewing machine. He frowned down at the container brimming with colored thread. How had he attached himself to woman's work? Her brothers best not tease him. Envy wormed through him at the sight of Thomas and Rabb lifting bags and trunks like they weighed no more than a feather. If not for his healing wound, he'd be doing the heavy lifting too.

Muttering under his breath, he tossed spools into each of the drawers but paused when he got to the last. It was different. Shallower.

He lifted his gaze, only to find her watching him. His heart did a strange leap. He straightened. Time to leave.

He approached Sallie as she rubbed the table with a cloth. "Need me for anything else?"

Her smile was genuine. "I give you permission to leave if that's what you need. Thanks for helping me."

"Didn't do much, thanks to this bum arm. Just drove you here."

"And that's what I needed. Do me a favor. Check on Mama, will you?"

He agreed and kissed her on the cheek before nodding at Thomas and Rabb. He avoided looking at Delia, though it was hard. But why stoke the embers of a relationship destined to fail? Too much had passed between them to ever start anew.

Delia walked to the window and watched Clarence pull the wagon away from the building. He left so abruptly.

Disappointment settled on her like a heavy blanket. She turned away and trudged up the stairs. What a mess. Clothing and boxes were strewn everywhere. With a huff, she picked up the box that had come in the mail. Clarence had left it in the middle of the floor. Men!

With an exasperated sigh, she tore the paper wrapping. Inside, a sealed envelope sat atop dozens of silk fabric swatches in a beautiful array of colors. Her fingers itched to begin a new project.

She slid the correspondence out of its envelope, and gasped when paper money floated to the floor. So many bills. In her mind, she totaled the amount as she picked each one up and stared in wonder. It was a third more than the wealthy client agreed to pay. A mistake? Or gift?

Either way, it was provision. "Lord, thank you."

She tucked the bills away in her bag and slid the box of silk scraps underneath her bed. She went downstairs in search of someone with whom to share her news. But the shop was empty.

Laughter rose in the distance. They must be in the back. She hugged herself. What a glorious day. And this place. The repairs brought a freshness to the space that hadn't existed before the break-in and vandalism. Fresh paint covered the walls, and plaster patched the holes. Even the curtains that separated the front area from the back room were crisp and cheerful, thanks to Aunt Mary's gift of red calico. The drapes meant her clients would have a proper dressing room, something the shop had lacked before now.

Her customers would find this place charming in this light, airy space. The teakettle she'd purchased to replace the damaged one stood proudly on the stovetop.

"Rabb, Thomas, this is amazing."

Thomas peeked around the curtain. "Happy to help you out."

Sallie smiled as Rabb passed, hauling Delia's trunk. "It looks mighty nice in here, you two."

He lifted his chin in acknowledgment and Sallie's face turned red.

Delia crossed to the Singer sewing machine where Clarence had worked only moments before. Running her fingers over the solid machine, she admired the oak cabinet encasing it, and the curlicued embellishments on the four wooden drawers. Gorgeous. It had withstood the vandalism, miraculously. Or perhaps the men hadn't found it before Clarence discovered them. Regardless of the reason, the Singer sewing machine stood at the ready, and she was thankful not to be forced to order a new one.

Who can find a virtuous woman? For her price is far above rubies. Proverbs 31:10

Just as she had the first time she saw the engraving, she wondered about the story behind the inscription. She straightened, brushing the dust from her fingers. Eleanor was indeed a virtuous woman. The prospect of filling her shoes was daunting. What this town had missed when they chose to forsake her.

She grabbed a soft cloth and made quick work of cleaning. Curious, she pulled out a drawer. Just as she thought, Clarence had filled it with no thought of organization. She should've directed him to sort like colors together.

One by one, she emptied the spools back into the wooden bowl and withdrew the drawers from the sewing cabinet, placing them side by side on the table-like arm of the Singer. She paused, frowning, as she peered at the one drawer not quite like the others.

She glanced up to find Thomas beside her. He gestured to the drawers. "I wanted to clean the machine up real nice for you, but we ran outta time." His dirt-smudged overalls testified to his hard work, along with the lock of dark hair pasted to his sweaty forehead.

"You've done more than enough already. But take a look at this." She pointed to the line of drawers. "Are my eyes tired, or is one of these a little different?"

His eyebrows arched. "They look alike to me. Why?"

She lifted the third drawer in the lineup and tapped on the bottom, then did the same with the others. She tapped on the others in the same fashion. "Hear that? It's a little muffled. I think it has a false bottom."

He took it from her and examined it. "Hold on a minute." He fished out a small pocketknife and withdrew the blade.

"Do be careful not to scar it."

He stuck the blade along the edge. "I'm just gonna try to get up under there, see if I can pop it out."

After several tries, Thomas sighed and put the knife away. "If it is a false bottom, I'd like to see the man who springs it."

"Or woman." She grinned.

After her brothers left and peace descended upon the shop, Delia served Sallie a cup of tea. They sipped in comfortable silence until Sallie said, "I sure appreciate you asking me to live here."

The words held more gravity than was typical for Sallie. Before their disagreement, Sallie had been agreeable and lighthearted. The Sallie who sat across the table from her seemed to save her smiles for Rabb. Perhaps it was just the thawing friendship, or maybe it was more.

"I was a little surprised you agreed."

Sallie studied her fingernails. "Your offer came at a good time. Things aren't good between my parents."

"Yes, you said something about that. I'm sorry."

"Ever since Clarence got shot, they fight all the time."

"Why?"

"At first, Pa wouldn't let Ma go help Clarence when he was hurt. I doubt their marriage has ever been a happy one, but after that ..."

Her words trailed into silence. Images and words floated back to Delia, the bitter words Mr. Parker lashed at Clarence the day he'd taken ownership of the hardware store. Her own papa had his share of flaws, but at least he loved her. There'd been no sign of affection or admiration in Mr. Parker.

Her gaze flitted to Sallie. She carried the weight of her parents' problems in her downcast expression. Surely there was something Delia could do to turn her from her moody thoughts. Maybe the little treat from Eleanor would cheer her.

Excusing herself, she went upstairs and grabbed the brown paper parcel, inhaling the vanilla sweetness. This would surely do the trick.

Downstairs, she said, "Look what I've got! Treats from Eleanor."

She made a show of unfolding the paper. Sallie moaned at the sight of sugar cookies laid atop the golden crust of a peach pie. "Smells divine." She reached for the envelope. "What's this?"

Delia took the packet, surprised at the weight. It clinked

musically. Lifting the flap, she gasped. "Why, there's five silver dollars!" She jiggled them in her hand, loving the sharp tinkling sound they produced.

"Look, there's a note. Read it."

Delia admired the elegant handwriting before reading aloud.

> Girls, I'm delighted you are inhabiting my little shop apartment. I pray you will enjoy blessed fellowship. On this first evening, please treat yourselves to dinner at the cafe.
> Warmest regards,
> Eleanor Baskin

She lowered the note. "How wonderful! We can finish our tea and cookies, then let's have dinner at Minnie's!"

Sallie clapped her hands. "I can't remember the last time I ate in a restaurant."

Chapter 29

"Some early influence has made him erratic, I'm sure." "He was born under a crazy quilt, I've been told."—Judge.—C New Oxford Item (New Oxford, Pennsylvania) August 25, 1921.

Once again, Clarence had missed supper at the boarding house. After delivering Sallie and her things to the seamstress shop, he'd left in plenty of time to wash up and be seated at his landlady's table. But instead of going home, he'd decided to drop in at the hardware store and see how the afternoon had fared in his absence. By the time he left, the meal was long concluded, and apparently, his landlady's good grace upon him had ceased.

Just as well. He'd come to think of Minnie's Diner as a home away from home. As he pushed open the door, the woman herself called out, "Come on in, Clarence. Always got room for one more."

He hung his hat on the rack and ambled to the long dining table, where his friends greeted him. He rounded the table, shaking hands with each of the five men before settling into a chair. This was sure enough better than the boarding house, where mealtime conversation was frowned upon. "Nice to see you fellas."

Minnie laid a cup of steaming coffee in front of him. "Pot roast, gravy, green beans, and mashed potatoes coming right up, hun."

"Sounds fine."

Cal Michaels clapped him on the back. "Dooley was just about to tell us about that oil well up Corsicana way."

Clarence nodded as he took a sip of coffee. No doubt, Dooley McFarland's account exaggerated the oil strike, but that was okay. That was part of the fun. Like him, these men had no one waiting at home, whether through the misfortune of widowhood or the ongoing search for the perfect woman. This lighthearted group lifted his spirits.

The door opened, and his friends turned to see who'd walked in. It didn't much matter to him. He sipped his coffee, content to let the day's pressures slide from his shoulders.

Beau Galloway, the barber, leaned across the table. "Ain't that your sister and your girl?"

Clarence glanced up and almost choked. Sallie and Delia stood just inside the door, rubbing their arms.

Great. He just couldn't get a break from that woman. "Delia's not my girl."

Beau perked up. "No kidding? Hey guys, did you hear the news?"

Clarence moaned when his friend waved at the women. Reluctantly, he stood, intending to invite them to the table. The men sprang to their feet. George Kaufman, a middle-aged attorney who lost his wife to influenza the year before, rushed to usher the women to seats beside him, at the other end of the table. "These men won't mind scooting over."

Clarence stood. "Now, there's no need for that. I've got two empty places right here." He waved to the women.

Rumbles of complaint followed, but he ignored them. Sallie beamed at him and settled in the seat he held out. "What a happy surprise!"

Clarence turned to Delia with a tight smile and rounded the table. But he was too late.

Beau pulled a chair out for her, giving Clarence a wicked grin. "Here you go, Miss Delia," he said.

She smiled shyly. "Thank you, Mr. Galloway."

"Aw, I'd like it right well if you was to call me Beauregard."

Hoots rang out all around. "Beauregard?"

Beau's face blossomed a deep red. "Don't mind them, Miss Delia. Jealousy is an ugly thing."

Clarence sat down and gritted his teeth as the man talked fast and loud to Delia.

He turned to his sister. "Are you all settled in now?"

She pushed her spectacles further up her nose. "It's coming along. I'm so glad I moved in with Delia." She included the others in her wide smile and chattered on, causing the men to hang on every word.

Clarence glanced at Delia, who watched Sallie with wide eyes. She met his gaze and lifted her shoulders as if surprised. Leaning toward him, she said, "This is the most she's talked all day."

Minnie appeared with his dinner. "Here you go, hun."

His mouth watered at the savory aroma. He sank his fork into a big hunk of meat and shoveled it into his mouth, moaning in delight. The hearty food hit the spot. He washed it down with a swig of coffee. "Delicious."

He spied Delia observing him from across the table, eyebrows arched questioningly. "Please don't wait to eat on our behalf." Sarcasm dripped from every word, but he saw the gleam in her eye.

He glanced down at the empty spot before her and hastily

set down his fork. "I'm sorry. I don't know what happened to my manners."

Just at that moment, his stomach let out a loud growl, noticeable even over the fellows' banter.

Sallie gasped. "Was that your stomach? By all means, eat."

He shook his head. "Nope. Not till you both have yours."

It wasn't long before Minnie brought two more heaping plates to set before the ladies, and Clarence tucked in without guilt.

He couldn't help but notice the mirth that danced in Delia's eyes. She'd probably never let him forget his *faux pas.*

The thought jarred him. It was as if he'd assumed they'd be sociable once more. Which, of course, they wouldn't.

Delia made herself right at home, conversing easily with the men around the table. Well, sure. She was a beautiful woman, and those lug heads weren't stupid. He sopped up his remaining gravy with his biscuit, barely tasting it. Beau Galloway's flirtatious ways irritated him. The man acted like he'd never seen a pretty female before now.

Dooley commenced with his story. "I'll start all over again for the benefit of our lovely supper companions." The story held little in common with the original version, making Dooley out to be some kind of hero. Clarence's leg bounced impatiently. Soon, he'd escort the girls back to their home. These fellas might get the wrong idea and think they could come calling on his sister and Delia, just because they were unmarried. He'd set them straight, that's for sure.

Finally, the women rose from their chairs. The men jumped to their feet and lined up to wish Delia and Sallie a good evening. Clarence glared at the men. Fools, all of them. They'd best back away.

To make sure they got the message, he placed a protective hand on each woman's back. "Ladies, I'll see you safely home."

Before crossing the threshold, Clarence looked back at the men. Their crestfallen expressions made him grin.

Delia gathered her wrap closer as the three stepped into the chill of the November evening. "What a delightful group of gentlemen."

Clarence harrumphed.

Sallie giggled. "They certainly knew how to welcome a lady."

"I agree. Clarence, you have charming friends."

He made no reply. She spotted the pulsing muscle in his jaw as if he were clenching his teeth. She smiled to herself. So, he was a little jealous, was he?

At the door of the shop, she dug her key from her bag. "We have a peach pie, if you would like to come in."

Sallie clasped her hands together. "Please join us."

He hesitated. "I really need to get home."

Sallie wilted. "Do you have to? Can't you just come in for a minute?"

Delia unlocked the door. She hadn't expected him to join them, but still, disappointment blanketed her when Sallie kissed his cheek in farewell. "At least we got to eat with you at the diner. Now that I'm in town, maybe we can see each other more."

Sallie waggled her fingers and stepped past Delia into the shop. Clarence gave a half-hearted wave and called, "Good night," over his shoulder.

A sudden impulse overtook her. "Clarence, wait."

He turned, and she said, "I have something I want to give you."

"I'm too full for pie."

She swallowed. "It's not ... Will you please wait just a moment?"

Before she could change her mind, she darted into the shop. Her fingers shook when she picked up the quilt. Was she really doing this? Her heart raced. It might be foolhardy, but something deep inside her insisted. At the door, she thrust it at him.

His jaw sagged. "Isn't this your crazy quilt?"

"I want you to have it."

He accepted it and held it in both hands as if measuring its weight. Then he shook his head and returned it. "I'm honored, but I want you to keep it. Put it in the window with that blue ribbon you earned. People should see how talented you are. This is something to be proud of, Delia."

Clarence lit a lamp in his room and sank down upon his bed. Delia had wanted him to have that quilt. A sweet and generous act, to be sure. He didn't deserve her kindness, not after the way he'd treated her. And all that fuss over a necktie. One that couldn't bring his brother back, no matter if he kept the tie near or never saw it again.

It was just a strip of fabric meant to make a man look his best. The significance he'd attached to that necktie verged on idolatry. Joe would hate that. If he made an appearance at this moment, he'd say people were more important than things.

He'd messed up. In his efforts to memorialize his brother, he had granted that tie priority over everything. Everyone.

He raked his fingers through his hair with a groan. He'd thrown away the love of a wonderful woman because of a worn-out piece of fabric.

He owed her an apology. Whether or not she allowed it was

the question. Or maybe he ought to behave as if nothing had happened.

Except, too much had occurred to ignore.

First thing tomorrow morning, he'd apologize to Delia. It was the right thing to do.

~

Delia stood with her back against the door, frowning at the quilt. If not for this quilt, she and Clarence would still be sweethearts. But she'd allowed her stubbornness and insensitivity to come between them.

Was that the reason he'd not taken it when she offered? Was this one more way to reject her? It hadn't seemed so. In fact, his expression when he gave it back was so tender, she'd almost reached up to stroke his cheek.

Sallie yawned. "I'm going up to bed. I'm exhausted after all that excitement."

Delia nodded. "I'll be up in a bit."

The footsteps ascended and faded away, leaving Delia alone to lay the quilt in the window. She did exactly as Clarence suggested and pinned the blue ribbon to it.

With a sigh, she turned away. Everything she'd done with that tie, her saving it from the rubbish bin, securing it into her quilt, hearing about his distress at losing it, and most of all, not telling him immediately of the tie's whereabouts ... all could have been brushed off as unfortunate choices.

But it went deeper than oversight. She'd been selfish, and her selfishness had divided her from a good man.

Yet when she'd placed it into Clarence's hands just now, a weight lifted from her shoulders. Maybe God had prompted her to surrender an object too important to her. *Is that it, Lord?*

Did you want me to give it away, even though he didn't accept it?

Eleanor's words from long ago drifted through her mind. *"What brings me joy is serving the Almighty."*

Delia couldn't imagine giving away her crazy quilt could be called service. But then, she didn't have faith like Eleanor's. She was just a girl from Georgia who'd messed up her fresh start in Texas.

Chapter 30

A lover's quarrel, like a crazy quilt, is generally patched up.—
Cambridge Jeffersonian (Cambridge, Ohio) August 8, 1901.

Delia rose from her seat at the table, ready for bed.
Despite the sudden onslaught of fatigue, it thrilled
her to check the doors, bank the fire, and put out
the lamps. One day, this would surely seem a mundane act. But
this first evening, she'd stifle her yawn and enjoy making the
rounds, like her father did at home.

Dark now, she peered through the front window at Main
Street. Clarence was long gone. She longed for one more glance
at him, feeling as empty as the street outside.

She let her breath out in one long whoosh. It was right,
giving him the crazy quilt, even though it had been a sudden
inspiration. Some would call it impulsive. But it seemed to her
the Lord himself had compelled it.

She grimaced at the few boxes she hadn't unpacked. Plenty
of time tomorrow morning if she woke early. She admired the
red calico curtains, fingering the playful gold flowers, then
parted the drapes to step into the back room.

Her step faltered. Something was not right. The light from the front illuminated the small area, showing the back door ajar.

Had it been that way all evening? She pushed it closed. Or she tried. Something kept it from meeting the jamb.

Splintered wood from the doorframe stuck out at odd angles. Ice crept up her spine. A break-in.

A strong hand grabbed her from behind. She gasped, struggling to free herself. A deep, gravelly voice chuckled in her ear. "Ain't nobody told me you's such a purdy thing."

He spun her around, leering as he let his eyes wander suggestively up and down her body. A ratty brown beard concealed most of his face from her except for his bloodshot eyes. Inches from her face, he sneered. "You gonna give me all that money, you hear? Then you and me, we gonna have us some fun."

God, help! She wrenched from his grasp and screamed. In a flash, he pinned her to the wall. Pain radiated at the back of her head, edging her vision with pulsing colors. His rancid, alcohol-laced breath made her stomach seize. "You wanna die? Quit whining."

Overhead boards creaked and her friend called from the top of the stairs. "Delia?"

Sallie.

The man's mouth sagged, and he shifted to look over his shoulder. Delia shoved him away and ran through the curtain, screaming. But her attacker was right behind. Growling, he yanked her by the hair. She yelped and fought against him.

"Gimme the money or I'll kill you!"

All at once, a shriek cut through the air and something landed on him, rocking them precariously. Delia fell hard to her knees as his attention turned to his attacker. Sallie clung to his back, her bare white legs girdling his stomach.

Profanity spewed as he swatted at her. "Get off me!"

Delia scrambled toward the front door. She could escape.

The man roared, then came a sound like something hitting the wall. Sallie moaned. Delia shot a terrified look over her shoulder. Sallie struggled to get up.

The man lunged for Delia. She ducked, and grabbed for anything to toss in his path_ Wood clattered. Curses bellowed. Her fingers clawed for the doorknob. He jerked her back from freedom, and with a grunt, he flung her against the wall.

Shrieking from the pain, she struggled to get up. Sallie's ghostly form blurred. Silver glinted in the lantern light as she lifted her hand. Scissors. Sallie plunged them into his back. Delia watched, horrified. He screamed and turned on her friend, like a bear. Metal clattered on the floor near Delia. The attempt to stab only enraged the monster. He grabbed the shears and raised them over Sallie.

"No!" Delia lunged for something, anything, to throw his way. The orange glow and licking tongue of flame registered as the lamp flew toward the monster.

The lantern sailed past him and crashed into the stove. Glass and flames exploded. The sickening odor of kerosene filled the air. The man shoved Sallie, then ran out the back.

Fire roared to life, greedy and relentless. Spilled kerosene ignited the wooden floor. A colossal swoosh sounded, and the curtains ignited in a terrifying spectacle of destruction. Wood popped and crackled as the fire consumed her shop. Delia's eyes stung as she gasped for oxygen.

Through the dense smoke, she spotted her friend lying in a heap like a rag doll, flames eating away at her skirt.

"Sallie!"

Delia had to help her. Coughing, she spotted her crazy quilt in the window and grabbed it. Holding it against her mouth and nose, she staggered to her friend. Over and over, she beat the flaming skirt with the quilt. She would not let Sallie die.

Church bells snagged Clarence's attention. Cries filled the air. "Fire! Fire!"

He tore down the stairs and out onto the street. Dread fueled him. Commotion sounded from the middle of town. He rounded the corner to Main Street and saw the eerie glow coming from the seamstress shop. Someone screamed when glass shattered. He pumped his legs, barely aware of men joining him, tugging on shirts and suspenders.

Orange tongues flicked out the front window, quickly consuming the overhang above the walkway. "Delia! Sallie!"

He had to get them out.

A man carried a limp body and gently laid her on the ground, across the road from the fire. Panic shot through Clarence. He fell to his knees beside her. "Delia!"

She struggled to sit up. "She's still in there!"

"Sallie?"

Pushing him, she croaked, "Get her!"

He scrambled to his feet and rushed across the street, where a bucket brigade had formed. "My sister's inside!"

Most were too intent on their job to answer, but one man shook his head. "That girl's the only one we found."

A scream pierced the roar of the fire. By the time he leaped onto the walkway, the heat seared, making him balk. He plunged into the blaze.

Black haze engulfed him. His shouts were swallowed in the roaring inferno. How would he find her? All around him, flames danced and greedily consumed everything they touched. He choked, trying to breathe into his sleeve.

Somewhere overhead, lumber clunked and crashed, reverberating underneath him. He shielded his face from the shower of sparks. "Sallie!"

Clarence sputtered and tried to inhale against the burning in his lungs. He pressed on, calling her name. Movement on one side caught his attention.

"Here!"

He dodged another avalanche of sparks to get to her. She lifted her arms, and he scooped her up, just like he'd done when she was a toddler. She clung to him as he groped his way toward freedom. Cool air kissed his skin, and he gulped the oxygen.

A coughing fit overtook them both. Someone guided him across the street, and he collapsed on his knees beside the two women. Delia reached for Sallie and the two women wept. Only then did he notice smoke rising from Sallie's dress. Clarence used his hands to beat the fabric despite her cries. Satisfied any threat of fire was gone, he scooted even with her face. Hoarse whimpers caused his chest to tighten.

"Where does it hurt, Sallie girl?"

Delia pointed to the right arm, where angry red skin showed where fabric had torn away.

"Am I going to die?"

The words pierced Clarence. He took a ragged breath and gently clasped her upper body in his arms. "You're safe."

Her eyes rolled back, and her head lolled. Panicked, he screamed, "Doc! She needs help!" It took forever before Dr. Taggert was there, and at the man's urging, Clarence carried her to the clinic.

Once inside, he laid her on the examining table, where the physician took over.

Coughing overtook him when he walked outside into the hazy night. He drank from a cup someone forced into his hand but refused another. He managed to choke out, "I'm fine." Another spasm choked off his reply.

When the hacking subsided, Clarence took an unsteady step. Rubbing at the familiar pain in his upper arm, he scanned the chaotic street for Delia.

She was by his side in an instant. He held her tight. He'd come so close to losing this woman. No notice, no hint of pending evil. His emotions threatened to overflow.

In a voice that barely resembled his own, he said, "What happened? Everything was fine when I left you two."

Struggling with emotion, she recounted the break-in and the fight with the stranger. "I've never seen him before." A sob caught. "It was awful."

Tipping her face to the light, he winced at the bruises and scrapes. Her lips had swollen, so that she was almost unrecognizable. What kind of monster did this to a woman?

At the clinic, he tenderly cupped her cheek. "You go on in and tell the doctor what happened. I'm gonna find the sheriff."

"No! Don't leave me."

Taking her in his arms, he said, "You'll be safe. But you've got to let me tell the law."

After a moment, she nodded, and he released her. As he turned away, she gasped. "You're bleeding."

Sure enough, blood soaked his sleeve.

"You need the doc to look at that." When he objected, she took his other arm and propelled him to the clinic. "I'm not taking no for an answer."

He submitted, and as they made their way to the door of the clinic, a fresh peal of church bells rang out. Turning, they gasped when fire consumed the building next to the shop. A brick wall crashed to the ground, producing a tall cloud of dust.

Blooming Grove was burning, and they were helpless to stop it.

Chapter 31

"Well, I should like to know," continued Fred, "what could be more idiotic than the way you spend your time, you girls, fitting those ridiculous, catty-cornered pieces of silk together, and working them all over with bugs and cobwebs and caterpillars, and little boys in Mother Hubbard dresses! You may call 'em crazy quilts! I don't believe there was ever anything crazier, unless it was the lunatic who first invented them!"—Linda's Crazy Quilt, Sun-Journal (Lewiston, Maine) Saturday, October 29, 1898.

Delia jerked awake, heart pounding. Blinking at the dimly lit parlor, for a moment her surroundings didn't register. Then, with relief, she recognized this beautifully appointed parlor as belonging to the Taggerts. Mrs. Taggert had urged her to rest until her family came. She must have drifted to sleep, if it could be called that. Images of towering flames and the desperate search for freedom tumbled through her dreams. She brought her bare feet to the floor, moaning softly as she pressed fingers to her temple.

The odor of smoke made her stomach roil. She brought her

smudged sleeve to her nose. Oh, she reeked. The shirtwaist looked nothing like the crisp white blouse she'd donned yesterday. A tear at the shoulder caused the puffed sleeve to hang limply, exposing her tender, purpling skin. What a sight she was. She'd make a trip to her apartment first thing for a fresh change of clothes.

Memory jolted her. She had no fresh clothing. Everything had perished in the fire.

A button from her blouse hung by a thread. She plucked it free and examined it, rubbing it clear of soot. "Well, hello there. Aren't you tenacious?"

Wonderful. Now she talked to inanimate objects. She rubbed the smooth button before slipping it into her skirt pocket for safekeeping. Maybe she was going mad.

She tucked her chilly feet underneath her skirt. Where were her shoes and stockings?

Everything, gone. She covered her eyes.

"Delia!"

Surprise and relief mingled as Mother and Papa hurried across the parlor. "Are you all right?"

"Yes, fine." She tried to smile, but she couldn't force her swollen, sore lips to cooperate.

"You certainly are not fine." Mother's embrace made Delia wince. Every part of her ached.

"Please, sit here beside me."

Sandwiched between her parents, their presence warmed her. Though it hurt to do so, she turned her head one way and the other, just glad to see their comforting faces.

Mother laid a gentle hand on hers. "What happened?"

Delia squeezed her eyes shut. Couldn't all this wait? Reliving the nightmarish evening was like going through it all over again, and she just wanted to forget. But one look at the concern lining her parents' faces, and she knew she had to try.

She'd say it quickly and get it over with. "A man broke in while we were at supper. He wanted money. He jumped out and ..."

The image of his face caused her pulse to gallop. How could she tell them those suggestive comments? How he'd tried to kill her. Her throat stung. "May I have some water?"

Mother rose. "I'll get it."

When it was just Delia and her father, she turned to him. "I don't want her to know everything."

His face sagged in grief. "Can you tell me?"

She related the nightmarish events, averting her gaze so she didn't have to see his horror. "Had Sallie not distracted him, he would have done unspeakable things ..." She touched the neck of her blouse with trembling fingers.

Papa's gaze fell to the floor. After a moment, he cleared his throat. "You both were very brave." He kissed her messy hair. "You survived a horrific attack, and I'm so thankful."

"Oh, Papa. I threw the lantern at him."

He sandwiched her hand in both his. "You are a fierce warrior. Times like these I'm thankful for your strong will."

"But don't you see?" She swallowed, wincing at the sandy dryness lodging in her throat. "I caused the fire, Papa." She choked on the words.

Mother returned and offered a glass of water, which Delia gratefully gulped. She longed for more, but first she needed to know about Sallie.

Mother lifted her shoulders. "The doctor's with her, but she isn't conscious. She has burns all down the right side of her body." A sob caught in her throat. "That could've been you."

"Sallie was amazing. She jumped on the man's back and beat him with her fists so he would release me."

Mother gasped. Delia winced at her thoughtlessness. "I'm sorry to shock you."

"My poor, sweet daughter. I knew you never should have

moved to town. In no time, the unthinkable happened. You need to be home, where you are protected and cherished. Not alone in the city."

A retort sprang to Delia's lips, but she smothered it. After this, they would never permit her to live on her own. But maybe that wasn't so bad. The dogtrot's safety appealed to her, especially as a place of refuge, with her father and brothers as fierce protectors.

She looked at her father. "Where are Rabb and Thomas?"

"They're with the rest of the men in town."

Tending to her shop, no doubt. Or what little remained. She ran her hand up and down her arm, reminding her once again of the torn shirtwaist.

Mother touched the ripped sleeve. "Let's see if we can get you new clothes. Robert and Mary are outside. They'll be glad to help."

A rap sounded on the open door, and they turned to discover the sheriff, hat in hand. "Mind if I come in?"

Papa crossed to shake his hand and gestured for him to sit. The lawman looked at Delia. "How are you doing?"

She gestured to her appearance, tempted to say she was fine. But she doubted they would appreciate her wry humor. "I'm a mess."

At Mother's invitation, Sheriff Akin sat on the chair opposite Delia. "Can you tell me what happened?"

She repeated what she'd told her father, glancing at her mother uneasily. It had been terribly brutal. When she finished, the sheriff said, "My deputy saw a man running in the alley about the time the fire broke out, and he took him in for questioning. But I need you to identify him."

"You don't mean she'll have to face this animal?"

"I'm sorry to say she will, ma'am, especially if there's a trial." He shifted his gaze away from her parents and looked at her. "If you say he's the intruder who beat you girls, we'll charge him with two counts of attempted murder."

Delia swallowed. She never wanted to see that evil man again. The sheriff must've sensed her reluctance. "It may not even be the same fellow. Why don't you tell me what you remember?"

Papa placed his hand on her back. "Just do your best."

She rubbed a finger. "Taller than my father, and heavy." She swallowed. "Dark eyes." Evil. "A front tooth was chipped. Long beard." Putrid breath, hot against her skin. Face contorting with rage.

Sheriff Akin looked apologetic. "Could be our man. Or a dozen others. I hate to say this, after what you've been through, but I need you to look at the man we're holding in the jail."

Her stomach roiled. She couldn't look at that monster. Not again.

Mother's strident objections caused her head to throb. She just wanted to get this over with. Put the whole thing behind her, forever. "Fine, I'll go." Standing with all the dignity she could muster, the objections ceased. Or maybe the voices didn't register.

Though it was surely after midnight, the street outside teemed with people. She ought to thank them for helping her, for leaving their warm homes and putting out the fire. She turned her head as they passed what was once her shop. Mother's shawl enveloped her. Her father walked beside her, his hand protective as it rested on her back. The gesture brought her pain, but she didn't have the heart to tell him.

Sudden movement made her start before her body sagged with relief. "Clarence."

She'd not seen him since he accompanied her to the clinic. "How are you feeling?"

The same question everyone asked. "Fine."

His eyes grew assessing. "Where are y'all going?"

Papa answered him tersely. "Sheriff Akin wants Delia to identify the varmint who tried to kill her and Sallie."

Clarence drew up short. "He caught him?"

The sheriff kept walking. "Hope so. Miss Truitt's gonna confirm it."

"Sheriff, she just went through an ordeal. Don't you think you're pushing things, making her face that outlaw?"

She shot him a grateful look.

The lawman's eyes narrowed. "You want justice, don't you?"

Clarence quickened his step to come even with the man. "I didn't mean to question your business, sir. I just hate for Delia to go through that, especially this soon."

"Gotta be done."

Dread weighed her as the sheriff held the door open for Delia and her father.

Behind her, the sheriff said, "Wait out here, Parker."

Before the door shut, Delia looked over her shoulder at Clarence. "Do I have to do this?"

Papa drew close to her, glaring at the sheriff.

"I'm afraid so." The lawman exchanged a meaningful glance with his deputy before speaking to Delia. "Your friend's unconscious, maybe dying, because of what someone did to her. If we're holding the man responsible in the cell, your identification will keep him from doing it to some other woman."

The words stunned her. She'd be protecting some innocent woman from the beating she and Sallie had endured. The heartbreaking image of her friend lying unconscious made her clench her fists. "I'll do it."

The deputy unlocked the passageway that led to the cells. He stopped beside one, causing the man inside to growl.

"When you gonna let me outta here? I didn't do nothing."

Delia hugged herself, trembling at the sound of the raspy voice. "That's him." Her teeth chattered, and Papa's arms shielded her. The deputy gestured for her to step forward. "You gotta see him before we make an identification."

Forcing her feet to cooperate, she stood before the cell. Him. Bile rose in her throat.

The hulking man stared at her before an evil grin spread across his face. "Missed me? I knew you took a shine to me. Pretty little thing, ain't you? Feisty too. I like 'em feisty."

Papa roared and charged forward. He grabbed the man's collar and jerked him against the iron bars. Delia gasped as her father hissed, "I'll kill you with my bare hands! Don't you ever come close to my daughter again."

It took both lawmen to pry her father from the cell. They propelled him back to the office. Cackling laughter trailed Delia as she hurried behind them. She rushed out the door and heaved the contents of her stomach into the bushes.

Hours later, Sallie still hadn't regained consciousness. Clarence prayed she would wake up and everything would be fine. She'd made it out alive, hadn't she? Surely she would live.

At least Delia was safely tucked away at her aunt and uncle's home along with the rest of her family. The night felt endless. Even now, the sun was two hours from rising.

The sheriff had formed a posse to bring the gang in and put an end to the violence. Delia's brothers sat their mounts alongside Clarence and others who ignored the bite of the wind to bring in the criminals. Moonlight gave a silvery hue to the street.

The sheriff strode to the middle of the road and held a lantern high.

"Appreciate your help, men. Y'all did good work on the fire. Because of your quick response, we lost only two buildings. One of them is Delia Truitt's business, where a no-account broke in with the purpose of robbing her. It ain't a secret she's had a lot of business here lately." He glanced at Clarence before continuing. "When Miss Truitt and her friend, Sallie Parker, got back from dinner, this fella was waiting. Beat them up pretty bad. Sallie's still out, right, Clarence?"

Clarence jerked his head once. The less said, the better. But he reckoned these fellows needed to hear the whole sordid story before they put their lives on the line.

"A fire started, and when my deputy saw the varmint running from the building, he arrested him. Miss Delia identified the man. Name's Jim Megolin, and he rides with Big Jake's gang."

The sheriff shifted on his feet. "Let me tell you, I'm mighty fed up with that bunch. They're like weeds. They'll keep spreading until we stomp out the root. Men, I'm ready to arrest every last one of them. That's what you're here for, to join the posse. Thanks to ol' Jim Megolin, we know where the hideout is."

How'd he get that information? Probably wouldn't say. No matter. As long as they rounded up all the outlaws, he'd be satisfied.

"Who is it we're chasing down, Sheriff?" Dooley asked.

"After Big Jake died, a guy named Virgil Mason took over. Got a couple of men with him all the time, so we'll expect a fight from them."

Virgil.

A horse shook its head restlessly.

Rabb asked, "How you know if he's telling it straight about that hideout?"

"Matches what Big Jake's widow told me about an old cabin ten miles south of here."

Dooley asked, "Who says we can trust her?"

"I say." The sheriff's eyes were stony as he stared down Dooley.

"No offense, Sheriff, but did you ever think maybe she ain't so trustable? Could be they's in it together, and we're gonna get ambushed."

Clarence clenched his fists. "That's not gonna stop me."

"Same here," Thomas said.

Rabb scowled at Dooley. "One of them yellow bellies tried to kill my sister and Sallie. We gotta put a stop to that gang. Track their sorry hides and make 'em pay."

Dooley pointed to the sheriff. "I'm just asking if we oughta trust that Baskin woman."

Thomas leaned forward. "That woman's like family to us. We trust her to take care of our mama and baby sister. That tell you anything?"

Sheriff Akin's gaze traveled from one man to the next. "If you aren't up to the task, any of you, declare yourself here and now."

No one spoke, and the sheriff nodded once. "We leave outta here at a pretty fast clip. Then we'll slow down. Don't want to announce ourselves."

Clarence adjusted his place in the saddle of his rented horse, grimacing at the painful nip from the bullet wound. He'd pulled his sister from a burning building. He'd manage riding with a posse. No matter how much his arm hurt, he was going.

As if he'd read his mind, the lawman approached Clarence. "Think you can ride with that bum arm? We're heading out, and we won't be stopping."

Clarence recognized the doubt in the sheriff's tone. "Look, Sheriff, whether I ride with you or behind you, I'm going. Mason murdered my brother, and one of his bunch tried to kill my sister and my ... Delia." Despite the pause before her name, it came out more like "my Delia." But in his heart, that's exactly what she was—his Delia.

Sheriff Akin sucked his teeth. "Suit yourself." He turned his horse to face the other riders assembled on the dark road. "Let's head out."

They rode hard for several miles, and Clarence was relieved when the sheriff signaled a stop. Massaging his bandaged arm with tender fingers, Clarence watched a group of riders approach. Adrenaline pumped, making him tense up. Was this a setup, like Dooley had said?

The sheriff drew his gun, and others followed suit. Clarence reached for his rifle, keeping an eye on the riders as he spoke soothing words to his uneasy horse. When the men got closer, the sheriff visibly relaxed. "It's all right, men. They're friends."

Clarence released pent-up air and tucked his gun back in the scabbard. He stared at the approaching men, many who were reliable customers and fellow church members. His blood went cold at the sight of Pa.

Why'd he have to come?

They advanced the horses at a brisk walk. Pa fell in beside him, saying nothing.

He didn't have to. Clarence read the body language clear as day.

Finally, Pa spoke. "You're bleeding."

"So?"

Pa spat tobacco juice on the dried-up path. "Go home. Leave this to us."

"I aim to see this through."

340

"Boy, you gonna get us killed. That wound makes you a liability."

"I'm not your boy."

Pa's mouth slackened for a moment. He'd shocked him. Well, who cared, anyway? He'd had enough of Pa's surly company. Clarence urged his horse ahead.

He trailed Rabb, who was unusually subdued as they rode out. Maybe the gravity of what could have happened tonight settled in the quiet predawn.

He shook away any suspicions. Rabb might not be a saint, but he had a noble heart, especially when it came to Delia. Underneath all his teasing, admiration and affection were easy to see. If anything, Clarence had to keep him from doing something reckless to avenge Delia.

Sheriff Akin signaled a stop. "We're close. We'll divide into four groups." The lawman made the assignments, adding, "We want to take our spots while we still got moonlight. Get as close as you can without being seen. We won't do anything until sunrise, then be ready. I'll fire one shot from the south to draw out the gang. If we're lucky, they'll surrender when they see they're outnumbered."

Not much chance of that if Virgil Mason was in charge.

Thomas gestured for Clarence and Rabb to follow on horseback while they slowly circled to the west side of the land. The full moon cast shadows where tree trunks and bushy evergreens dotted the land, giving the scene an eerie feel. Thomas held up one hand, and they halted.

Wordlessly, the three men dismounted and tied off their horses. Rifles in hand, they crouched under a tree. Not more than fifty yards away, a square log structure sat in the middle of a clearing. Smoke rose like an apparition from the stone chimney. So that was the gang's hideout. If he didn't know better, he'd think the cabin belonged to a family. Only, families didn't post armed guards like the one against the back wall of the building, discernible only by the orange tip of his cigarette.

The sky gradually took on a grayish light. The lookout was easier to make out now. Tall and skinny, the man leaned against the shack, rifle pointed to the ground. Thomas signaled to get closer, and they moved with stealth to a set of shrubs. A twig snapped beneath Clarence's foot, and he dove onto his stomach. The guard brought his gun to his shoulder, cigarette abandoned in the dry grass.

Clarence held his breath. Body taut, he waited for the inevitable discovery. His heart pounded against the silty dirt.

"Clear."

The word was so soft, Clarence didn't trust his hearing until Rabb shifted his weight and whispered, "Let's take him."

Thomas said, "No."

"Come on. We can do it."

Thomas glared at his brother. "No telling how many guns are in there. We're not thumping a hornet's nest. Just wait."

Rabb muttered. Although Clarence agreed with Thomas, to say so now would only heighten the tension between the brothers.

In strained silence, they watched as the lookout moved to the back of the cabin and vanished from view.

Rabb whispered, "When's the sheriff gonna signal? Sun's comin' up."

Thomas shook his head. "Wanna get mowed down? Don't know about you, but I got a sweetheart wanting me to come back alive."

Rabb said nothing in response, but his body lost some of its tension. Clarence rubbed his eyes. The waiting was maddening.

The sun peeked over the ridge of trees to the east. "Let's get to better cover." Thomas pointed to the path.

They shifted to a position better hidden within the brush. Thomas shoved a canteen his way, and Clarence took a long gulp before passing it on to Rabb.

Clarence wiped his face with his sleeve. "Why hasn't the sheriff signaled yet?"

A bullet whizzed over their heads, and they dove for their weapons. "That came from the hideout." Thomas checked his ammunition, grim-faced.

Heart thumping like a skittish colt, Clarence's chin hit the dirt as more bullets zinged through the air. He kept his head low, waiting for a lull in the gunfire so he could return fire. If they'd held their position, they wouldn't have been spotted. Now they were pinned.

Chapter 32

The truly good get their reward! It may come early, it may come late. But it comes. Boston's pulpit darling, the ex-pounder Downs, has been presented with a crazy quilt by his silly female admirers.—Davenport Daily Gazette *(Davenport, Iowa) December 12, 1885.*

Clarence's chest pounded. The barrage of bullets stopped. His body tense, he waited. Had the men left, or were they creeping in for the kill?

Thomas got his attention and motioned for Clarence to give cover while the brothers dashed behind an oak tree. As they moved, he fired toward the cabin. When Thomas provided cover, Clarence ducked behind a cedar bush, rifle drawn to return fire.

But no shots came. In the tense silence, they waited. The only movement was the flapping curtains in the window below.

After a few minutes, he whispered, "Think they're still in there?"

Thomas didn't look away from the cabin. "Reckon so."

Rabb blew air through his mouth. "What're they waiting for?"

"Probably watching us," Thomas said.

"What you want a bet I got a couple of them?"

Clarence stole a glance at Rabb. "But don't go down there and check ... Best to stay safe."

Rabb curled his lip. "You don't gotta tell me that. Think I'm an idiot?"

More like impulsive, which might be worse.

Thomas grunted. "Look there, fellas. You see something moving to the north?"

Keeping his head down, Clarence peered across the clearing and focused on the bordering trees. A mixture of evergreens and bare-branch trees gave just enough camouflage to hide people or animals. Then a flicker of movement caught his attention. "I see men. Don't look like ours."

Rabb looked at his brother. "The gang's getting away."

Thomas squinted. Sheriff's got men on all sides, remember?"

Rabb gnawed a fingernail. "Reckon we oughta spread out a bit so those weasels don't get past us?"

Thomas nodded once. "You all right with staying here, Clarence?"

Clarence jerked his head in the affirmative.

The brothers skittered in separate directions, Thomas to the north, Rabb to the south.

Clarence let out a slow breath. He could protect them better from a distance and keep at least one alive to head back to their family. If he couldn't protect his own brother, at least he could protect Delia's.

He squinted at the distant spot where they'd seen movement. All still. Too quiet. Not even birdsong. His stomach clenched. He hated not knowing.

Glass exploded and sharp cracks sounded. Clarence ducked, heart pumping, prepared to return fire. But all around him, the dirt was undisturbed. They weren't aiming at him. He peeked at the hideout below. The barrel of a rifle protruded from the back, barely visible. The outlaws were shooting north then. Return fire pinged the metal roof. Who, besides Thomas, was up that way? He breathed a prayer. Bullets fired from the south. The sheriff's group. Finally. Clarence sighted in on the window facing the west and squeezed the trigger. With bullets coming from three sides, the outlaws would think a hundred lawmen surrounded them instead of two handfuls of farmers and businessmen.

Something hard and cold jammed the base of his skull. He froze.

"Drop it."

He swallowed and released his rifle. A grubby hand snatched it, cackling. "Woo-wee, looky here, Boss. Mighty fine rifle."

A man's voice snarled, "Quit your talking and get back."

Clarence closed his eyes. He knew that raspy voice. *Lord, help.*

Feet rustled in the rocky dirt. The toe of a heavy boot struck his ribs. Clarence cried out as pain threatened to rob him of his breath.

"Get up."

Gasping for air, he slowly pushed his body into a crouch. Despite the dizzying pain, he climbed to his feet, looking for anything he could use as a weapon. Nothing but twigs and sand and small rocks. He held his hands away from his body and turned to face the man who'd murdered Joe.

"Virgil Mason." Less than ten years since he'd seen him. The man had aged twice that.

347

The outlaw snorted. "Well, if it isn't Clarence Parker. Thought you knew better than to shoot at your own gang."

The scrappy man who held Clarence's rifle spit in the dirt. "He one of us, Boss?"

Virgil's lips lifted. "Once an outlaw, always an outlaw. But some men's stupid enough to think they can run."

The other man grinned, showing a gap where his two front teeth had once been. "Can't run. Not from you, Boss."

"That's right, Forrester." Virgil pressed his revolver into Clarence's chest. "Big Jake let you go. But he turned out to be a softy, and softies don't last. Now it's me who hunts down traitors."

Clarence gritted his teeth. He itched to grab the gun. A stupid move with a couple of broken ribs. But what did he have to lose? Virgil was no respecter of life. Killing came easy. Like that day in Fort Worth. Joe's face flashed in his mind.

Virgil shoved the gun barrel into Clarence's temple. "Forrester, get the rope."

Fear sliced Clarence. Would they hang him, or drag him behind the horse? Shooting him would be too civilized. He schooled his breathing as the little man tied his wrists behind his back.

Ahead, bullets whizzed, piercing the cabin walls.

Virgil sneered. "Idiot sheriff. Thinks he can come in here and take us all to jail. Not a chance. Know why? 'Cuz heroes won't shoot their own."

Clarence scowled. "What does that mean?"

Virgil popped one of Clarence's suspenders. "You and me's gonna walk outta here, like the good pals we always been."

"No."

Forrester's surprised guffaw grated. "You ain't gotta choice."

As if to emphasize his point, he rammed his fist into Clarence's middle. He doubled over, sucking in air.

"Walk."

Clarence stubbed his toe on a stump in the path leading to the clearing but kept himself upright. "Was it you behind the fire last night?"

Virgil chuckled. "Pretty good, huh? Knew I could get you out here if we killed your girl. Told you I'd get even."

"But you didn't. Nobody died, Virgil."

"Shut up and walk."

Clarence allowed himself to be prodded to the edge of the brush and onto the cleared land. He sank to his knees on the rocky dirt, only feet into the clearing. The outlaws shouted and slapped him, but Clarence focused his efforts on loosening the binding on his wrists. Was the sheriff watching?

Hand under Clarence's armpit, Virgil jerked him to standing, screaming obscenities. "Pull something again, and you die, Parker."

Clarence spit in Virgil's face. He steeled himself for the bullet.

It was the fist to the chin that caught him off guard. The jolt made him dizzy. Warmth oozed, metallic and thick. Rage filled him. With a roar, he lunged. "You killed my brother!"

Virgil lost his footing and fell to one knee. Clarence dove at him again despite the awkwardness of hands secured behind his back. This time, Virgil dodged the attack.

Forrester grabbed Clarence by one sleeve. "Want me to shoot him, Boss?"

Wordlessly, Virgil reached into his pocket and produced an object that glinted metallic in the dappled sunlight. He grabbed Clarence from behind. With his other hand, he held a knife against his throat. "No more games, you hear me? Now walk."

Virgil forced him forward, using Clarence as a shield to walk awkwardly across the clearing. With the knife against his throat, he dared not swallow or turn his head. But he had to live at least long enough to kill this man. Long enough to protect Delia. He strained against the binding. *Lord, I'm defenseless here. Help me.*

He stumbled with every forced step into the clearing. Sweat trickled down his back. *Please, God.*

Then Akin shouted, "Far enough. Let him go, Mason."

Virgil held him close, turning them both to see the lawman standing ten yards away, rifle at his shoulder. Virgil moved so that the blade pricked Clarence's throat. Something warm ran down the length of his neck. He was going to die. That's how this would end, wouldn't it?

A bullet from the cabin door started a chorus of whistling bullets going both directions. And here they stood in the middle of the volley. Someone inside the cabin screamed. Virgil's body tensed.

"Gene? You all right?"

Above the whistling bullets, Clarence heard no movement in the house.

Virgil grabbed a fistful of hair and jerked Clarence's head back. He sucked air. Another prick, another trail. "See this, Sheriff? I'll kill him if you don't let me go."

Tense silence layered the air. Gray sky was all Clarence could see. Virgil's hold tightened, and Clarence grimaced. His peripheral vision caught the black wings of a crow beating the air.

"What do you want, Mason?"

The sheriff sounded closer. But maybe that was fear making him imagine things.

Virgil yelled, "I want outta here, me and my men."

"Your men are dead."

Virgil yanked his head back again. This time, Clarence couldn't keep from yelping. "Want me to slit his throat?" His voice was higher. Too high. The man was panicking.

"Now, settle down there, Mason. Just let the man go. He ain't done nothing to you."

No doubt this time. The voice was louder. Closer.

Pulling Clarence backward, Virgil called, "You get on back, Sheriff. This here is a turncoat. A deserter."

"I'm stopping right here, Mason."

Virgil screamed, relinquishing his hold on Clarence to wave the knife toward Akin. "Liar! You're tricking me! Get back—"

A rifle cracked, and Virgil dropped without a sound, leaving Clarence unbalanced.

Forrester howled. He fumbled with the rifle's shooting mechanism. "I'll get you!"

Clarence slammed his body into the man, leaving both to roll on the ground. Screaming obscenities, Forrester scrambled up and delivered kick after kick to Clarence's ribs. Clarence rolled away, trying to wrench free of the rope while crawling to the gun. He couldn't allow Forrester to get the rifle. But the man scooped it up and brought it to his shoulder.

"Drop it," the sheriff yelled, aiming his revolver at the gang member. Forrester fumbled to get off a shot but not before two posse members knocked him off his feet, intercepting the weapon. Sheriff Akin ordered men to clear the hideout, and waited until they emerged, declaring everyone inside dead, before he holstered his gun and arrested Forrester, the gang's only survivor of the shootout.

Relief flooded Clarence. He sagged against the prickly dried grass and panted. Was that it? Was it really over?

Someone tugged at the bindings still cutting into his wrists. "Looks like you need a hand." Pa untied him. Clarence sat up and rubbed his wrists to get the blood circulating. Pa swiped moisture from his leathery cheek before pressing a neckerchief to Clarence's neck. "Here. This'll stop the bleeding."

Clarence hissed. "Stings."

His father crouched beside him and, with a gentleness he'd never witnessed in the man, secured the fabric around Clarence's neck. "There." His father's steel-blue gaze met his. "You all right?"

The rare question caused emotion to lodge in Clarence's throat. "I'm good." He pushed off the ground, breathing in the crisp air.

Pa squeezed his shoulder. "Go easy, son. Just lean on me."

While the others ate breakfast in her aunt's dining room, Delia slipped out the back door to find a space to pray under the wispy gray skies. Food didn't interest her. She'd forced a cup of coffee for the sake of appeasing Mother and Aunt Mary, who insisted she needed something on her empty stomach. "To sustain you," they'd said.

Could anything sustain her, after such loss?

Whenever she closed her eyes, images from the night before came unbidden. Now she faced them, trying to accept the horrible truth that would forever alter her life. Sallie's too.

At least they were alive.

The soft autumn sun couldn't erase the wind's chill, making her grip the shawl closer. She couldn't remember who gave her the wrap. Mother, or Aunt Mary, or perhaps one of the town women who'd come by to share clothing and food. In the hours since the fire, people had sprung into action to help.

The wheezy rasp of the backdoor opening arrested her attention.

Gert Waldrop stood on the small covered back porch. Delia registered the showy feather chapeau, the garnet, high-collared dress with puffed sleeves, the patent leather lace-up shoes. As always, she looked like a fashion plate straight out of *The Delineator* magazine. Envy sliced Delia.

Delia straightened, preparing to combat the inevitable smirk that accompanied the cutting phrases.

Gert stopped before her. "I suppose I'm the last person you expected to see."

"I'm in no mood for your sarcasm."

"I'm not terrible, you know." Gert lifted her chin. "I'm honestly sorry about your tragic circumstances. When I heard you'd lost everything, Mother and I packed a few of my things to give you."

Well, that was a surprise. "That's very kind."

Gert lifted her shoulders uncertainly as if she didn't know how to respond. But within seconds, the mask of haughty indifference slipped back into place. "It's not like I wear them anymore."

Ah. Delia took a deep breath, measuring her response. "I appreciate your thoughtfulness."

Gert looked down. "I know that shop was important to you." Her cheeks colored again. "I'm not proud of the things I did. But that reporter was begging for a story. I gave him a good one."

Delia's lips parted in astonishment. "So it was you?"

"Surely you are clever enough to figure that out."

"I had my suspicions." Because no one else would stoop to such a thing. But she hadn't known for sure until this moment. "But why? What did you hope to accomplish?"

"I wanted you to leave."

Delia almost choked on a laugh. "It'd take more than a half-true news story to make me run away."

"At the time, it seemed a way I could regain the attention you stole from me. It rather backfired, though. People around here are absolutely fascinated by you, though I can't think why."

"Yes, it did work out well for me. But must we be enemies?"

Gert adjusted her hat. "And be friends? I'm not sure it's possible."

"I'm not talking about friendship. I'd be happy with civility."

"We'll see." With a nonchalant lift of her shoulders, Gert walked out the garden gate.

Delia rubbed her eyes. Exhaustion was catching up with her. If only she could collapse onto a nice soft bed. But first, she had to see what remained of the shop.

How short-lived that dream had been.

She followed the path Gert had taken around to the front side of her aunt and uncle's home. Checking over her shoulder to be sure she'd eluded Mother or Hazel, she set off at a quick pace up Third Street, turning on Kerr toward the center of town. She was thankful for the two-story storefronts that stood along her path.

Past the barber, who rushed out to offer condolences. Past the print shop, past the bank. Around the next corner. She inhaled a shaky breath and pushed herself to keep walking. Cold wind brought the odor of burned wood, halting her. The stench made images flit through her mind. She grasped the hitching rail and forced emotion down.

Behind her, a woman spoke. "Miss, are you feeling unwell?"

Shaking her head, she murmured, "I'm fine, thank you."

The stranger continued on her way, leaving Delia resolute. *No stopping now.*

Delia waited for her knees to stop wobbling before she stepped off the boardwalk and onto Main Street.

She forced herself to turn around and face what remained of her little shop. But no matter how much she'd prepared herself, the sight gutted her. She clasped a hand over her mouth.

Smoldering bricks spilled over the charred lumber and unrecognizable blackened clumps amidst rubble. Only part of the second story remained, eerily jutting across empty space. Nothing but a ghostly specter of lost dreams.

Delia wiped the tears from her cheeks. She tried to recall where each item had stood before the fire swept through. There, right there, a beautifully painted Singer had proudly stood, ready to produce the whir of a well-oiled machine. Now it sat topsy-turvy, half hidden within a heap of cooling wreckage. The flames had scalded, pocked, and discolored the shiny black casing, its delicate mechanical parts now forged together for all time. Nearby, the iron treadle's familiar waffle weave jutted from the rubble.

She shielded her nose and mouth from the wafting smoke, eyes burning. The loss was enormous. No more shop. Upstairs apartment. Pretty dresses hung on pegs. Bolts of bright, cheerful fabric. The box containing two quilts' worth of silk, velvet, and satin. Gone.

Along with every bit of cash money she had to her name.

Just like the springtime afternoon when she and her family stood as mute witnesses to the disassembling of their lives in Georgia, her efforts to take control of her life were in vain. Nothing more than piles of seared rubbish. She kneeled and held her hand just above the still-warm residue. Suddenly, a gust of wind stirred the hot ash. Delia sputtered and whirled away, blinded and coughing.

Someone forced a handkerchief into her hand and led her away. "Maybe it's best if you didn't stand so close to the remains, Miss."

When she could see again, she turned to find an older man watching her with concern. She managed a thank you before a fit of coughing overtook her again.

"Oh, dear. Are you in need of water?"

What a question. She nodded and before long, the man returned with a cup. "I'm sorry, I am afraid some of it spilled. I tried to hurry, you see."

She gulped it down and handed it back to him, breathing shakily. "Thank you."

"I'm just glad I was here to help. Uh, which brings me to my point. I'm wondering if you are the owner of this unfortunate business?"

"I am."

He introduced himself, a name Delia promptly forgot as she blinked against the gritty sensation in her eyes. He spoke quickly, and words like "loss" and "destruction" flew past. His manner was blessedly impersonal. A show of sympathy might just break her.

When he took a breath, she said, "I don't understand."

"Fire insurance, Miss Truitt."

Her gaze strayed to the piles of stone and bricks. She hadn't thought of insurance. It was probably something Papa and the banker had discussed while she seethed in an upholstered chair.

Maybe she could rebuild. Even if she did, would her customers have the patience to wait?

Though she hated to admit her ignorance, she was forced to

direct the man to her father. He scurried away, and she was left to stare at the rubble once more.

Vanity of vanities; all is vanity.

The verse from Ecclesiastes was one she'd heard in a sermon not long ago. At the time, the message wasn't personal to her. But life had changed, and she had an inkling of what the passage meant. After all the time, effort, and heartache, the only thing she had to show was a heap of rubbish.

Where did that leave her?

As if compelled by some invisible hand pushing her forward, she walked back to the crumbling brick. A hole in her shoe allowed her tender flesh access to the gritty ash and glass that lay beside the partial wall. If only she could hunt through the rubble for any fragment the fire hadn't destroyed. She sank to her knees. Tears dripped from her cheeks onto her sooty skirt.

The words of Pastor Swenson floated through her mind. "There is nothing of worth apart from God. We were made to fear Him and keep His commandments. Apart from Him, we are nothing."

Delia brought her grimy hands to her face and wept.

She couldn't say how long she sat beside the ruins of her shop. Long enough for her bruised flesh to protest when she stood. But the clean-up must begin, and now was a good time.

She reached to lift a blackened piece of wood, whose surface rippled with the effects of fire. She hissed at the heat, letting it fall.

Several voices called to her as she worked, offering to help, but she turned them down. For now, this was her mess to put right.

"Miss Delia, what're you doing? Get away from that mess."

She peered at the man who spoke. If only her mind wasn't so spongey. She'd seen this man somewhere. "Oh, you're Mr. Pendergrass, from the diner."

"That's right. Why don't you come on over and we'll feed you?" He looked askance at her clothing, almost as if he wanted to take his words back.

"Oh." What time was it? "Maybe a little later. I need to clean up a bit."

He nodded. "A good idea. But I doubt them clothes will ever wash up."

She looked down at her smudged hands and streaked shirtwaist. When had she gotten so dirty? "You might be right about that. I might have to make myself a new dress."

Mr. Pendergrass winced. "Reckon so?"

Her shoulders fell. Of course she wouldn't be making a dress. "Oh."

Under her feet, the ground shook. The sensation grew stronger, accompanied by the sounds of running horses. Shouts jabbed the November air like exclamation marks.

"They're back!"

"Let's go see!"

Suddenly chilled, she retrieved the shawl from the floor and waded through the debris for a better look at what had people so excited.

A growing multitude swarmed the sheriff's office. Was the posse back? Her heart thudded, faster and faster. She joined the flow of townsfolk hurrying to hear the news. Her chest tightened with anticipation. She gave into the impulse to run, gripping her ash-covered skirt with one hand and her wrap in the other.

The throng of people surrounding the jail buzzed.

Breathless, she grabbed a gentleman's sleeve. "Sir, what's happening?"

The man did a double take at her, wrenching his arm from her ash-laden fingers. "Lady, you take a dip in coal dust? I never see'd nobody so dirty in all my born days."

"Is it news of the posse?"

"They's back. And I'll thank you to keep your hands off me."

She scanned the crowd for sight of Clarence or her brothers. Dread filled her. Had they been successful? Were they hurt? She elbowed her way through the dense crowd. Maybe he was up at the front.

The sheriff stood on the top step, just outside his office door, seemingly perplexed by the mob before him. His gaze connected with hers, and he waved. "Miss Delia, come on through."

The crowd parted for her, mutters rolling through like a tidal wave. He met her, hat in hand. "Miss Delia." He paused, his gaze taking in her attire. "You doing all right?"

She nodded. "Tell me." A band around her chest squeezed. Did she want to know? What if the worst had happened? She couldn't take much more.

Sheriff Akin's voice had a confidential tone. "I wanted you to know before everyone else."

Lord, please ... "Is Clarence all right? And my brothers?"

His gaze fell to the ground before he nodded. "We got 'em. I want you to rest assured, the gang has been apprehended, hideout's been cleared, and there isn't a trace of those crooks anywhere within one hundred miles. You're safe."

Narrowing her eyes, she let a puff of air escape her lips. "I seem to recall you assuring the town of the same thing last week."

He winced. "Reckon I got ahead of myself. This gang is a

mite bigger than anybody thought. But thanks to brave men like your brothers and Clarence, we got all of them outlaws."

Relief made her knees weak. "Thank the Lord."

"Rabb saved Clarence Parker's life. I heard he was a crack shot. Saw it for myself when he took out Virgil Mason."

The sheriff turned to the crowd, and Delia shrank against being swallowed by the horde. She pushed against bodies until she could breathe. Then she walked back the way she came. If she had to wait for Clarence, it wouldn't be here.

Chapter 33

The ladies of the Congregational church presented Rev. W. J. Jacobs and wife with a very handsome silk quilt, which could not fail to please, on the old principle that "a thing of beauty is a joy forever."—Elyria Republican (Elyria, Ohio) December 30, 1897.

Dog tired, Clarence pulled the horse to a stop at the sheriff's office. Nothing like a big crowd looking for juicy gossip to make a fellow want to turn and hightail it for the woods. After the day he'd had, they'd best not step between him and a steak supper with the woman he loved.

Before he could bolt, the crowd descended on him. Questions pelted him like hailstones.

"Did you take the outlaws down?"

"We heard you almost got killed!"

"You gonna be the next sheriff?"

He couldn't hear himself think amidst all this ruckus. One thing was for sure, though. He wanted no credit for bringing down Virgil. He turned to locate Rabb. He and Thomas stood to the side of the throng, speaking with the sheriff. Clarence pointed to his friend and shouted, "Rabb Truitt's the hero, not me."

Rabb's head jerked up, eyes wide, looking more like a scared rabbit than town hero. The fickle crowd turned their adoration to him. For a fleeting moment, Clarence regretted calling attention to his friend. Despite Rabb's gregarious nature, his somber expression now told a different story. Taking a life had that effect.

He'd be dead if it weren't for Rabb. Something shuddered deep within Clarence.

On the ride back, he'd taken time to reflect. Life was precious and fleeting. He'd not waste one more minute disputing silly things that, in the end, didn't matter. Like a quilt and a tie. He might not know all the answers, but he was sure of one thing—he needed Delia Truitt.

He sure wished he'd taken the quilt when she offered it. It had most assuredly burned in the blaze.

At the sudden roar of the crowd, Clarence shook himself from his musings. Dooley McFarland and Cal Michaels hoisted Rabb to their shoulders, singing "For He's a Jolly Good Fellow." Clarence folded his arms against a whip of cool wind, laughing softly. Rabb lifted his arms like a champion, drinking up the attention.

Dooley shouted, "You're looking at the best shot in Texas."

Cal Michaels guffawed and almost dropped Rabb. "Just don't bet against him. You'll lose all your cash, gents!"

Rabb's golden complexion turned red. "Hush up, Cal. My ma'll skin me raw for betting, even if it was a sure thing."

So, the cash Rabb had flaunted last summer he'd won in a shooting match. Delia would not be surprised.

Clarence scanned the street for any sign of her. Surely, she wasn't missing all this revelry. Yet she was nowhere in sight, even though it seemed the whole town flocked to this impromptu celebration.

Not that he shared in the high spirits. True, the hideous gang had been taken down, once and for all. For the first time in eight years, he didn't worry about Virgil Mason getting away with Joe's murder. He was dead.

Heavy sadness filled him. Long ago, they'd been friends. But unlike Clarence, Virgil never turned his life around. A wash of relief and gratitude made his eyes burn. If not for the Lord's grace, Clarence might have followed the same crooked road.

A hand squeezed his shoulder, and he turned to see his manager, Bill Graford. "Hey, Boss, why're you standing all alone here? Party's that way."

Emotion made him mute. This reliable, honest man before him was proof of the good life he'd been given. He'd come so close to a different kind of life. Like Virgil.

Without a word, he enfolded Bill in a tight hug.

"Whoa, what's all this? You all right, Boss?"

Clarence winced at the word. "I'm good. And call me Clarence, will you?"

Frowning slightly, the man responded. "Sure, B—I mean, Clarence. You coming to the celebration?"

Clarence shook his head. "I'm looking for someone."

Understanding dawned on Bill's face. "Ah. I might have seen that *someone* down the road. Good luck."

All at once, the prospect of coming face to face with his love caused his steps to freeze in place. Last night, they'd clung to each other as if they'd never gone separate ways. But in the clear light of day, did she have second thoughts about him?

His feet moved automatically down the now deserted street until he stood across from the charred remains of Delia's shop.

Her dream, reduced to a pile of scorched lumber and velvety ashes.

He braced himself as the tidal wave of mourning washed over him. It wasn't fair. She'd worked so hard, only to have it disappear in minutes. What would this loss do to her?

Pebbles skittered ahead, and he tensed, on guard for an attack. Then he laughed softly at himself. No dangerous outlaw stalked him here in the street. Just a poor, bedraggled beggar woman digging through the debris.

Blooming Grove had no beggar women ...

He sharpened his gaze. "Delia?"

She straightened slowly and looked at him. "Clarence!" With a cry, she waded through the rubble and launched herself at him. Clarence caught her in an embrace and held her close, soaking up the way she fit in his arms. Like home.

"I was so worried you would be hurt."

"I'm all right." He gently pushed her from him, wanting to drink in the sight of her. He took in her soot-streaked face, tousled hair, and blackened dress. "What's all this?"

Delia held her arms aloft, turning full circle, eyes twinkling. "It's the latest fashion from my shop. Like it?"

"I like *you*." He pulled her to him, growing somber as he traced her smudged face. "Delia, I was a fool for letting a tie come between us. Will you forgive me?"

"As long as you forgive me for keeping the truth from you."

In answer, he kissed her forehead. "I promise. Your dream didn't burn down like this building did. We'll build another, and we'll do it together. I won't rest until you have everything you want."

Her eyes pooled with unshed tears. She pressed her hand to her heart. "Sitting here, in the ashes of my dream, I realized something important." She gestured at the rubble. "A brick building, or silk fabric, or basking in my independence, those things have worth. But they don't bring me joy." She cupped his cheek. "You do."

His grip around her waist tightened. "I can't live without you, Delia. I love you. I want to spend the rest of my life with you."

She uttered a small gasp. "You want me to marry you?"

He drew back to search her face. "If you'll have me, I promise to honor and cherish you all the days of my life."

In answer, she tugged him closer. "I love you with all my heart, Clarence Parker. Of course, I will marry you."

He captured her lips in his, sealing their betrothal, and silently thanked the God of second chances.

Epilogue

The craze for a piece of wedding cake, to place under the pillow to dream upon, has given way recently to the mania for pieces of the wedding dress for crazy quilts. The demand on the dressmaker for pieces far exceeds the supply. It is suggested that the bride get two or three yards extra for crazy quilt pieces.—The Daily Courier (San Bernardino, California) January 1, 1888.

January 1, 1896

On the morning of her nuptials, Delia stood before the cold shell of what once was her little shop.

She and Clarence were to be wed in her aunt and uncle's elegant home this afternoon. Her family buzzed with excitement, and Mother forbade her from lifting a finger. "This is your day, one you'll remember forever. Let me spoil you a little."

So, she'd slipped out to say a final goodbye to the dream that had once occupied her every thought.

That night bound her forever with Sallie. They'd fought

367

hard against evil, and with God's help, had won the battle. They'd both walked away with scars, some visible, some not.

Thomas and Lucy would be married in a few days. They would settle down at the farm he'd purchased from Uncle Robert. The very piece of land they'd been mortified to view the first day they'd arrived in Blooming Grove, Texas. With the improvements Thomas had already made to the place, the farmland was not the same as it had been back in June. Thomas had put his heart into cultivating the land and his documentation of the cotton, wheat crops, and animal care was earning him a reputation as a purposeful, strategic farmer.

Something Papa had never been.

When Mother and Papa announced at Thanksgiving that they were moving into town to run Uncle Robert's dry goods store, no one had been more surprised than Delia. "Seems your uncle wants to expand the business to the space next to them and make it Truitt's Groceries. Besides, he wants to put Clive Waldrop out of the mayoral seat by running against him this spring."

Wouldn't Gert love that? Delia could imagine her fury if Uncle Robert succeeded. Some people never changed. Despite their truce after the shop burned, there remained a guardedness between them. Delia hoped one day, they would be at peace with each other.

"Red."

Delia turned at Rabb's call and fluttered her cold fingers in greeting. He came to stand beside her, his deputy badge pinned like a banner to his outer coat. He pulled her to him in a brief side hug. "What're you doing out here? Reckon you'd best be getting ready for the big shindig this afternoon, don't you think?"

She poked his chest. "It's you I'm worried about getting to

the wedding on time. Sheriff Akin assured me you'd have the time off."

His shoulders lifted for a moment. "A lawman ain't never off duty. Gotta look after the town."

"Regardless of whatever heinous crimes occur, you *will* be at my wedding."

He grinned as he tipped his hat in mock surrender. "Since you're so all-fired bossy, might I have permission to walk this down to Hazel?" He lifted a small book for her perusal.

"Another one? That girl's shelves are overflowing. Fine, go on. I'll be home in a bit."

She watched him saunter down the street, tossing the book and catching it. If their sister witnessed that, there'd be no end to her lecturing.

Down the road, he stopped to talk to a woman so bundled she was almost invisible. Eleanor, most likely, judging by the outrageous amount of covering. She smiled when the woman hurried to her side, teeth chattering. "Mind if I join you?"

Delia pulled her close. "Eleanor, why are you out here in the freezing cold?"

The woman puffed a steamy breath. "Looking for you." She thrust a small box at Delia. "This might be the only time to speak to you alone on this glorious wedding day. Besides, I wanted to give you my gift in private."

Delia studied the box in her gloved hand. "How kind. You didn't have to do that."

"Actually, I do."

"That's mysterious."

The skin around Eleanor's twinkling eyes creased. "I suppose it is. Open it, dear."

"Here?"

The older woman's smile faded. "I thought perhaps this was a place where you could appreciate something gained."

Delia considered the box. "Until that day, I never realized the most important possessions are the things one can't own. Like people. Family. The Lord."

Eleanor nodded in agreement. She pointed to the box. "Open it."

Delia removed the pretty paper in a way that kept it intact. Inside, a colorful enamel hinged box took her breath. "How beautiful."

Eleanor's smile held wistfulness. "My father gave it to me long ago. It's Japanese cloisonne."

Delia held it up, turning it around. "It's remarkable."

"Even more so if you open it."

Delia gently shook it. She lifted the top and gasped at the twinkling red gems inside. "What are those?"

"What do you think?"

Delia snapped the lid shut. It couldn't possibly be what she suspected.

Yet the woman beside her nodded her head. "Rubies."

Delia stilled. "Why do you have jewels?"

Eleanor laid her hand on Delia's arm. "May I tell you a story?"

What could she do but nod her head?

"That beautiful Singer sewing machine that once graced my shop was a gift from my father after I married. Papa didn't approve of Jake and tried in vain to talk me out of my decision to marry him. He gave me the sewing machine to provide a way out, if ever I should need it."

"You mean, a way for you to earn a wage if you left Jake?"

"Yes, partly. I didn't find out until much later that there was something else."

Tingles danced up Delia's spine.

"Remember the inscription on the cabinet?"

"*Who can find a virtuous woman? For her price is far above rubies.*"

"That's right." Eleanor sighed, sending out a puff of cloudy air amidst the chill. "Whenever I visited Papa, he always asked how I liked my machine. After he died, I couldn't rid myself of the feeling he'd meant something deeper. So, one day when Jake was away, I took it upon myself to solve the mystery." She cupped her hand around the small cloisonne box and opened the lid once more. "That's when I found the rubies in a small velvet pouch. It seems he'd had a carpenter create a false bottom in one of the cabinet drawers, so the rubies would be a secret."

The soft winter sun made the jewels twinkle. "I put them back in the drawer, where they've been ever since. Until the fire, that is. I hoped they weren't lost, that I could somehow locate them underneath the rubble. When all the big debris was out of the way, I found almost all of them laying not far from where the sewing machine had sat." She held them out to Delia. "They're yours now."

"I can't take these. If nothing else, Clarence would never approve of such an extravagant gift."

But Eleanor shook her head. "If you don't take them, they'll go to waste."

"But you could use these, the way your papa intended."

"I have no need for them. I inherited my father's estate. I think Papa would want me to pass his blessing onto someone deserving of it."

Delia's jaw dropped. "But I thought ..."

"You thought I was poor?" She laughed. "No, dear, just frugal. And perhaps a bit timid at the notion of people knowing I am a woman of means."

Delia forced herself not to gape. "I just can't believe it." Any of it, really.

"Please don't deny me the pleasure of giving in the Lord's name."

A cold wind whipped her cheeks, and Delia rubbed her arms. What would Clarence think of the rubies? Would he be suspicious that Eleanor harbored these as part of the gang's loot? As Delia had, much to her shame.

The old Clarence would have. But her fiancé had softened, especially toward Eleanor. He, like Delia's parents and siblings, accepted her as part of the family.

But Eleanor held a greater role in Delia's life. If not for the woman's wise counsel, she wouldn't be standing here with a sense of peace, that she stood in the middle of God's perfect will.

Turning, her gaze held Eleanor's. "Thank you. It's an honor to accept your gift."

Eleanor's eyes sparked as she placed the small box in Delia's hand and closed her fingers around it. "Be blessed, dear one. Take these and use them for good." She planted a kiss on Delia's cheek. "Now, let's go. Your Clarence will wonder where his bride has gone."

The End

Acknowledgments

The germ for this story began years ago, when I inherited my great-grandmother's crazy quilt, stitched around 1900 using velvet, silk, and satin fabrics. The fancy stitches embroidered on the randomly sized pieces were beautiful, but what interested me were the names stitched on it. I've always been a nut for the history of my ancestors. A few decades after I received the crazy quilt, this story was born, inspired by the bits and pieces I've learned about my family, and sewn together with historical research combined with my wild imagination.

Speaking of family, my first thanks goes to my wonderful husband, Rick, who pulled more than his fair share of work so I could meet my deadline. His love and encouragement kept me going, as did the love and cheering of my daughters Kristen, Katy, and Sarah, son-in-law, Austin, and grandchildren Lyric, Lily, and Fletcher. I'm so grateful for the ongoing encouragement from my mother, Eloise, and stepfather, Ray, and in-laws Don and Freda.

In memory of my dad, Joy Green. I wish he were here to hold my book in his hands. A quiet man, his love and silent support were constants I took for granted until he left this earth. I miss him. Every Christmas, I add a *Joy* ornament to our tree in his memory. I can't wait for our heavenly reunion.

To those who feel like family—my community group, ladies' Bible study, and steadfast friends: how could I have done this without your prayers? This book underwent so many transformations, and your prayers paved the way. I humbly thank you all.

To the ones who helped refine this story, a huge thanks. My huddle buddies, Liana and Lori, and my critique sisters Paula, Peggy, Nancy, Ally, Connie, and Cindee. I'd be nowhere without your insight and truth-telling. Iron sharpens iron in the best way.

I am humbled and thankful for the guidance of talented authors Sandra Byrd, Becky Wade, Lynne Gentry, and D'Ann Mateer, as well as My Book Therapy and American Christian Fiction Writers, national and my local DFW chapter.

Thank you to Linda Fulkerson for taking a chance on me. It's an honor to be part of the Scrivenings Press family.

Thank you, dear Reader. I hope this book has inspired you to hold the things of this world with a loose grip, and to trust the God who loves you more than you know.

And most of all, to Jesus, the Alpha and Omega. Your name is above every name, so that at the name of Jesus every knee will bow—in heaven and on earth and under the earth—and every tongue will confess that Jesus Christ is Lord, to the glory of God the Father. (Philippians 2:9-11)

About the Author

Teresa Green Wells is a native Texan who, while loyal to her home state, longs for the lush mountains of Western North Carolina. After getting degrees from the University of North Texas and Texas A & M, she did what her grandmother did: she taught children (though not in a two-room schoolhouse) before becoming a school librarian, surrounded by hundreds of books and kids hungry for a good story. Some of her favorite memories revolve around reading aloud to a group of wide-eyed children.

Teresa's love of reading and writing developed early, when she would retreat to her bedroom to write her epic novel in her red glitter looseleaf notebook, inspired by Nancy Drew, Little Women, and Caddie Woodlawn.

In her free time, she enjoys cross stitch, studying the Bible, and dreaming of one day owning a grand Victorian home. But she takes the greatest joy in sharing laughter, meals, and a game of chicken foot with her husband, her children and grandchildren. *What Brings Us Joy* is her debut novel. You can find her at www.teresawells.com.

You May Also Like ...

A Troubling Suggestion

by Betty Woods

Clarisse Matthews still grieves the tragic loss of her fiancé and doubts she'll ever love anyone again. Particularly if she has to divulge the secret abolitionist ideas she keeps hidden deep inside that only her beloved knew.

After the lady Luke Williams loved spurned him and married another man, he will never risk giving his heart to another woman. Especially not to Clarisse who had to have known about her best friend's ruse and helped the woman to conceal it from Luke. He doesn't need a lady by his side to manage his family's plantation or forge a path to become an attorney.

But when Luke's cousin is deceived by a rogue, who only Luke and Clarisse know the whole truth about, they form a reluctant alliance to protect his cousin. Their feigned attraction grows into genuine love.

But will the differences between them become a wall too tall to climb or can they find a way to go around?

Get your copy here:

https://scrivenings.link/atroublingsuggestion

~

No Leaves in Autumn

by Terri Wangard

Marie Foubert grew up in an orphanage and struggles with feelings of rejection. As a Red Cross recreation worker, she interacts with the American men based in Iceland during World War II. Her growing attraction to seaplane pilot Stefan Dabrowski excites and concerns her. Won't he disappear from her life like everyone else?

Stefan hears his commanding officer describe him as exciting as last night's bathwater. One of his colleagues constantly berates him because of his Polish heritage and his superior flying skill. Despite being the squadron's most productive pilot, he is threatened with court martial. A showdown approaches to prove who's the better pilot and the better man.

Marie's cousin, passing through Iceland, tries to see her after spotting her photo in *Life* magazine. She declines to meet him, but Stefan encourages her to do so and learn why no one wanted her. She may gain a family after all.

Get your copy here:

https://scrivenings.link/noleavesinautumn

A Slight Change of Plans

by Denise M. Colby

She believes she doesn't matter

Jenny Millard's hopes for security and stability as a schoolmarm out west are dashed when her schoolhouse closes, and no positions are available nearby. With only enough money for a one-way train fare, Jenny heads to her friend's home, uncertain of her next step.

His scars have made him an unlovable outcast

Newcomer Ren Lyman prefers to keep to himself, hiding in the back of the blacksmith shop to avoid the stares at the scars left by a childhood accident. When he comes across a lost stranger, he's surprised when she doesn't recoil at his appearance and even more so at his eagerness to assist her.

As Jenny settles into the welcoming but small town of Washton, she can't help but come across Ren, especially since his daily constitutional takes him along the same path. It doesn't take long for them to form a connection that breaks down the walls erected by years of hurt. But when strange occurrences unsettle the townspeople, it seems their chance at happiness might be at risk.

Will Jenny and Ren discover that they're enough—for God ... and each other?

Get your copy here:

https://scrivenings.link/aslightchangeofplans

Stay up-to-date on your favorite books and authors with our free e-newsletters.

ScriveningsPress.com

www.ingramcontent.com/pod-product-compliance
Lightning Source LLC
Chambersburg PA
CBHW060616100726
47907CB00006B/1648